Inner Dragon
A Yin Chen Novel

SHANGHAI
East China Sea
CHINA
TAIWAN
MYANMAR
LAOS
THAILAND
VIETNAM
CAMBODIA
Andaman Sea
South China Sea
PHILIPPINES
MALAYSIA
KUALA LUMPUR
SINGAPORE
Celebes Sea
INDONESIA
Java Sea
JAKARTA
AUSTRALIA
Great Australian Bight

Inner Dragon
A Yin Chen Novel

By Richard Giudice

With Tim Brost

Author's Notes

Inner Dragon - A Yin Chen Novel is a collaboration between military and commercial airline pilot Richard Giudice and novelist Tim Brost.

Rich began this project with questions and ideas born from tragedy. What happened to Malaysia Flight 370? Investigators have worked tirelessly for over a decade, yet as of May 2024, speculation continues.

Rich's journey in aviation is a testament to his dedication and passion. He began as an F/A-18 Hornet fighter pilot for the United States Marine Corps in 1988, participating in multiple combat deployments. His commitment and skill earned him the title of Squadron Commander and Deputy Group Commander. During his years of service, Rich logged nearly 5,000 hours in the F/A-18, a testament to his long and faithful service.

In 1997, Rich became a commercial airline pilot and continued serving as a United States Marine. He retired from the Corps as a Colonel in July 2013. He has accumulated over 20,000 hours of flight time.

The World Trade Center attacks in 2001 had a visceral effect on the entire world and a significant impact on Rich. Rich, who had previously worked for a Wall Street firm on the 67th floor of Number Two World Trade Center, The South Tower, knows what would have happened if he had been there that day. The threat of another 9/11 has been on the minds of our intelligence community and the military for over 20 years.

When Malaysia 370 disappeared, Rich wanted answers. Could a mechanical issue have been the cause, or was it taken down by a sinister actor or actors? He viewed the event through a pilot's lens and followed investigations, making copious notes and trying to understand.

No one knows precisely, but a great story emerged when Rich began drafting the what-if scenarios that led to this novel.

Tim Brost writes. His novels Trade: Bangkok, Trade: Azerbaijan, and High-Rise Crew Dirty Money are available on Amazon, along with samples of his commitment to short stories in the Dying Breed Writers Group series. Tim's wife is an international purser for the same commercial airline as Rich. What began as a conversation between a purser and her captain in 2022 became an exciting collaboration in which drafts were exchanged, modified, and rewritten dozens of times. Our mission throughout has been to entertain.

Richard Giudice and Tim Brost

Acknowledgments

Contributors: Thanks to my brother Michael, who lit a spark inside me to deliver the best possible story. A special thanks to Jody Berger's keen insight into Yin and Li. Last but certainly not least the father-daughter duo of Scott and Aubrey Campbell whose contributions are immeasurable.

First Readers: Matt Prinkey, Rob Maki, and Jonathan Brostrom.

Introduction

Futurists predict massive technological and economic shifts, mind-bending bioengineering advances, and intense, potentially violent resource competition. Many stressors are already here. Sino-American relations continue to deteriorate. Terrorists learn from each other in corners of the Internet as nation-states pump out misinformation. Bad actors see innovative defense techniques applied in Ukraine and other conflict areas then use them worldwide.

This novel explores a matrix of unexpected coalitions through the point of view of an exceptional Chinese woman. Follow her to the nexus of organized crime, terrorism, and the intelligence communities we know as Five Eyes. The authors fell in love with Yin Chen. We think you will, too.

Prologue

2024 Chinese Year of the Dragon

The empty Red Bull can Bao Gu throws from his 13th-story balcony tumbles through gusts of wind toward an open garbage can. The projectile ricochets from a lamppost onto the hood of a Mercedes-Benz sedan and clatters to the sidewalk yards from a trash bin. Passersby look up in unison at the façade of a landmark building on Avenue Vieira Souto, across from Ipanema Beach in Rio De Janeiro, spitting expletives at a solitary, unapologetic figure leaning over his railing. Bao doesn't react to their expletives. He returns to the kitchen for another energy drink and other stimulants. Dozens of pills are scattered across counter surfaces, hidden amid takeaway cartons, dirty plates, and spent beverage containers. He finds two Adderall capsules and swallows them with another Concerta tablet while dragging a wet cloth across his face, exhausted from a two-month, drug-fueled technical sprint to complete his project.

A dozen programmers and renowned game theory experts anxiously await his return to their video screens. They work from exotic destinations across continents and time zones. The industry knows that working on a Bao Gu project means guaranteed success, but the work is always grueling. At every moment, someone is coding the next module, troubleshooting an issue, or reviewing user feedback from somewhere on the globe. Remarkably, Bao has been present and online for virtually all of it. He is 18 hours into day 51 of this scheduled two-month online game development project. The talent and purchased source code needed to fast-track a functional beta model of his latest game have cost him millions, but to him, these expenses are worth every cent. A private beta release has been in the field for only two weeks but already shows promise.

A video conference app has been streaming non-stop from day one. Participants must always live within feet of their laptops to hear and respond to notifications—and no one dares fail Bao. Frozen assets, manufactured crimes, and destroyed reputations are only a few of the weapons in Bao's retribution arsenal.

No one is more eccentric, driven, or challenging to work for in the gaming development industry than the legendary Bao Gu. He is the mastermind behind three of the most successful games on the international market, which is why this elite team of next-level programmers and technicians agreed to this project, and why not? As an incentive, Bao sent everyone to the luxurious location of their choice and covered all expenses from day one. They work from Hawaii, Saint-Tropez, North Bimini, Phuket, and other bucket-list locations. In addition to paying for their rooms and providing a daily *per diem*, Bao supplies his team with enough amphetamine and dextroamphetamine to stay solely focused on performance, day in and day out.

As everyone reconvenes on the video conference, he sees empty takeout containers, spent pizza boxes, and recyclables piled high in the backgrounds of most participants, each dedicated to one or another vertex of this extensive game. The dynamics of the gaming architecture are complex in the extreme, involving games within games within games, forcing player coalitions across the entire playing surface.

Today, the team will review feedback and user patterns among those invited to play in the beta version. The players were each given an edge, an advantage leading to some outcome. Players can work independently or form coalitions. If they can't reach increasingly difficult heights in financial returns, they face miserable game-over deaths.

Unlike most expensive development projects, Bao has no intention of moving into production with this game. He is harvesting ideas by placing beta users into predetermined segments to see what they do with their skills. Part of Bao's genius is gathering innovation from others. *It's a numbers game*, he often says. The beta testers will provide innovation and options, and this information-gathering phase of his work is nearly complete. At the end of this meeting, he plans to announce that the group can spend seven or eight days on beaches, in bars, sleeping in hammocks on verandas, or running naked in the streets for all he cares.

Growing up in China, Bao dreamed of making thousands of Yuan working for the government. As a gaming genius undercover in Silicon Valley, his goal became the accumulation of millions of dollars. For the past two years, he has enjoyed the rarified air of being a rogue mogul worth billions of dollars. Making money no longer interests Bao. It's too easy. Having the power that money provides, moving pieces on a global game board, is all he thinks about these days. Life is the ultimate game, and these brilliant gaming strategists have unwittingly helped him advance many levels.

Bao calls for everyone's attention. When he sees observant faces in their respective grids, he begins. "You look as wasted as I feel. Are you awake, Nick? You added the player interruptions we discussed, right?"

The programmer replies, exhausted, from somewhere in southern France. His Eastern European accent is evident. "Yes. There are now random earthquakes in China, hurricanes for Florida, drought in Asia, terrorist attacks—sickness, war, and famine with unpredictable outcomes—totally sick!"

"Token values rise and fall with these events?" Bao asks rhetorically, referring to currency fluctuations.

Nick laughs and then continues. "For sure, and social response is also in there. People cross borders, governments fall, some make money, and many lose their asses in the chaos. Like in real life, coalitions form. Nasty players do better than polite ones. And the code is good."

"Cool. Kim, what are the top earners doing? Any interesting groupings?"

Kim stumbles through her report from a hotel room in Amsterdam. The lack of emotion in her voice underscores her fatigue. "Yeah, one of the top earners last week. Do you remember the British hedge fund guy? He joined forces with a New York asset manager."

"For real, or as avatars?"

"The Brit invited his friend. I approved the invitation."

Bao laughs, and his sudden exuberance startles the group. "That's what I'm talking about. Fuck, yeah! Where are we on the stats?"

"Approximately sixty percent of the players go on random raids by themselves, thirty-five percent form localized coalitions to take over cities, but a few use the game for corporate takeovers. Their edge is buying stock in a company and then hiring mercenaries to sabotage competitors by blowing up facilities, assassinating essential engineers, infiltrating maintenance crews, and whatever. There's more but—" Kim says and is interrupted.

"More what? Be specific," Bao demands.

"They used a stealth token to penetrate an airline maintenance crew and mess with fuel mixtures to reduce efficiency and slowly damage aircraft components. The advanced players mimic real-world events. These two are near the trillion-dollar mark. On the other hand, weak players predictably create a little chaos, run out of tokens, and then get killed or give up. Your theories on targeted chaos seem validated."

"Give me another example," Bao says, leaning into his camera.

"They went after computer chips. I didn't know that most of the world's chips come from Taiwan. Take semiconductor manufacturers out of commission for a while, and the impact has a worldwide ripple effect."

"How did they do it? Did they attack facilities or mess with the supply chain? It would take a lot of resources to shut down that industry," Bao says.

Kim seems confused by Bao's zeal. "I don't have specifics, but I can look into it. Didn't seem important."

Bao reacts angrily. "Going after the chip makers is brilliant, but you can't tell me what the fuck the impact is? What's the point of beta testing?"

The confrontation deflates Kim. "Give me an hour."

Nick interrupts, his condescension obvious despite a thick accent. "What is point? Game works. You could send for animator rendering right now."

"I'm talking to Kim," Bao snaps. "What about other industries like mining, chemicals, or electronics? Anything more on avionics?"

"Not so much," Kim says, defeated.

As if anticipating this outcome, Bao shakes his head. "What do these idiots need? More incentive, or are they just stupid? Give them more capital. Double their resources. Hell, triple their free tokens. Let's see what nasty shit they do when money isn't an object."

Peter, one of the research engineers Bao uses for in-game financials, interrupts to reinforce Nick's suggestion. "Win or lose, they keep playing, right? You've got one of the best games ever. We should go live."

Bao continues to question Kim as if Peter said nothing. "Any players go after tourism?"

"Minimal interest," Kim says flatly.

"It's laughable. Players should have uncovered hundreds of startling strategies by now." Bao folds his arms and sits in awkward silence for nearly a minute.

Nick is the first to speak. "I thought this was a kickoff meeting."

"Not even close. If the game doesn't stimulate radical ideas, we've failed. If you're so intent on going live, Nick, then triple the resources for top players, and Kim, I need those reports. Everyone else, your accommodations are paid through the end of the week. Stay where you are to unwind or go home. I appreciate the effort. I really do."

Bao steps away from the video screen, secretly pleased by the day's results. As he mixes vodka into his Red Bull, he mutters. "The gloves are off, you beta warriors. One more round of tests."

He returns to the balcony in a maelstrom of racing thoughts. Learning from six failed attempts, Bao carefully aims at the garbage can and releases another projectile. Fluttering in the wind, the empty Red Bull can falls miraculously into the trashcan 130 feet below. A wry smile creases his face. "Game on!

Chapter 1

The silhouette of a majestic Boeing 777 departs Kuala Lumpur and ascends into thinning air and moonlight on its way to Beijing. Some passengers start videos on their phones, others read, and a few of them gaze at the cumulus clouds below before closing their eyes, hoping to sleep through the remaining six-plus hours of the flight.

Captain Khan commands the flight deck of his craft with the expertise and accuracy gained from a past life as a military pilot. He is one of the youngest at Inter-Asian Airways to earn the title of Captain and continually proves his worth with methodical precision. Adjusting settings and fine-tuning the controls, he repeats a mantra for his First Officer, Aisha. "Routine is necessary. It calms the mind, and this is what flying is all about. Best view in the house—"

"Best job on the planet," Aisha Al Shuja smiles, finishing his sentence.

Captain Khan is exceptionally predictable and obsessive-compulsive, and Aisha is his most frequent copilot. He repeats the best-view-in-the-house observation twenty minutes into every flight and insists on lavatory breaks when they reach speed and altitude, as if nature borrows from his schedule. He also goes through a bizarre stretching routine midway, squatting and breathing heavily. It's annoying behavior, but Aisha respects Khan's competence and commitment to excellence.

Furthermore, he's a gentleman. There's nothing more uncomfortable than being hit on while strapped into the First Officer's seat at 37,000 feet. Aisha is five feet seven inches tall, slender, and dark in complexion, with full lips and elegant hands. She is always attractive, but Aisha is beautiful when her broad smile reveals high cheekbones above soft dimples. Her sense of humor delights coworkers. Unlike other copilots, Aisha sees Khan's quirks as endearing, and their relationship and respect for one another allow comments on his quirks without fear. For example, Khan has an obsessive need for hand sanitizer yet won't use a bottle opened by someone else. She chides that it's a lotion moment.

The most troubling of Khan's quirks to upper management is prayer in the cockpit. He doesn't use a sajjāda rug except when flying with Aisha, but it remains in his kit, along with the pair of black slippers he wears as soon as the cabin door is locked. Aisha often hides them until he catches on and shakes his finger at her.

There is one Khanism that requires frequent negotiation with his managers. The captain requests more fuel than is necessary on every trip. His motto is: *Why leave extra gas on the ground when you can bring it just in case?* His supervisors argue that excess weight reduces efficiency. They've done the calculations a million times but Khan is an otherwise exemplary employee. Sending him airborne with extra fuel is a small price to pay for competency, especially since Khan's argument involves safety.

Captain Khan levels the 777 at 37,000 feet fifty minutes into this flight. He methodically monitors and cross-checks all systems to ensure peak performance. Then, like clockwork, he suggests the First Officer take a bathroom break. Aisha obediently calls the flight attendant stationed in the forward cabin to arrange for the first scheduled interlude.

Following terrorist attacks on the World Trade Center in New York in 2001, flight attendants now prepare for lavatory breaks by placing a barrier between the passengers and the flight deck door. This is not always done in Asia, but a flight attendant trades places with the First Officer, ensuring that two people are always on deck.

Aisha locks herself into the forward lavatory. While washing her hands, she glances into the mirror. Her clothes are neatly pressed, and her emblems remind her of her accomplishments thus far in her career. Malaysia has only recently opened its doors to more female pilots, and Aisha wants to make Malaysia her home. As she admires her emblems, her image in the mirror blurs. There is commotion in the galley outside the door, and she experiences sudden weakness. It's as if she has had a mild stroke. Is the cabin losing oxygen? Has she succumbed to hypoxia? Thinking she needs an oxygen mask, panicked that death is imminent, Aisha opens the door and lurches forward.

There are no audible alarms and no apparent reason for her dizziness. Oxygen masks don't dangle above passengers, yet two of the flight attendants in the galley cling to equipment, unresponsive to her pleas for help.

Most passengers seem sound asleep in the first-class cabin just beyond the barrier. Fear has gripped the few passengers that are still awake. Their eyes are wide with terror, and they call to her. The only man to get out of his seat calls to her in Chinese but then collapses in the aisle.

Something is dreadfully wrong. The flight deck door is locked. Aisha pounds desperately, but there is no answer. Captain Khan must be in trouble, scrambling with controls, desperately trying to resolve a problem that Aisha cannot even identify. She can't breathe. Her motor skills fail while hunting for a cockpit door key, but it's useless. What is she thinking? There is no key anymore.

Seconds from succumbing to whatever their problem is, fighting to draw breath from dead air, a bizarre sense of euphoria envelops her.

The commotion that alerted her has ceased. The cabin is quiet. All she needs is to rest. Everything will be okay.

As Aisha falls to her knees and slumps against the bulkhead, Inter-Asian 957 continues its journey as a graceful projectile high above the ocean, a fading blip on someone's radar, destination uncertain.

Chapter 2

February 10, Morning | Present day.

Identical twin sisters Yin and Li Chen ride a city bus through Shanghai streets in their final days at Shanghai Jiao Tong University. Apple trees blossom all around them, sending fragrance into the sunlight. The bus is as crowded as Shanghai, a sea of 25 million inhabitants bound into a single organism, shoulders pressed into each other, some sitting three to a seat, others gripping handholds in the crowded aisle on the thirty-minute bus ride. Yin hears conversations in Mandarin, German, English, and Shanghainese. A married couple behind them argues over money in Cantonese. As a trained linguist, Yin has always delighted in dialects, but with her first trip to America just days away, she realizes for the first time how obsessively conscious she has become of her surroundings—who is behind her, who might be taking pictures or recording her conversations, who gets on or off the bus she rides today, and who may be working for her government or another. Many postgraduate students participate in government research projects, but her connection with the Shanghai State Security Bureau may have been a poor decision.

Thoughts about freeing herself from the watchful eye of intelligence communities and her pending trip to America will have to come later. "Let's concentrate," Yin says to herself, acknowledging that she, too, should be mindful of the present.

Yin has many rare cognitive gifts Li did not receive, including eidetic memory, ease with math and hard sciences, exceptional computer programming abilities, and a penchant for languages. But Yin also has a dark shadow lurking within. As a child, she inappropriately taunted other children, pulled pranks, and worse. Her parents forced diverse learning approaches on her, cautioning that she be positive and not give in to the darkness she'd always been capable of. Yin has done her best to heed their warning.

Looking curiously at her sister, Yin witnesses an anxious thumb traveling repeatedly across the fingertips of Li's right hand, and her lower lip twists as it does when distraught. "You'll be back in time for our 26th birthday, right?" Li asks, revealing the fear and vulnerability she can no longer hide. The twins have never been apart for more than a few days—the separation anxiety they drowned in when their parents and 12-year-old brother died under mysterious circumstances was too strong to ignore.

Yin sometimes wonders if her government's interest in her abilities and her parents' fate are somehow connected. They had just turned 20 when the automobile accident happened. Yin suppressed the memories of the crash and buried herself in endless academic pursuits to cope with unanswered questions and growing frustration. On the surface, she is a well-adjusted, successful academic. Her quiet moments alone are anything but.

For Li, however, losing her brother and parents is still fresh. Their time at SJTU is ending. Yin might move to America. The prospect of being separated weighs heavily on both sisters, but Li talks about this incessantly.

Yin rests a hand on Li's shoulder, stroking her long hair to comfort her. It's something their mother did whenever her daughters were troubled. She leans in and whispers. "When I return, we'll spend a day on the beach, dancing in the park, doing whatever makes us happy. I promise."

In five whirlwind years at SJTU, Yin accumulated a bachelor's degree and three master's degrees, and as of last week, earned a doctorate in applied computing with an emphasis on international finance.

In the same period, Li struggled through undergraduate studies and is about to receive her graduate degree in social work. The joke between these monozygotic twins is that Yin got the brain, Li got the heart, and both got the looks. Differences in appearance between these women are nearly impossible to detect. Li and Yin run, but Li does more with resistance equipment at the Gym. Li also has scars on her left knee, but they are tall, slender, proportionately lovely, and beautiful in the extreme. The only observable difference comes in conversations and academic performance.

As Yin's trip approaches, Li reflects on their relationship. "I held you back," she says, as tears form.

Yin showed exemplary intellectual potential as a child and advanced rapidly through the educational system, leaving sister Li behind. Yin never mentions the dissimilarity, but Li often hints at feeling inferior. Intellectual gifts are measurable, but measuring gifts of the heart is problematic.

Yin takes Li's face in her hands and brushes a tear with her thumb as they gaze into each other's eyes. "You have never held me back, pretty girl. You lift me."

One of the many stereotypes about twins is present in the Chen sisters. Yin and Li have a deep emotional connection bordering on the paranormal. Yin has shared Li's deepening sorrow for days. She kisses Li's forehead and pulls Li's face to her shoulder.

A man pressed into the aisle immediately in front has faced the twins for blocks, shamelessly studying them. Seeing the twins embrace brings a twisted smile to his face, and Yin gives him a piercing look. Ogling is a constant. Being inappropriately propositioned is a daily occurrence, yet lovely and gifted as they are, these women are impervious to base instincts. Anyone planning to engage with the Chen sisters must be confident yet humble, intelligent yet respectful, attractive both inside and out, capable of minding his own business, and above all, kind—traits that this ogler has never enjoyed. "Turn away," Yin snaps, the darkness in her voice surprising even Li. The man's eyes avert immediately.

Yin fights the impulse to tell Li she is emotionally frail and naïve. At the same time, she hides many of her ambitions and activities. Li sees the good in everything around her. Yin suffers no delusions. She is practical, socially distant, and instinctually guided to see things exactly as they are. Unlike her sister, Yin verbally decimates anyone who has it coming, and lately, that's been everybody.

Yin spends hours each week hacking foreign companies on the dark web, sometimes for work, often for the challenge, and always for the excitement. Nefarious exploits are soothing, partly because they occur in the evening while sipping tea or wine. She is also relieved to appease her inner demons. Penetrating someone else's firewalls somehow makes her feel more secure. The structure and demands of perpetual collegiate commitments keep Yin grounded. She is loved by academic instructors and celebrated by government project supervisors. In short, Yin believes she is a good person who sometimes does questionable things and is at peace with her future. During the day, she honors the family ethos of hard work, kindness, and gentility. At night, Yin exercises inner demons. Dual existence comes naturally to Yin. From a very early age, she hid aspects of her personality that elicited disfavor.

"Have you checked into your flight? I could ask Haitao for his roller bags," Li says as their bus approaches the campus stop.

"That's not necessary, Li, but thank you. I won't check in until tonight, and I'm traveling light."

"Where will you be when I finish my exam?"

"I'll say goodbye at work and have my Visa interview at the US Consulate this afternoon. We should do something tonight."

"What if you can't get off of work?" Li asks.

Yin smiles. "Focus. This is your stop."

"Could you take my exam for me?" Li says, laughing as she stands. There was a week, years earlier, when Li was ill. Yin went to classes in her place. She'd aced an exam and pop quiz for her sister, and no one knew they had switched places.

"Not this time," Yin laughs, waving goodbye as Li gets off the bus.

When their parents and brother died in the accident, Yin took care of the arrangements, found a place for them to live, helped Li get into college, and became a parent overnight. Li emotionally flattened. While Yin attacked the problems at hand, her sister fell into depression. It took months for her to get on with her life, but she did. Yin thinks it's time to get on with hers. Perhaps there will be a way to bring Li with her to America one day, but it's unlikely. They both have secrets. Yin hopes to live in America for a few years. Li and her boyfriend Haitao talk about marriage. The twins may be parting but will remain emotionally close wherever life takes them.

After Li departs, the bus carries Yin to the Xuhui District Shanghai State Security Bureau building, one of the most active bureaus within the Ministry of State Security. MSS is the counterpart of America's CIA and similarly exercises close attention to the histories and activities of its employees. The word security in the names of various Chinese agencies is appropriate, but Yin didn't fully understand the implications when she agreed to do postgraduate projects. It's common for advanced students worldwide to be involved in government-funded research. They get a stipend and experience. It looks good on resumes. Large projects are gateways into corporate life, government work, and, for some, an introduction to careers in the intelligence community.

On paper, Yin works for the Shanghai Academy of Social Sciences, but multiple bureaus have used her acumen in finance. The project she worked on most recently created dozens of the thousand shell companies China uses for gathering intelligence and advancing their business and military interests around the globe. Yin navigated the mountain of legal and financial strictures imposed upon corporations in different countries. She's signed non-disclosure documents and is sworn to secrecy, no matter what. The government paid for her education, they paid for ongoing assistance, and they openly acknowledged surveillance of her when tasked with collecting classified information. Some in China say there is no way out of the intelligence community. Yin hopes to prove that understanding wrong.

Yin makes one bus transfer before crossing the Lupu Bridge onto Ruining Road. As she's done many times in the past two years, Yin walks from the bus stop to the towering high-rise office building, badges her way up the elevator to a reception lobby, and informs the project leader's administrative assistant that she is there to turn in her badge. She gave notice days earlier. Her immediate supervisor, Mr. Fang, begged her to stay, but Yin had other plans.

At the same time, it is unwise to burn bridges in China. "Is he available?" Yin asks Fang's assistant. She could have left her badge with guards at the entrance, but a farewell to friends and supervisors seems appropriate.

"He wants to speak with you," the administrator says with a smile. She gestures for Yin to take a seat.

CCTV cameras scan every room and hallway of the SSSB building. Yin waits below one of them for a few minutes before dropping her badge on the administrator's desk and asking her to say goodbye for her—she doesn't have this much time to waste. She's about to get into an elevator when Mr. Fang finally sticks his head out of his office and calls her name.

Fang is a gregarious and often humorous man in his late forties. He manages dozens of students and professionals. Though she and Fang often joke that he should pay her for the work of ten employees, it's never happened. Now, he is uncharacteristically tense.

Seeing the shift in mood, Yin is reserved. His encouraging and often flirtatious interactions are gone. She follows him to a meeting room.

When they enter the room, Fang points to a seat. "We'll begin when the Director arrives," he says, surprising Yin.

"Why?" Yin asks. It's inexplicable that they would even have a meeting. Furthermore, the esteemed Director has hundreds of dedicated professionals below him, and they have never spoken in person.

"I told him you were leaving, and he wants to meet. I think he—"

Before Mr. Fang can finish his thought, the door opens. Both Yin and her supervisor snap to their feet and bow slightly. Introductions are brief. The Director drops a folder on the table and says, "Fang reports you are the best employee, but you are leaving. Why?"

"Small correction. I am a student, not an employee, and my studies have ended. I am grateful for the great experience here, but yes. I am leaving to pursue other opportunities."

The Director's face sours. He pages through the documents in his folder, which Yin sees include her collegiate records and work history. Dropping the documents to the table with a thud, he says, "To America?"

Yin instantly regrets having said anything about her upcoming travel to coworkers. "Thank you for your kind words. I plan to attend a week-long conference on artificial intelligence. I'll consider all options when I return to Shanghai."

"MIT? I'll need a report," the Director says.

Yin sees snakes in the grass and is judicious in her response. "I can give you a report on the conference, but to be clear, I am leaving SSSB. My future is in academics or business."

"You can't be serious. Academics? You have many degrees from the best school in the world! It's time to put that brain to good use," the Director says. He has a way of looking displeased even while smiling.

Yin doesn't hesitate. "SJTU ranks 12th worldwide in computer science. MIT ranks higher in that discipline and other disciplines of interest. We should know why. What do they know that we do not? We are the rising sun, not them. Anything I can do to help seems appropriate, and of course, I will return to China. I am Chinese, not American."

A smile of recognition crosses the Director's face. "How long were you in the League?" he asks. *We are the rising sun* is a famous phrase in the Youth League anthem, synonymous with pride and commitment in the Chinese Communist Party. Yin could care less about politics, including the rhetoric of the CCP, but feigning loyalty is often necessary to successfully navigate social situations. Speaking to a man with strong party connections is one of those situations.

Fang interrupts by also demonstrating his commitment to party and security. "Our work is classified, Yin. The Americans will ask questions."

"Questions about my clerical skills? That kind of thing?" Yin asks, smiling.

The Director catches her meaning more quickly than Fang. He laughs. "Precisely. When you return, I'll need a full report on your experiences. Who are the influencers? Where do they see AI taking them? How is the West applying AI to human capital, finance, military operations, and intelligence? You're an attractive young woman. Find a way to meet their thought leaders."

Yin understands spies better than most. It's one thing to disclose publicized conference material, quite another to divulge who is sitting beside whom, where they work, their traits and interests, and whether they can be coerced into providing corporate or governmental information. Yin draws a line at corporate espionage, though there have been multiple instances where she's attacked computer networks. When she started working on government projects as a teen, her family considered it a great privilege. She was on her way! As the years passed, this *esprit de corps* faded into gray. Was she still doing good for her people and country, or had she crossed a line?

"It's just a conference, but I'd be happy to send a report to Mr. Fang," Yin says, already deciding to compose a generic overview of the sessions and nothing more.

The Director shakes his head and laughs at the suggestion. "Fang's group has nothing to do with artificial intelligence. AI is handled elsewhere. Send the report directly to me."

"Not yet anyway," Yin counters.

Richard Giudice

"AI? Yes. Not yet. After you send the report, get some time on my schedule. We can discuss your future," the Director says, smiling broadly. He slaps the desk with the palm of his hand as if he's just given Yin a wonderful surprise.

Yin exits the building for a quick bite before her appointment at the US Consulate but doesn't enjoy her meal as anxiety and fear of an uncertain future dominate her thoughts. Despite her reservations, MSS remains an option. Fang lives very well. The perks and privileges the Director and his family enjoy could be hers, but the culture frightens her. Since signing up for government projects, she has been under constant scrutiny. Wherever she goes, she feels surveilled. Her financial transactions, social habits, and especially the few friendships she maintains are all watched. Her contacts, phone calls, and the texts she sends and receives are archived in a database within the intelligence community. As inviting as the perks may be, her future is not with the security services. Constant surveillance is not what she wants for herself and Li.

Or is it? A strange and inexplicable blanket of comfort washes over Yin as she muses on how predictable the CCP has become.

Yin enters a neighboring cafe, orders Xiaolongbao dumplings and Chrysanthemum tea, then sits in the sunshine by a large window to mentally prepare for her visa interview. She expects to see familiar faces in the crowd of passersby and does. When reassigned to classified projects, a surveillance team began following her from the SSSB building to her apartment, and in the past year, three team members became familiar faces. At first, it was frightening, but Yin turned the experience into a game of surveillance, countersurveillance, and cat and mouse. She'll almost miss the excitement.

Today, the Anglo Yin dubbed the reader, sits at a bus stop across the way with an open newspaper. He brings a smile to her face. Leaving the college and research projects behind will likely end daily overt surveillance, but spotting the surveillance team makes her wonder what threats lie outside the protective walls of China.

Yin walks to the bus stop with a small bag of egg tarts. The Anglo appears uncomfortable as she sits beside him and starts a conversation. "I've seen you in the neighborhood many times. My name is Yin," she says, bowing slightly.

The reader nods politely but doesn't answer.

"You should be more friendly. It's a lot easier to keep an eye on your subject if they are happy to see you."

"Excuse me?" he says, eyes fluttering in confusion.

"You and two others have followed me for months. If a university student can spot you so easily, your jobs are probably in jeopardy. I could give you a few tips if interested."

He denies everything even after she mentions the places he was spotted, but a telling smile says he respects her.

When Yin's bus arrives, she hands over the bag of tarts and says, "It's been fun, but I'll be traveling for a while. Good luck."

Chapter 3

Yin read that Visa interviews typically take ten minutes or less, especially where the intent to visit America is tourism. The process will be quick and painless if she doesn't acknowledge working for the government in any capacity, but Yin decides on transparency. She hopes to eventually attend or work for MIT, at least for a year or two. It's better to be denied access to America now than be expelled once enrolled for not mentioning the research projects in which she was involved. The American government sent numerous Chinese students from the US for not declaring university affiliations during their Visa application processes.

SJTU is dubbed the Eastern MIT for its expertise in science and engineering and is a member of the elite C9 League of Chinese universities, comparable to the UK's Russell Group, Canada's Group of 13, and Ivy League schools in the States. Getting into any of these schools takes a lot of work. Chinese-born scientists, engineers, and even academics living or visiting the US are targets of the Department of Justice under what was initially called the China Initiative. Yin understands why. The Chinese intelligence community relies on human beings over technology to gather information and has thousands of loyal citizens and skilled professionals worldwide. Yin imagines the US intelligence community works in similar ways. Will the IC investigate her as a traitor for visiting the US Consulate General building? Will the Consulate see her as a spy? Recollections of hacking for the government, and often just for fun, send chills through her body, but she reminds herself that these are her memories alone. The Americans don't need to know more than what is necessary for her purposes.

All the same, Yin is on guard from the moment she approaches the Consulate until she leaves, noticing who may be across the street, comparing images of pedestrians to people seen in the past, studying the position of cameras, and analyzing the tone of voice used by guards at the entrance.

Worry subsides when she meets her interviewer. The woman is pleasant, approachable and professional. She begins their conversation casually. Yin wonders why she was ever concerned.

As they continue, the woman's demeanor shifts from the welcoming, bubbly persona that greeted her to body language implying suspicion. The transformation occurs as the Consulate Officer discovers how Yin participated in projects for the Shanghai Academy of Social Sciences. "Students all need a little extra cash. Are you still involved?"

"Participation is compulsory for many post-graduates, but no. I've given notice. I feel free! If that makes sense to you," she says, chuckling.

The Consulate Officer laughs back but continues her line of questioning. "While in college, I worked in a department store and waited tables," the interviewer says, eyes cast towards her computer display while typing furiously. Eyes still averted, she asks, "Were any of these projects for Unit 61398 or the Institute for International Strategic Studies?" Yin should have expected a person in her position to be aware of Chinese cyber intelligence centers, but the directness of her questioning is off-putting.

"No," Yin says flatly, laughter gone, smile remaining as a gesture of innocence.

The interviewer looks up from her keyboard and locks eyes with Yin.

"Bureau Four? Counterintelligence? Any of that?" the officer inquires, clearly hunting for a reaction.

Yin tries not to appear evasive but is cautious. "My most recent projects involved research and documentation of financial processes. We educate companies so they can conduct transactions in other countries—wire transfers and that kind of thing."

"I see. And you were invited to the US by MIT? That's impressive—advanced degrees in computer science, finance, linguistics—may I see the invitation?" The interview officer holds out an expectant, chubby hand.

"I'll be attending a conference," Yin says as she presents a printout of her invitation from one of MIT's department heads. The response seems to satisfy the officer, but the interview process isn't over.

"Thank you. I need a moment to confer with my supervisor," she says, leaving the room with Yin's application form and invitation letter.

Minutes later, the Consular Officer returns with a young man who also smiles. He is courteous but spends a few minutes reading Yin's visa application while glancing alternatively at Yin and the female officer. Setting the paperwork aside, he says, "How long have you worked for the government?

"I'm not sure what you mean. I am not an employee. I'm a student," Yin says.

"A student working on government projects. Am I correct? Counter-intelligence?" The young man asks.

"I don't understand how finance and AI connect with intelligence. There is no hidden agenda for wanting to attend a conference if that is what you are asking," Yin says defensively.

"Of course. The US welcomes anyone who wants to learn. How long do you intend to stay in America on this trip?"

"It's on the form. About ten days."

"You aren't applying for a work visa. Is there a chance you may want to stay in America to work or study?"

"If MIT offers a position, I might consider it, but I don't expect they will. I've never been outside China, so I'm just looking forward to a new experience."

"You should stick around for a while, see the sights. Boston is a great city. I grew up there," he says, which Yin believes to be a lie. His diction is that of the Southwest.

"I won't be staying beyond the conference," Yin says.

"Pity. Friends there, fellow students, anyone that can show you around?" The young man asks, clearly probing.

"The conference schedule is very tight. No time for sightseeing," Yin says. It's a common technique among Chinese human intelligence officers to explore connections their persons of interest have with family, friends, and associates. The officer's body language and line of questioning say to be careful. He continues in a quick tempo. "Place to stay? Transportation?"

"I'll figure it out when I arrive. The conference director says she will help if I need it," Yin says, feeling an urgency to be brief.

"Right. It sounds like a great opportunity. Wait in the lobby. We'll call when the visa is ready. Have a great trip, Ms. Chen."

Yin thanks the young man and wonders if his rank is similar to the Anglo watcher she met earlier. The thought amuses her.

• • •

Universities across the globe are fertile recruiting grounds for intelligence agencies, and what the Director said at SSSB resonates in Yin's mind. Multiple bureaus within the Ministry of State Security, called Guó'ānbù in China, have followed Yin from the day she scored 748 on the national college entrance exam, and she accomplished that score eighteen months before most candidates even considered taking the test. Gaokao, the nine-hour equivalent to the SAT in America, is the world's most challenging academic entrance exam. No one has ever perfectly answered the 750 questions organized by province. With her scores, she could have attended any university in China, including Peking University or the other C9 schools, but she remained in Shanghai with her sister.

Yin recalls when MSS's first, fourth, and eleventh bureaus approached her. When she completed a master's degree in computer science at 18, the Eleventh Bureau asked her to participate in a research program for cyber intelligence. When Yin expanded her education to include artificial intelligence and cybersecurity, the Fourth Bureau said she had a duty to join them. Logic dictates that Yin's mind is best suited for counterintelligence, but counterintelligence will have to wait. Her strategy with recruiters has always been to feign interest while justifying additional studies. If she were less gifted or unable to assist the government with various research projects, the strategy might not work. Instead, the state allows her to continue self-directed education for free. They even provide a stipend for expenses, but they also call on her frequently to assist with what they call research. Yin participated in many ethically perplexing projects, including covert activities, that she found incredibly stimulating.

After securing a travel visa, Yin returns to her apartment and finds Li eating lemon ice sorbet. She says, "Your exams went well, I see. Let's celebrate."

For Li, lemon ice is already a celebration, but she smiles broadly and bounces on the balls of her feet as she does when excited. "No more school for me and no more work for you. I feel like dancing!"

"Dancing, teasing, and men that pay for drinks! Shall we dress to kill?" Yin asks with a mischievous grin.

"You're so nasty!" Li laughs, and the two women practically run to their respective closets. Forty minutes later, the twins are dressed to impress in matching charm bracelets and identical dazzling sequined blouses above black leotards and high-heeled red stilettos. They take DiDi, the Chinese equivalent of Uber, to their first destination for a night on the town.

Beautiful women often attract attention when they enter a nightclub, but when the twin Chen sisters enter Mai Road Disco-Bar, a seismic ripple of turned heads surrounds them wherever they go.

The night begins in the punk health tradition with Peddlers Gin and sugar-free alcohol seltzer before heading to the dance floor. Four hours and thousands of burned calories later, they laugh uncontrollably at the lock to their apartment. "Stick it in," Li says as Yin fumbles with the key alignment.

"Now, who's being nasty," Yin giggles.

Inside, they collapse onto their sofa, lifting their tired legs to the coffee table, shoes off, hand in hand. Silence settles onto the twins.

"I'm going to miss you," Li says as tears emerge.

"Me too. Every day." Yin gently squeezes her arm as words form in her mind. *Life goes on no matter what. Who knows, maybe we both end up in America someday.* Instead, she says, "It's only a one-week conference. Besides, you have Haitao now." *Too much.* Yin has played the parent role for so long that it flows without awareness.

"You don't have to do that anymore. It's okay," Li says, brushing at a stain on the knee of her right leg.

"Do what? What do you mean?"

"Remember Fandong?"

"I never liked that dog. He got hair on everything," Yin says.

"You did, too, like him. He slept at your feet almost every night." She gently pushes Yin to emphasize the point.

"And I brushed his hair off the blanket every morning. What about him?" Yin asks suspiciously.

"When he died, you cried. You cried more than after Mom and—after. After the accident," Li Manages to say with quivering lips.

"I did?" Yin knows full well what happened. When their parents and brother passed, she had to be strong for her sister. She hid the crying and grief in those days, turning inward for strength and protection. Just as she's doing at the moment.

"You did, and I know why. You think of me as a child," Li says, crying. "You don't have to do that anymore."

Yin studies Li's face for a long moment before kissing her on the forehead as she often does. Without notice, Li hugs Yin and won't let go until they are nearly one.

Yin begins to cry with Li and doesn't see the smile that comes to Li's face. For the first time since being very young, they share a trembling moment of grief and sadness, tears merging on their cheeks, Yin relinquishing her role as a parent.

They reach for tissues and settle back onto the sofa. Li says, "Promise you'll return to me."

"We're both going to cry, but you know what? It's okay. It's only temporary, and I promise I'll be back."

Li stands, picks up both pairs of shoes, and says, "That was so much fun. Thank you. I enjoyed dressing up, hitting the club, all of it. Do you want eggs? We should eat something to counter the alcohol."

"With pepper jam and toast?"

February 11th

In the morning, Yin feels exceptionally excited. Though her flight to Boston doesn't leave until nearly midnight, she packs, unpacks and packs again multiple times. In some ways, luck gave her the travel visa. Yin did things as a student contractor that blocked some from leaving China and might have stopped her from entering the US. She found excitement in helping to compromise the affairs of foreign governments, lending her understanding of AI and localization of languages for social media campaigns. She assisted as a translator, performed as an interpreter in a financial group, and worked deep into many of her nights learning to attack networks and compromise electronic devices. The side projects conducted as a geopolitical analyst were a natural gateway to a career in the MSS. She knows she can always return, but for now, it is over. Either she will become a tenured professor in the West or climb the ladders of multinational corporations. The last time her academic advisor spoke with her, he asked what she wanted out of life, and she gave him the only answer that made sense at the time. She'd said, "I want it all. I want to experience everything life has to offer."

As Yin settles into her economy seat for the seventeen-plus hour flight to Boston, she feels a sense of exhilaration coursing through her veins. She feels liberated by traveling to an unknown land, even though nothing is more exhilarating than penetrating the private communications of prominent foreign dignitaries.

Stop it, she scolds herself and opens an American Audiobook to improve her pronunciation. She's seated next to a New York businessman. In their few conversations, she attempts to sound like a native of Wisconsin or Illinois, but it's difficult. English uses an alphabet whose letters have no individual meaning, whereas Mandarin is written in symbols, each standing on its merit. The sounds are also very different.

Yin practices the sounds of V and L, which are as foreign to her ear as the tones in Pinyin characters are to Westerners. Her astounding gift of eidetic memory allows her to recall nearly anything she wants to retain, but making sense of English idioms and other turns of phrase is challenging—sick as a dog, clean as a whistle—so much about America is nonsense, but not their science and technology.

Yin's enthusiasm rises significantly during the flight's descent, but Boston is much smaller than anticipated. 27 Bostons could fit within the city limits of Shanghai. Boston has a distinct dialect, but Shanghai has a unique language, Shanghainese. The two cities couldn't be more different. Even so, Boston Harbor, the Charles River, and the city streets below are bustling with early morning traffic and expectations of things to come.

Their plane meets the tarmac at 5:42 am, and while taxiing toward the terminal at Logan International, she leaves airplane mode to text that she has arrived safely. Li responds immediately to wish Yin luck, then follows up with a WhatsApp call.

"You sound so happy, pretty girl," Yin says as she answers. It's a silly thing they have done for years. Mirror images in nearly every physical way, they often compliment one another on how attractive they are, especially in the morning when their long black hair is a mess. It's especially fun to do as they stumble into or out of the kitchen in frumpy pajamas and slippers.

There is a twelve-hour difference in time, and Li is giddy and chatting with friends on another night out. "I am celebrating with Chyou and her new friend. Guess what we are going to do? Just guess," Li says as her friend Chyou blurts loudly in the background that they will see belly dancing. Li barks at Chyou for spoiling the surprise, but they are having fun.

"Where in Shanghai could you possibly?" Yin asks, Li quickly stepping on her question.

"1001 Nights Restaurant and then—" Li says, apparently turning away from her phone momentarily to ask a question of someone. "Oh. He says the M1NT Club. I'll tell you about it later."

"Haitao has such a tight wallet. That Club is expensive," Yin says, feeling her sister's joy.

"Not Haitao, Chyou's friend. Haitao is working late all the time! So boring, but he will come to the apartment after. I'll send pictures. Love you," Li says and ends the call.

Yin floats through the busy airport and berates herself for being so concerned about the American intelligence community. No one in Logan Airport seems interested in her, and she merges perfectly into the broad spectrum of ethnicities and social status. No one appears to be looking for her or taking pictures. "Foolish girl," she whispers.

Surprisingly, the two Chinese MIT PhD students she recently corresponded with are there to greet her at baggage claim. An older woman named Ling is with them. Yin is immediately cautious of Ling, due to the age difference and her general demeanor. While the students seem ecstatic to meet, Ling is reserved, folding her hands at the waist, as women did in previous generations.

Nearly in unison, the students say they have arranged accommodations for Yin at Copley Square Hotel near campus. If it hadn't been depicted in this way by students she trusts, Yin might have thought it the work of an intelligence community officer. The IC in Shanghai would place her where they can observe, but Yin doesn't believe she is all that important.

Laughing and conversing in English, the four women share an Uber ride to the hotel. As they move through the streets of Boston, one of the students signals Yin when she asks about encounters with American authorities. The women switch to Mandarin to avoid including the driver, but the gesture carries a deeper meaning. She needs to guard her thoughts.

"Did you ever meet Gang Chen in person? It's terrible what they did to him," Yin says. It's her way of broaching a subject while demonstrating loyalty to China. Gang Chen headed the mechanical engineering department until he was arrested in the DOJ's roundup of Chinese academics. The department shut down without him, and fear spread through the American academic community from coast to coast. All charges were dropped one year later, but it was too late. Gang returned to China, where the CCP used his experience as an example of how the Americans are out of touch with reality.

"When they thought we were gadget makers, everything was okay. Big surprise," one of the students says, prompting laughter. Yin laughs, too, but cannot fully enjoy the moment. The academics who want her attention in America could be as covert and controlling as those she worked for at SSSB. Are the professors at MIT strictly academics or connected to the government? Knowing that MIT conducts government research projects leads her to believe obligations and back-room agreements are in place. What will they want from her in return for what she wants from them?

The nexus of technology and international finance training prepared Yin for the highest performance levels in the global economy. Adding artificial intelligence to her computing, cybersecurity, and finance expertise means that virtually any multinational corporation will consider her for a position, and she's willing to have those conversations. If not that, then she might launch a consulting firm.

Yin slept briefly on the plane and is not as tired as expected, so when asked if she would prefer to rest or tour the campus, she chose the latter, if only for an hour or two. They arrive at the hotel, and she checks in with the front desk before her tour. Pleased she brought a warm coat for the cold winter days, Yin smiles. The walk to campus is short but joyful. It rarely snows in Shanghai. Winters are dry and marked with sunshine, but here, puffs of steam follow their words into the air, and a thin sheet of snow rests on everything that has not been shoveled. She's seen pictures of MIT's Stata Center, with its cartoon-like angular buildings, but never one taken in winter. The buildings rise at crazy angles as if pushed by a great wind or slammed by wrecking balls.

The Ray and Maria Stata Center for Computer, Information, and Intelligence Sciences is a capriciously bold concept, but the activities that take place inside are anything but playful. Stata is home to the Laboratory for Information and Decision Systems and the Department of Linguistics and Philosophy—all disciplines Yin pursues. She senses billions upon billions of neurons firing on this campus, and the thought of being at a university known worldwide for innovation excites her unexpectedly.

Finally, after feeling the weight and exhaustion of her trip, Yin has had enough. She is about to download the Uber app when Ling says that won't be necessary. "It's not far, we can walk. I'm heading in that direction."

Yin smiles, thinking her government is so predictable. "That would be wonderful," she says, thanking the students again for their assistance.

"You must be very excited. Your first trip to America?" Ling asks as they walk.

"I am more tired than excited, but yes. How long have you been here in Boston? Your English is excellent."

"Two years. I was in Houston when I first came, but that was ten years ago. What has the esteemed Director asked you to do? Maybe I can help," Ling says bluntly.

Chapter 4

February 12th

Half a world away, Deputy Chief of Station posted at the Australian High Commission Defence, Singapore, Nigel Rainer, sits on a hotel balcony near Barwon Prison in Victoria, Australia, reviewing notes. He prepares for a challenging interrogation. Nigel glances at his phone, which tells him it's time to return to the prison. He's been in the country for days. The park across the way and the scent of familiar plants on the breeze remind him of how close he is to home, and how much he misses his family, but he won't visit relatives on this trip. In the true sense of the word, he is an Australian native. His mother and father, aboriginal Australians, ensured his upbringing was deeply rooted in their culture. His grandfather was a Noongar tribal leader from Nigel's early childhood until his death, and he brought Nigel to unique places, relayed the history of their people, and acquainted him with their customs. For the Noongars, pride has nothing to do with accomplishment or wealth. It is a gift resulting from living honestly, reverently, and simply.

The work he does in Singapore conflicts with his upbringing. The Noongar sometimes use words like migaloo and wadjela to describe white people, but Nigel's family is open-faced and kind to everyone they meet. His childhood was spent just outside Ravenswood, in the Peel region of Western Australia. Nigel misses fishing the banks of the Murray River for Redfin, golden perch, and Murray Cod with friends and the elders, listening to stories and telling some of his own. He's often retold the story of catching a 20-kilo Murray Cod using cheese as bait, eventually leaving cheese out of the story because no one in Singapore believes him. He's recently dreamed of leaving the duplicitousness of his career to spend a few years at his father's side in a fishing boat, but boats are expensive.

Family traits have carried Nigel through years of disciplined training and casework. His skin is dark as sandal leather and nearly as durable, ideally suited for Western Australia. His pearl-white teeth and thick black hair atop a muscular, athletic frame set him apart from coworkers, most of whom are of English and Scottish descent. Solid in their way, Nigel's coworkers are saved from the damaging effects of an equatorial sun by Singapore's frequent clouds and rainy days.

At the start of his career in law enforcement, Nigel endured discriminatory remarks based on race. What comes his way these days, even from mates, is rooted in envy. Nigel doesn't play by the book. He uses common sense, and to the ire of his immediate supervisor, William Essex, often relies on gut instinct to get the job done. Essex has twice threatened to send Nigel back to Australia for being unorthodox. If Nigel were not so valuable to the organization, Essex would fire him. The two coexist in an uncomfortable state of disrespect.

This week, Nigel was immersed in interviews with men he helped put away at Barwon. Two things happen in the first weeks of an inmate's imprisonment. The first is the system decides where inmates will be housed—in the general population, where prisoners are not considered at severe risk to each other, or with the most dangerous men in specialized units like Hoya, Banksia, or even Acacia, the highest security areas. The second is that a criminal's perspective shifts from denying participation in a crime to negotiating for early release, better conditions, or safety from other men in the prison.

After their trial, Nigel requested that the Triad inmates go to the Banksia section, where they were placed in individual cells and kept under close supervision. He used their temporary housing situation as a bargaining chip. The strategy worked well on two of the prisoners. As he worked through the group, it became clear which of the convicted was in charge. Their leader is Chuanli, and he saved this interview for last. Part of the strategy is that Nigel runs translation software on his phone in case this prisoner talks back in Mandarin as he's done with others. Feeling mentally prepared, Nigel collects his things and heads back to Barwon.

• • •

Nigel and Chuanli have been in the interrogation room for over an hour. Usually, the prisoner is positioned on one side of a metal table, confined in cuffs, while the interrogator sits safely on the opposing side. Nigel made a conscious decision to remove all barriers. He sits face to face with Chuanli, indicating he is neither impressed by nor afraid of the man. However, in the past 67 minutes, Nigel's tenacity has not yielded the desired result.

Chuanli wears scars on his chiseled face. His head is shaven, and tattoos rise from his chest onto his neck. In contrast, Nigel wears a starched white shirt, sleeves rolled up his forearms. He doesn't suit up for the criminals. He wears the suit to command respect from the warden and guards.

Nigel has always seen defiance as a mask to be removed by cleverness and patience. To a trained interrogator like Nigel, even simple gestures tell a story, and it's time to press. "Here's what's going to happen. Your men will go into the general population where they have yard privileges, access to television, and each other for company. I may even give a few of them early release for cooperating. But you? You're a dangerous bastard, mate, an ugly bloke with those big ears and shit tattoos. I'm sending you to maximum security. It's Acacia for you, and guess what? You'll fuck up, which will add time. I'll see to it. My guess is you'll never again be on the streets. What do you think about that?"

Chuanli spits expletives in Chinese, cursing at the men who ratted on him, screaming that he'll kill those dogs, but then, in broken English, says, "I know my rights. You can't do that, so piss off."

"Yes, we can. You have a brother in China named Jiao Long, and Jiao is a Dragonhead. I bet you call him Ji, am I right? You're a kingpin, mate, a transnational criminal, which means we have every right. We can't have you back on the streets helping carry out this ten-year plan of yours. You're going away for a long time."

Earlier in the week, Nigel verified that the crew are all Triad members from the Hong Kong area. Two of them attempted to trade information for lighter sentences, claiming they knew of a big plan. They gave up names, human trafficking methodology, and more, but in the end, they had no idea of what the big plan was, except that it was called the ten-year plan and involved weapons. For all Nigel knows, the Triad could be seizing territory from another criminal enterprise. It could be taking place well outside his jurisdiction, in China or Taiwan, but he uses the information to his advantage.

Chuanli sneers at Nigel and snarls, a guttural sound, as if he were a cornered dog. If he weren't in cuffs, the man would attempt to rip Nigel's face from his skull, but Nigel is undaunted. "I don't know what you are talking about," Chuanli growls.

"You don't know Jiao's plan? He's your brother! What is it? Are we going to war? Do you want to blow things up? Where? You help me, I help you. That's how it works."

Chuanli barks profanities and shakes with rage but shuts down. Nigel has hit a nerve. Chuanli won't divulge anything until he feels the pain and isolation of maximum security. Until then, Nigel will have to use other methods.

Nigel calls for the guards to return Chuanli to his cell. As they leave, he says, "I thought you'd be more intelligent. You had your chance and blew it."

In Mandarin, Chuanli screams, "You're a dead man."

"Maybe. I'll let your brother know we had a nice chat. You know what that means, mate. Good luck."

Chapter 5

February 12, Evening

Glacial runoff did not form the Huangpu River. A notable Chinese excavation project connected the Yangtze River with the Baoshan Waterway and the East China Sea. Seventy miles long and averaging 30 feet in depth, it is a central feature of the Shanghai cityscape, dividing east from west and providing transportation, shipping, and a water supply. Huangpu also offers impressive views in multiple districts, including the Xuhui District, where Chyou and Chyou's new boyfriend took Yin's twin sister Li to enjoy the evening. Why not? Yin is in America. Chyou's new friend has deep pockets, and Li's years of studying are finally over. Within a few weeks, she'll be working in the same hospital where her boyfriend Haitao practically lives these days.

The trio has dinner at Lost Heaven, and as the evening lengthens into the night, Chyou gets restless. She wants to dance. They have to hit the Vue or maybe a club in the Changning District near her boyfriend's residence. Li thinks it would be better if she went home, but Chyou insists, and they end up at the M1NT Club dancing and enjoying far too many drinks. Three hours into the club experience, Li sits in their booth, pressing ice cubes to her temples and trying to sober up for the trip home. She's exhausted from dancing and fending off the boyfriend's associates, an assertive group of inebriated young businessmen.

Chyou emerges from the crowd of happy bar patrons with a drink in each raised hand, yelling, "No more school!" She drops awkwardly into the booth across from Li, nearly spilling the cocktails as she pushes one of them toward her friend.

Li laughs and pushes it back. "I'm drunk but not crazy. It's time to go. Haitao will be worried."

"It's too early—one more. The sun hasn't even risen," Chyou says as she nearly consumes her entire drink in one swallow.

"You're funny, but maybe you should slow down, too."

"You know what you are? Thirteen o'clock. I don't understand why you'd want to go home to that successful, handsome doctor fiancé and waste the night making love when you could be here brushing off losers, but whatever. Come on. I can get one of the guys to drive you, but you should stay. Please have more cocktails with us and sleep it off on my boyfriend's couch. No problem."

"You are such a good friend. Thank you and thank your friends for the night."

"You and Yin mean the world to me. If she were here, we'd party into tomorrow. You know that, right? Just one more," Chyou says, pushing the drink across the table.

Li doesn't refuse the drink this time, but she doesn't drink it either. "I also wish Yin were here," she says, her voice tinged with a hint of sadness.

"Whatever. I'll get one of the guys to drive you. My boyfriend is too drunk. Be right back," she says while sliding out of the booth and nearly falling to the floor in a drunken stupor.

Li chases after her to say no thank you but instead edges through the crowd, past the busy bartenders, and out the door, thinking she needs a Dīdī Chūxíng driver or the bus. She and Yin take the Metro and public transportation all around the city, rarely this late, but she needs to be home.

Two blocks down the street, she joins a woman wearing work clothing at a bus stop. They converse about the evening, the woman complaining in florid language about cleaning bathrooms for the rich. They are there for a long while when a DiDi driver approaches them and offers Li a ride. Having little money, she says no. The driver is insistent until the working woman loudly intervenes. "She says no! You mangy dog! Go away," she barks, and as the driver leaves, they laugh.

The bus eventually comes. Li makes one transfer and arrives on Changii Road, which is within blocks of her apartment, exhausted. As she walks through the canyon of tall apartment buildings and decorative saplings, she dials Haitao's number. The air is sweet, insects buzz in the light of lampposts above, and all is well, but he doesn't answer the phone, which is common when working late. As she records a video message to her boyfriend, a DiDi pulls up beside her. It's highly unusual to see these drivers in her neighborhood, and it's alarming that one would stop next to her without being summoned.

The alarm turns to dread as she recognizes the driver from earlier. Has he followed the bus?

Li quickens her pace. The apartment complex is not far away, but as the driver follows, fear grows, and she runs. Accelerating and then screeching to a stop, yards in front of her, two large men jump from the back seat and give chase. It takes only seconds for them to reach her, time enough for her to yell once for help before being taken to the ground. Falling hard, a heavy man lands on her chest. She is helpless and stunned. As breath escapes her lungs, Li succumbs to panic.

Fighting with all her might to regain composure and control, the assailants grab her hair, neck, and legs. A vicious man slaps her violently across the jaw and then again on her ear as they force her into the vehicle.

Wrists taped together behind her back, her mouth gagged, and rope wound tightly around her neck, Li's body becomes trapped at an awkward angle. Her head and back rest on the seat, but her legs are pinned beneath the man's thigh and folded onto the floor. In this position, she is unable to resist the man as he explores her breasts and thighs at will. Getting orders from the front seat, the man holding her down presses his fingers into her empty pockets. "It's not here."

The driver yells back. "It has to be there. She was carrying it when we took the bitch. Look on the floor!"

Li has never been this terrified. The men scream at each other, cursing that no one grabbed her phone. They want to know what she did with it, but Li cannot speak. Even if she could, there is no answer. She'd been recording a message to Haitao. They chased. She ran. The phone must have dropped during the fight.

The driver's impatience becomes evident as a flurry of expletives explodes, and the car accelerates. They hide her beneath a blanket and wrestle a hood over her head. It's nearly impossible for her to breathe, and she often battles to remain conscious. An hour of groping, physical pain, and emotional distress later, the men drag her from the vehicle into the belly of a boat headed for a terrifying and uncertain future. The hood is removed. Li keeps her head down but realizes there are other women in the boat—eyes glazed, bound, gagged, and fearful.

When the boat clears the harbor, threats demand she stay silent, and her gag is removed. Despite being warned not to do so, one of the women yells. She is violently beaten.

The boat travels through the night. When they finally reach their destination and are docked, another group takes over. Men argue over her price on the deck above. They speak an odd mixture of Chinese and Cambodian. She is unique, they say, and her captors demand more money for Li than the other women.

When the negotiations end, Li is approached, held down, and feels a pinch on her arm. Before she can react, her senses drift into oblivion. She has just received the first of many injections of heroin before a thug forces her into the back of a truck, where she will spend the next few days traveling through sections of Vietnam and Laos on her way to Cambodia. The last thing she hears from her captors is a phone call. One of the men comes into the back of the truck, looks through the women, and takes a picture of Li.

In the following conversation, she hears the man tell someone, "I told you we have her."

Chapter 6

February 12th

During Li's terrifying ordeal in Shanghai, the clock strikes 2:00 pm in Boston as Yin is introduced to the MIT Director of Computational Science and Engineering. She's only communicated with Margaret Buchannan through email, but upon meeting, thinks of her as a woman she can trust. During a tour of a computer laboratory, an indescribably uneasy feeling grows in Yin, triggered by seeing a reflection of herself on an idle monitor. For a moment, she sees herself as Li.

The department head is calm and professional. She doesn't promise anything but implies that Yin could join one of the MIT programs and perhaps even be offered a fellowship. If not in Computational Science, then perhaps in linguistics. In many ways, studying linguistics is less stressful. The CCP will be less interested. Hoping to make her trip fruitful, she applied for multiple programs online. Everything sounds positive, but she worries that her work history of assisting in research projects for the government will become an issue.

Worry seems irrational to Yin at this point in the process. She dismisses thoughts of the intelligence communities in China and the US, but her dread is more profound, insistent, and intimate. She had a similarly deep and foreboding sensation one day as a child. She was inconsolable, insisting that twin sister Li was in dire trouble. Screaming that her father must do something, young Yin Yin, as her parents called her then, convinced their father to drive through the neighborhood looking for Li. He'd done this to prove that nothing was wrong, but within a few minutes, they came upon a group of people at the side of the street. Li had lost balance and ridden her bicycle into traffic. A passing motorist attempted to swerve out of her way but hit Li. The motorist was emotionally distressed, repeating that Li just rode straight into the road. The incident broke Li's leg and arm and Yin never forgot the sensation that alerted her.

Walking through MIT, that horrible feeling returns. Yin interrupts the tour in midsentence. "Please excuse me for a moment." Apologizing profusely, she steps a few feet away and places a WhatsApp call. No answer. She texts. No reply. Li would have awakened from a deep sleep to take her call, but nothing. Perhaps she's on a dance floor somewhere and cannot hear the notification through loud music. Her phone, logically, would be in her handbag.

But Yin can't shake the feeling that something is very wrong. When she returns, her eyes have moistened. Director Buchannan is appropriately concerned and asks if everything is all right, adding, "We can do this at another time."

Yin wipes her cheeks and forces a smile. "Please continue," she says, bowing slightly. Recovering quickly as the tour continues, Yin eventually follows Margaret to her office. For nearly an hour, they discuss the emphasis MIT places on global perspectives and innovation, how she can't remember when a student applied for multiple PhD programs at one time. Eventually, their conversation touches on what Yin has done in the research programs. Yin explains how she needed extra money when her parents died and that these projects offered the highest compensation. She admits that some of these programs involved aspects of cyber intelligence.

"Has your government asked for anything since? It sounds like you are here on your own accord. If so, those projects shouldn't be an issue. Anything you need to tell me?" Margaret asks.

"If you are concerned, I can just study linguistics," Yin says respectfully. She recalls her conversation with Fang and their superior, how he asked for a detailed report on her experiences here in Cambridge. It's not her intention to become a spy for anyone.

Nearing the end of their conversation, Margaret touches a printout of a Graduate Record Examination on her desk. "We require applicants to take the GRE. Based on our conversation today, I don't think you will have any difficulty with the quantitative and verbal sections. We'll even waive the cost if you want to take this while in America."

"Is that the exam?" Yin asks.

"The old one, yes. We've updated everything for the coming semester. Many of our admissions take the GRE multiple times before they score high enough. How do you think you would do on short notice?"

Though Yin continues to feel dreadful, she reaches for a diversion. "May I?"

Margaret slides the exam across her desk, and Yin thumbs through pages while their conversation carries them into cultural differences and what life is like for PhD students on campus. Five minutes later, Yin returns the document.

"What do you think? Are you willing to take the exam in the next few days? It's a lot to ask," she says, eager to see what the genius in front of her is capable of.

Yin answers confidently. "If I can take it for no charge, yes. I can answer all the questions except for 18, 44, and two at the end. I would need the language explained better for those two."

The director smiles at Yin's confidence and then chuckles. "We don't expect anyone to complete the exam perfectly, especially coming from a foreign country without study. Given your history, however, I'd like to see how you perform."

Yin takes the director literally. She says, "Now?" and immediately begins quoting questions word for word, giving answers. Her impeccable recall of the exam and the ability to answer very challenging questions without hesitation seemingly astounds the director to the point where she leans forward, picks up the exam, and follows along. After the first dozen questions, Margaret interrupts. "And which questions are an issue? I think you said eighteen, and what was it, forty-four?"

Yin recites question eighteen from memory and listens to the explanation. She answers the question and begins reciting question forty-four, but the director raises her hands in surrender. "I didn't mean for you to answer the questions right now, but my God. If all of China's students are as gifted as you, her future is bright. Astounding. A fellowship is yours if you want it. We may even find a budget for moving expenses. Welcome to MIT, Ms. Chen. I will finalize an offer tomorrow or soon after. Do you have any further questions for me?"

Yin beams. "Thank you very much. Before I can accept, I must discuss it with my sister."

Margaret is surprised by Yin's reply. "You must be very close. Anyway, that is acceptable. There are people I would like you to meet. If I arrange a dinner for tonight, can you be available?"

"Absolutely," Yin says smoothly.

Walking briskly to her hotel, Yin is overwhelmed with dreams for the future. The probability of having moving expenses paid and coming here to study exceeds expectations. She feels she could easily work on two PhD degrees simultaneously. Smiling, she tells the frigid Boston air, "The opportunities are endless." But the thrill doesn't last as she remembers her sister's lack of replies, and dark thoughts overtake her.

As Yin arrives in her room, the generalized sensation of dread turns to panic. It's early morning in China. Li has never been a heavy drinker, and even if preoccupied with her friends, she would want to know what Yin is up to in America. They talked briefly about Yin studying abroad one day. That day has come. Li should have replied to text messages. Hadn't she promised to call?

Yin dials Haitao's number. Li's boyfriend picks up immediately to say he's worried. "Li went out with Chyou and some guy to a restaurant, then maybe dancing. I should have been there, but she promised to be home by 10, and I haven't heard from her since they left. I've called her five times in the past hour. I even went to your apartment and banged on the door, but there were no lights or answer."

"She's such a foolish girl sometimes. They were going to see belly dancing. Did she mention anything else? What do you know about Chyou's boyfriend?"

"We've never met, but you know what Chyou is like. She's all about the money. He's probably rich," Haitao replies.

"You have his number? Maybe you can reach Chyou."

"No answer. I'll keep you informed. There's probably a simple explanation."

"I hope so, Haitao."

• • •

Exhausted from travel, anxious about Li's whereabouts yet jubilant with the day's activities, Yin collapses onto her hotel bed. Eyes closed, nearly asleep, Yin gets a phone call. Ms. Buchannan invites her to have dinner with a group of faculty members. Yin agrees, but her mind spins like a child's top, losing momentum. She sets her alarm and focuses on possible explanations, such as that Li may have celebrated a bit too much, that her phone is lost, or perhaps left in a restaurant. Speculation seems useless. An innocent explanation is the best. Li probably left her phone in a car or taxi and will use Haitao's to connect when she awakens.

Seconds later, Yin has an idea. She opens a map that geo-locates Li's phone via GPS, and it's right there! According to the tracking feature, Li's phone is at the apartment building, and Yin experiences a deep sense of relief. "Silly girl!" she says aloud, believing now that Li did make it home and has fallen into an alcohol-induced slumber.

The realization that Li's phone is at the apartment allows Yin to focus on other matters. She is in America. She will meet with faculty members for dinner and likely will be awarded a fellowship. That thought returns her to Li, but in a different way. For weeks, she'd imagined their conversation, how she'd inform her sister of the opportunity, how Li would resist leaving her boyfriend and her new job at the hospital. Li is change-averse, but separation is inevitable. Yin will come to America while Li remains in Shanghai. Who knows, she reasons. In time, maybe Li will join her in Boston, or Yin may return to China after a year or two in the West. Moments into imagining a bright future for her and Li, she is sound asleep.

Two hours later, a phone alarm frightens Yin awake. It's 6 pm in Boston and 6 am in Shanghai. Checking for messages, she finds nothing from Li. Rising, she decides to present her best look. She'll wear an intelligent business outfit, slit skirt, silk blouse, and jacket. The occasion calls for exceptional makeup. When Yin wants to use her looks to provide an advantage, she does. Men are instantly attracted, and women become envious. *Why not?* Opportunity awaits.

As a taxi takes her to the restaurant, Yin attempts to reach Li and Haitao, but there's no response. It's understandable, as it's only 7 am in Shanghai. Li is probably sleeping off her night on the town, and since Haitao was up nearly all night looking for her, he must be exhausted and resting.

Through appetizers and a glass of recommended Pinot Grigio, Yin listens to the professors praise her abilities. In turn, they arrange for moments of her time in the coming days. She smiles and agrees, but internal conflict builds as the night progresses. Yin worked for years to get into this exact position. If MIT doesn't work out, Technische Universitat Munchen in Germany or Oxford in the UK might. Every instructor in China encouraged her to think big, reach for the stars, see the world, and accomplish great things. Great things are happening, but she cannot fully relax until she hears from Li, which is a problem. Everyone at the dinner table assumes she is coming to Cambridge.

"Oh! I almost forgot. I talked with friends, and we have arranged a moving stipend. I'm so excited for you," Margaret says.

"Me as well but remember that I still need to discuss this with my sister."

The director and faculty members seated near her stiffen. "I rarely have everyone together in one spot, so let's take full advantage. What time is it in Shanghai? Is there a 12-hour difference? I'm sure your sister will be excited for you. Make the call, and then we can discuss how you fit into various programs."

"In America, as you say, there is no timing like the present," Yin says, inviting smiles and chuckles from the faculty. Stepping away, she sees an urgent text from Li's boyfriend Haitao, *Call me as soon as possible.*

"What now," Yin whispers as she steps out of the restaurant into the frigid evening and places the call. Haitao answers on the second ring, clearly distraught. "Li's phone is not in the apartment. I found it in the street and called the police."

"I don't understand. Where is Li?"

"If she's in the apartment, she is not answering the door. I banged for a long time. I doubt she would have passed out from drinking, but as I walked to my car, I dialed her number one more time and heard ringing. Li's phone was out here on the pavement beneath a parked car. The glass is cracked, Yin. The police are on their way. And there's something else. It isn't good, Yin," Haitao says, but silence says he is reluctant to go on.

"Haitao! You can't just say there is something else and leave that hanging. What?"

"I really need to get into your apartment to verify that she made it home. I'm worried."

"That's it? That's the something else that isn't good? You are overreacting, Haitao, but I'll call the building manager and have him meet you, okay? Try not to worry."

She imagines logical explanations. Li became intoxicated, fumbled for her keys, and dropped her phone without realizing it was gone. The phone bounced off the curb into the street, but this is fear-driven speculation. Yin has more important things to do than focus on her sister's foolishness. When this is all straightened out, she'll give Li a piece of her mind!

Two men approach the restaurant entrance while Yin is on her call. One of them turns back. "Ms. Chen? Yin Chen?"

"You'll call now? Haitao says. Then, reluctantly adds, "There is a smear of something on the phone."

Distracted by the men talking to her, she doesn't catch everything Haitao says but agrees. "Yes, I'll call now. Don't worry. I have to go."

Yin ends her call with Haitao, and the men approach. They introduce themselves as a professor and a consultant. "We've heard amazing things. You're like some mysterious genius from China, but I had no idea you were so good-looking. Welcome to Cambridge," the Professor says. Yin overlooks the sexist comment and gives the intruders minimal attention before strategically tapping the call button for her apartment complex building manager. When the manager answers, she dismisses the men with a raised finger, saying the group is in the restaurant.

The men politely nod and leave to join the others.

Yin describes the dire situation to the building manager, and he agrees to meet Haitao and the police for a wellness check.

Yin returns to her hosts and nearly forgets the situation at home. Concern evaporates amid lively discussions about the future of artificial intelligence, including what AI means to the global workforce. Some believe it will increase efficiency, while others are more concerned with the social and economic effects of replacing millions of workers with technical solutions. Yin doesn't comment on speculations involving autonomous weapons. At the tail end of every discussion, Yin's opinions are solicited. Her assessments spellbind the group.

As it turns out, the consultant she met in the parking lot is a former student and one of the speakers at the upcoming conference. His role on a panel is to discuss AI applications in governance. Choosing to be politically neutral, Yin uses a trick she learned during casual debates with students of the Philosophy department at SJTU. She borrows from scholars and experts to advance points, quoting articles, noting the author and date of publication for the materials found in the *International Journal of Information Management*, the *Journal of Business Research, Government Information Quarterly*, and numerous other scholarly sources as she describes the intersection of machine learning and embedded code, disruptive innovation within higher-level thinking, and how AI will soon parse the workforce into silos based on emotion-sensing algorithms, disease forecasting, and statistical comparisons with corporate and governmental goals.

"Governments face social and ethical challenges that too few people are working to solve. Your Google scientists, for example, think their machine has attained consciousness, but look at what is already in place. AI is a buffer between large companies and their employees. Applying for a job requires satisfying AI first before meeting an actual human being," she says, interrupted mid-thought by yet another text from Haitao: *Li is not in the apartment. Call me!*

This new message sends observable chills through Yin as the simple explanations conjured about Li's well-being cascade into dark speculation.

"Are you okay?" Margaret asks.

Yin places her phone on the table and attempts to remain cheerful.

"Might you be willing to sit on the panel? You can explain the latest advances in China. I think it would be fascinating. Have you been involved in any of that research?" The panelist asks.

Yin has not come to America to disclose her country's technology.

She is about to reply and ask the consultant probing questions of her own, such as who he works for, but the words don't come. All that Yin manages to say is that her sister is missing. Despite the stoic demeanor she attempts to present, tears flow.

Surprise and concern envelop the table as Yin describes an empty apartment, the phone found in the street, and her deep sense that something horrible has happened. As is her culture and personal style, Yin apologizes for bringing emotional problems to the table and then is interrupted by another text.

"So sorry. Please excuse me," Yin says as she leaves to call Haitao.

"The police think there's blood on the phone and want to open it. Do you have the passcode? It's hard to see through the display, but the phone still works," Haitao says.

Yin struggles with the implications but focuses on the passcode. She's seen Li open her phone a thousand times using facial recognition, but sometimes Li's fingers fly thumb over thumb in an X pattern. "Try 357159," Yin says and waits.

Moments later, Haitao confirms access. "We're in. The police will go through the phone looking for evidence. I'm so sorry, Yin. It must be tough for you, being so far away."

"Difficult for both of us. Make sure they have my number when they find something," Yin says and returns to the dinner table.

The conversation continues, but Yin cannot focus. While feigning interest in her dinner partners, her mind travels elsewhere.

Forty minutes later, as her hosts sip coffee and after-dinner drinks, Yin gets another phone call and again steps away. In the parking lot, Yin listens to a police officer describe the video Li was recording when taken. "Taken?" Yin asks in disbelief. Her thoughts tumble one over the other.

She hears the steps the police will take, is promised a video copy, and firmly implores the officer to do everything possible to keep her informed. "She may have come home on the bus. The CCTV cameras on Changi Road will show if someone followed her. Also, she may have been at the M1NT Club with numerous cameras. You should contact her friends. Haitao has their names and numbers," Yin says, prompting the policeman to say he knows his job.

When Yin returns, her hands shake. She explains that Shanghai police are calling her sister's disappearance an abduction, then asks if everyone would be all right if she retired early. No one argues. They all stand to say goodnight and wish her well. Ms. Buchannan drives Yin to her hotel, and they talk momentarily, but Yin has already decided.

In the hotel room, Yin logs into Scandinavian Airlines to change her flight schedule. Li was abducted. That is her highest priority. Whether MIT understands or not, she will return home and begin a search. Nothing else matters.

Chapter 7

February 13, evening

Deputy Chief of Station Nigel Rainer is familiar with the long history of Triads in China and Taiwan, but he recently encountered a significant operation in Australia. The prospect of having interrogated the brother of a Dragonhead has him on edge. Why would they send a high-ranking member to Australia? Are they planning something on his home turf? Prisoners he's interrogated claim there is a five and ten-year rolling plan, and Nigel's gut says their capabilities and outreach are more sophisticated than his intelligence community imagines. He's heard stories of brutal retribution to Triad members and their families and even more violent attacks against outsiders, but professionals like Nigel don't cower to anyone.

Dragonhead's brother Chuanli doesn't care what comes. He's vile, arrogant, and thinks of himself as untouchable. Nigel would typically be cooling down from a gut-wrenching gym workout or 20-mile cycling run along Singapore's East Coast Park coastline at this late hour. However, having just returned from Australia and fueled by unanswered questions, he finds himself at work instead. He sits in a dark operations center catching up on classified material showing Triad activities over the past decade. His boss, Essex, would be incensed at this diversion from other projects, but he doesn't understand the enemy. Why has this Triad expanded its arms business? What could he do if he controlled 20,000 members and wanted to make a statement? If the Triads are moving toward more advanced weapon systems, that is especially worrying. They've existed for centuries and are well organized, so Nigel is in for a very long night of research.

The operations center turns off air conditioning late at night to conserve budget. The air is stale, the humidity is rising, and Nigel's is the only light in the otherwise dark room. Where to start?

Nigel's methodology may be unorthodox, but many facts are found in the margins of research. He dives into classified internal documents that all point to the Triad drug trade and then into the history of the regions where they have extensive operations, beginning with a history of activities in the Golden Triangle.

Shan State Province in northern Myanmar is beautiful, rugged, and impossible to govern. Naypyidaw cannot control the regions of the north, no matter what they tell themselves or the international press. Nigel finds that the United Wa State Army, Warlords, and Jihadist-leaning organizations reign supreme in two large enclaves.

Shan State is among Southeast Asia's most beautiful yet dangerous areas for foreigners. Nigel's government has long warned citizens not to travel there unless necessary, and it makes sense. Corruption is rampant and ongoing. The province is a stronghold of resistance against the central government, and Nigel imagines it is possible the Triad trades weapons for drugs and drugs for weapons. At one time, the region provided most of the world's heroin supply, bringing billions of dollars into the pockets of warlords. The Golden Triangle region encompasses the northern areas of Myanmar, Laos, and Thailand. He reads that chemicals used to transform poppies into heroin come mainly from China. Specifically, the Guangdong and Hong Kong underworld supplied growers with equipment and manufacturing supplies. In return, they became one of the prime exporters of finished products.

Heroin is still produced and shipped from the region but has lost market share to Afghanistan. Today, yaba rules the streets, even in Australia.

Nigel speeds through additional background material: yaba is a mixture of methamphetamines and caffeine, is easier to produce, more lucrative to sell, more challenging to enforce, and rapidly gaining popularity. The cost per dose is minimal, and the manufacturing process is simple. Nigel is astounded to discover that a single small manufacturer can produce 10,000 tablets per hour and may have his extended family working 24/7.

Nigel leans back in his chair, hands clasped behind his head. Sipping the last drops of cold coffee, he laughs at one of his findings. UNODC, the UN's effort to unify drug enforcement agencies across borders, still publicly touts their interception of a million-plus tablet shipment of yaba. The calculator on his phone shows the hollowness of that win. Furthermore, the batch UNODC bragged about was seized in Bangladesh years earlier, headed for India. Quantities above that one confiscation leave Myanmar daily and travel uninterrupted throughout the region. Yaba, sometimes called crazy medicine or Nazi speed, is unstoppable, and the organized underworld knows how to leverage drugs to their full advantage. Nigel's smile fades to worry as he gazes at the map on the wall. The Triads are masters at moving people and materials undetected through their networks. They are well established in the drug trade, invested heavily in human trafficking and prostitution, and have, based on his research, increased their presence in the arms trade. Dragonhead has a ten-year plan. Speaking aloud, he mouths his mounting concern. "What the hell are you blokes up to?"

Meanwhile, nearly 1,800 miles away in the region Nigel is researching, workers package 100 kilos of yaba for transportation. The drug is weighed, wrapped, and then concealed in vehicles. Crazy medicine has an immediate rush, a meteoric rise in energy the user craves, followed by an equally dramatic crash. Long-time users are helplessly addicted and will do essentially anything to maintain supplies, which means that the Triad has a nearly endless flow of cash. The humidity in the waystation where these men work is a concern. They bag the tablets quickly to avoid damage from the moisture.

It takes longer to move a few dozen small amounts across borders than to transport it in one load by truck, but if one or two transporters of these small quantities get arrested, Triad losses are minimal. Furthermore, transporters know very little about operations and are intimidated enough to keep their mouths shut.

This batch of yaba is divided between waterways, sent through jungle trails on pack animals, loaded onto ATVs and motorcycles, and hidden in the wheel wells of inconspicuous vehicles. Voluminous shipments leave Myanmar weekly for a warehouse near Jinding Town, Guangdong Province, and underworld Hawala financial networks facilitate transactions.

Tu, a leading figure with a fierce reputation in the Pearl Triad, oversees acquisition, transportation, packaging, and distribution. The organization operates primarily throughout the Pearl River Estuary, with operations in Zhuhai, Shenzhen, Hong Kong, Macau, and surrounding areas. It is often also called the Hong Kong Triad because this is the most recognizable city within their domain. Dragonhead trusts Tu to oversee shipments with a street value in the tens of millions, and as such, he inspects every batch as it arrives in China, but this shipment has an issue.

One of Tu's intermediaries arrives at the warehouse from his collection point in a tuk-tuk. He unloads 85 packages, claiming that one of his transporters arrived 15 bags short. Tu pulls a pistol concealed in his belt and points it directly at the man's head, prompting the intermediary to fall to his knees with hands clasped in front of his chest. "You dare to steal from me?"

"No sir," the man says with begging eyes and lips quivering in a toothless mouth. They are feet apart, shadows merged, Tu towering over the transporter. Even the insects seem to sense tension in the room as the man begs.

Tu barks at the driver's assistant. "Is he stealing?" Tu is stout, muscular, and unflinching. As Dragonhead's right-hand man, Tu is the Triad's enforcer and, in that role, one of the most feared men in the region. His skin glistens with sweat below a hanging light.

The assistant glances once at the driver and then back to Tu. He says, "I said it wouldn't work. His wife has the pills."

The driver is shocked at the betrayal. He pleads, palms pressed together. "Wait. Please wait! I can get it all back. It was a mistake I'll—"

Without warning, Tu fires a round into the driver's forehead mid-sentence. The bark of his round echoes through the warehouse, and blood floods from the man's skull onto the floor as he collapses. He points his pistol at the young assistant. "You helped him?"

The assistant spits on the dead driver and says, "No, but I know where she lives. I will get the drugs back for you." He doesn't wince, beg, or run as Tu assesses his options.

As quickly as it was drawn, Tu holsters his weapon. "You have twenty-four hours. Get the shipment back, and you can have this fool's job."

"Yes, sir," the young man says. He quickly bows and then hops into the tuk-tuk.

"Wait," Tu says.

The young man steps out of the vehicle. Tu lifts a steel machete from a nearby table and tosses it to the young man's feet. The clatter and scrape of steel on concrete startles the man, but not as much as Tu's demand. "Bring me her hand."

"Her hand? The wife's hand?"

"Do you want the job or not? Her hand or yours," Tu says, glaring.

With a nod and bow, the assistant takes the machete into the tuk-tuk and speeds away.

Tu was young when he joined the Triads, just 14 years old. He quickly learned that his superiors expected ruthless loyalty. Jiao Long is Dragonhead. He heads Pearl Triad operations worldwide. He is brilliant, pitiless beyond measure, and under his leadership, annually supplies billions in methamphetamines to the world. When Tu finishes his repackaging work, he checks the time and opens an email client on his phone to modify a draft message: *I'm finished with the rice but had extra housekeeping to take care of. I'm returning in a few hours.*

The draft resides on a private server in a penthouse atop one of two casinos Dragonhead controls in Macau. The Las Vegas-style casino is the crown jewel of Dragonhead's vast enterprise. He opens the draft Tu created using the same login credentials, reads the message, and closes the file with a smile. Their shared message is never actually sent. Even if sent by accident, the email would go nowhere. The message describes shipments of rice and housekeeping. Neither rice nor housekeeping fit into the algorithms of prowling search engines used by governmental agencies.

To celebrate yet another successful shipment of yaba, Dragonhead pours a short glass of expensive aged Scotch and sips it while standing at the floor-to-ceiling windows of his penthouse, gazing at the Flor de Lótus Estrada below. His wealth is indescribable. Liquid assets are hidden in bank accounts across the globe and stashed in cryptocurrency accounts. Like many Russian oligarchs, dubious wealth managers, and underworld figures, Dragonhead embraced crypto early. It remains a simple way to facilitate large transactions secretly. The introduction of blockchain inhibits some nefarious payments, but BitCoin and Ethereum are not the only options. Wealth buys talent. Dragonhead has purchased some of the best talent in the world to help him secure and grow his fortunes.

From his penthouse in Macau, Dragonhead manages hundreds of projects as pedantic as fishing pens for illegally harvested ocean fish to ransomware attacks on unsuspecting Westerners watching porn in the privacy of their bedrooms. Dragonhead digitally tracks his earnings but carries the bottom line in his head. From an early age, he's been good with numbers and has a mastery of calculating risk vs. reward. When his foolish brother was captured in Australia, he hired a hacker and his crew to investigate. It was the first time he heard the name Nigel Rainer. According to his hackers, Rainer's dogged research ended his foray in Australia, accelerating his plans to increase digital capabilities.

Drink in hand, Dragonhead forgets about his shipment of yaba, pushes Australia out of his mind, and goes to his desk to follow up on a more relevant and stimulating project. Dragonhead's portfolio of legitimate businesses has expanded exponentially in the past decade. At the same time, recruiting and retaining members in his organization is more complex. This Triad remains strong, but factions and decentralization have undermined stability. Social media and the internet entice the vulnerable young men who once took to the streets to fill social needs. The Triads offer money, position, and a sense of belonging. Today, these young men sit in isolation, playing online games.

Furthermore, many members no longer adhere to the old ways. The noble ceremonies, spiritual overtones, and familial bonds that held the seven Triads in power for a century barely survive. Dragonhead is more cunning and resourceful than his competitors. He lives in a bigger picture and has mapped a ten-year strategy for regaining the honor and dominance of his predecessors. China is undoubtedly regaining supremacy, and so is he.

Dragonhead reviews reports from one of his legitimate import and export companies serving the international arms trade. Like many of his coded communications, he uses predetermined terms to discuss the tracking technology built into recently purchased and highly specialized weapon systems.

Jiao Long never implicitly trusts anyone and worries that he doesn't understand the technologies he relies upon. The complexity of contemporary tools forces him to study robotics and algorithms rather than people and events. He borrows concepts and terms from one expert and uses them with another to convince those he hires of his capability. He's manipulating a daunting weapon system. When manufacturers construct surface-to-surface or surface-to-air missiles, they embed sophisticated tracking technologies. Militaries enforce digital and physical security measures to prevent weapons of mass destruction from being released into the wild. Fleets of specialized satellites track these weapons until they are used or dismantled. Personal phones, truck fleets, and virtually anything can be geocoded and tracked. Jiao would love to use shipment tracking technology for drug transportation but fears law enforcement could somehow identify his specific tracking tags. The tracking tags used in weapons of mass destruction are more powerful, welded into the ordnances, and very difficult to defeat. Disarming tracking systems in surface-to-air and surface-to-surface missiles is critical to the big plan. It's difficult, but the spirits of his predecessors are with him.

Dragonhead logs into an encrypted virtual private network to check the progress of a competent team of underworld engineers. It has cost Dragonhead millions for them to design specialized GPS jammers. Their bolt-on low-profile design has been tested and works flawlessly. It would have been less expensive to disable tracking, but he demanded the ability to toggle tracking signals on and off from the comfort of his office. As soon as he's given a demonstration, the engineers will receive the balance of their payment. They may even live to spend it. Then again, why should he trust these men to stay silent? Trust is a weakness. He prides himself on being strong. The initial phase of his ten-year plan is nearly ready for execution. It's time to cash in on years of work.

Where is Tu? Dragonhead looks at his watch and impatiently awaits the arrival of his enforcer. Tu is the only man allowed to enter Dragonhead's office without first seeking permission. When he enters, Dragonhead sizes up his lieutenant as if confirming his tenure or contemplating his replacement. Tu smiles. He's intimidated, beaten, and even killed for Dragonhead. Though under six feet tall, Tu is rock hard with thick hands, mentally tough, and emotionless in the face of adversity. Even Dragonhead is unsure if Tu is trustworthy, but the man's loyalty has been unwavering. "Housekeeping?" Dragonhead asks.

"A transporter gave our product to his wife. I've dealt with it," Tu says.

Tu's father grew up in Hong Kong. His mother came from Yunnan Province in the Southwest of China, home to many who embrace Islam. Tu has the appearance and background to interact casually with Muslims. It's one of the traits Dragonhead relies upon while dealing with warlords and Jihadists in Myanmar. Tu's quiet demeanor and don't-mess-with-me physique earned him a spot in numerous negotiations with Islamists along the drug routes he relies upon for the yaba trade. Dragonhead is undeniably in charge, but Tu is the sword and his gateway into the Muslim community.

"What happened?" Dragonhead says gruffly, raising his glass in a silent offer to procure a glass of scotch for Tu. As always, Tu declines.

"One of the intermediaries. The amount was insignificant, but the act is unacceptable. I shot him and ordered his replacement to bring me his wife's hand," Tu says flatly.

"These peasants think they can do whatever they want."

"Others will think twice before trying something like that. Trust me," Tu says.

"You confuse obedience with trust. A man in my position trusts no one!" Dragonhead snaps.

Tu has heard this rant a thousand times. He stiffens out of respect but shows no fear.

Dragonhead lets his words settle for a moment and then changes the subject. "I'm creating a second cyber team and data center. You will manage the project. I want them operational within one month or else. It's all in there," Dragonhead says, pointing to a folder on a nearby table.

Tu is unshaken by Dragonhead's veiled threat of—or else. He studies a summary of the project before replying. When he does, his tone is perplexed. "I'm no technologist, but for a project of this size, one month isn't long."

"I have a man for the technology. His bio is in the back. Just keep him motivated."

Tu jumps to a section on the project leader, Bao Gu. After reading some of it, he says, "Are you sure we can trust this guy?"

Dragonhead laughs. "What did I just say about trust? You insist on using that word. No matter. I understand the man. He thinks like I do. Remember the girl I had you take? It was a request from Bao. You questioned why it had to be done. He didn't say, and I don't care. He has his reasons, and that is the end of it. It's important that we keep him happy and motivated for now."

Tu questions how taking the girl from Shanghai connects with Bao and the data center, but his thoughts are interrupted by a wave of Dragonhead's hand.

"Let it go, Tu. She's just another bitch in the system. Bao is an extraordinary hacker and crypto expert, so whatever he wants is approved. He trained in Beijing and was a former protégé with MSS. He has the skills I need."

"I understand," Tu says. "Bao spends most of his time in the West, which has made him unruly. You know the type, but I've tested him on three projects."

"If you have confidence in him, so do I. What kind of man is he?" Tu asks, thumbing through the dossier.

"He sounds more like a boisterous Westerner than a Chinaman. I need to meet him in person. Set it up as soon as possible. If that goes well, we will proceed. There's no room for error as we move forward. I hope you know what that means." Dragonhead says, with emphasis on yet another threat.

"Understood. Meet here or somewhere else?"

"Downstairs, and Tu, he doesn't need to know this is my casino. That's all," Dragonhead says and turns again to the window. He increasingly ends their conversations with a curt dismissal, which concerns Tu.

Tu rereads Bao Gu's CV and technical documents at home. He was born in 1983, the same year the Communist People's Republic of China formed its Ministry of State Security. It was the year of the Pig, which implied good fortune and hard work leading to prosperity. Bao should have been sociable, reliable, patient, and a loving and humorous child. But he was born in an emerging China where a billion people struggled against each other for positions and rewards. Fortunately for Bao's family, his father was reassigned from the Central Investigation Department to a prominent position within the Fourth Bureau of MSS, where he trained recruits in gathering information, analyzing trends, and counterintelligence. The CCP rewarded the family with exceptional housing and ample income, but they were not wealthy.

Wanting a better future for his son, Bao's father ruthlessly trained him to become a national treasure, a prodigy in computer science. While the neighborhood swelled with the laughter and sounds of children learning Chinese football, Bao worked through tutorials on programming and robotics. He spent hours at his father's side learning ultrasonic, RF, acoustic, and optical wiretapping techniques by hacking their neighbors. Young Bao was enthralled with intercepting domestic communications and soon extended the practice to the international stage. Learning to compromise others led to advanced encryption techniques and trading hacks on the deep web. By the age of 15, his father's plan took root. Bao was on a path toward specialized schooling and a position within the intelligence community.

The dossier reads like an official intelligence briefing. In Tu's estimation, Dragonhead paid generously for the information or traded something of intense value. He would love to know where the information came from, but questions are dangerous. The next document reads as an analyst's assessment of Bao's childhood and work history. According to the writeup, he was pampered, arrogant, self-absorbed, and disruptive in his youth—traits the CCP exploited. A lesser talent may have been arrested and sent into a reeducation program. Instead, Bao was moved to higher challenges, eventually leading to an international assignment in Silicon Valley that yielded detailed information on corporate expansions. Unfortunately, the move inspired Bao to pursue self-interest.

The dossier says he spent a year programming games for a major US firm in California. Tu knows that a few phone calls to trusted individuals in the Triad's network can verify that, but Bao worked for himself from California forward. A hand-written note on one of the pages asks if Bao has gone rogue. The implication is that Bao no longer works for MSS. On the next page, there is a brief entry saying he was the founder and president of a private cryptocurrency corporation.

Another scrawled comment in Dragonhead's hand says Bao is wealthy and cannot be effectively motivated by money. This second message tells Tu all he needs to know. That Dragonhead calls Bao wealthy is a powerful statement. Dragonhead is close-lipped with everyone about his finances, even Tu. He claims to own a small house on the outskirts of Hong Kong and a condominium on a golf course, talking about them as if he were financially overcommitted and living a commoner's life. Meanwhile, he often spends weekends on a yacht, owns two casinos, and, as Tu knows, pockets much of the cash generated by years-long trading in drugs, arms, illicit seafood, and dozens of other nefarious activities. None of these activities matter much to Tu. He gets paid handsomely and has a 10-year plan of his own. If Dragonhead says Bao is wealthy, then Bao is very wealthy.

Dragonhead insists the Triad needs to leverage cutting-edge technology better to survive, and the goals for this new cyber team address that strategy. Bao's proposal is detailed and visionary. But who is leading whom? As Tu scans the equipment and skills needed for a new data center, he realizes how important Bao is to Dragonhead's plans. Business requirements include the manipulation of cryptocurrency, expanding their corporate digital espionage programs, gaining a foothold in China's move toward mobile money, penetrating or otherwise compromising governmental anti-crime units, and pursuing new technologies useful in transnational trade. Tu knows what that last requirement implies. Dragonhead seeks to use the dark web to service illicit commerce.

The Triads are specialists in moving drugs, undeclared produce, arms, and people undetected across borders and around the world. Establishing a super cyber team in support of these activities is brilliant. But becoming dependent on someone like Bao Gu worries Tu. It's risky, but it is not in his job description to question Jiao's judgment.

In just five years, Dragonhead created multiple successful online gaming sites serving millions of Chinese and international customers. Operations of this size attract intense scrutiny from the CCP and others, but he is protected. Protection is quietly paid for in trade, as Dragonhead provides personal data to the government. The Triads also move spies from neighboring countries in and out of China, so their passports don't show return trips. Dragonhead has a database that he calls his dirty dossiers. There's no better place to gather dirt than at the nexus of digital technology and vice, and Dragonhead has collected extensive material on visiting professionals, corporate giants, and party leaders.

Bao will need to know intimate details about Dragonhead's plans. Tu knows that trust is a dangerous commodity, and in the case of the Triads, it comes with high expectations and potentially lethal consequences. People who betray Dragonhead's trust are visited at night and missing in the morning. Families receive anonymous funeral expenses before a husband or wife goes missing, and while Jiao Long remains in power, no one is exempt. Always watching, never forgetting, Tu understands that even Dragonhead's brother is no longer trusted. He knows too much. Anyone can break. Dragonhead asked him to collect information on Barwon Prison. He wants to know the precise location of Chuanli in the prison, which can only mean one thing.

Tu knew Dragonhead's sibling had great ambition, which is a good thing in Triad culture. People who want things are easy to manipulate. Chuanli's appetite grew too quickly. It wasn't enough for him to run drugs and prostitution in Shenzhen, so Dragonhead put him in charge of Australian operations. If he'd been smart, he would have cautiously developed friends in high places before taking risks, but he hadn't listened. The Triads have long developed intel on law enforcement and counterintelligence groups through human assets. He'll investigate this person Nigel Rainer, but that's not what worries him. Tu foresees being called upon to clean up the mess at Barwon Prison.

At the end of a long day, as Dragonhead locks his office and summons his driver, he reflects on his progress. Recent communications with Bao reveal untapped potential in his plan. When people can't trust institutions and leaders to keep them safe, they turn to authoritarian principles and vice. In Dragonhead's business, desperate people become profitable targets. Real estate values plummet in periods of crisis, markets fall, law enforcement becomes preoccupied, and the distance between haves and have-nots grows. The underworld fills that temporary gap. In time, the market rebounds, and property values rise again in the cyclical nature of economies. In good times, the Triads do well. In bad times, they do even better. The key to making money is working both sides of the economic equation—creating chaos in times of stability and stability during crisis.

Dragonhead enjoys his ride more today than usual. Everyone he passes on the streets is a potential source of revenue. As a young man, Jiao learned from his elders. From the earliest days of the five monk fighters, through the secret societies, and until today, the Triads have been influential in China's culture. They help leaders rise to power, serve as advisors and generals, and remove players from the political landscape when necessary. The regional chaos he plans will undoubtedly exacerbate the worsening state of US and Chinese relations, which suits Dragonhead very well.

There's nothing more chaotic than terrorism. Jiao has anonymously funded small regional attacks for years through intermediaries, building trust and gradually increasing his support among those intent on attacks. Coordinated attacks on specific targets will lead to a higher demand for the services he provides, including the diversions of sex, drugs, gambling, the prevalence of backdoor loans, and a heightened demand for conventional weapons.

"Never let a good crisis go to waste," Dragonhead often says. The Triads earned over a billion dollars in the US during the COVID crisis simply by manipulating the availability and distribution of masks and related PPE. Beijing made 100 times that amount. He'd sold masks he didn't have, claiming problems with shipping. He manufactured three-ply masks from inferior materials, created knockoffs of European goods, and flooded markets with diluted disinfectant. His gambling and prostitution operations, command of the drug trade, and ability to control select politicians at every level of government through payoffs and extortion are, to him, tested strategies in need of replication and scaling. Years of incoming personal wealth will come if he executes his plans flawlessly. To do so, he needs men like Tu and Bao.

During the limo ride to his yacht, Jiao studies the Macau skyline and imagines buying additional properties in the harbor, opening more casinos, and one day retreating to a private island. Anything is possible.

• • •

Back in Singapore, staring blankly at a map encompassing the golden triangle, Nigel Rainer realizes he is more interested in the golf podcast playing on his phone than in researching Triad activities. He's tired. He's learned a great deal and knows where he wants to take his investigation next.

Nigel has a friend in the CIA who plays golf. They use golf to get illicit favors from each other, so before going home, he books a tee time at

Marina Bay Golf Course. His friend will probably comply with a minor request if he pays for the round and dinner afterward.

Chapter 8

February 14th

Yin's flight from the US to Shanghai Pudong International Airport lands at 8:45 in the evening. She anxiously gathers her luggage and flags a Dazhong taxi. Yin and Li's apartment is 30 minutes away in the Zhoujia Ferry residential district, which gives her time to call Haitao and the police for updates. Unfortunately, Haitao has nothing new, and the detective is unavailable.

The restless flight home included bouts of hypervigilance and fear, leading to exhaustion. She napped when she could but spent most of her flight outlining strategies, beginning with research on abductions. She planned to reach out for help, but to whom? The police say they are doing everything in their power. She may be able to retrace Li's steps, which prompts a call to their friend Chyou.

"Why would you let Li go on her own!" Yin snaps when Chyou answers.

"You're back?" Chyou responds, startled.

"Of course, I came back. What happened?" Yin says, trying desperately not to eviscerate her friend before hearing her side of the story.

"She wouldn't listen to us. I tried everything. My boyfriend said she could stay with us, and one of his friends volunteered to drive Li home. She wouldn't listen. I'm sorry, but please don't assume it's my fault. I feel terrible already. We were all dancing and having a great time. The next thing I knew, someone said she was gone. What do the police say?"

"She wanted to be home at 10. What time did she leave?" Yin asks, still swallowing her anger.

"I'm not sure. Sometime after midnight? Haitao says she was kidnapped. I can't believe this is happening," Chyou says. The sincerity in her tone disarms Yin. Every woman fears aggressive, deranged men. As upset as Yin is, this is likely Chyou's nightmare, too.

"Wake up, Chyou! If she refused the ride from your friend, he was no gentleman."

Chyou doesn't answer, and Yin continues. "You shouldn't have kept her out so late, but never mind. I'm just upset with her foolishness."

"The police?" Chyou asks.

"Nothing yet. I'll let you know when I hear something. I have to go now, though. I've just arrived at our apartment."

As Yin exits the taxi and opens her front door, her resolve stiffens. There is her sister's favorite chair. Photos rest in frames on tables, selfies mostly of the twins at Sanjiagang Beach and their trip to the Great Wall. Nothing seems out of order. The chair where Li often drops her handbag is as empty as she feels and somehow looks pathetic. The lemon ice Li is so fond of still waits for her in the freezer, untouched. Knowing Li so well, she would have immediately reached for that treat upon returning from her night out, but Li didn't make it to the safety of their apartment. Someone grabbed her in the street. Had she been targeted at the dance club and followed? Who would do such a thing, and why?

Another thought comes. Could Li have been taken by mistake? Yin imagines that she might have been the target, not Li. She recalls the sights and sounds leading up to her Boston trip, sifting through the faces of men and women she suspected of following her from the SSSB building, people she and Li call party lackeys, but it's useless. Nothing relevant occurs to her.

Forcing herself through a shower, Yin fries an egg, makes toast and tea, and then opens her laptop. She hunts for the few people she knows on the dark web who might be knowledgeable about human trafficking, but minutes into the hunt, her eyes begin to blur with fatigue. Yin fights to stay alert but cannot think clearly. Reluctantly, she curls onto the sofa and, within minutes, sleeps.

But the sleep isn't restful. In a dream, she imagines receiving a ransom note. The note demands 3M Yuan, roughly the equivalent of $1.4 million US, a ludicrous request. Li and Yin live as students, occasionally skipping meals to cover rent. Yet in her dream, she hunts the universe for ways to get the ransom money.

In the morning, the nightmare of a ransom demand is replaced by the soft hues of light filtering through the curtains. There's so much to do, but apologizing to the MIT director seems an appropriate first step. She hesitates over the keypad. What if Li is found soon? What if MIT is unwilling to wait? The director said she understood how family comes first, but there was an unspoken urgency in the director's voice that implied an immediate decision was needed.

While sighing, Yin asks how long the fellowship offer is available. A reply comes quickly. Ms. Buchannan repeats that she understands Yin's complicated situation and writes that, at most, Yin has a week to ten days. Yin is at the top of their list for this budget cycle, but she is not the only applicant. Buchannan goes on to say that if things don't work out this time, perhaps they can discuss options for fall.

Yin's takeaway is that the MIT opportunity is open-ended. Even if this doesn't work out, other colleges and opportunities await. Right now, there are more pressing issues to deal with. She again calls Haitao. "Sorry, but I still don't have a copy of Li's video. I'm frustrated. Can you call them?" Yin asks.

Haitao's voice immediately betrays his stress on the phone. "I thought they sent it. I'll send you my edited copy."

"Edited?"

"The recording goes on long after the phone dropped onto the pavement. I went through the entire video, but there is only the sound of an occasional car passing and someone's dog barking. The important section is in the beginning."

"Thank you, Haitao. Send it now."

"The video is on its way. Let me know when you receive it. It's horrible that this happened while you were on your trip."

"Li is the priority. Nothing else matters," Yin snaps.

"Of course. Police checked the CCTV in the apartment building. There was nothing. She never made it into the building."

"What about the street cameras? There is one that covers our apartment. Any reasonably intelligent person would go through that video," Yin says accusingly.

"The police checked it all. Nothing."

"Sorry. You're doing all you can," Yin says, trying not to take out her frustration on Haitao.

"I also pushed the detective to look at the video on the busses to see if anyone made the same transfers. They're not doing enough."

"I'll look into it," Yin says, softening.

"I love Li with all my heart, and she loves you. When you talked about going to America, she and I spent a few hours looking at job opportunities in Boston."

Yin feels a burst of love for her sister that causes words to choke in her throat. "She was willing to move?"

"Both of us. I just thought you should know."

"Thank you," Yin whispers. "That means a lot to me."

The video recording arrives seconds after their call ends. Yin braces for what will surely be a horrifically emotional experience. The video begins with Li speaking directly into her phone. She looks tired but happy and apologizes to Haitao for being late. She should have sent her message earlier. As she explains how everyone got so drunk and that she took the bus, she turns in panic to her left. The camera angle falls to her midsection and the frames blur wildly as she runs.

The audio track is all Yin has for the next few seconds. Rapid footfalls and the guttural grunts of a man chasing and catching up to her sister rip into Yin. In a nanosecond of frames, a taxi is partially visible. Li yells in broken Mandarin for someone to stay away. "No!" she yells just before the phone bounces to a stop on the pavement. The audio recording continues, but from then on, the recording takes place in total darkness. She hears Li's muffled screams as one man angrily instructs another to grab her legs. She hears a car door slam shut, then another, a moment of a car running at idle, and then the distinct sound of an automobile speeding away followed by unbearable silence.

The visceral effect of watching her sister's assault is gut-wrenching. She curls into a ball, arm hanging over the sofa's edge, phone in hand. She is helpless there for a long while, defeated, but then she watches the video again. There has to be something there, perhaps some clue in the voices. The men yelled at each other in a dialect of Mandarin she associates with the border regions of Myanmar and Thailand. If they'd been local hoodlums, their language might have been Shanghainese or a dialect of Mandarin more common in her surroundings. Mandarin is the lingua franca of China, but the tones are subtly different by region. There's not much to go on, but everything she encounters gets her full attention and joins the growing list of clues in her memory.

Yin recalls her conversation with the detective. He'd said something disturbing that she should have followed up on. She'd asked if this happens often and whether there might be ransom demands. Before he could answer, she'd barked questions the detective couldn't possibly have answered—what happens to abducted women? Where are they taken?

When the detective spoke, he said, "It could be a ransom kidnapping if we are lucky. Call right away if you get a demand."

What had he meant when he'd said if they were lucky? Yin sits upright and remembers the detective asking if they were, in fact, identical twins. He'd asked for a selfie, saying it might be helpful in the search, but what kind of search? Where might they begin?

Yin's logical mind races through dark possibilities, and she explores those on the Internet. She reads that over 2,000 women go missing from Shanghai every year. Some show up a few days later, traded for ransom, but too many are smuggled out of the country through underground networks, never to be seen again. The thought frightens Yin, but it also encourages her to act quickly. If she is to find Li in the underground, she needs help. Yin opens her laptop. A sense of calm washes over her as she dives into the familiar comfort of the dark web. The domain is rich with predators, but Yin has never allowed herself to fall prey.

Chapter 9

February 15

Yin has been at it for hours and finally finds what she's looking for. She traded exploits, insults, and compliments with an underground network cracker named EEL a year earlier, eventually winning an unspoken duel by penetrating his server. Some of what she discovered there repulsed her, especially the folders of sexually explicit photographs and videos. Recalling his proclivity for buying sex workers and frequenting unthinkable fetish sites makes him the only person she knows who may understand sex trafficking. Anyone with a three-letter online handle is an accomplished hacker. The most accomplished hackers have been online since the late seventies. As a result, they have three-letter handles but Yin doubts that EEL is a set of initials, especially since the man has previously posted photographs of naked-back knifefish. EEL boasted of once taking an 800-volt charge from the mysterious Electrophorus Electricus while snorkeling in the Amazon. He has a penchant for hyperbole, but EEL is an authentic, proficient hacker well-connected in the underworld. EEL claims to have left the boredom and restrictions of our everyday world to exercise his craft in dark places, analogous to actual eels. When his prey least expects trouble, he emerges from the dark in a shocking display of skill. Given his word choices, Yin believes EEL to be in his forties.

Yin also stalked prey through an alias. EEL could have used established companies including CyberGhost, IPVanish, and ExpressVPN, but he did everything himself and missed a pinhole in his firewalls. EEL's notoriety in the hacking and hacktivist communities was legendary. Penetrating his systems was a great accomplishment. She could have owned him but did the honorable thing. Leaving a private message disclosing his mistake.

From that day forward, Yin fended off numerous phishing attacks, each time smiling to herself that the EEL had been hunting her and failed. However unsavory and arrogant, she needs him now. If anyone in her network of contacts could get information on who was operating a kidnapping operation in Shanghai, possibly for the sex trade, it would be this disgusting individual.

Yin hunts through Tor and gaming sites to relocate EEL. When she does, he replies to her alias within minutes.

What the Fuck? Where have you been?

Busy. I need your help.

I doubt that, but shoot.

What can you tell me about human trafficking out of Shanghai? Not just smuggling people to other countries, but sexploitation?

What turns your knobs, male or female?

Not for me. Somebody grabbed a friend's sister.

Fuck. Nothing happens in Shanghai the Triads don't know about. They have Snakeheads for that kind of thing. Not sure I can help, though. You're on your own, dude. You'll need a hell of a lot of money to go hunting. Good luck.

Can't help, or won't? No one has to know.

I'll look around, but damn. You know as much as I do about research. Look into gaming, prostitution, drugs, and loan sharks. It's all tied together. I probably can't help, but I'll go nasty and get back.

LMK what you find. You already did help some. Thx.

Yin logs off Tor and sits with the information. Her mind revisits the few articles she read about the Triads—they've been around forever, are well organized, and impenetrably secretive. Every other article uses words like brutal, pitiless, and dangerous. Some say they are dying out, but others say they are still a force in China, Taiwan, and many other locations worldwide. Their longevity speaks to sophistication and perseverance.

The thought of her sister being in the hands of Triad thugs terrifies her. It would be far better to receive a ransom demand. Women have been grabbed in the Philippines, Vietnam, Cambodia, and virtually every ASEAN country and used as barter or sold into servitude in other parts of the world. If that's her sister's fate, by now, she has probably experienced needles in her arm and been subdued by drugs.

Yin finds that over 14 million people have been snatched in India alone, but the number that worries her most is the 3.2 million victims in China. One article says that Cambodia is a clearing house and transit station where traffickers buy and sell.

As the detective pointed out, Li is an attractive woman. She will be highly valued. His reasoning sickened her, but the detective said that beautiful women don't end up as street-level prostitutes. Li speaks three languages. She would be worth much money to someone, but how would traffickers control someone like Li? What goes on in the minds of people who trade in people?

Yin needs better questions, more information, and quick answers. Anxiety fuels her research as she races through the Internet, absorbing everything she finds about the sex trade. Early in her quest, Yin discovers the concept of Snakeheads, which, in China, means the Triads. She recalls something said at work years earlier. A coworker asked another for the quickest overland route to Bangkok, joking that he needed a vacation. In reply, his friend said to call the Triads, and they laughed. Given the dialect of Li's attackers, is it possible? Could she be on her way to Cambodia and some dark underground auction site?

Drugs are a probability. It may not be enough to find and rescue Li. She may need to wean her off of street drugs, and what if Li becomes infected with AIDS or Hepatitis C? What if, and what if, and what if.

As fear morphs into near mental paralysis, Yin races to the bathroom mirror and stares at her reflection. When young, she and Li would stand together in front of her mother's floor-length mirror, playing a game. She looked at Li as Li looked at her, both searching for what the other was thinking.

Yin mouths the words, *Pretty girl. What if I never find you?*

She imagines seeing Li instead of herself in the mirror, and her reflection says, *"What if they were after you and not me?"*

Chapter 10

February 16

For a time, Bao Gu invested heavily in property developments worldwide. He moved among them to experience different cultures, but his residence in the barrio of Belgrano, Buenos Aires, Argentina, is extremely secretive. Luscious foliage, a meandering creek, and neighborhood restaurants wrap around the three contemporary buildings. If asked, he rents, but the complex was purchased through a series of shell companies.

Stricken with a youthful, unattractive babyface, Bao, at 40, looks 26. He's never attracted a woman by his looks but often garners attention through wealth. They all disappear when they get to know him. While living in San Francisco, it bothered him immensely to appear so youthful and innocent. At one point, he'd endured a full-sleeve tattoo to look manly. It didn't work. Having billions in hidden investments and crypto wallets, he's reconciled the conflict between inner strength and outer weakness. He's learned to live with white skin, disobedient hair, lack of muscle, and being somewhat unsightly. In Bao's mind, he's changed what power looks like. He uses his weak appearance as a disarming weapon against those approaching him for business.

Today, he posts a legitimate help wanted ad on the open web, then sinks into Tor and underworld markets to recruit talent for a new data center. Explicit personal invitations travel to their destinations through droppers he's worked with for decades. In addition to routing communications through dozens of servers, bouncing them like pinballs from one node to another, droppers provide manual interruptions in communications. The dropper receives a packet of information from the sender, copies it into a different message, and sends it to the intended recipient for a fee. The interruption in routing makes forensic tracking much more difficult, but the dropper must be trusted, and Bao knows who to trust.

In addition, he uses semi-legitimate channels like Telegram to invite applications from loose contacts, directing them to his postings on the open web. Within hours, numerous queries arrive for a Hong Kong data collection enterprise position. Techs receive the same invitation that Yin and two of his friends will receive, with a significant difference—his friends are exempt from pre-hire testing. Their invitations exactly fit their experience.

He sends invitations to a pair of hackers he's worked with frequently. Peter is a network engineer living in the UK. That's his day job. At night, he exploits corporate server farms. Nicolay lives in a rural area of Bulgaria. He doesn't need a day job. Bao used his incredible capabilities to build his short-lived BRICS crypto empire. They became close, taking money from Russian oligarchs, and more than once, Nicolay alerted Bao as Interpol tried to penetrate his network. As a result, Nicolay has made millions of dollars and Bao pays handsomely to keep him.

Bao needs Yin's financial acumen. He learned about her through MSS contacts and periodically received updates on her career through those duplicate contacts. He thinks her expertise in establishing shell companies will fit nicely into the data center. Bao has additional long-range plans for Yin.

All uninvited applicants get vetted for technical expertise. Being abrupt, driven, and even intolerant of employees worked perfectly for Bao in California. He was the baby-faced tyrant of Silicon Valley, but that aggressive approach brought success, leading to the confidence required for bigger things. Bao lives by a personal philosophy—*the next opportunity hides in the margins of what most believe is essential.* He'd thought graduating from Beijing Tech was important, that gaming when he should have been studying was wrong, but gaming led him to Silicon Valley and the millions he earned there. Becoming an MSS prodigy was exciting, but going rogue was his first taste of genuine thrill.

Lately, crypto has become his obsession. He's experimented with every aspect of that technology, beginning with utility investments, then digging into payment systems and security measures, and eventually investing heavily in the underworld use of stablecoins. The greedy venture capitalists who funded his first three games wanted more online gaming code, but coding had become dull child's play for Bao. Life had become a game with a new set of rules and limitless opportunities.

Bao reimagined stablecoin. Instead of linking it to a commonly agreed valuation like the American dollar, he created a stablecoin backed by the vision Russia and China proposed, a valuation dubbed BRICS. There was momentum in BRICS at the time. It just needed a push, a seed crystal of legitimacy. This new underworld cryptocurrency was based on the aggregated currency values of Brazil, Russia, India, China, and South Africa, ergo, a BRICS-based digital currency.

It took five programmers with experience in financial technologies, including blockchain, four intense months to make Bao's vision a reality. PR firms and marketing executives spend millions daily introducing ideas and driving demand in commercial markets. Bao lacked the inclination to follow that traditional path, so he turned to disruptive innovation and gorilla marketing. Dark crypto was now his bread and butter, the most secretive means of exchange in the underworld.

The crypto marketing team identified Russian oligarchs and unscrupulous wealthy Chinese businesses, all of whom used crypto in one way or another to hide and move capital. Intermediaries quietly offered prospects an opportunity to be on the ground floor of something unique, intimating that the BRICS nations secretly funded his cryptocurrency.

Over 70 percent of his stablecoins were purchased, sold, and bought again within a few months. He'd evolved from writing and coding first-person shooter fantasies to manipulating global markets.

As the wealth housed in BRICS currency grew, so did its notoriety among wealthy underworld clientele. One of those customers was Jiao Long. Like others, Jiao wanted personal assurances before investing. The ensuing dialogue took place over months and drifted from cryptocurrency to financial management, eventually leading to a discussion about what each of these men might be able to do for the other. Dragonhead wanted specialized assistance and was willing to pay handsomely. Bao wanted access to a broader network and claimed he could launder money. Ultimately, they agreed on a trial project. They planned for a highly specialized data center, a gateway to grand vistas. Jiao's only interest was in making money and protecting his operations. Bao always wants to advance a level in his private game.

Bao knew Jiao to be a Dragonhead, one of the most powerful underworld figures on the planet, but he never said as much in their communications. Dragonhead presented himself as a simple entrepreneur, and Bao was just a programmer and businessman. As their duplicitous relationship developed, they brainstormed a data center project. Dragonhead hinted at a 10-year scheme. Even without hearing details, Bao decided to piggyback on whatever the Triads planned.

Very few crypto transactions are fungible. The value of coins varies widely, given the whims of political and economic circumstances. Bao gambled and won on the underground's need for untraceable financial tools. As investors purchased his inventory with real money, he bought legitimate stablecoin from industry leaders like BitCoin and Ethereum.

Bao issued four million coins, not 21 million like BitCoin. The value of his coins rose sharply when in short supply. As designed, investors lost faith and began to sell his coins as the economies of Russia and Brazil fell into ruin. The beauty of his plan was that investors became angry with Brazil and Russia, not Bao's system. They bought in at high rates and sold low.

Bao processed every sale without complaint, and why not? If an investor had purchased 100 M worth of BRICS stablecoin and wanted to sell at a fallen rate of 68 M, so what? Bao refunded investors from his legitimate reserves and kept the remainder. The meteoric rise of BRICS stablecoin reached 22.6 B, at its peak. When he liquidated the company, its value was 8 B, netting residual earnings close to 14.3 B, which resides in dozens of legitimate crypto accounts and diversified investments worldwide. Bao liquidated much of his crypto before the FTX meltdown, moving his wealth into commodities, land grabs, and various social startups. Bored with crypto, he closed shop and wandered off the grid to consolidate his earnings and plan his next big adventure.

Sitting in his Buenos Aires apartment, Bao receives an expected message from Tu that Jiao wants to meet in person. He knew it would come. Jiao is the only investor Bao fully refunded. Jiao invested 600 M and watched it grow to 1.1 B, but didn't pull out in time. The value of his holdings dropped to under 500 M. When he called, he was angry. They negotiated. Bao refunded 900 M, 300 over market value. It was a small price for what Bao hoped to gain in return—friendship, opportunity, and a chance to manipulate an underworld kingpin.

Bao taps one of his lesser wallets to hire a G700 flight. He boards the magnificent jet in a hand-tailored suit, then flies directly from Argentina to *Aeroporto Internacional De MaCau*, Macau International Airport, Macau, China, where he exits the plane in faded black jeans and a Pink Floyd T-shirt. A worn brown leather laptop case with a bright yellow frown-face sticker on its side rides on his shoulder. His Italian shoes are gone, replaced with sandals. The laptop case holds a computer, a change of shirts, and an electric toothbrush, but little else, perfect for the image he wants to present.

He grabs the first available driver and enjoys the two-mile ride along Wai Long Avenue, through barren industrial park scenery, to do Istmo Estrada, the Cotai Strip. The limo stops at the front entrance of what Bao knows to be one of Dragonhead's casinos. He tips the driver and looks for a man dressed in a black suit and white shirt. Three men fit that description.

"Tu!" Bao shouts. Everyone within listening distance turns, but only one approaches. He looks Bao up and down, irritated.

"What did you expect? Giorgio Armani?" Bao asks, rolling his eyes. "Let's do this."

They enter the rhythm and flow of the casino, with its slot machines, laughing customers, and the smell of freshly baked bread flowing through the HVAC system to entice customers into one of the fabulous in-house restaurants. Like Las Vegas, the music is loud, and the atmosphere is electric with manipulated excitement.

Bao asks unanswered questions as they walk to a quieter, private area at the back of one of the exclusive bars. Two young bottle girls greet them dressed in white blouses and short black skirts, and Tu gestures for Bao to sit at the table of his choice. "Jiao Long will be here as soon as he is through with a private matter. He appreciates your patience. Your drinks and food are complimentary."

Bao orders a double baijiu from one of the servers. He attempts to start a conversation about life in China today, but the server is all business. He hasn't had this liqueur since leaving China years earlier. Returning would be delightful, but then again, he'd severely disappointed the CCP when he left Silicon Valley. If he'd flown on a commercial flight and used his birth name, he'd probably be in detention by now.

When Dragonhead arrives, he looks unpleasantly surprised but smiles as the men shake hands. He dismisses Tu with a wave, instructing him not to go far. Tu sits across the room in this otherwise empty section of the restaurant. As Dragonhead sits, he says, "Thank you for coming. I will reimburse your flight. Which airline?"

"Not necessary. I'm here to contribute to your plans. How much do you need?"

Dragonhead is caught off guard but quickly recovers. "Shared risk leads to mutual reward, but our interests differ. One does not invest in the data center like a property."

Bao laughs. "Semantics. I'm not just talking about the data center. How you use the money is up to you. Call it a gift if that feels better, but I want in on the action. How much?"

Dragonhead hides his inner thoughts by looking away. "We are here to discuss the data project. I want you to—"

"We'll get to that. I want to piggyback on your action, but it has to be spectacular. Feel me? You're a frigging genius buying up properties, stockpiling munitions—you have the whole Rih Aleaqrab terrorist thing going on. What the hell does Rih Aleaqrab even mean? It's all cool with me, though. Let's tear it up. How much?"

Dragonhead's face reddens. "Be careful with your accusations. You don't know what you're talking about."

"But I do, and if I can find out, so can MSS and the CIA. You need me, Ji. Can I call you Ji, or does it have to be Jiao? You should let me tighten your digital security when the data center is up and running. You have a ten-year plan, right? Outstanding."

Bao knows too much about his affairs, causing Dragonhead to be visibly upset. He inches his chair backward and nearly spits his words, "None of your concern! This meeting is over. You'd better hope your luck doesn't run out."

Dismissing the threat, Bao continues. "I made you angry that easily? What do you need, one hundred million? Two hundred million? Let's go big. I'll drop a half-billion into your account right now, no questions asked, and we'll go from here. Sit down, Ji. Please. I've come a long way."

Dragonhead rises from the table and waves Tu forward. "Look at yourself. You dress like a street tramp," he says.

"You're seriously going to blow off a half-billion because of a pair of jeans? You don't like Pink Floyd? What is it? How much? I'll transfer the funds right now," Bao says, unzipping his laptop case while calling for another cocktail. "You have great taste in servers, I'll tell you that much. I really miss young Chinese chicken sometimes. Do you want anything, a steak? I've got it! Scotch. You're a Scotch guy, right?" he says absentmindedly to Jiao, apparently unflustered by Dragonhead's growing rage.

Dragonhead lifts a hand to his face and rests an index finger on his upper lip, but then, as if he's changed some internal calculation, he waves for Tu to stand down. Dragonhead sits and says, "For that kind of money, you want something I cannot give."

"Will I be working with Tu in the data center?"

"Yes. Stick to the point. What do you want in return for that much money?"

"Here's my offer. I'll give you 200 million US right now, no strings attached, and another three if you include me in some of the planning. I've got some talents and ideas you may not have considered. Is it enough? A single Hellfire missile costs that much. Let's make it 600 million and figure out what to do later. I like how you think, Ji. I will make a ton of cash in the aftermath of your big move either way, but it would be way cooler to work together. You in?"

Dragonhead sighs. Apparently calculating the offer and its risk, his demeanor cascades from anger through skepticism into curiosity and finally settles into acceptance. It takes him nearly a minute to do this, but in the end, he quotes an American film. "You got some balls on you, kid."

"I thought so. A Scotch guy. Do you trust your guy, Tu? That's his name, right?" Bao asks, placing a period on Dragonhead's thoughts.

"Explicitly."

"If you do, so do I. We need people we can trust." He begins tapping instructions into his keypad, fingers moving impossibly fast. "What I'm going to do is transfer funds into Tu's wallets, differing amounts, different sources over a few days—30M tonight, 45M in the morning, and so on, but let's keep an eye on that little fucker. Half a billion is a lot of money. Maybe he retains a percent or two for his troubles? What do you think? Keep him honest."

"He can be the conduit for the first 50 million, but I have other accounts. I'll have him give you his account numbers."

"Makes sense, but it's crypto for now and I already have his information," Bao says, and then beckons the waiting women to bring a bottle of whatever Jiao prefers. "I'm going to need some coffee as well. It's going to be a long night. Want some? Let's get Tu over here and transfer the money."

Without waiting for Jiao to act on his suggestion, Bao waves for Tu. Tu looks inquisitively at Dragonhead and gets the nod.

As Tu approaches, Bao dominates the conversation without looking up from his phone. "I hope you don't mind, dude, but I just put some cash into your wallet. You can keep one percent for your trouble, but the rest goes to Ji. You good with one percent? Anyway, which of you oversees facilities? Will the center be here in Macau? What are you thinking? I like Hong Kong."

Dragonhead takes a moment to catch up, then exerts himself. "Singapore."

"Wow! Okay, surprises the dookie out of me, but sure. Singapore. Are you good with that, Tu? Of course you are. When do we get started? I've cleared my calendar. We need a shitload of equipment. I'll buy that and the talent, but the location is up to you. Remember, Tu. Physical security is just as important as a firewall, so think it through—maybe a tech park, someplace with fiber to the door." Bao rambles. His pace is unsettling to Dragonhead and inappropriate to Tu, but as Tu takes a seat, the conversation gradually settles into objectives, goals, and timetables.

An hour later, as Bao finishes his fifth drink and a second cup of coffee, he checks the time. "You know what? I'm going to Singapore right now to look around. I can take Tu with me if he's ready," Bao says, rising to his feet and offering his hand to Jiao Long.

Dragonhead rises as well and takes Bao's hand. "Tu will stay here, but you should have a facility within a week." It pays to have Triad affiliates worldwide.

Tu accompanies Bao out of the building to a waiting limousine. Bao extends his hand again, but Tu doesn't reciprocate. "I don't know what you are up to, but if you hurt Jiao's operations, I'll cut your eyes out. Understood?" Tu says.

Bao is not intimidated. He never is. "Clear enough. See you in Singapore."

Chapter 11

February 16

Yin spends the next six days in focused isolation. She imagines three possibilities. Li was abducted and murdered, Li is a hostage somewhere in China or, Li was smuggled across the border to another country altogether. If held in China, there is little she can do but wait for a ransom request or for the police to find her. If smuggled out of China, who would do this? Who is capable? She guesses there are networks, perhaps gangs of men experienced in human trafficking. The logical move is to identify the gangs that do such things regularly, but how? Who tracks this behavior besides the Shanghai police, who are already working on the problem?

She hunts for leads on the dark web, often getting fewer than three hours of sleep before springing out of bed with new ideas. In these marathon sessions, Yin becomes more determined to accept the life-altering risks required to find Li. She is physically and mentally exhausted. Everything she encounters becomes evidence of human trafficking. Most troubling are the dialects used by Li's captors. They are not native Chinese. Chinese Triads, Japanese Yakuza, and many underworld figures throughout Southeast Asia use the term Snakehead for gangs that run trafficking and prostitution operations. Snakeheads create false passports. They bribe and intimidate border officials and manage networks of trucks, boats, and planes to move people from one country to the next and across continents. Laborers commit to steep fees for safe passage and then pay the balance of their journey at the point of destination, often in service of these Snakeheads. Sweatshops worldwide use people who fled Asia only to be locked into intolerable working conditions.

The Taiwanese Triad is notorious for this form of trafficking, but according to Yin's research, the Chinese mainland Triads and the Taiwanese Triad do not get along well, so she believes the Pearl Delta Triads were involved.

Port authorities don't monitor fishing vessels in the way they do container ships and aircraft, as the Triads dominate the seafood industry and have numerous connections with officials. Fish harvested illegally from Philippine and Indonesian waters are smuggled into Victoria Harbour near Hong Kong and stored in pens. When fish costs rise, they are harvested and brought to markets virtually inspection-free. Drugs and people alike are frequently smuggled into and out of coastal cities on Triad member's fishing boats. If Triad affiliates took Li out of the country, it's possible she rode in the hull of a fishing boat, but to where and to what end? To the Triad Snakeheads, women are just another commodity.

Yin's mind races across the subtle, nuanced canvas of clues, acting on every thread of evidence, beginning with a hack of the CCTV cameras positioned on the streets between the M1NT Club and their apartment. Within hours, she identifies the relevant cameras and accesses recordings of that night. She finds Li at a bus stop with an older woman. They speak to someone off-camera, the older woman threatening that person with her bag before following Li onto the bus and, eventually, off the bus where her observable trail ends. Yin hunts for another hour but cannot identify who followed her sister that night. Believing this to be a dead end, she moves on to the next area of research.

Yin imagines that men who take women either drug them into prostitution or sell them at auction. The buyers use aliases just as hackers do, so she creates an alias in the profile of a narcissistic wealthy businessman shamelessly seeking an attractive Asian woman. Cost is no object. The woman must have long black hair, be tall and thin, be in her mid to late twenties, and be athletic. The alias prefers that she speak Mandarin and English as he conducts business in Guangzhou, Shenzhen, Shanghai, and multiple English-speaking countries.

This persona finds wings in the dark web, where traffickers may see it. The exercise opens her eyes and darkens her perspective on humanity as hundreds of women, ages as young as 12 and as old as their sixties, are portrayed in recordings as ripe for marriage, servitude, and worse. She encounters on-camera beatings and terrified women reading scripts about the sexual things they supposedly enjoy doing. There are women from Croatia, Bangladesh, India, Vietnam, China, and Latin America. Blond women from Europe and the United States are highly valued in Asia, while Westerners seek Asian women.

What Yin doesn't find is Li, but among the victims from China are two women born and raised in Shenzhen. She attempts to unravel these threads, but large amounts of cash are required to enter seedy underworld auction sites. Not having enough money to participate and no history of visiting similar destinations, she gets booted at every attempt.

EEL warned that the search would require money. She needs a view of the participants and access, but time is not on her side. Where are the shortcuts? How can she get cash, and who has the precise information she needs? Indeed, the Ministry of State Security has information, but if trafficking continues in China under the watchful eye of MSS, they don't know enough. Internationally, Interpol claims progress, as does the UN. Nearby, Australia has a robust intelligence community that deals with trafficking and transnational crime. In China, it's unwise to petition the law enforcement agencies of other countries. The government will misinterpret her intentions, but covert options remain.

Australian intelligence teams possess decades of information on human trafficking. They share that information with other Western powers through embassies across Southeast Asia, so locating watch lists within the Australian IC becomes a priority.

As Yin probes the Australians, she discovers a vulnerability in Singapore. The field office there is run by William Essex, a family man with a wife and two sons. Like most parents, Essex has yet to learn what games his children play online. Terms like Battle Royale or MOBA are foreign to him—but not to Yin. Multiplayer Online Battle Arenas require access to a keyboard, webcam, and audio devices so players can communicate during missions. Like most teenage boys, the young gamer is susceptible to social engineering, and Yin poses as an attractive girl his age with considerable skill. Yin convinces her prey that his computer needs more speed to capture higher ground in their gaming partnership. All he has to do is accept a Remote Desktop Connection, and Yin will optimize his download speeds.

While penetrating the laptop, Yin adds keystroke logging software and can soon view snippets of Essex's email communications and calendar. She also has access to his downloads.

Though the Chief of Station uses an outdated virtual private network model, critical data inside the firewall is segmented. Access to classified document folders requires biometric logins. If the Australians hadn't evolved to use micro-segmentation, she could probably see critical files with Essex's credentials. Access to stored files aside, Essex has a bad personal habit. Pressed for time, he often downloads work files to his home hard drive and prints them. Essex is the vulnerability Yin hoped for.

Through scanning personal emails and studying downloaded documents, Yin learns that the man heading the interdiction of trafficking efforts in Singapore is Nigel Rainer, Deputy Chief of Station Singapore, Australian Intelligence Service. His primary areas of expertise and responsibility are human trafficking and cyber. In one of the documents Essex downloaded, she finds Nigel's report on the capture of multiple suspected Triad members convicted of trafficking in Australia. These criminals are imprisoned in Victoria, Australia.

Nigel becomes her primary law enforcement target. Unlike his boss, however, Nigel is somewhat tech-savvy, and his digital footprint is airtight. Working in Cyberspace, Nigel is undoubtedly immune to social engineering tactics. If she wants what he knows, creativity is required.

Yin imagines dozens of possible exploits. She might ask the man for help, but she's not an Australian citizen. She could seduce Nigel, but she's not in Singapore. If she were, she would identify the bars and restaurants he frequents and somehow seduce or compromise him there. What would happen if she confronted him on the street? Yin feels her energy shift. The Australians know things. Nigel knows how the Triads operate and could inform her about how a Chinese woman from Shanghai might end up in another country. Nigel and the Australians are worth pursuing, and the thought comes to fly into Singapore and camp on Nigel's doorstep until he gives her what she wants, but why would he? She's a Chinese national, and there is no way he would hand over what he knows. Thoughts of extorting Nigel cross her mind. She closes her laptop to breathe and consider what she's doing. Whenever she got angry as a child, her father would say she'd unleashed the dragon, which made no sense then. Dragons are protectors.

When she was twelve, Yin verbally attacked a group of tweens for disrespecting Li at school. She'd been absolutely convinced Li would appreciate how she devastated those other children and that her parents would be proud of her, but revenge prompted Li to say something unforgettable to her.

"We need to control it, Yin Yin." Control it, as if Li also knew about the inner dragon.

Fortified by these memories, Yin returns to EEL's social pages with purpose, prepared to trade the information she's gained from the Aussie Intelligence Unit in Singapore. Dealing in network hacks is devious and bold, but if this encourages him to help her, why not proceed?

What she discovers when returning to EEL's site astonishes her. The synchronicity of thinking about Nigel in Singapore and EEL's job reposting of a data center job in the same city transect perfectly, but coincidences trouble analysts. The post hints at working for a powerful family organization based in China, followed by a separate post showcasing EEL's favorite tattoo, the head of a dragon. There is no rational link between the two components of this discovery. The data center is in Singapore. Nigel is in Singapore. Even if she could find a link to justify her apprehension, she'll stop at nothing to find her sister. The quest will inevitably bring her higher stakes and darker water, but she doesn't hesitate. Her dragon has joined the quest to find Li, no matter what.

Yin revives the alias she'd used when hacking EEL, the year before and responds to the job notice, asking what skill sets EEL's friend needs. A reply comes immediately:

> *Dude! I can't believe it's you. You're perfect for one of his positions, but he needs a legit CV forwarded to the address below. Please include the word Artifact somewhere so he knows it's you. I told him you're fucking awesome, the only person ever to have hacked me. He can't wait to meet you. Pack your bags!*

Chapter 12

February 22

If not for Li's abduction, Yin would have pursued an apartment in Boston before flying home. Instead, she's packing for Singapore and a descent into the underworld.

Yin updated her CV as instructed, including the word artifact and hinting at various mastered exploits. A reply and offer came quickly, confirming speculation. EEL and Bao are the same person. If she is correct, she'll meet EEL soon enough, and he'll be even more surprised than she is now.

Friends unwittingly borrow phrases from each other, forming a quasi-unique subculture. Even the written word becomes a fingerprint to linguists. Bao's sentence structure, word choices, and distinctive phrases are consistent with many of EEL's online rants. But who hired her is secondary to the mission. In this new narrative, she is near Nigel and earns enough money to penetrate the underground.

The Australian intelligence community has one central mission: to gather and analyze information from disparate sources. They do this surreptitiously when necessary, so discovering a mole in an organization known for transnational crime would grab Nigel's attention. Yin imagines Nigel reacting to an insider, a whistleblower in the Triads. To pull it off, she'll have to operate well outside the boundaries of her comfort zone.

Yin uses her research into Triad history and activities to fabricate another identity. She becomes a Triad insider so offended by the activities of their Dragonhead that he may be willing to disclose critical information, but the informant will need credibility. Yin goes to the document she captured on Essex's computer and copies a paragraph she believes will startle Nigel into reacting. He'll have to accept her claim that Australian systems are vulnerable.

Yin masks the traceroute of her email. The Australian forensics team will spend days, if not weeks or months, trying to find the author of what she sends. As they get deeper into the investigation, Chinese authorities will stonewall progress. Australian forensic teams may identify the machine address of the computer used to send her message, but a shared device in the university library at SJTU will lead them nowhere. Yin includes the paragraph she copied from the report she found on Essex's computer and signs the message.

Mr. Nigel Rainer,

As evidenced in your report, we share an interest in finding justice. I'll be in touch soon.

Sincerely,

Incense Master

In early Triad tradition, the Incense Master was second in command under the Dragonhead. As she hits send, she experiences a rush of exhilaration.

Luggage is packed, and Yin spent all but a few hundred dollars she saved from her days with MSS to pay up their rental agreement through the end of their term. Nothing left to do but catch her flight, she heats tea water and empties a milk container into the sink and drain. She pens a note at their kitchen table while sipping her tea. It's an emotional moment darkened with conflicting thoughts about her future and fear for her sister. If Li somehow breaks free, she'll return to the apartment. The note explains where Yin has gone and why, ending with *I love you, my beautiful sister.* She holds the note against her cheek and closes her eyes.

Yin updated her passport before going to the US, and as she rolls luggage through Pudong International heading for yet another long flight, she experiences separation anxiety. Her sister is missing, her academic aspirations are on hold, and she is leaving the routine and familiarity of Shanghai. She doesn't study or work to enhance her linguistic skills during this flight. Instead, she leans against the bulkhead of the plane's interior and closes her eyes, hoping to gather enough energy to push on.

Singapore is one of three inspiring city-states in the world, a melting pot of ethnicities, cultures, cuisines, and finance. Their banking laws cloak billions of dollars in the ways Switzerland and the Cayman Islands do, and the government protects that information from the world. In the margins of her research, Yin found that the government punished an Australian academic publication for reporting on potential corruption among members of parliament. The government can be oppressively strict at times, especially when its good name in the global community is challenged, but the streets are clean, buildings well kept, and public transportation abundant.

If Yin had not rushed to find an apartment, she might have hunted nearer the data center in Queenstown. However, she was unaware of the street address and instead explored living quarters in Chinatown.

Money is tight. Yin checks into the Wink Capsule Hostel. A guest cooks ginger rice and vegetables in the communal kitchen just down the hall from the lobby. Garlic, scallions, star anise, and a hint of cinnamon accompany her to the second floor and a room with individual cubicles. Cube Six is the upper berth nearest the door. She lifts her luggage into the space, closes the curtain, and receives a short tour of the facilities—numerous areas for computing, a shared bathroom, and a spacious balcony overlooking a busy one-way street. The sheets on her bed are clean, and a cooling breeze flows through the room.

The day is overcast, but for a few minutes, the sun shines. It is a good omen. Sitting on the balcony above Mosque Street, Yin eats three of the remaining seasoned rice crackers she brought on the trip from China, pleasantly distracted by the traffic below and the sounds of the city. She notices how soft shadows inch down the neighboring wall toward the pedestrians and cars below as the morning turns into the afternoon and realizes she'll go hungry if payday doesn't come soon after work begins, but she must persevere no matter what.

Before texting the data center team leader to announce her arrival in Singapore and requesting particulars, Yin closes her eyes for a few minutes of reflection and meditation. All she can think about is her next steps. The message asking for an address and start time ends by asking when she will get paid.

Bao responds immediately with a building address and room number in Singapore Tech Park 2, suggesting workstations and servers need attention. Any help will be paid in cash at the end of the day. Her response: *OMW.*

After acquiring a NetPay card, she takes the SG Bus to the technology park. As she approaches the building, she's greeted by a man who appears to be her age and Chinese. He's ingested either speed or far too much caffeine. Upon seeing Yin, Bao nearly doubles over in laughter. When he recovers, he says, "Total surprise. When I read your CV, I nearly shit myself, and here you are. Before reading the CV, I thought for sure I'd been trading hacks with some hairy dude, not a woman, but shit. Come in."

"EEL?"

Bao laughs, finger to his lips as they enter the building. Inside, he says, "Busted, but that's our secret. Around here, I am Bao."

A retaining wall separates the small reception area from a large central room. It's a contemporary office setting with high ceilings, glass-walled offices, and chest-high and partially assembled cubical dividers arranged in a maze across the carpeted floor. Rows of expensive-looking office chairs rest in boxes.

Bao leads Yin to the center of the room and nods toward a room at the back where two men are running cable and installing blades into server racks. "I'll introduce you momentarily, but first, pick an office."

Only one of the five walled office spaces is occupied. Bao claimed it as his own. His walls are hung with gaming posters and a life-sized photo of Bao standing next to a man she believes is an American or Latino guitarist, Carlos Santana. "Does it matter? I'll take that one," Yin says, pointing to the largest of the remaining offices with a view into Bao's office.

As they walk into Yin's office, Bao speaks to her over his shoulder. "You're the full package, Yin. How much do you need?"

"Need?"

"Money? Keep up, yeah? Fuck worrying about where to live and what to eat. We'll get you a company card or something, but for now, this will work," Bao says, tugging a thick wad of Singapore Dollars from his jeans. He doesn't bother counting the currency. Instead, he randomly grabs approximately one-third of his cash and drops it on the desk.

"For me? Is this how we get paid?" Yin asks, very quickly thumbing through the bills with feigned indifference. If Bao is casual about money, she should be, too. She drops the cash onto the desk before folding her arms.

"Let's call that a moving bonus. You'll get cash, crypto, and a paycheck. We'll talk about that later. If you want different furniture, chairs, or whatever turns your gears, ask, but for now, I need to get back to the guys. Follow me," Bao says.

Singaporean dollars have roughly 70% of the value of US dollars and five times the value of the Chinese Yuan. The bills she was given are S$1,000 notes. Yin has never received that much cash at once—not even close. She'd been so focused on getting this job that she'd never even asked about compensation. Given Bao's personality, maybe that was a good thing.

Before entering the server room, Bao touches Yin's arm and whispers, "We'll have over a dozen people working here, but only four of us will ever know why. These dudes are not on that list. We good?"

"You're the boss."

"Fucking right I am, but I'm also a hired hand. You'll meet the guy we report to next week. His name is Tu. He's as close as anyone ever gets to the big dog." Bao says. He opens the server room door.

Inside, Bao is a different man. The change surprises Yin, but she maintains a smiling, resolute, professional face while being introduced to two Middle Eastern-looking technicians in English. The mercurial nature of Bao's personality shifts on demand into that of a deliberate and strategic technologist. The irreverent street-smart banter she encountered was already more subdued than EEL's posts, but Bao's personality transforms as he shifts. His diction and gestures are academic, calm, articulate, and firm. Every sentence arrives with a reassuring smile and a sense of ease. It's as if Bao understands the psyche of these techs at a deep level and knows precisely who to become for maximum effect. Personality aside, Bao is supremely competent. For a moment, Yin wonders how well he would have done on the MIT exams and decides he would have excelled, though perhaps not as well as she. More importantly, Yin wonders what type of person can seemingly change so entirely from one moment to the next.

When the introductions are complete, Bao provides instructions to the technicians.

"How can I help?" Yin asks.

In calm English, Bao says, "We need to pen test everything—routers, switches, firewalls, and eventually the user devices. These guys are good, but they don't have our level of experience, and—oh fuck. We don't have payroll set up yet. You can record your hours, but screw that. I'll give you an extra $1,000 for every vulnerability you uncover. That should be enough incentive. We could sit side-by-side and trade exploits, but unfortunately, I'm stuck babysitting. Good to go?"

"Of course, but if you're still configuring—"

"The architecture has segments, subnets, and virtual local area networks. The guys you'll meet in a few days handle digital security. You know all this shit, so do what you do. Find vulnerabilities. Need anything?"

"I don't think so. Let's start with low-level access, something a receptionist or janitor might have, and we can go from there."

"Done. I'm glad you're here. It's going to be fucking epic," Bao says.

Yin laughs at his language, but it's a ruse to project comfort she certainly doesn't feel. She's never been this close to a criminal organization or worked with a devious genius like Bao. Even the shifting eyes and careful speech patterns of the two techs in the server room are concerning. She must appear to be a willing participant to survive this environment long enough to get what she needs.

"What?" Bao asks, acting as if he doesn't know why his Silicon Valley lingo would elicit her laughter.

"You are the first Chinese man I know that can perfectly imitate a Western rock and roll star."

"I'll take that as a compliment. Rock on!" Bao says emphatically, adding a grand gesture of striking the strings on an air guitar.

Yin enters her office, opens her laptop, and finds network vulnerabilities within minutes. Craziness. Bao invited a known hacker to penetrate systems at their most vulnerable stage during development. Bao could be testing her, watching to see what she does, but he could also trust the process. Twenty minutes into her tests, Yin reports the first two vulnerabilities, both easy fixes. An hour later, she discovers another opening in the firewall and hacks together lines of code that, if buried deep in the network, might create a back door available to anyone with administrator status, a role she believes she will have later. Dropping this code into the network would be the ultimate betrayal. Whether she finds the courage to go through with the exploit at some point is uncertain. Unsure and anxious, she sets the code aside and continues penetration testing, leaving this vulnerability unreported.

Three hours into the day, Bao receives a phone call and steps away from the servers. Yin studies his expression as he quickly moves to his office, shuts the door, and frantically taps his keyboard. The guy seems happy at work. It's an uncharacteristic moment, and Yin uses the distraction to place her code in the network. As Bao exits his office, she approaches to discuss another of the minor vulnerabilities.

Bao interrupts her. "That was the boss. You'll be moving the little fucker's money around the globe. I think he's on his way to Dubai, or I might have introduced you."

"I see," Yin says neutrally, unsure of the reaction Bao was hoping for.

Unperturbed, he continues. "Anyway. Find something?"

Chapter 13

February 23

Tu has conducted dozens of special missions for Jiao Long to enforce the will of the Triad. Today, he flies to a city with two faces, the social heart of the United Arab Emirates, Dubai. He is to meet an Emirati businessman named Rashid and present lists of goals and demands.

Dubai is infamous for tracking the interests and behavior of its visitors. Many hotels embed surveillance gear throughout the building. It's a popular cosmopolitan destination where guests feast in expensive restaurants, drink alcohol, play golf, and dance the night away amid the incredible sights. Wealth is on display in Dubai. The UAE is among the world's ten wealthiest countries, yet nearly 20% of its citizens live below poverty thresholds. The country is also predominantly Muslim. As such, Tu conducts himself as a believer but is careful not to overdo it. He and Dragonhead don't yet know enough about Rashid to manipulate him on a personal level. Money is their only lever for now.

Tu understands that Rashid is wealthy. He often contributes to worthy causes, but some of these causes are off-book and nefarious. Militant contacts in Myanmar and the Philippines gave Dragonhead Rashid's name. Why these warriors should know a handsome middle-aged Emirati multi-millionaire can only mean one thing, and Tu is to verify their assumptions. Tu's Islamist contacts report that Rashid is a funding conduit, and if Dragonhead is serious about supporting them, he should move the money through this intermediary. Tu aims to evaluate the man and earn his trust with a sizable donation.

Rashid's driver brings Tu from the airport to the popular Dubai

Mall. Perhaps concerned with being overheard, Rashid begins their conversation off-topic. Tu patiently listens to irrelevant plans for Dubai Square as they walk past stores and restaurants to the foot of a giant four-level waterfall feature. There, water plummets loudly from near the ceiling to a ground-floor pool. Statues of divers gracefully extend their arms in perfect form mid-stream, heads down, as if suspended mid-air in swan dives.

Facing the noisy flowing water, Rashid changes subjects. "I believe you are here to help my friends and their cause. Look around you. What I see disgusts me. People imitate the West, luring our children to sin and telling our brothers and sisters that the one true religion is just a myth. If you want to help, talk to your leaders. Make them understand that Islam is not the enemy."

Tu is cautious in his reply. "My mother read from the Holy Quran every day. I am unworthy of the Al-Raheem—praise be upon him, but your interests and the interests of my employer overlap. He is not a righteous man. There will be much to answer for. We are only conduits, and the people who brought us together expect results."

Rashid seems momentarily eased by Tu's use of Arabic, equating Allah with eternal mercy, but he is also a businessman who collects fees for his services. In so many words, Dragonhead has told Tu that if Rashid isn't forthcoming in his assistance, he should go directly to the end recipients of their funding in Myanmar, Indonesia, and the Philippines. Never mind that they want Rashid to be an intermediary.

Pointing to the waterfall as if the two men marvel at its construction, Rashid says, "There is a camera behind us and a Security Authority photographer on the third level. Our government believes you are here to discuss the Dubai Square project. Please keep this in mind for the rest of your time here."

Tu directs his attention to the waterfall and keeps his expression blank.

"You are a very cautious man. I appreciate your situation, but we also require speed. Are you up to the task? I suggest we work together."

"Moving money quickly is not a problem. These are difficult times. I'm pleased your employer wants to help impoverished children in underdeveloped Muslim countries. Your donations will be greatly appreciated. Transfer funds to the accounts on this card." He pulls a business card from his suit pocket. "The door will be open for 24 hours. If your employer is as capable as you suggest, this should not be a problem."

Tu accepts a card with a long internet address with random characters printed on one side.

Rashid says, "Only Allah can judge your employer's lifestyle. Is there anything else?"

"I would like you to consider helping similarly trusted groups in other ASEAN countries. We may want to support them as well."

Tu expects the request to illicit suspicion, and it does. Rashid stiffens, but Tu produces his own card before he can respond. "Trust is earned. Allow me to show our appreciation for your commitment. Assalamu alaikum."

As Tu leaves, Rashid glances at an amount worth roughly 525,000 dirhams, or $50,000. "Are you sure?" Rashid calls out.

In response, Tu nods and says, "May blessings be upon you all the days of your life."

• • •

While waiting for his flight to depart DXB, Tu takes a picture of the address Rashid gave him and attaches the image to an email draft located on a secure server at the new data center. His work is done. It will be up to Bao to initiate the transactions. Then, while boarding his flight back to Macau, Tu receives a text message from Bao: *Done. Have a safe flight.*

Rashid's mouth drops open when he returns to his office and sees the transfers already made by Tu's people into various accounts. For a fleeting moment, he considers not forwarding the money to the intended recipients, but it's only a passing thought inspired by Satan. The 6% he negotiated as his fee for handling the transactions, plus the significant gift from Tu's employer, is more than sufficient.

Rashid sends a carefully worded encrypted message to a network intermediary who will undoubtedly pass the information up the chain of command:

The All-Compassionate One gives us water to drink, air to breathe, and land upon which we build. You can help many with his blessing. Find an island of serenity in the troubled sea and go forward in faith.

Translated—the message confirms that funding is finally in motion.

Chapter 14

February 24

Yin wanders the streets of Singapore's Chinatown, looking for a rental opportunity with a minimal footprint, carrying the burden of Li's fate on her shoulders. Shops and eateries line the streets. It's colorful here, and a hint of jasmine incense on the air reminds her of Li. There are many reasons to be grateful for being in a beautiful city, but Yin's mind races through hypervigilant assumptions about what comes next. Enthusiasm accompanied every aspect of her life until now. Academic excellence and pleasant routines filled her days, but that's not the case in Singapore. The darkened reflection she encounters in a storefront window one block later is etched with uncertainty. She pauses to search the image for hidden meaning, but there is no hidden meaning in despair.

Academic pursuits provided a sanctuary and the illusion of control. Yin now sees the natural world as cruel and unkind. The mantra of saving her sister propels her, but what comes next? For the first time in her life, she is terrified to share personal information with the people and institutions around her, and for good reason. The person she presents to Bao and others exudes confidence and competence, but she has never been quite so anxious, hyper-vigilant, and untrusting. She indirectly works for an international crime organization. Bao says a legitimate cover business hides them, but what is hidden now will inevitably be discovered by authorities. Where will she be when that happens? A more determined reflection in yet another storefront window reassures her that Li is worth any price.

Yin notices a face across a busy street that she saw twenty minutes earlier. Has paranoia followed her to Singapore? Is she being surveilled?

Suppressing aspects of her inner psyche takes effort. The other self wants to wreak havoc on the people, places, and events that challenge her. At times, she's allowed this force to act, but seldom has this helped her situation. Li's calming influence has saved Yin from inappropriate outbursts for over a decade. Routines are also an effective buffer against internal turmoil. She acknowledges that daily tea, running five days per week, and looking forward to Friday nights with her sister and friends were all anchors, but Yin's routines are gone, and so is Li.

Before Li's abduction, there was less to be angry about and seldom a need for rage, but this afternoon, smiling and pleasantries require effort. Too many questions don't have answers, and even the simple task of finding a place to live seems overwhelming in this mental state. "Finding you should be easier. I'm talking to myself now?" Yin mumbles aloud, amused by her predicament.

Yin has the cash Bao gave her, but what about payment records? There will be checks or direct deposit, taxes, a formal record linking her with the company. She doesn't want that. None of the insiders should want that. They should work under assumed names and collect payment in crypto or cash. *What good is it to find Li but spend the rest of my life in prison, and why is that person across the street following me?*

Yin read up on SDRs because she was the target of the Chinese surveillance detection route network. Fear sets in as she turns a corner to see if her shadow follows. As far as she can tell, he does not, but she's only just arrived in Singapore. A team might have handed off the package.

Ann Siang Road is a winding, narrow street of shops and restaurants. One of the small restaurants has a For Rent sign on its second floor, and she quickly ducks into the building to evade surveillance and investigate housing. She meets the owner, a Chinese immigrant pleased to deal in cash.

Yin pays a damage deposit and three months of rent in advance, leaving plenty of money from Bao's initial payment for other things. Having secured a place to live, a smile creases Yin's lips. *I am a person of action. Action breeds control. Control is needed to find Li.* The experience is cathartic.

An hour later, Yin sits near a windowsill in the dusty and dimly lit room, lost in thoughts about recent choices. Until coming to Singapore, she'd been eager to continue her studies, but why? Pride? Why does she need to be the best in the world at something? There have been dozens of very lucrative opportunities presented to her in the past few years, all arising from what she's already accomplished, all passed over in a bizarre, mindless pursuit of excellence. A superior education opens doors to great projects, but perhaps there are other more suitable priorities, beginning with wealth. She knows how to manage money. Money is coming. She confesses that money solves problems but is just as capable of creating them. Looking at the street below, Yin knows all this is unimportant. Li must come first. *Be a person of action.*

Equipment and furnishings will continue to arrive at the data center in the next two days. Yin is perpetually surrounded there by the shuffling of desks, the whir of power tools, and the clatter of cubicles, chairs, and meeting room tables being assembled and positioned. The workdays are more extended than even Bao expected, but he assures her and others that they will soon settle into a more reasonable rhythm. Yin doubts the claim. Bao has a cot in his office. He's at work when she arrives and nearly always starts a new project when she leaves. She offers to stay every night, but he says no, exposing a secretive element in his workflow. Yin manages her tasks with ease. Focus is maintained, but she is also interested in Bao. There are inconsistencies in his demeanor, persona, and actions. Understanding the man and shaping their relationship could help her find Li.

Due to the long hours, nearby restaurants are closed when Yin returns to her apartment. Her choices are to eat at a bar or find something in her refrigerator. Like Bao, she has secretive projects, and her research often continues deep into the night.

Before Yin begins her covert evening tasks, she paces in her apartment, frustrated by her dependence on others. She texts Haitao, but there is nothing new from the Shanghai police. Yin thumbs a harsh reply message, telling Haitao he needs to be more aggressive. She writes: *The police are stonewalling. Where is your courage? Do something!* She changes her mind. The message is replaced with encouragement to keep trying.

Familiar with exploit tools employable on various devices, Yin configures a tablet for exploits and carries it while walking the neighborhood and sipping wine at a bar. The process is complicated, but soon, she is picking and choosing between unsuspecting users. The strategy is simple—find a suitable target, take control of their equipment, verify that they do not live in Shanghai, and use the victim's device to send a message to the Australian Deputy Chief of Station, Nigel Rainer. When convinced she has a suitable mule, she composes a short text message on the phone of a traveling French businessman. It reads:

Nigel. We will talk soon about trading information.

Incense Master.

• • •

Yin spends two days assisting Bao with equipment configuration, probing for weaknesses in Triad digital security, and always looking for opportunities. Exhilarating dark intent counterbalances her anxiety about potentially being discovered. She grows weary but continues creating shell companies and strategizing with Bao on projects. She occasionally mentions the plight of her friend's missing sister. It's troubling to Yin that Bao seems uninterested.

At night, she steals files from the Australians. For all she knows, a digital security team may already know someone lurks on Essex's home computer. Essex himself may be under suspicion for lax security practices.

She no longer wonders if she is followed to and from the data center. It's a fact. She's identified at least two persons. The question now is, who do they work for? If the Chinese man with crooked teeth and the woman obsessed with feeding birds surveil for the Triads, it's not a problem. Surveillance is expected. But what if they work for INTERPOL or Singaporean police? If so, she's already in trouble. Australian or American spies would likely be of European descent. But then again, her shadow could be MSS, which would complicate everything, or would it? Whatever the case, she needs to be alert.

Before returning to Essex's computer, Yin reviews her procedures. She imagines digital forensic experts sorting through event logs, discovering her malware, and conducting endpoint analysis of her attacks. The thought is frightening, but she's been here before. In a government-funded research project at the university, she worked with teams that attacked or defended various networks. Accomplished technicians created the laboratories where this work took place. These were digital warfare scenarios, and yet just a game. Being caught there was part of a process employees and contractors readily endured.

In Singapore, government agencies have the right and ability to tap private phones and computers without oversight. Law enforcers can detain persons of interest for up to two years without a judicial hearing. Conducting espionage, knowing that authorities will assume she is doing this for MSS and not for personal reasons, renders her vulnerable. There will be no legal recourse for Yin if caught, and yet she continues to steal and analyze information obtained from William Essex and other Australians. *I am a woman of action*. Action is control! It's as if Li encourages her to carry on.

Gathering intelligence is slow, requires meticulous attention to seemingly random details, and can only be achieved with patience. Initially, there is only the goal of finding and freeing her sister, but there are thousands of steps, perhaps millions of decision points, between her and the goal.

Essex and Nigel eat breakfast together weekly. Anyone else might dismiss a flurry of emails surrounding birthday and anniversary announcements, but to Yin, these are valuable pieces in an elaborate puzzle, and every new piece of information contributes to her planning.

Nigel's birthday approaches. Workers often get takeaway from a nearby restaurant, and many go to a particular bar after work. Nigel seems to enjoy golf, but with whom? He is recently divorced and will travel back to Australia soon to conduct another series of interrogations associated with trafficking.

Yin's focus is not limited to Aussie intelligence services. She hunts for factual or fabricated information suitable for trade with Nigel. That she is inside a Triad-funded data center is already a major bargaining chip, but she wants more. She wants specific information that will lead Nigel to believe she is an important Triad member. She needs leverage. She wants enough money to enter underworld sex trafficking and auction sites and desperately needs Bao or the Australians to assist her in the quest.

On day five of the data center buildout, Bao calls his teams together, pours champagne, and declares the center operational. Minor touchups will continue at the facility. Workers have yet to install cabinets in the common area, and the women's bathroom needs paint, but it's time to get serious about building a company.

The announcement comes midway through the afternoon, and to celebrate, he hands out S$100 notes before inviting everyone to go home early. As coworkers collect their belongings to go, he whispers that Yin should stay. He does the same with two other employees. Peter, a network engineer from the UK, and a Bulgarian named Nicolay, whom everyone calls Nick. Their common language is English, which is where Bao starts.

"I sent everyone home so the four of us can talk. I'll answer your questions, like, what the hell are we all doing here, right?" Bao pauses, grinning, until he gets nods and smiles. At first, Yin found this playful aspect of Bao's personality strangely endearing, but now she sees it as manipulative acting. Bao continues. "We're here to make a shit-ton of untraceable money. Everyone will get a standard paycheck with deductions and all that BS to keep up appearances. See? Just another company. Our cover is data collection and aggregation, but the four of us know better.

"If what I'm about to say makes you uncomfortable, the door is right there. Keep your mouth shut after you leave but fuck off. No hard feelings.

"On the other hand, if you stay with me for a year or so, you'll have enough to retire in style. Considerable risk, big reward, right? Nicolay and Peter know I live up to my word on pay. They also know we'll be doing some nasty shit, and whatever you think that means, it's probably worse.

"The other question is, why the hell are we in Singapore? I can't answer that one. I've protested, but the big man has his reasons, so being here means no screwups. Singaporeans monitor mobile devices, SMS, and most of the apps that we believe are secure. They record our credit card transactions. CCTV cameras feed facial recognition software. They can track your movements through bus cards. If we were selling gummy bears, no problem. But that's not what we're doing."

"So, how do we communicate?" Peter asks. Of the four, he seems most anxious.

Bao implies he is surprised by the question, though his surprise is overly theatrical. "What did I just say? If it's about anything important, we don't. Nothing digital. If you stick around after tonight, we'll discuss protocols, but here's the thing. We never discuss operations in the open. We don't use phones, email, SMS, WhatsApp, none of it. Hold that thought."

Bao jogs into his office and returns with a digital surveillance wand. "We'll scan the facility before any serious conversations. I did that earlier."

"Aren't there any carriers we can trust?" Peter asks, referring to the service providers that deliver telephony and digital messaging.

"You're on SingTel, right? I am. It doesn't matter what service. The government monitors everything coming into and out of Singapore. It pisses off the neighbors if you know what I mean. Nearly all digital communications in Southeast Asia run through hubs in Singapore. The Singaporeans tap into all of it for themselves and their friends in Five Eyes. Singapore is like a sixth eye. Australia, Canada, New Zealand, the United Kingdom, and the United States all get intelligence from Singapore, so I ask again," Bao says, now gesturing with arms wide and rolling eyes, "Why are we in Singapore? Only the boss knows, and he's not talking. I suspect it has to do with laundering money, but who knows? With the shit we're going to attempt, we should be in East Bum-Fuck Africa, but we're here, and I say all this to let you know the seriousness of our situation.

"Enough about the downside. Fuck that. Risk is sexy. We'll hack and push money around the globe. You will get your hands dirty and make tons of money doing it. Details will come if you stay, but if you walk, I'll understand. Anyone?"

Yin looks at Peter, and Peter and Nicolay look at each other, but no one leaves. Their attention returns to Bao, who says, "I need verbal commitments."

Yin says, "I'm definitely in. That's my verbal commitment, but I have a question. Who do we work for, and what's the goal?"

Bao holds up his hand to wait. "Peter? Nicolay?"

"Yes," Nicolay says immediately.

"Yes. It sounds like a bit of fun," Peter adds, though his twitching eye and shaking fingers suggest reluctance.

Bao doesn't seem to notice or doesn't care. He rests his backside on the edge of a desk, folds his arms, and seems relieved. He clears his throat as if emptying his mind. "Good. You're all in, so here it goes. There are no Chinese families more famous than the Triads. In time, one of their big shots will probably show up here. When that happens, heads down and eyes averted. Blend in with the other clueless coworkers, and yeah. We'll have a smokescreen. If the Singaporeans or any other intelligence agency gets on to us, they will drop us in a hole and throw away the hole, but if we are careful, there is no reason to worry. Peter is a network genius, Nicolay has hacked more corporate and governmental sites than anyone, and Yin is the queen of techno-finance. I have a few skills myself, especially in cryptocurrency. In short, we are the A team for the Triad's digital activities. Did I mention that I am the boss?" Bao says, laughing at his bravado before continuing.

"When I tell you to do something, for fuck's sake, make that a priority.

I don't need any whiny little bitches in my company. If I tell you to hack the F fucking BI or the Kremlin, just do your best, and don't get caught."

Nicolay and Peter's faces show anxiety, but not Yin's. To her, it's all bravado from a showman. Bao must have sensed Nicolay and Peter's concern because he adds, "Okay, maybe not the FBI, but you know what I'm saying. No matter what I ask for, do your best."

"Where do we start?" Nicolay asks.

"Your first job, Nick, will be to hack the shit out of our boss's firewalls. I did some unauthorized pen testing and found tasty Swiss cheese. You'll have details in the morning.

"When you're convinced we have it all, Peter and I will help them tighten network security, and Nick, I need that list of law enforcement hacks. I appreciate wanting to keep that to yourself—Snowden-level shit—but you're here now. We can talk numbers later if that's the hitch."

"You need everything?" Nicolay asks. The tone in his voice and the surprise on his face suggest he has deep information, probably collected over years of attacks. Yin realizes that Nick could be very helpful to her if he's willing, but the emerging sentry in her says trust no one. From this moment forward, she must safeguard every action and scrutinize every decision before acting.

"What the hell, dude? Yeah. If you're here, you're all in. I'm interested in ASEAN countries, but if I ask you to help move drugs or money through, like Guyana or Armenia, I'll need information on law enforcement to be readily available. Don't worry about compensation. I've got you covered. Right now, I'm interested in the Australian prison system. Tomorrow, it could be financial institutions in Cambodia or Zimbabwe. Next week, maybe something in the Middle East. Are we good?"

Bao mentioning Australian prisons sends shockwaves through Yin's frame. Nigel Rainer is interrogating suspected Triad prisoners in Victoria. Bao wants information on the Australian prison system. She considers how to use this information, but her thoughts are interrupted.

Nicolay nods his understanding, and Bao continues. "That leaves you, Yin. I need you to create dozens more shell corporations—Africa, Vietnam, Latin America, the Cayman Islands, wherever. The criteria will include whether a country is friendly with the international Financial Stability Board, whether the government regularly surveils transactions, and how often they mess with people like us. If they don't have a sense of humor, move on. When the big boss asks us to move funds, that will be on you, and we're not talking about thousands. Think hundreds of millions. There could be a billion in transactions before we're through."

Yin responds with a grin, unsure why she's so anxious to get started. Regardless of the mission, being on a covert team again is exciting.

"I thought you were the boss?" Peter says wryly.

"Wiseass. I let them think they are in charge. You are looking at the grand wizard, captain of your universe. It's better if you focus on me and forget the Triad connection. I'm serious about that one," Bao says emphatically.

"What is timeframe?" Nicolay asks in his Bulgarian accent.

"Does yesterday work for you? We're not on a clock until I say so, but there's no vacation time, no PTO or any of that other corporate BS. Show up for work and kick ass until I say stop. The gig could last months or years."

Peter raises his hand, and Bao goes ballistic. "Fuck's sake, Peter! Don't do that."

"What?" Peter asks as surprise and embarrassment twist his face into an impish expression.

"You raise your hand like a wimpy schoolboy? If you have something to say, say it."

"If it's just us four doing the real work, why so many employees?" Yin would have asked the same question. At last count, 26 people have cycled through the center hoping to claim one of the 30 cubicles.

Bao laughs. "You'll love this one. Each of you gets a handful of employees to manage as our cover. There are a few guidelines, but I don't care what they do in their little cubicles. We're a data center, right? The Singapore Data Centre. We have the budget, equipment, and talent for a big-data shop, so we put them to work on whatever makes sense. You might study the impact of technology on sports, research urban traffic patterns, and look at how climate change will affect Singapore, but avoid topics that might draw unwanted attention. Pharmaceuticals, tax shelters, and anything about law enforcement or corruption are off the table.

"Actually, wealth management might be a good cover for Yin as long as we don't get into hiding money, but you know what I'm saying. Your people should generate enough digital noise to hide our work. Done properly, we will be just like every other greedy business. Five Eyes is watching. Don't give them anything to act on."

Chapter 15

March 1

Nigel returns to Singapore late in the evening from one of his frequent trips to Australia. There is urgency in his step, and even though the workday has long ended for his coworkers and boss, he's tempted to call Essex for what should be tacit approval to approach his contacts in the CIA for assistance. Unfortunately, Essex doesn't work that way. Six months earlier, Nigel relayed signals intelligence data suggesting that human trafficking was on the rise in Queensland. There wasn't much to go on, more of a hunch, but his reasoning was verified. Arrests were made, a case developed, and convictions ensued. That could have been the end of it for Nigel. Trusting his instincts, Nigel made another trip to Barwon Prison to speak with the more malleable of the convicted Triad members. Essex considered his actions frivolous, a desperate man grasping at straws, but it paid dividends.

These men were charged with and convicted of human trafficking. Nigel had seen something on a few of the men's faces during their trial and initial questioning. Subsequent interviews revealed unexpected sophistication and confirmed a ten-year plan. That plan is indeterminate, but Singaporean SIGINT surveillance of Triad activities might help.

Signals intelligence is the core of counterintelligence. Singaporeans share intel with everyone, but especially with the US and Britain. They are aligned with the West more than with China or its neighbors. It's time to press Essex into action. Looking down the corridor into his boss's dark office, Nigel decides not to approach Essex until morning.

• • •

Daybreak arrives quickly. Nigel picks up a coffee and apple crostata on his way to the office and sighs heavily upon returning. Sticky notes cling to his desk and lampshade as he drops into the chair behind his desk and rereads an email from one of the corrections officers he'd met at Barwon. According to this guard, as soon as Nigel left the prison yesterday, he intercepted a kite, a prisoner's note passed from one cell to another. Jiao Long's brother made sure every man convicted with him read his note. Penned in Mandarin, Nigel has one of his assistants translate:

> Guard your tongue as you would guard your family. The sage never speaks of the great things to come.

The message ends with the character for Hexagram One of the I-Ching, which Nigel looks up. *Qian*—Heaven is in motion.

There is a moment in casework when the lights come on. This was that moment. Jiao Long's brother, who is very likely in charge of this Triad, threatens the families of his men. If they snitch on the great things to come, Dragonhead will kill their families.

Nigel thanks the guard who sent him the message and loads Essex's calendar to get on his schedule. An hour later, he joins his boss to discuss his findings.

• • •

"Have a minute?" Nigel says after tapping on Essex's open office door. The big man has his back turned, stirring sugar and cream into his tea with a plastic spoon, "Good trip?" Essex asks, with a quick peek over his shoulder, barely acknowledging his second in command.

"A few of them were more cooperative than last time, so yes. Good trip. I've stumbled upon something that warrants requesting assistance from our friends at the CIA. This guy, Chuanli, has a brother named

Jiao Long in China. He's a Dragonhead. Chuanli will do five years, maybe longer, but a guard intercepted a communication. Something big is coming with that group. We can probably crack it if we go all in on this Jiao Long character for a while."

"And this guy is here in Singapore?" Essex asks.

"Well, no, China. We think Macau."

Essex shows his displeasure by nudging a stack of paperwork and sighing. "I'm not going to burn favors for some guy in China. Anything actionable?"

"Not yet actionable, but credible. We're talking about Dragonhead's brother," Nigel says.

"What was it, six bad guys and a dozen prostitutes?"

"Twenty girls in two locations, two of them underage."

"Wow!" Essex says, the comment drenched in sarcasm. "I stand corrected, but we have other priorities. Does the war on terror sound familiar? We're fighting to keep people alive, not lock them up for a little dick action." Off Nigel's stony reaction, Essex backtracks. "Sorry, mate, you didn't deserve that. It was a good bust. You followed through on this last trip down under, but the bad guys are behind bars, all done. I'm denying the request. Anything else?"

"Nothing else," Nigel says as he leaves, but for him, the information is too valuable to dismiss. He taps contacts on his phone. The Deputy Chief of Station for the CIA Singapore is more than an intelligence contact. The two men play golf often, have been known to drink themselves into oblivion, and have repeatedly broken rules to help each other. Justin Wright answers on the third ring.

"Let me guess. You finally broke 100," Wright says when he answers. Nigel dreams of breaking 75, but they chirp at each other for fun. Wright is a tall, muscular African American who played defensive end for the Navy football team. He is a fitness freak capable of driving a golf ball over 300 yards, though seldom in the right direction and not strictly through the air. Brilliant, connected, and singularly responsible for Nigel's sense of inadequacy off the tee and in the locker room, Nigel thinks of Wright as a friend. That his short game sucks, gives Nigel an edge on and off the course. Furthermore, both men agree that Nigel's supervisor should be replaced.

"Are we talking about your goal or mine? Next time we play, I'll give you ten strokes, and you still won't break 90. What are we doing for lunch? I'm buying," Nigel says.

"It's about time. Fusion Bistro or the Fat Cow?" Wright asks.

"I like the veranda at Red Dot." Asking to meet outdoors means Nigel wants to talk shop in private.

Two hours later, the men sit opposite each other, sharing plates of Satay, Bangkok Pork Sticks, Grilled Prawns, and custom summer ale beers. They open with banter about golf and where they should play next and inevitably move to the women Wright has dated recently. Nearly done eating, Nigel asks for a favor. "A few weeks ago, we put away some Triad members operating near Melbourne."

"Sounds like an internal matter," Wright says as if the subject were irrelevant in his domain.

"They're a transnational operation."

"No shit, Sherlock," Wright replies, chuckling.

"I have intel that something big is in the works, and before you ask, I don't know what. I need more intel on a guy named Jiao Long in Macau. We have his brother in custody."

"This a formal request? Essex has your back?" Wright asks, setting his fork down and leaning back in the chair.

"Screw him. It's just me for now. Don't stick your neck out if you don't feel up for it, but there's something big here. Jiao Long is the head of the organization. Anything you can find will be appreciated." Nigel says. Even though these two are friends, there's an unwritten protocol when asking for off-book favors.

"It's interesting that you would bring up that group right now. There's a buzz about some nasty cyber stuff coming from Macau." Opening his phone and tapping the keys, he asks for the names of the probable Triad boss and his brother. "Give me a week? What you got to trade?" Wright asks, knowing he's holding all the cards.

"What? Lunch isn't enough?" Nigel asks with a look of disbelief. "What do you need?"

"What I need is a fat-ass Wagyu steak, two inches thick on a bed of grilled onions. You know what I'm talking about." Wright says, grinning, signaling that he shares Nigel's concern.

"Get me something I can use, and you're on."

Chapter 16

March 3

In the aftermath of the New York World Trade Center attacks of September 11, 2001, those intent on spreading terror realized their communications were being hunted, identified, and monitored by the US and its allies, notably through cooperation within Five Eyes. The Western alliance formed these alliances during and after World War Two and continued their collaboration through the Cold War. These days, the war on terror hardens their resolve. The intelligence apparatus of these nations is more committed than ever. They have to be. Terrorists become more sophisticated every year.

Tactical discourse between terrorist organizations exists on the dark web, hides in game chats, and often relies upon encrypted and secured applications available to everyone. Critical communications between major players disappeared from the digital landscape altogether. Trusted hawaladars pass funds and information in a closed network using face-to-face couriers and sometimes carriers like FedEx and DHL.

The network Rashid participates in takes additional steps to ensure secrecy. Many long-distance communications still move through common carriers, but for critical messages, either the sender or recipient or both are disassociated. Faithful friends are used to send and receive sealed packages, which are then delivered in person to their intended destinations.

In the dim light of the dawn rising over Kuala Lumpur, Nasr Rakmani faces the Kaaba and dutifully completes morning prayer before any other activity. The Fajr prayer has new meaning today because the evening before, he received a coded text message requesting five and a half pounds of goat meat be ready for pickup at precisely 7:30 this morning. The text came from someone he's never met, but the language verifies the recipient.

Nasr carefully carves goat meat over a sealed plastic bag containing his latest report. The courier will forward his report in a different package, but the final recipient is Almudir, the man above him in their network. For all Nasr knows, Almudir could have someone above him and another after that, just as Nasr now has two cells below himself, but that is unlikely. Having met Almudir in person, it doesn't seem possible. Almudir is the most confident human being Nasr has ever encountered—with a frightening demeanor and clear vision of the enemy, he's no one's subordinate. Almudir is as well known among elite holy warriors as Bin Laden was in his early years. He knew Bin Laden. He helped form Bin Laden's plans and has been secretly active ever since. History lists holy warriors dating back to Sayf Allāh al-Maslūl, the Drawn Sword of Allah. Almudir wants to be the next great name on that list.

Nasr follows orders and doesn't ask questions with the goal that someday, he will make the plans, secure resources, and give the orders.

When Nasr met Almudir, he knew what he wanted to be. He also knew he had to do everything asked of him without wavering because failing Almudir could end his life. In five short years, inspiration drawn from Almudir shifted to caution and then aspiration. But Nasr wonders if his view of Almudir will change again as they prepare for what's to come. Almudir trusts him with delicate matters. He's been promoted for his loyalty and commitment and feels as if he is fully engaged in the struggle.

Nasr prepares his shop for the day ahead. Distracted by wrapping cuts of meat, he forgets the time. At precisely 7:30, someone knocks on his door. Nasr unwittingly yells that he doesn't open until 8, then snaps into awareness. There is a van parked in front of his shop. A woman wearing a simple sarong and tudung head scarf, atypical in his neighborhood, is accompanied by a solid-looking man in black cargo pants and a matching tactical shirt. Glancing at the wall clock, Nasr rushes to them and unlocks the door. The woman softly taps her chin twice. "Assalamu alaikum. Is my goat meat ready?"

"Yes. *Wa alaikum salaam*," Nasr says, gesturing to come in. Nasr quickly returns to the counter and lifts a package to the countertop.

The woman steps forward to receive her package. Her escort, a broad-shouldered man who appears to be well-trained in deadly arts, waits at the door, hands clasped at the waist. Money couriers occasionally travel in pairs for heightened security. The chiseled face and menacing presence of her escort today indicate danger, which tells Nasr that whatever she brings is valuable, extremely sensitive, or both.

"Prepare to travel soon," Nasr's contact says as she opens her shoulder bag and hands him a thick parcel.

"Thank you," Nasr says, placing the package under his counter.

"How fresh is the lamb?" she asks, gazing at prices posted on the wall behind Nasr. Nasr is momentarily confused but decides this additional request is not code. She's simply thinking ahead, planning a meal for her family. When Nasr began his journey into the network, he was just like this woman—innocent, happy to help, unaware of the significance. Nasr cuts lamb to her specifications but refuses to accept payment.

When they've gone, Nasr reengages the bolt lock of the shop door and carries the package into the back room. The envelope is heavier than usual, which makes him smile. This time, the weight is from dozens of blue envelopes, which have more money than the green envelopes he is accustomed to receiving. He slides them into a wall safe and opens a folder of instructions from Almudir.

Almudir is slightly older than Nasr, and physically intimidating despite a noticeable congenital defect. His right arm is shorter and leaner than his left. Though the disability doesn't render the arm useless, Nasr knows he must have endured endless mocking during his tough childhood. Almudir has spoken before about his father's early disappointment. Early in their friendship, Almudir described how the man had been brutal, and how they lived in the Xinjiang Uyghur Autonomous Region in Northwest China. His father had been outspoken and angry about being governed by the Chinese. Why should anyone live in a country governed by infidels? Before they met in person, Nasr expected Almudir to be Arab, but his features and accent were Mongolian. He was mesmerized by the towering sixty-something militant's thick hands, dense beard, and penetrating eyes. Almudir's voice was gruff, bordering on viciousness, and the strongman had an unmistakable odor from incessantly smoking clove cigarettes. The paper Nasr reads now carries this scent and conjures memories.

There are days when Nasr thinks of himself as a rising star in Almudir's Jihadi network and that Almudir is the greatest mastermind of all time, but lately, he's had doubts. He's been quietly carrying out seemingly meaningless and unrelated tasks for months. The activities made little sense until now. This new set of instructions encourages Nasr to redouble his recruiting efforts and focus on men with military training.

Nasr exhausted his contact list in the first round of recruiting. The new task is daunting. How can a simple Halal butcher be expected to accomplish so much in such a short time? Even worse, Almudir's technical instructions elude him. He must familiarize himself with the regulations at Port Kelang. He has a glossary of terms and a complex workflow diagram for moving containers into and out of the port. Most disturbing, he's supposed to understand how to move sensitive equipment through the maze of electronic detection instruments installed at the port. It's a frightening prospect. But Nasr is more afraid of disappointing Almudir than of getting caught by port authorities, so he will work day and night, fulfill each task, and keep Almudir's trust.

When he received his first set of complicated instructions, Nasr didn't know what an HLV was, but he learned to acquire a Heavy Lifting Vessel. He'll work on this new set of instructions until he understands what it is required.

A section of Rashid's message to Almudir helps Nasr form the big picture. The coded message reads: *find an island of serenity in the troubled sea and go forward.*

Nasr studies an aggressive timeline and sighs at the calendar on his wall. Almudir has often said that secrets are like marbles on a tabletop. It's easy to control a few of them, but the more there are, any disturbance scatters them in every direction. The details of Almudir's plans are secretive, divided among many participants. Nasr knows his part and nothing else, but the timing of his tasks has accelerated significantly. There is little time to waste. He's always known that Almudir's plan is big, but it was always in the distant future. Receiving so much money with explicit instructions implies that a countdown has started.

The final line of Almudir's extensive instructions underscores how critical heavy equipment and pilots are to his plans. Overwhelmed by the gravity of new tasks, Nasr closes his eyes and prays for strength and guidance. He also thanks The Omniscient One for giving him the foresight needed to hire an extra person for his shop. Sensing that demands on his time would increase, he posted a simple *Now Hiring* sign in his window and got immediate responses. Within hours, he'd hired a nearly destitute but brilliant young woman named Syhala. Two other applicants came through his door, either of which might have been capable, but Syhala speaks multiple languages and is a member of the nearby mosque. Moreover, when he implied that his time might be limited because of all the work he does to help Muslim refugees, she nearly begged him to let her help. Syhala wore some makeup when she came in to apply, which Nasr found off-putting, but as they talked, she said she didn't know what he would be like, and so many business owners are secularists. She prays five times per day, observes Ramadan, and persuaded him with her enthusiasm and friendly banter, teasing him, calling him uncle, and practically begging for the opportunity.

The butcher shop now has three employees. Two young men work as butchers in training while his new hire manages the counter. It troubles him that she is of birthing age and unmarried, but customers love her, and she understands the technology at the register. She often clowns with him for being so serious, which has lightened his mood. They trade jokes and, during lunch breaks, often tell stories.

This afternoon, Nasr closes the shop early to talk with his employees. Syhala says. "I hope this has to do with refugees." Nasr winks at her, a hushing index finger to his lips.

When they've locked the door and gathered in the back room, Nasr claps his hands together to show enthusiasm. "This won't take long. Please sit. You all know I do extra work for Islam. We help refugees and move people and equipment for our brothers and sisters. I am told more time is needed, which is one of the reasons I hired Syhala. Well, guess what? I have no choice but to promote all of you. Everyone gets a raise, even Syhala, but there will be extra hours. I'll also pay more for evening deliveries.

They all smile while agreeing to more hours at better pay, but family

Richard Giudice

commitments prohibit the training butchers from working evenings. Nasr turns his head in disappointment.

"Uncle. No problem. If you pay for the gasoline, I can make deliveries on my scooter. The scooter has baskets and they drink less gas. How often?" Syhala asks.

Nasr laughs and brightens. "Yes, yes. I pay the gasoline, and we can work out the schedule. I'll have one steady customer and three food shelters to take what we cannot sell, so three nights per week for the shelters and four nights for my pilot friend. Do you remember seeing Captain Khan in the shop? He's a commercial pilot."

"I don't think so. He must be rich if we bring him food," Syhala says with a gleam in her eye. She's never known a wealthy person.

"Of course, he makes money. Pilots make good money, but our food is a gift. He does important work for Islam, so I support him the only way I can. Do you have any questions? You boys will open the shop, and Syhala will close."

"What exactly do we do for Islam?" Syhala asks.

"Right now, we relocate refugees of war, drought, and persecution. We also fly supplies to those in need, but first things first. Let's go through the procedures for opening and closing the shop, and then you can all go home."

It takes only minutes to show the butchers how to open the shop, and they leave. "I'm proud of you, uncle," Syhala says as Nasr relocks the door.

"Thank you, but why?" Nasr asks.

"For helping people. For helping me," Syhala says with gratitude.

Nasr places a hand on Syhala's shoulder. "You're a gift from Allah, a blessing just for being here."

Kissing both cheeks, Nasr looks into Syhala's eyes and says, "I must stress, the deliveries for my pilot friend are our highest priority."

Syhala beams and asks, "Does the pilot have someone to go home to?"

"He does not," Nasr says, laughing and shaking his finger at her insinuation. Syhala smiles widely, and Nasr changes subjects. "When you close, check the back door. Then, print the day's transactions, count the money, put the cash into an envelope, and drop it in the security slot. The empty register drawer stays open."

"The deliveries?" Syhala asks.

"The boys know the pilot's schedule. Khan is very particular, so we don't make substitutions without talking to him."

"I call him Mr. Khan?" Syhala asks innocently.

Laughing, Nasr says, "I see right through you, my niece. I will not interfere but know this. He is critical to our cause and must remain focused. Captain Muhammad Khan is a former fighter pilot but now flies commercially. He's an important man. Call him Captain Khan."

Chapter 17

March 4

Rain flows gently down the window of Yin's apartment, and sparse traffic outside sounds notably different when the pavement is wet. Showers are common in Singapore, something Yin finds soothing, but she awakens startled, physically drained, mentally exhausted, and later than usual. The unimaginable suffering that Li must endure has penetrated her subconscious mind and frequently returns in the form of nightmares. She dreamt of being tied to a bed. A dark, faceless figure approached, causing her to awaken. The dreams come more often, and the rage she hoped would subside has turned warriorlike and calculating.

An app on Yin's phone says it's been 20 days since Li went missing. There is power in anger and energy in plotting revenge, but the police have nothing. Haitao quit calling. For everyone else, hope wanes. But every morning Yin arises with enough energy to continue, no matter what. Her sprint has turned into a marathon fraught with distractions and obstacles.

When Yin left the apartment in Shanghai, she packed Li's clothing instead of hers and took the small Buddhist shrine in their living room. Li had a morning ritual that Yin now performs. The smell of Li's incense, the sound of the bell, and the image of the statue on the windowsill remind her to keep going, no matter what. Yin dresses as Li. She wears her sister's makeup and perfume. Before leaving the apartment, she places a small durian fruit on the improvised shrine.

Yin walks two blocks from her flat and boards a bus destined for the data center. She scans the passengers, cataloging them as she tends to do out of habit—or *is it survival?* A mother and infant sit across from her. The child inquisitively stares at Yin as if solving a riddle. Yin smiles and waves. It makes the child happy, but the infant hasn't yet learned to return gestures. Still, the interaction has an unanticipated cathartic effect.

Infants have but one identity, a singular point of view. Yin has long felt that she has multiple identities, each in different stages of development and often conflicted. The most stable of these identities is the exceptional student with a bright future, but there's this other, more secretive identity she consciously hides and, at times, is at war with. This inner warrior, this dragon her parents sought to suppress, wants control, but Yin fears letting go. The child embodies innocence. Yin is slipping into darkness, spending her days angry, hunting for the men who abducted her sister, wanting to lash out.

Live among demons, and you become a demon. How long can Yin work for the Triads, hack law enforcement agencies, and send millions around the globe for nefarious activities without becoming irretrievably tainted? Daily, Yin undermines the person she believes she is in favor of the person she fears becoming. The identity that carried her so far into the academic world is fading. Is this disassembly, or does momentum feel like this?

When Yin arrives at the covert data center today, it's bustling with activity. The enthusiastic interns and young technicians are there to earn paychecks, get extracurricular college credit, or advance their careers, but the week begins with the dreaded Monday morning all-staff meeting. The level of deception is nearly untenable for Yin, and surreal. They are a criminal enterprise. As the meeting starts, she hears herself say, "If it weren't for the money." The thought shocks her. She is here to find her sister, right?

Bao stands in the center of the office, feet wide apart, chest out, fiddling with the security fob and keys he wears on a lanyard around his neck. Yin likens Bao to a miniature Napoleon when he postures this way, a small man trying to appear virile while leading his minions into battle.

Nicolay has quickly evolved into Bao's confidant and task manager. It makes sense. He's the only true alpha male in the group, something Yin has noticed as she's sized up her coworkers' weaknesses. There are winners and followers in every society, and Yin is not beyond using the stereotypes of social constructs to her advantage. Hard men prefer to dominate through intimidation. Yin has something they long for. She is attractive and intellectually gifted. As such, her arsenal of social tools includes flirtation, dismissal, feigned allegiance, and, above all, cunning. She is far more powerful than all these men combined and willing to do whatever fits the situation. It's a game Yin's caged dragon longs to play. Both Bao and Nicolay notice her sensuality. It makes them susceptible, but that move will come later, if at all.

Gruff, muscular, and square-jawed, Nicolay calls for everyone's attention with a whistle and the pronouncement, "Overlord!" It's a moniker Bao gave himself at the first all-staff meeting, a carryover from a game he'd programmed. In this context, however, the sophomoric idea of calling oneself an overlord is somehow appropriate. Staff gather in a crude semicircle around their leader, and the meeting begins with more of Bao's nonsense.

"We need a name," Bao says, gesturing with open arms. To gain the trust of his underlings, Bao manipulates, leaning on inspiring platitudes, encouragement, and juvenile interactions. The interns especially respond well to these ruses, believing the head of the company is like them—approachable, intelligent, wealthy, and humorous. He's respected and emulated.

Yin has no interest in playing Bao's games, but the salesman on her team is confused. "We're the Singapore Data Centre, right?" He asks.

"Not the company, dog breath. This," Bao flaps his open arms. "What do we call this cluster-fuck of cubicles?"

"You mean the maze?" someone says from the back of the room.

"Cool. We have the maze, the rack room, and our orifices," Bao says, pausing for effect. The scatological comment provokes modest laughter, but Yin is embarrassed for him. Bao continues. "Enough of that. Team leaders, give me the overview. Nick can start."

Nicolay reads from notes. "We've loaded and parsed the first three terabytes of purchased data, and our bots are now crawling 24/7. The team made six sales this past week, so kudos to everyone."

"How many calls?" Bao asks. The question startles Nicolay, but it shouldn't. Bao repeats his line about making calls to make money every day.

Nicolay turns to a young woman on his team, and she whispers back. Turning back to Bao, Nicolay says, "Call record shows 341 calls or texts."

"Email?" Bao asks, but as Nicolay again turns to an employee, Bao stops him with a sharp comment. "Stop it. Just stop. Next time, come prepared. Peter?"

Peter speaks from notes as well. "We're researching urban traffic congestion and the availability of electric charging stations. We've contacted numerous municipal planners and are finding good interest. The team directly contacted 112 prospects this week, qualified 76% of these, and has gone on to identify 25 decision-makers. We pitched 18 prospects and have five pending sales."

"You guys are kicking ass, Pete! Excellent. Yin?"

Yin reports without notes: "Our focus is trendlines in wealth management services. We rank financial services providers like banks, private firms, and independent consultants, then apply geocodes to the findings. Where these institutions are located is a rough measure of wealth concentration. Numerous marketing firms have shown interest in our white papers. We have yet to convert prospects, but we are receiving calls and collecting leads."

Bao smiles. "The white paper thing was brilliant, especially when you described blockchain in the context of Web3. Give them the elevator speech."

"It's technical, I'm not sure," Yin says, but Bao interrupts.

"Doesn't matter. You're not telling them how to climb, just where the mountain is."

Yin hesitates as her mind races into the complicated subject matter. No one in the office, except perhaps Bao, has spent any time at her level in the financial sector. The document Bao referenced informs wealth managers on the proper use of stablecoin vs. other volatile cryptocurrencies. It describes digital dollars as fungible assets and how the speed of global transactions is streamlined. Even a cursory understanding of the content requires familiarity with blockchain technology and knowledge of significant players, such as Solana, Avalanche, Hedera, TRON, and Ethereum. She's been here before, trying to explain the Foreign Exchange Market to her sister, Li, and decides to dumb things down. "The paper addresses decentralized finance. Banks are no longer the only place to store and move money. In these new DeFi ecosystems, there's no centralized authority. Without meddling intermediaries, blockchain allows anyone to send and receive information directly, one person to the other."

"Like PayNow," one of the interns says.

"PayNow, PayPal, and Venmo are intermediaries, connecting one bank to another. Recipients can immediately use what you send them to make purchases, but sending is routed through the banking system. A company called Circle takes that concept to a higher level. Our mission is to explain digital dollars in the context of Web3, which will soon facilitate decentralized transactions. Blockchain promises transparency, but at the same time, these transactions protect personal information by using public and private keys. In theory, no personal data is discoverable by seeing the public record, but I'm off track.

"The thing we are selling is geocoding of wealth. We also offer advice on how to survive in the emerging digital landscape. Financial institutions have the data. They know which countries, regions, and cities have wealth concentrations. Naturally, they position offices there. I'm warning that people don't care to drive to an office and talk with their bankers any longer. They control their finances in a browser or app."

"Cryptocurrency isn't even real money," one of the interns says. Yin hears this often.

"Money isn't real either," Yin says. "Not these days. Our currency is fiat, meaning it is only valuable because someone says it is. Most currency is valued against the American dollar because it's currently the most stable, but things are changing. China represents over one-third of the worldwide GDP, has the most companies on the Fortune 500 list, and one day the Yuan may replace the dollar in valuations."

Yin looks to Bao, indicating that she's said enough, and he takes over. "Thanks, Yin. Peter, I'd like you to lend your sales guys to Yin this week. We'll talk later. Okay, everyone. That's a wrap. If you haven't updated your time slips, do it now. Yin, my office," Bao says, and the meeting ends.

Yin reluctantly follows Bao to his office. As they walk, she worries over how to think about him moving forward. Yin finds it necessary to regard coworkers as friends or enemies. Triad members are enemies, but where does Bao fit? Is he trading his time for a paycheck? Yin doesn't think so. Nick and Pete are valuable idiots. Although it's too early to tell, Nigel is either an ally or a waste of energy.

They enter Bao's office, and he closes the door. "What a fucking shit show, but let's keep up the front. You did good work in there. This week let's land a few legit clients. Pete's guys will help. Maybe you offer a free trial. I'll send you a list of qualified prospects."

"I'm masking IPs, building shell companies, and managing the nerds. Do sales matter at this point?" Yin says.

"Don't tell me how to run things. Just do it," Bao snaps.

"Understood." Stiffening slightly, thinking that Bao fits in the enemy column, she realizes that he's also in deep with the wrong people. It happens.

"Sorry. Where are we? Tu's stuff, I mean." Bao asks apologetically.

She relaxes. "I conducted forty-seven transactions last week for $92 million, but converting crypto at the going rate is expensive. What do you want to do?" Yin asks.

"What about India or my friends in China?"

"Even there, we're selling at cents on the dollar."

"They'll beg for crypto in a few months, but I'll make some calls. Tu will be in later today, so prepare a report and stick around."

"This afternoon?"

"Afternoon, Evening. What does it matter? You have somewhere to be?"

Yin turns to ensure no one is just outside Bao's window. "You asked for information on Australian prisoners. I found something."

"Lay it on me," Bao says, dropping into the chair behind his desk.

"I've gotten access to some Australia Intelligence Service files through the Singapore field office. Their Chief of Station is lax and prints reports at home. I might be able to bypass network segmentation, but I decided to ask first," Yin says, hopeful she's not overplaying her hand.

"Why? I mean, it's cool and everything, but that's not your fucking job."

Yin has miscalculated. Bao is in one of his moods, but she quickly recovers. "I was inside before Singapore trying to help my friend find his sister. I go back in occasionally. Do you want me to go ahead or let it go? Speaking of that, you once said you would go nasty and get back with some information. Or was that just an empty promise from EEL?".

Bao studies her for a long moment, then reaches for his phone. "Your friend's sister? Hold off on that because Nick may already have access."

Yin doesn't like Bao's tone as he repeats the phrase "your friend's sister." It's as if he doesn't believe her, but she decides not to follow up. Having Nicolay penetrate the Australian Singapore office is enough. Better Nick takes the risk than her. Smiling, she says, "Good Idea. I'll be in my office."

Within the hour, Nicolay arrives at Yin's door carrying a laptop. He enters without knocking. "Bao says you need help with prisons in Australia. Some guy is named Chuanli?"

"Yes. Help with that and other things. Tu is coming later today. What do you know about him?" Yin says distantly.

Nicolay smiles as if he knows things he's not going to divulge. Nicolay thinks he is physically desirable and every woman's dream. He reinforces that narcissistic misogyny daily, rendering him vulnerable in ways he doesn't understand. Yin fights to keep her expression pleasant as he opens his laptop and positions it on Yin's meeting table. "This is not the right question," he says. Who is Chuanli, and why is Tu interested?"

Though not attracted to Nicolay, Yin uses his inflated ego to her advantage. *Shuai jiao*, Yin says to herself. She smiles broadly, thinking of Essex as scorched earth. "You're brilliant! Let's start with their Chief of Station?"

Nicolay is a native Bulgarian, Yin from Shanghai. As is common in cosmopolitan settings, their conversation is a collision of accents laced with phonetic misshapes and the overuse of common idioms. Even if Nicolay hadn't been introduced as Bulgarian, Yin's linguistic skills would have placed him in one of the southern Slavic countries by the trilled "r" sounds he makes and his intonation of the letter "t".

"How long have you known Bao?" Yin asks.

Nicolay responds from the side table where he's positioned his laptop so she cannot see his display. Typing as he answers, Nicolay surprises her. "EEL or Mr. Bao?"

"Either, or any other names he's used," Yin says, laughing, hoping Nicolay will slip up and disclose something useful about Bao.

"I am putting it this way," Nicolay says, turning to face her. When you hacked into his computer and left a message, I was one of the first ones he called. We have done things together for many years, but please focus on the task. What have you got?"

"I'll tell you what I've done with AIS Singapore, if you tell me what you have on the AFP and Barwon Prison. Let's work the problem together so Bao is ready for Tu," Yin says, referring to the Australian Intelligence Service, the Australian Federal Police.

A smile of recognition appears on Nicolay's face. It's not uncommon for underworld hackers to begin a conversation in this way—I'll show you mine if you show me yours. Hackers trade exploit kits and technical information when they reach an impasse, but the more accomplished they are, the less likely to trade secrets, and Nicolay is a consummate hacker. With the hesitation one might use talking to a federal agent, Nicolay says, "Eight men of some special organization that is for sure Triad were captured, only six are in prison, which means two have done something for police or were unimportant to Triad. The important one is Chuanli, brother of big boss. I know this from various activities I am doing, and Bao has confirmed."

"The police know these are Triad members," Yin says, not volunteering how or where she got the information.

"Maybe yes, or maybe nothing. Bao wants to know if these guys are keeping mouth shut. I don't see how you can help in this situation," Nicolay says dismissively as he turns back to his laptop.

"Bao says Chuanli is a brother of the Dragonhead?" Yin asks, acting surprised.

"Like you said, we trade information. What do you have to trade?" Nick says.

"I'm inside the home computer of the Chief of Station, Australian intelligence community outpost, Singapore. His name is Essex, and I've learned through that hack that their Deputy Chief flew to Victoria to interview these men several times. It's possible I can get a copy of his report when he files it, but I'd really like to penetrate via Essex's

VPN. I've got the password, but he's using multi-factor—fingerprints I assume. Is that something you could help with?"

For the first time since they met, Nicolay glances at Yin with respect. "Is Windows? Windows for sure. What other devices?"

"I believe he has an Android phone, and I know a few places he frequents, but there's no time for that before Tu comes. We should focus on court records and newspaper articles. For example, what were they convicted of doing? What landed them in prison?" Yin asks innocently, setting the hook.

"Sex traffic, prostitution, drugs, all what Triad is doing in other places. They know things the big boss does not want leaked to police," Nicolay says with a shrug. No emotion.

Yin's heart quickens as ideas race into her mind. "What happened to the women when they were captured? Will they also be interrogated? One report I read said some came from China."

"Doesn't matter. They don't know anything. I suppose if Chuanli has a big mouth, but they aren't our concern."

Disappointed that she can't press for more on the women without making Nicolay suspicious, she says, "What do we have for Bao's meeting with Tu?"

"You are a very pretty woman. You have a man?"

Laughing, Yin says, "Stop it. What do we tell Bao?"

"I am handsome man, you are pretty woman." Nick shrugs. "But okay. We say what he wants to hear. Report is coming. Take me inside Essex computer."

Nicolay uses public trial records and hacked information to identify Corrections Reference Numbers assigned to all six Triad prisoners in Barwon Prison. This leads to specific cell numbers and entries for visitors. Nigel Rainer appears frequently, which is all they need for Bao's meeting.

Bao meets with Tu privately for a half hour, then calls Yin and Nicolay into his office. Bao is typing away on his computer when Yin enters. Tu rises to greet them. Their eyes meet, and for a second or more, Tu appears to be deeply shaken at the sight of her. "Tu, meet Nicolay and Yin. Have a seat," Bao says, finally looking up while gesturing toward two empty chairs.

"*Nǐ hǎo,*" Yin says, a common greeting among Mandarin speakers, adding in English, "I am pleased to meet you." A cool façade and disingenuous smile quickly replace Tu's reaction to meeting her.

"Tu and I have gone through your reports, and he has a few questions, but tell us what's happening in that prison. Nick?" Bao says.

"Eight men were captured, six in prison. Chuanli is separate from the others and all have been interrogated by Australian intelligence guy named Nigel Rainer, Chief of Station from Singapore. Chuanli interviewed many times," Nick says immediately.

"It's Deputy Chief," Yin corrects, then adds, "There is a chance we can intercept his field report soon."

"Fuck yes. Hacked the Aussies. How did you pull that off?" Bao says, tapping fingers on his desktop in delight.

Nicolay glances at Yin and says, "Is long story. More important is intelligence professional flying there means this is no longer just police.

I can give prison number and cell if you want, but until report, no more informations."

"Nigel's expertise is transnational crime and specifically human trafficking," Yin says, and then looks directly at Tu, "Some of the women released after this group was captured are Chinese, possibly from Shanghai." Yin hopes for a micro expression on Tu's face. His reaction is to stare blankly, but for a flash, his pupils enlarge.

Bao says, "Your man being isolated from gen pop and the Australians interrogating him on multiple occasions—that's not good, Tu."

Tu slumps forward, resting his elbows on his knees. He is silent for a long moment, staring at the ground, but then turning to Nicolay and Yin, he says, "Thank you. Yes, I would like his ID number and cell location. How are the money transfers going? Any concerns?"

"Yin?" Bao says, wanting her to give her report.

Yin defers. "Maybe you should tackle this one."

"Whatever. Yin has done a great job moving funds on our end, but there's a problem. Your guy says the amounts will draw too much attention, and he might be right. He can only convert so much crypto without raising flags. We need the kind of cash that flows through our mutual friend. I think you know what I'm saying."

"That may be difficult, but if he can't move more quickly, we must do something. Anything else?" Tu asks.

Bao is emphatic in his response. "Tu, it's not a question of if. Your guy isn't performing! We can buy cash in multiple currencies, but let's work around this guy."

"I'll get back to you on this," Tu says.

"Thanks, Tu. Yin, you can leave," Bao says dismissively.

While Bao is distracted reviewing Nicolay's report, Yin strategically closes one of the idle shell companies she created, waits an appropriate amount of time, and then stands just outside Bao's office with an urgent expression. Even smart men make mistakes when events don't align with their plans. Yin wants to introduce doubt. If the recipient of their money funnel is compromised, what will they do? When Bao looks in her direction, she nods for him to come.

"Excuse me a moment," Bao says to Tu and joins Yin in her office. They close the door.

"One of our transactions was just now flagged. The amount was under $10,000 US, so it shouldn't have been an issue, but that tells me that someone is watching Tu's man. I scrubbed our corporation but thought you should know."

"Interesting. That's something Tu needs to know, but what was that BS about women from China? These guys get suspicious. They'll mess you up. Understand?" Bao says, turning to leave.

"He knows something. I could see it in his eyes," Yin says defiantly, and Bao turns to her.

"Do you think Tu gives a rat's ass about you or anyone else? Challenge him, and your friend's sister becomes a pawn. You want to get in his face? Go ahead. Become a target. We'll talk about this later."

Yin realizes the potential depth of her overstep as she watches Bao return to his office.

Chapter 18

March 5

When Tu returns to Macau, he relays what Bao's team said about Rashid. "His paranoia and ineptitude make moving money on their schedule difficult, and there is another issue. Authorities blocked a transaction. Nothing can be traced back to us, but I don't trust him as an intermediary. The schedule has been set back."

"I committed a quarter billion, and he's moved how much?" Jiao asks.

"He claims to have disbursed 65%."

"Amateurs. I'll have to personally get involved," Dragonhead says threateningly.

"With respect, that is too much exposure. It's what you pay me to do so I'll take care of it," Tu says.

"Has the group received our weapons?"

"Only a partial shipment. They are training men on a secluded island somewhere and impatient with the financial situation. If we want them to widen the scope and depth of the attacks they need money," Tu explains.

"Then eliminate the bottleneck," Dragonhead snaps.

"Of course. It would also help if we knew their plans. Are the attacks simultaneous or launched over time? What weapons are needed at each location? If they can't even handle money transfers, how can we trust them with complicated weapons?"

Dragonhead takes a long moment. "Do it this way. Set a meeting with the man in command. You say his name is Almudir?"

"There may be others. But is this wise?" Tu asks.

"Let me worry about that. Meet with Almudir and this man, Rashid. I want you to use Bao in my place. Do it on the island to see what our investments are used for and threaten to end funding if things don't move swiftly. I want targets, timing, and expected results, but make sure Almudir sees Bao as the investor. No. Make Almudir think Bao is the Dragonhead. Do you understand?"

"I do."

"Rashid must go. Do it during the meeting if necessary. He's the only one that can directly tie us to any of this. Anything else?"

"Rashid is already compromised. Is it wise to include him?" Tu asks.

"It isn't a risk if you are careful. I want everyone to know what happens when people fail me. He won't be around afterwards to compromise anything." A trademark Dragonhead promise. Now, if that's all, I have work to do."

Tu knows what comes next will displease his boss. "One more thing. An Australian intelligence agency is interrogating your brother."

Dragonhead is again visibly concerned, this time appearing to be more defeated than angry. "The IC? Not just police?"

Tu nods. "What do you want me to do?"

Dragonhead stands, turns his back to Tu, and walks to his in-office bar. He pours Scotch, his shoulders stiff as he shakes his head, then angrily throws the glass against a wall. "Who came up with this? Bao?"

"The woman. I believe her. What do you want me to do?" Tu asks again.

"Why would you even ask? You know what to do! Get background information on all of Bao's people, especially those that handle money."

"We have background on all of his people," Tu reminds him carefully. "But I will dive deeper just in case."

"Who handles my money?" Dragonhead demands.

"That is also the woman. She sets up shell companies and moves money. According to Bao, as you know, she's highly skilled and competent."

Dragonhead stares blankly into space as he often does when calculating risk versus reward. "And she's the one that compromised the Australians? Maybe she's too competent."

Chapter 19

March 7

Between northeast Indonesia and the southern Philippines, a remote island shaped like a crescent moon rises from the remote sea in the Sangihe Arc region of the Celebes Sea. The island's peak reaches 1,500 feet in height at the center, and land gradually tapers downward for three miles in either direction. It's one of many geological marvels formed at the intersection of the Eurasian, Indo-Australian, and Philippine Sea tectonic plates. Volatility in the region is not limited to the violent rumble of underwater volcanic activity. The Filipino insurgents and seafaring pirates that live among the gentle indigenous populations that have inhabited the islands for so long share one indisputable law—survive.

A 2.6-mile-long road ascends the southern arc of the island. It forms a remarkably straight line from the small harbor lagoon to an uphill cluster of small buildings. The lowest section of the road is a suitable runway for the planes and small jets that once airlifted executives and workers to and from the island. Fish in the surrounding reefs and underwater mountain tops were harvested to near extinction, leaving the harbor, processing plant, and small hangar nearly idle. Boats still anchor here in storms. In emergencies, they can refill diesel tanks, but the facilities that once processed tons of fish have been empty for a decade. It's the perfect location for Almudir's plans. This morning, however, Almudir is anxious.

"This is foolishness." Almudir spits vitriol at his second in command. "Before you say anything, I don't care how much this man gave us. Meeting here is an unnecessary risk."

"We can still call it off, but we need that money. Reassure him with a few facts, and everything will be okay," Junaid drawls, far too relaxed.

Almudir considers this for a moment. "I don't want them near our sheds. We meet, they leave, that's the end of it."

Junaid nods in understanding. Unlike Almudir, who incessantly barks at the men around him, intimidating with vulgarities and threats, Junaid earned respect on the battlefield and during extraterritorial operations with the Quds Force, an elite unit of Iran's Islamic Revolutionary Guard. He rarely speaks. Dark in complexion and demeanor, Junaid does things for Almudir that no one else is willing or capable of doing. He is the sword Almudir wields against anyone, or anything, that stands in his way. Junaid is the enforcer and head trainer for Almudir's growing army of fighters. Whatever Junaid needs to carry out the missions is supplied through Almudir's numerous connections and seemingly unlimited budget—men, equipment, munitions, explosives, logistics, and a network of well-placed spies are at his disposal.

The two men have driven in a golf cart to a section of road undergoing reconstruction. A bulldozer and a dozen laborers widen it from 18 feet to over 80 feet, blasting through uneven terrain and filling low areas with pulverized volcanic rock. Newly finished portions of the road are obscured from aerial observation with tufts of foliage, the growing deception verified each day by a video drone sent 8,000 feet above the island.

Angered by the slow-moving bulldozer, Almudir says, "They're driving too slowly! When our guests have gone, do something about it." He presses his foot into the throttle of the cart that carries him toward the harbor.

To the man in charge, everything moves slowly. Almudir complains from morning to night about progress with the road, building construction, and training. He hired an architect to redesign the fish processing plant, adding a false second story to the building and creating two new outbuildings that appear from the sky to be independent structures. Inside the structure, welders and metalworkers work 24/7 as they hoist I-Beams and install trusses to remove central support posts. When complete, what was once a processing plant will become a camouflaged hangar capable of hiding a commercial aircraft. From the air, the island is nothing more than a road, a small harbor, and a few buildings. It will be much more, but only if the work continues faster.

As they drive by, Almudir shouts at metal workers in the nearly finished hangar, blistering them with unjustified expletives. His SAT phone buzzes, and he answers in the same condemning tone. "What's taking so long? Where are you?"

"Our friends have just landed. We depart soon," Nasr says. He's called Almudir from Sam Ratulangi Airport, Manado City, North Sulawesi, Indonesia, 200 nautical miles south of the island. He stands with Rashid, who arrived from Dubai via Kuala Lumpur. They have waited in the airport for hours, preparing for the inevitable tongue lashings of Almudir. As Nasr talks with Almudir, Rashid sweats. His eyes twitch. He's failed to complete multiple financial transactions.

Almudir barks at Nasr through the satellite phone as if the man were a child. "Don't talk in front of the pilot. Do you understand me?" Bringing people who may be under surveillance together in one spot, especially having them travel as a group this close to their attacks, is reckless. Almudir is vehemently against this meeting. But Tu is equally relentless in his displeasure in sending money that does not reach the intended recipient. He promised that an in-person meeting would fix everything and implied that more funds would be available once they met. If Almudir had his way, no one would know anything about his activities, but even in service of The Almighty, money talks.

Rashid and Nasr expected Tu's boss to be an imposing figure. But the boss Tu introduces is a short, somewhat chubby man in a crisp white shirt and expensive black suit. He wears dark glasses, and a menacing dragon tattoo writhes upward beneath his shirt collar encircling his neck. The tattoo seems out of place below rounded cheeks, but Tu introduces Bao as *wǒ de shàngjí*. Nasr thinks this is his name and offers his hand, welcoming the man by that name. Bao doesn't shake hands. Tu translates. "*Wǒ de shàngjí* means my superior, but if you wish, address him as Friend. We all speak English."

The group boards a private plane. During this time, Rashid prattles nervously about unrelated subjects, clearly trying to form a bond. Neither Tu nor Bao shows interest.

Before landing, Bao asks for a low flyover. They see the aqua lagoon and vine-covered rock cliff at the center of the island's crescent, a break wall, dock, and harbor with two fishing vessels near a cluster of processing plant buildings. A runway travels partway up the side of the short mountain to a cluster of tin-roofed buildings. The most prominent building up there is easily visible from the air. Hut-sized dwellings surrounding it are nestled among the broad-leaf shrubbery and large eucalyptus and teak trees. "Workers and their families stayed up the hill when the plant was in operation," Nasr explains. "The big one was a food kitchen and used for entertainment."

When Bao has seen enough, the pilot lands, taxis the aircraft, and rolls across the tarmac to the front of the former fish processing plant. Unless visitors are told otherwise, the facility appears to be dormant. If Almudir had his way, the hangar would already be complete, and the runway expansion would be easier to conceal from overhead aircraft and nosey charter pilots. As has happened on previous flights, the pilots must wait in or near their plane to avoid inadvertently seeing dubious construction.

Nasr exits the plane first, followed by Tu, Rashid, and Bao. They are met by Almudir and Junaid, who stand by as a few workers move materials in and out of the building. The echo of power saws emanates from the plant's interior.

"Assalamu alaikum," Almudir says, embracing Nasr and shaking hands with Rashid. Nasr introduces Tu and then Bao, not referring to him by name but as the man with all the answers. No one introduces Junaid. Instead, Almudir gestures toward the golf carts, and they ride uphill together.

They pass the bulldozer and workers and soon arrive at the sizable tin-roofed building overlooking the harbor below. All the buildings are in disrepair, including the largest, which features an expansive lanai prepared with chairs and a long teak table set for their meeting. The sounds of gunfire meld with the constant low rumble of machinery and the occasional chirp and buzz of birds and insects in the nearby trees.

As they sit on an odd assortment of rattan, folding, and plastic chairs left behind by the plant workers, a woman in a headscarf emerges from the building to attend to them—silent, demure, efficient. No one acknowledges as she places a tray laden with tea, nuts, and dates on the table, and Almudir dismisses her with a wave of his hand and turns to his guests. "The property is owned by one of your pretend corporations. We need it for training and other operations. Tea? Make yourselves comfortable."

As the men settle into their meeting, Junaid drags his chair away from the table, exchanging predatory glances with Tu. His stoic demeanor presents a silent menace that's hard for the others to ignore. Almudir's tone is firm, and his speech is terse. "There will only be this one meeting. You should not be here at all, but now that you are, what is on your mind?"

Tu bows slightly before speaking. He is gracious but also firm. Without wavering, he says, "There will be as many meetings as are necessary. First, we must address a problem before releasing additional funds." He glances at Rashid before speaking bluntly to Almudir. "We could send you two or three times the original commitment, but Rashid is too slow. How much have you received of the 350 million sent, and how was it spent?"

Rashid is shocked at the brazen condemnation of his efforts, stunned into momentary silence. Almudir's face reddens. Pointing at Rashid, he nearly shouts. "Where is it?"

"It's on its way, Almudir. You will have it very soon, I promise. Another 30 million this week."

Before Almudir can respond, Bao interjects. His words are calm but unwavering in their denunciation of Rashid. "Don't take the money. The intelligence community is watching Rashid. He's a burned asset. For all we know, Rashid may have spent some of your money on his causes."

"Not true, Friend, I have spent nothing! I've been meticulous," Rashid insists, rising to his feet in frustration.

Bao ignores him. "Please listen carefully. If you tell me how you've spent our funds thus far, we will find a way to fund you directly. What could you do with an additional 500 million?"

Rashid surrenders his calm to fear and frustration. "Almudir! My friend. What he says is not true. I would never take what is not mine, and the companies are not a problem."

Bao shakes his head, rattling expletives in Mandarin to Tu before naming four shell corporations in Rashid's portfolio. "You are compromised. I've ordered my people to distance themselves from your incompetence.

You're done. For security reasons, Rashid cannot participate in the next conversation."

Rashid is enraged, going so far as to step in Bao's direction, but Almudir snaps his fingers, and Junaid intervenes. He restrains Rashid, and Almudir rises to his feet restlessly pacing across the lanai with anxious footsteps. Everyone but Bao is on edge. He casually leans forward, grabs a fist of dates, and calls to Almudir. "Please sit. How much do you need, and how will it be spent? I also have plans in motion. We need to coordinate."

Almudir continues pacing. His eyes are locked on Bao's, but he points at Rashid. "Are you sure he was compromised? How can you know this?" His tone is accusatory.

Bao is deliberate in his response. "Assets in two of Rashid's corporations have been seized. We know this because it's our fucking money!" Bao says, raising his voice for the first time. The effect is immediate. "It's just a matter of time, so please, Almudir, sit. Focus. We must work quickly. What is the plan, and how much do you need?"

Nasr is unnerved, eyes fluttering back and forth between Bao, Almudir, and Junaid. No one speaks to Almudir this way.

Almudir's response is guttural. He growls at Rashid through bared teeth and then barks the words, "You've failed! Useless garbage!" Then turns towards Bao. "You knew of the situation with authorities and still insisted he come here? Of all people, you should understand operational security."

Without prompting, Junaid takes Rashid by the throat and violently presses the panicked philanthropist against a wall, denying him oxygen. Veins on his forehead expand, and his skin darkens, hands clawing uselessly at Junaid's grip. Junaid looks to Almudir for direction, but direction doesn't come from Almudir as quickly as from Bao. "If you don't, we will."

Degrees of shock envelop the table, but no one is more shaken than Nasr. He spins away from the violence and brings his shaking palms to the side of his head, tapping his skull in distress. Almudir looks at him with curiosity, throws a smile at Bao, and watches Junaid drop Rashid's corpse to the floor before dragging him away by the arm.

Almudir sits, sips his tea, and reaches for a date. "I assure you. Money is spent wisely. As for our plans, we have trained and outfitted numerous cells. Each works independently. None know what the other is doing, and we will strike in ways that surprise everyone."

Rashid's legs bounce on the stairway as Junaid drags his body to a golf cart. Bao says, "We're here to contribute, Almudir, but we must coordinate. Specifically, what targets, when, and how?"

"You want something we do not do," Almudir counters. "I can't give you specific targets. Here is why you shouldn't even ask that question. What happens if the police capture one of my cells? I might think you are the leak. I can say that we will hit the infidels in prominent locations. If you have extra money, we can strike simultaneously from the air, land, and sea. Does that answer your question?" Folding his arms across an expansive chest and midsection, Almudir goes silent.

Tu is the least shaken by Rashid's murder and now becomes the most direct. Speaking to Almudir, he says, "If you want our help, you need to be more specific. Are you planning for consulates, military installations, and soft targets? What specifically do you intend, and when?"

"Yes!" Almudir says emphatically. His patience has observably worn thin, and an uncomfortable silence follows. Tu rises. Junaid is gone. Almudir has no bodyguard at his side, and he recognizes, perhaps for the first time, how formidable Bao and Tu are. He raises his hands in surrender. "I understand why you want to know, so let's do it this way. Tell me what targets to consider, and I will say what is possible. We have 18 cells operating in multiple countries. Praise be to the All-Powerful. We operate independently. Each cell will attack one target for us, but they are also free to attack other targets. American, British, Canadian, and Australian Southeast Asian embassies are all possible targets. Some of these are more vulnerable than others. Ports and military bases are on the list. Did you hear the gunfire here today? We have equipped and trained over one hundred and fifty men and women on the island alone. We will have an air strike in the first round, and wave upon wave will follow, each more capable than the last. The world will soon see how weakly the West defends its corporations and government spies. Television and social media will replay the destruction for many years to come. Trust me. The attacks will be unprecedented, but that is as far as I will go."

Bao surprises everyone with what he says next. "Eighteen cells in multiple countries. Very impressive. What you don't understand is that you, too, are a cell. In the way you coordinate your forces, I coordinate mine, and you are one of mine. Do you understand now? Defeating the West isn't only about military action, Almudir. Flooding the streets with counterfeit euros and dollars will do more to undermine Western currency than any bomb. Did you know that telecommunications throughout Southeast Asia flow through Singapore? They are a regional hub for Five Eyes. We should coordinate attacks there to disrupt communications between Western allies during and following your attacks. You handle physical elements while we attack them digitally. I've planned a massive disinformation campaign targeting the shareholders of major corporations. Random attacks create havoc and terror, but altering the course of history requires strategy."

Almudir takes Bao's comment personally. "We have already changed the course of history. I would have perpetrated additional attacks, but look what we did to the World Trade Center."

Bao smiles. "It's interesting that you mention 9/11—a mere half-million dollars funded that entire attack. We have committed over 400 times that amount based on your promise to get the job done, so I'll ask again. What are your plans? When will the attacks take place? What is the expected outcome? You say this operation is need-to-know. I agree, but Almudir," Bao says, also rising to his feet before nearly barking the rest of his sentence. "I am one of those that needs to know, and don't ever again imply that I might leak information." Standing resolute, Bao checks the time. "A fishing boat will arrive within the hour. Tell your men to let it dock."

He sits. Tu sits. Almudir calms himself.

"If you had money today, how much could you effectively absorb?" Tu says.

Almudir seems confused. Nasr starts to explain, saying, "He means —" But Almudir dramatically points a finger at him to be silent.

Almudir says to Bao, "Our fighters are nearly in position, and we are prepared to utilize all resources available. Moving the money and weapons you promised will only take a few weeks."

Tu abruptly interrupts. "Nothing comes from us."

"Of course," Almudir says, waving apologetically. "I misspoke. No one will know about our arrangement. What is on the boat?"

Bao grins as if explaining something to an idiot. "What are we talking about? Money and weapons. It will be a long day of trading ideas and coordinating activities, so I suggest we all have more tea and get to work. I will give you my suggestions," Bao says, removing his dark glasses. "Tu, bring me the satchel we brought to the island."

Bao stands. Turning toward Almudir, he finally responds to an unanswered question from earlier. "As to why we wanted Rashid here," Bao gestures with his head to the retreating golf cart carrying Rashid's lifeless body. "No one could have tracked him. I oversaw his travel plans. I needed to see how committed you are. Let's do some business."

Chapter 20

March 9

Bao frames every discussion in his favor—the data center is his baby. He's accomplished more at forty than anyone else achieves in a lifetime. Everything good is the direct result of his leadership and generosity. Yin has learned not to question anything Bao claims he has done or will do, at least not to his face. She believes he broke from being pushed to perform beyond his years in childhood. There is no better explanation for a man so obsessed with personal recognition.

There is a term Bao uses to describe the exhilaration encountered while absorbed in a complex challenge purely for the sweet thrill of achievement. She most recently felt the juice while at MIT. Finding Li is now her biggest challenge, but she needs help. As EEL, Bao could help her dig into the underworld, but she hasn't seen that persona in Bao since arriving in Singapore. The EEL in Bao surfaces anytime a hacker challenges him, and the best way to awaken and catch an EEL is with bait and hook. *You like games? Let's play.*

Bao has the undisciplined habit of leaving his phone at his desk while getting more coffee or meeting with team members in their offices. She's also noticed that his auto-lock feature is set to minutes rather than seconds to avoid constantly passing authentication. Believing that Bao will respond in kind, knowing it is a way to grab his attention and reinvigorate an earlier bond, she enters Bao's office while he talks with Nicolay and changes the wallpaper used as his background to display a frowning face icon with the words 'Tag, you're it!' emblazoned in red.

Returning to her desk, she watches for Bao's reaction from across the room. When Bao is visibly surprised and upset, she goes to his office window and presses her face against the glass. The grotesque but humorous image causes Bao to laugh.

"Get your bitch ass in here," Bao barks, but it's innocent fury. When she enters with her hands up in surrender, he throws a muffin in her direction. Yin shuts the door behind her.

"Just saying. Keep the phone with you at all times," Yin says.

"You got me this time, but beware. Take a seat. Remember Tu? I've got one for you."

"What's with the tattoos? Are they permanent?" She asks, referring to the dragon that encircles his neck.

"Hell no. Just having a little fun. Henna."

Bao's eyes and hesitation ask a question before it comes out of his mouth. "Hacking my shit aside, can I trust you?"

"If that weren't the case, I wouldn't be here. How can I help?"

Hands clasped together on the crown of his head, Bao says, "Since our financial pipeline is temporarily compromised, we will use cash in some situations, but we obviously prefer a digital solution. Here's the challenge. The big boss is sending a hundred or more subcontractors into Southeast Asia to configure and repair HVAC systems. The repairmen need to pay travel and equipment purchases. We're talking five or more countries."

"For real? Air conditioning."

Bao laughs. "Hypothetically."

Smiling, Yin says, "Cryptocurrency isn't yet fluid enough for incidentals, at least not until Web3, so he needs to use a recognized payment network with globally accepted card-issuing capabilities. He'll need robust policies and procedures and enough centralized control to ensure legitimate expenditures."

"I was afraid of that—Visa, Mastercard, or American Express? What if a repairman needs to purchase something expensive, like a truck or car? They might need a hotel for weeks at a time, book flights, that type of thing. I have a $100,000 high-limit card in the US, but someone is always watching. I need minimum exposure to authorities."

Yin has assumed the large money transfers she's undertaken were related to the drug trade, but this scenario opens different possibilities. Forcing their hand by claiming a transaction was flagged has worked perfectly. She hides her exuberance. "Legitimate corporations can issue credit cards under their name. It takes time to go through the process, but it always happens. You mentioned high limits. People with those cards look and act a specific way. We could create a repair company in one of the non-CRS countries and run the cards through them," she says, referring to countries that do not yet comply with international banking Common Reporting Standards. "I'd probably use prepaid ghost debit cards. It's a way for companies to manage expenses in the field. We'd have to implement very strict policies, but it's possible."

"Like where? Use that big brain of yours to give me options."

Probing, Yin says, "The cards will be used in Southeast Asia though, correct? Not Europe or the United States"

"Does it matter?"

"Speed and efficiency of reporting. We could form the company in Cambodia or the Philippines, but there are other options that might slow down forensic teams—the Dominican Republic or Paraguay in South

America, maybe Armenia, Macedonia, or Georgia in Eastern Europe. The Ukraine was preparing to participate with banking standards, but the war may have interrupted their plans," Yin says effortlessly.

"And you have shell companies in those countries?"

"Not the Ukraine, but yes. I'm about to burn a few of them. What's the timeframe?"

Bao curses to himself in a muttered tone while reaching for his phone. He asks Peter to join them. When Peter arrives, Bao says, "I want you to work with Yin. There will be multiple shell companies issuing Visa cards to employees. These will be prepaid cards with limits from $300 to $100,000. It gets complicated because the users travel under more than one name and should have cards issued from each shell company Yin creates. There could be as many as 200 users, traveling under 400 names."

"Damn. How many companies are issuing cards?" Peter asks.

Bao looks to Yin. She says, "That's up to you, but four is all we can handle. To manage large purchase authorizations, you'll need a dozen phone numbers with call forwarding and buried trace routes."

"Can they be fake names?"

"Only for small purchases," Yin says. "Proper ID is needed at hotels, airport terminals, and for anything expensive. Amounts vary by country and store policy."

Bao mutters to himself again, a manifestation of mounting stress. "We create false IDs, which will be a fucking nightmare, or we use real names? I'll see what I can do."

Bao will eventually think his way into the policies she sees automatically. Suggesting the obvious does not make her more complicit than she already is. "The cards should only be used once and destroyed if you are trying to hide the movement of cardholders."

"That will have to come later. Focus on the system." Bao says dismissively.

Yin spends the rest of her day working with Peter, often connecting with Bao to make decisions. As they work, Bao periodically sends phishing texts to Yin's phone, some appearing to be authentic offers, others hilariously sophomoric: she's won a car and only has to click on a link to claim it! An NGO needs her help saving endangered sea turtles—click here to donate! The most bizarre phishing attempt from Bao sends a message claiming to show pictures of Nicolay wearing lipstick while riding nude on a donkey. Yin imagines these messages are more than Bao's twisted take on a hacking competition. He's flirting with her—this short man with unruly hair and deviant sexual obsessions lurking in his sordid history. The idea of it disgusts her—but what if? What might he reveal if he thought he had a chance?

Yin reminds herself to be cautious but prepares for this possibility and proceeds with a test. When their work is nearly complete, she sends Bao a risky message: *You're never going to catch me by phishing. I need a break. How about dinner tonight?*

Hitting send is accompanied by trepidation and remorse, but this could work. If Bao drinks heavily, he may slip. If he slips up, she may have leverage to get his help finding Li. But that requires mutual trust. His plans with Tu are nefarious. The idea of moving crypto from the shadows onto the street within a specific timeframe means something big is coming from the Triads. Or is it the Triads? Who is getting the money, and why would the Triads need them to mask delivery? Theirs is a closed network. No, they are working with someone. Yin's mind sifts through thousands of possibilities for who the Triads are working with but comes up empty. If she is right, an evening with Bao will yield valuable information.

Bao instantly agrees to drinks after work, suggesting they go to dinner at the Tipping Club on Tanjong Pagar Road. He includes a link to the restaurant, which Yin ignores. Perhaps he is still phishing. She explores the restaurant through her browser instead.

Two hours later, having gone home to change and once again push Haitao to keep after the Shanghai police, Yin stares into the mirror and reflects on her goals for the evening.

"What am I doing?" she asks, and the image of Li replies. *"Be careful with this one."*

• • •

Bao receives his third cocktail as Yin arrives at the restaurant. He says, "You have to try one of these Greenbacks. Fucking awesome cocktail."

She sees Bao's attempt at sophistication for the first time since arriving in Singapore. He wears a dark suit, a white shirt, a gold bracelet, and a Rolex watch. His hair is combed and apparently lathered in something sufficiently strong to press it into submission. He even smells cosmopolitan. It's an altogether different look for him, and the outfit comes with swagger—yet another version of Bao, Yin thinks.

A waiter quickens to her side and pulls out the chair for her. "Can I get you anything?"

"A Greenback cocktail for me and another for my friend," Yin says politely.

Bao waits until the waiter has left before saying, "Great work today. Any concerns?"

"We're not to talk about work outside of the office, but thank you."

Bao laughs. "That's for you all when I'm not around. I make up the rules. So, I'll ask again. Any concerns with the whole card thing?"

"We should all be concerned, but—" Yin begins and Bao interrupts her.

"I know why you're here."

Her heart falls into the pit of her stomach. "Why exactly am I here?"

"You think the Triads have your friend's sister? Clever. I get all that, but be careful. Why would you risk everything for this friend? You must be close."

"Everything? I should hope not. You'll have to explain someday. I only asked for help when I thought you were EEL. It's behind us."

"No, it's not. Just don't go over my head. It won't end well. These guys are animals. If they did take this woman, you'll never get to her," Bao says. His tone is caring, but there's no sign of a tell.

Controlling her emotions and avoiding a tell of her own, Yin takes a chance. "That's not my style, but you have their ear. Is it too dangerous even for you?"

"They'd never admit to taking someone, but I promise. Stick with me until the end of this project, and I'll do what I can. Is that fair enough?" He downs the drink in his hand.

"Thank you," Yin says, dumbfounded by the conversation.

Bao glances at Yin's untouched drink and sniffs. "A goddamn sipper, huh?"

Yin hopes to remain sober enough to recall their conversations frame by frame when she gets home but needs to keep the party atmosphere moving forward. She drinks about a third of the cocktail and compliments him on the choice. "Let's get our business over with. The longer these cards are in the field, the higher the risk."

"For example?" Bao asks, signaling to their waiter for another round.

"Airfare, for example. Let's say five or six users take the same flight. They should all act like they know each other and use only one card for all the tickets. If they don't know each other but have cards issued by the same corporation, that would raise suspicion. ATMs have cameras and the appearance of the cardholder should match the purchase. Imagine what would happen if a homeless man with a scruffy beard tried to purchase a watch like yours. Someone somewhere would want an explanation."

"Sounds like training issues more than technical problems." He pauses and glances at the fresh cocktail the waiter sets in front of Yin. "Do you really like it, or are you just being nice?"

Yin is not impressed. "The drink? It's lovely. I might try the Savoy Truffle next. Have you been here before?"

"Once. If something goes wrong, how quickly can we disappear?" Bao asks, setting down an empty glass.

"You mean the authorities?" Yin asks.

"I'm talking about the people we work for. Keep up." Yin notes that Bao's speaking has been reduced to an uncharacteristic mutter.

"You'd have to answer that one. What's going on? If you know something—"

Bao doesn't appear to be listening. He calls loudly and waves for another drink, dropping a thick wad of cash onto the table when it arrives.

"We're stepping out for a tiny phone call. When we return, we'd like to try—what was that cocktail?" Bao asks Yin.

"Savoy Truffle," Yin says politely.

"What she said." Bao stands. Motioning for Yin to follow, he says, "I may need you for this one."

Outside the restaurant and away from foot traffic, Bao places an encrypted call to Tu. "My girl has policies for card use. How long will they be needed?" Bao asks, gesturing to Yin for confirmation. She gives a thumbs up, and Bao continues. "I know it's late, but you know what, I got the job done because that's what I do. You pointed them at me, but I'm not unhappy. I got set up, okay? Don't care. It was epic."

Yin cannot hear Tu's replies but listens intently, hoping to discover something valuable.

"No. You set me up, you little fucker. They think I am him, but it's cool. I'm cool with it, just not happy."

He pauses. "What'd he say? No. The cards should only be in play for a month?" Bao says, looking again at Yin for confirmation.

Yin gives him a thumbs down this time and holds up two fingers. Bao continues. "Fuck that. We deliver the cards and tick-tock. Two weeks, and we pull the plug. Tell him that."

The call ends with Bao defending his two-week timeline, and they return to their table to sip cocktails and order food. As the conversation heads toward personal histories, Bao becomes increasingly inebriated.

"I know things about you," Bao says between bites.

"We know things about each other," Yin says, feeling the fire of inner demons longing to lash out. The conversation has darkened, and it's all Yin can do not to leave Bao sitting there alone.

"How long did you work for SSSB?" Bao says glibly. His expression expects a wild response, and she gives him one.

"How long were you with MSS? You worked for them in California. What about after that? BRICS Crypto, was it?"

"Wow. All right," Bao says, feigning surprise. "We come from the same team, but I've moved on. Have you? The truth is, we can't avoid it. Even when we're not helping them, we are helping. That didn't sound right. Helping Tu helps the CCP."

"How's that?" Yin asks.

"You think the government leaves these guys alone out of ineptitude? Fuck no. Their boats carry military-grade early-warning surveillance gear. Who do you think secretly smuggles our spies across borders? Tu and his friends. Whether we like it or not, we're all on the same team."

"I was never on the team. I just needed money."

"Everyone needs money. How much? I know what you're doing, you know," Bao says, repeating himself, slurring every other word. Maybe it's a good thing. Perhaps he won't remember the night.

"What's that?" Yin asks.

"Get me drunk and try to get into my pants," Bao says.

"The thought hasn't really crossed my mind," Yin replies.

"Bitch. How much? 100,000? Half a million?" Bao says, a grotesque smile darkening his drunken face, his hand reaching for hers across the table.

Yin withdraws her hand and casually says, "You've had too many Greenbacks. Find my friend's sister, and we'll talk. Until then, it's just business. Okay?" Yin would have verbally decimated any man who dared speak to her this way, but she still needs him.

"The guy is even more of an asshole than me," Bao says, a completely random, nonsensical statement that confuses Yin.

"Who are we talking about, Tu?"

"The other one. Come on, I'll give you a ride." Bao's words are barely intelligible.

"You're not driving in this condition. Taxis for both of us," Yin shakes her head, waiting for Bao to clamber to his feet.

"The other one," Bao mutters to himself as he staggers out of the restaurant. "The big boss. What a fucking asshole."

The city spins as Yin rides home in the first taxi she can find, stomach churning. She plays back their conversation, stumbling over a few of Bao's statements. How long did you work for SSSB? Did Bao know Yin was Yin even while he was EEL? If so, does he know that the friend's sister she talks about is Li?

Bao also asked how quickly they could disappear if something went wrong. Some big plan has come up more than once, undoubtedly fueled by the money she pushes around the globe. Though she's curious, she can't focus on that right now. Her priority is finding Li, and Bao's loose tongue has exposed massive bargaining chips she can use to motivate Nigel Rainer.

Chapter 21

March 10

Yin sits behind her desk at the data center, reviewing her team's work and thinking about her sister. She replayed her conversation with Bao and then returned to Will Essex's home computer for leads useful in contacting Nigel Rainer. She revisited the Barwon Prison website and reviewed information Nicolay hacked from Australian police personnel files. Nicolay had laughed with pride at his accomplishments. Like Bao, he has a twisted sense of humor. He explained NITRO to her, a program that collects and analyzes civilian reports on nefarious digital activities. While working together, he bragged of sending a message from one of the Australian corporate CEO email accounts he'd hacked, telling the head of that program that his computer was compromised. It had been, and he was the hacker.

Yin plans to trade information with Nigel Rainer after leading him to believe she is more connected than she is. If successful, Nigel will help her find Li. It's a complicated ruse, fraught with dangers but also exhilarating. The Triads are planning something big. Millions of dollars are pouring into their network and distributed to Southeast Asian players. Information is power, and she intends to wield it to maximum benefit.

It's 8 am in Singapore and 10 am in Geelong, Australia. Thanks to messages intercepted on Essex's computer, Yin believes Nigel has finally wrapped up his prisoner interviews in Australia. He is scheduled on a flight back to Singapore within a few hours.

The first email she sent Nigel would have led Australian digital forensic teams to a dead end in Eastern Europe. The second email she composes will also go nowhere. Touching the heart charm on her bracelet, Yin checks the time. She glances through her office window to ensure no one is watching.

She taps into a bogus email account she created months earlier. It is hosted in Bulgaria by a team of underworld administrators who never disclose who uses their systems, and this is the only way she can proceed. Manipulating a high-profile intelligence officer like Mr. Rainer is risky, but she closes her eyes and entertains memories of her sister dancing, jogging, laughing, cooking, and crying. *I am a person of action*, she hears herself say aloud and is surprised to hear herself say even louder, *I'll own you, Nigel.*

Three thousand miles away, Deputy Chief of Station Nigel Rainer sits at an in-room desk at Novotel Geelong Hotel, reviewing recorded interviews and transcribing notes taken during three days at Barwon Prison. He's often stayed on the waterfront while working as a police detective. He is well acquainted with the harbor, Cunningham Pier, and Wah Wah Gee restaurant, where he had breakfast earlier, but this trip is different. He conducted his third round of in-person prisoner interviews, and his effort paid off.

Chuanli is a hard man—arrogant, cocky, unshakable, as are all the prisoners with families to worry about. However, two of these criminals, having been convicted on multiple counts, showed a willingness to cooperate if the reduction in their sentences is significant. Through them, Nigel and his counterparts in Australia hope to secure valuable information on operations, including transportation methods, names of ships, and the location of Triad safe houses in Australia. Information flows slowly at first, but Nigel exerts pressure on a mission to wear them down. The strategy works.

Nigel's report is finished and sent but without any sense of accomplishment. He sullenly stands at the hotel window to take in the harbor view one last time. Seeing hundreds of boats reminds him of his father's dream to own a craft sufficient in size to launch his fishing guide business. His eye catches on an Invincible 36 leaving the harbor. He'd shown pictures of that vessel to his father, claiming he'd have the down payment within a year, two at most. He made that promise over a decade ago and now lives with guilt.

Even if he bought a boat today, his father would need help rigging gear, maintaining the craft, and running the business. Simple men need simple work, and his father is a simple man. He imagines presenting a set of keys on his father's next birthday, how they might get into his old truck and drive to the harbor for a quick run to see how his new boat handled. The thought of deep sea fishing with his father and hauling in Wahoo, Cobia, and Yellowfin tuna brings a smile to his face, but he's trapped. He doesn't have enough money for the boat this year, and if he waits a year or two, it could be too late. As the muse carries Nigel's dream out to sea, he realizes that he's been living in denial. Why would a simple man fight and claw his way to the position of Deputy Chief and stay on as an underling to men like Essex if none of it made him happy? He isn't just his father's son, he is his father, his grandfather, and all the men that came before them. Simple men need simple work.

Nigel turns away from the window to finish packing. Before closing his laptop, he receives an email from an unknown sender. It reads:

> *You must be tired after all those interviews. I could have saved you the trip, but no matter. I have information to trade, and you have the resources I need. When you get back to Singapore, let's meet.*
>
> *Sincerely,*
>
> *Incense Master*

Nigel reads the message multiple times and then forwards it to the cyber team in his office. He copies Will Essex. Incense Master will have made it untraceable, but even the best hackers sometimes make mistakes.

Before leaving for the airport, Nigel hits reply and sends a message saying he would like that, but when he hits send, the message is undeliverable. As before, the account is gone, evaporated in the digital landscape.

• • •

Back in Singapore, in the late afternoon, Bao enters Yin's office and shuts the door. "See," he says, holding up his phone. "I carry it with me at all times."

"Quick learner. Have you recovered from last night?" Yin says, smiling.

"I have the list of cardholders, but we need to talk. Can I trust you?"

"How many times do I have to say it?" Yin asks. Repetition of the can I trust you phrase doesn't make sense unless he's using it to create some secretive bond.

Bao looks away, chastened, and then back to Yin. "We're getting into next-level shit, Yin. It would help if you didn't freak out, but you'll see some Arabic names on this list I've sent you. I'd give you a simple bullshit explanation, but you're too smart for that. In short, the big boss is doing some things with a Muslim network. Maybe not Muslims, exactly. I doubt any of these guys do mosques, but you know what I'm saying. They're moving stolen goods, drugs, and whatever. I need you to be good with this, or do we have an issue?"

Yin's eyebrows rise involuntarily as she takes a breath. Her mind races through possible responses, settling on something she believes Bao can relate to. "As you often say, WTF? You seem to know what you are doing but is this worth the risk.?"

"It's part of the job, but I understand. There's an extra $50,000 in it for you if that helps. Are we good?" Bao asks, almost nervously.

"None of my business, right?" Yin suggests the spirit of cooperation in her voice.

Bao smiles, amused. "You're pretty smart, bitch."

"Don't ever call me that again, or you'll find out just how much of a bitch I can be. Are we clear?" A hint of the uncaged dragon let loose on Bao—the quickness and sharpness of the retort surprises even Yin.

"Crystal."

When Bao leaves, Yin opens the list and thinks she's never seen this many people named Muhammad in one place before—Muhammad El Amery, Muhammad Al Tamimi, Muhammad Al Tajir, Muhammad Fayed, Muhammad Najjar, and more, but this list doesn't map well. The surnames come from countries like Yemen, Saudi Arabia, Pakistan, and Iran. Half of the names are associated with Southeast Asia. Bao was either misled or is lying. But Bao is a liar, and the idea that he would offer a bonus on top of her fantastic salary says he knows more than he's willing to disclose. The realization rips at her conscience. How far is she willing to go in this hunt for her sister?

For inexplicable reasons, the Triads are funding Islamists from the Middle East for activities that will take place throughout Southeast Asia. She wants to believe it's an underground collaboration to move stolen goods, knockoffs, and drugs, as Bao said, but intuition says something else. What if the unthinkable is true? Could the Triads and terrorists be collaborating?

Yin wishes she had known this before sending her last message to Nigel. She could have told him about the potential terror connection while there was still time to react, but maybe it's not too late. The cards won't be manufactured and distributed right away. There's printing, shipping, configuring balances, setting up a call center, mailing, or some other means of distribution, and that all takes time.

The maelstrom of emerging events blurs her focus, but she knows one thing for sure. The list she has now is valuable. The thought brings a smile to her face, followed almost immediately by panic. How many people know the list exists? Yin knows of five people who are aware of the list. They are Bao, Tu, Peter, herself, and the person who sent it to Bao. Was that Tu? She thinks not. If she divulges the list, her name will be suspect. The Triads are incredibly ruthless with enemies. Turning on them and a potential international terror network at the same time will mean certain death or worse. She'll be running for the rest of her life.

Priorities collide with self-preservation, but ultimately, she decides to move forward. The list is valuable, and she needs to be of value to Nigel if she wants him to find Li.

Yin loads names, amounts, account numbers, expiration dates, and CVV numbers into a spreadsheet that will eventually be turned into money cards and sent to who? Terrorists? Yin feels her soul slipping away. She reads and rereads the entries, planning to recompose them from memory when alone.

Chapter 22

March 11

Back in Singapore, Nigel prepares for his debriefing with Essex. He's proven once again that his hunches are correct. The captured Triad men disclosed details on human trafficking, forced prostitution, and even enslaved labor. Though their leader was unshakable, the Australian Intelligence Community has enough information to make Triad operations in Australia much more difficult for years.

When Nigel enters Essex's office, the Chief of Station looks up from the mountain of papers on his desk with the same expression he always has when proven wrong about something—it never happened. He points to the only clear spot on his desk, indicating that Nigel should leave his report.

"It's in the shared folders. I came into a bit of intelligence we should discuss."

Essex holds up a finger, gesturing for Nigel to hold his thought. He pushes a pile of paperwork from one side of his desk to another and points to an empty chair. Before Nigel can proceed, Essex says, "I'll read it tonight. I know you're stoked about this prison thing, but we have a lot going on, so until further notice, you'll be taking no more trips back to Australia. Understood? I need you here in Singapore."

Before Nigel can reply, he receives a text message. It reads:

Welcome back. In three words, tell me what you wanted to get from Chuanli. You have 30 seconds— Incense Master

Nigel springs to his feet and fights with his emotions, staring at the message.

"What is it?" Essex asks, but Nigel waves him off and paces as he replies.

Nigel writes: *Who is Dragonhead?* But believes he already knows. He changes his wording to read: *10-year plan*. With his 30 seconds nearly over, he hits send. Chuanli never used that phrase or disclosed specifics, but one of the lesser captives implied as much, saying Dragonhead was operating on a two-part decade-long strategy. Phase one started five years ago and is nearly complete. The men working for Chuanli are too low in the organization to have sensitive information, but they'd overheard Chuanli laughing about the huge profits they would make in phase two.

Nigel continues to pace as Essex looks on. Within seconds, a reply comes to him that stops his pacing.

> *There is less time than you think. Look for a yellow envelope, your eyes only. If you share the contents with Essex, I will know. Don't make that mistake.*

Nigel rereads the message in disbelief. Whoever this is knows a great deal about the inner workings of the Triad and may even be watching him now, right here in Essex's office. He glances at the window, wondering.

"What the hell is going on?" Essex says.

Nigel slips his phone into a pocket and sits. "Sorry. Personal matter. A friend of mine has had a heart attack. That was his wife."

"Sorry to hear that. I hope he's going to be okay," Essex says, his face showing sincere concern.

"Me too. I guess they are taking him into surgery. Anyway, where were we?"

• • •

In the evening, Essex does what he often does at the end of a busy day. He downloads Nigel's report, unwittingly sending it to his printer and Yin. She scans pages of the report while sipping tea in her apartment.

Nigel's interrogation of Triad-connected prisoners exposed methods and tactics. He had detailed information on specific fishing boats and border agents used to move workers from China and Vietnam to Australia, Europe, and even South America. Attractive young women fleeing to find work or escape problems at home are often coerced into prostitution. No matter how much money they pay to be smuggled across borders, it is never enough. They are trapped.

Two summary statements stand out. Nigel recommends that the prostitutes be released without prosecution to the care of social services and repatriated—five to the Philippines, three to China, two of the youngest to Vietnam, and the rest to Slovakia. Li is not among the women freed from Chuanli's underground brothel in Australia.

Nigel also reports that Chuanli's brother pursues a ten-year plan involving collaboration with others and advanced weapons. The prisoners claim the weapons will be used, not sold. This differs from anything the IC has uncovered thus far about Triad activity. They are known to sell arms, but using advanced weapons in concert with others is different.

Intercepting the report is the opening Yin hoped for. She has already proven she can breach Australian digital firewalls. Now, she will show that their physical security is also vulnerable and make it personal.

Yin sends a document to her printer. Sliding Nitrile gloves onto her hand, she opens a large yellow envelope, slips the printout into it, and seals it with a damp sponge. She addresses the front of the envelope in Malay: *Untuk Perhatian—Attention Nigel Rainer.*

Yin opens the Uber app and feels unstoppable as she rides to The Grange Residences, blocks from the Australian embassy. Intelligence officers hide personal information from the public. It took digging through files on Essex's computer and exploring local resources to locate Nigel's exact home address and devise a way to reach him.

Just past 10 pm she is dropped two blocks from Nigel's condominium building. The air is cool as she carries three Amazon Prime boxes toward the multi-story complex, and the opportunity she planned for comes as a car enters the parking lot. Yin and a giddy couple home from a night on the town reach the entrance together. Yin is a delivery person and is running late. They have no problem letting her into the building.

Yin exits the elevator two floors above Nigel's address and backtracks through the stairwell. A bright yellow envelope slides from her waistband under Nigel's door, and she discards the Amazon props into the trash when she exits the complex. The rush of exhilaration stays with her for the rest of the night.

March 12

Energized by the excitement of her late-night exploit, Yin leaps out of bed at 6 am with an invigorated sense of control, and this empowered sensation follows her to the data center. Nothing in her life now fits into a classroom scenario. The feeling of being in control is like an addictive drug to Yin. She wants more.

At work, Yin deliberately leaves a few names off the list of card recipients. She goes to Bao's window for further instructions, and he waves her in.

"I dropped the spreadsheet on the server. What's next?" Yin asks.

"We still friends?" Bao asks, and Yin knows he's referring to the word bitch he used the day before.

"You're a funny guy," she drawls, imitating a phrase she picked up in the US.

"How so?"

"You use offensive words, ask if we're good, and repeat the offense. It's a pattern."

Bao's reaction is to laugh. "Sorry. You're right. We good?"

Yin closes the door and sits. "Who is that musician?" she says, pointing to the enormous image of Bao and Santana behind him.

"Santana? The dude is awesome. Listen to a few tracks. You'll love it. Dinner was fun. We should do it again. You pick the spot."

Yin smiles. The man doesn't recall half of what he did or said, and he wants more. "I'd like that. Did you look at all the names? Most of them originate in the Middle East. There's a lot of surveillance going on over there."

"Tell me about it. You asked what's next. I promised the big boss we'd help him tighten security. Nicolay is working on that right now, at least that's his assignment today. See if he needs help on the financial side."

"In what way?" Yin asks, teasing out as much information as possible.

"Good question. Look for tells in their transactions. Nick will do the heavy lifting, but he doesn't know a ledger from a shopping list. Make sure the underworld funds aren't bleeding over into his legit accounts. The little fucker thinks we're awesome. Prove him right."

"About dinner. I want to try Mott 32. If tomorrow night works, this round is on me. You paid for the last one." Choosing the venue and timing has little to do with Bao and nothing to do with preferring one restaurant over another. She's sent Nigel to that restaurant and wants to observe him without being noticed.

"I got a bit drunk last time."

"I didn't notice," Yin says with a wry smile.

"If you're buying, I'm definitely in. I appreciate you, Yin. Look for a bonus crypto key," he says with sincerity.

Yin stands, bows slightly, and leaves Bao's office. For all his bluster, the man is predictable. He picked the first restaurant. She picked the date, time, and location of their second outing. The men she hopes to involve in finding Li will be in the same restaurant, but hopefully unaware of the others presence.

Chapter 23

The name Li is never used here, and Li doesn't volunteer any personal information. She doubts that anyone knows or cares who she once was. Here, she's called China. Clients know her as The China Doll, a cam girl performing in a 10' x 10' bedroom.

Three sides of her prison are decorated to look like an elaborate penthouse. The fourth wall is made of cinder blocks with a video camera mounted seven feet above the floor. The camera is on 24/7. Deranged men pay for half-hour interactive performances. Unlike typical cam-girl sites, the women imprisoned here don't go home at night. They don't talk with each other or compete for bonuses. The slaves are condemned to their rooms until they are no longer saleable. Li decides daily to be as much like her sister as possible. She is determined to survive, and until she is rescued, she imagines Yin watching over her through the vanity mirror next to the bed. It is there for her to apply makeup, but Li sees it as a window. Every time she looks into that window, she sees Yin's face urging her to be strong.

Some men pay to watch the cam-girls sleep, hoping for an unscheduled performance. During sleep, the shock collar is turned off, and performances are less expensive and longer. Even the concept of time is warped in these rooms. Natural circadian rhythms do not exist. There is no morning or night, today or tomorrow, only the lights that signal when to sleep, eat, perform, and us the communal bathroom.

With some lights, a magnetic lock is released, her door springs open, and she moves quickly. Food is at one end of a long hallway. The restroom and shower stalls are at the other. She has learned to move quickly because bad things happen if she doesn't return in time and gets locked out. She dares not be locked out after what she's seen and heard.

Behind closed curtains down the hallway to the left of the showers, there is a frightening cage lined with sadistic implements. Li passed the cage three or four times while the curtain was open. Girls beg and scream from there while being beaten or whipped by the leather-clad monster that paces in the hall before each cage performance. Li fears the cage more than death. The cage is for women who disobey. China Doll never disobeys.

When Li arrived, she had little idea of the country or continent where she is located. She might be in Cambodia, Laos, or Thailand, someplace tropical because the air is always humid. During the trip from Shanghai to wherever she is men injected her arm with powerful drugs. Injections continued after arriving but were no longer intravenously administered into her arm. For reasons she didn't understand until later, she was injected between her toes.

As she emerged from the drug-induced stupor, she endured what her captors called training. The shock collar around her neck is riveted, not buckled. It cannot be removed. Li sat on a stool in front of demanding, heckling men for hours. Sometimes there was just one man. On occasion, there were as many as five. They yelled at her to undress, dress, and undress again. They barked orders, told her to smile, called her names, and demanded she perform unspeakable acts of perversion. If she resisted or failed, she was severely punished. Not one of the men touched her, which added to the surreal qualities of the horrifying experience. If she bruised herself or did anything to look less desirable, even if by accident, she would go to the cage and be shown what real bruising felt like.

Then, one day, a camera and overhead speaker replaced the men.

Instructions came in a calmer but firm voice. She had her own room, her own bed, and her own customers.

When the red light comes on, she performs, obeying the nameless voices emanating from the speaker above her head—no matter what. Survival depends upon sales, and sales depend upon performances. Li is determined to survive and every time she applies makeup, her sister's image in the mirror assures her that help is coming.

The Li from before had just graduated from the university, was planning a wedding, dreamed of a honeymoon, and enjoyed life. She is no longer a student and may never dance or play tennis again. She longs to be held but cannot afford to ruminate on loss. For all she knows, Yin could still be in America pursuing her dreams, but she doesn't think so. Yin has never abandoned her and never gives up. Li sits on a small chair, staring into her mirror. She applies makeup as if in a trance. She no longer sees her reflection. She only sees Yin, and Yin whispers, *I love you, beautiful girl. I'm coming. Stay strong.*

Chapter 24

March 13

Yin fights self-doubt. Sleep has been elusive, short-lived, and shallow for a week or longer. The inner dragon has no boundaries and doesn't sleep. It is always pushing forward, but Yin is physically exhausted. Stressful work at the data center, long evenings hunting in the underworld for signs of her sister, and the emotional rollercoaster of conducting covert activities for and against the Triads have taken their toll.

Yin hasn't gone running in a long time. She eats the wrong food. There are moments each day when she doubts whether she will ever find Li, but as happens every morning, she rises with renewed hope and determination. The difference between the Yin of Shanghai and the Yin of Singapore is that she trusts no one, calculates every action, assumes enormous risk, and is strangely closer to her sister than ever before. The most profound difference is that the woman looking back at her in every mirror is Li. Not long ago, she was willing to move to America and leave Li behind. The way she feels now, nothing will ever again separate them.

Yin goes to Nicolay's office as Bao instructed and taps on his door. For all she knows, the consummate network cracker is the next evolution in finding Li. His skills were obvious on day one, and he flies through Triad security on wings as she enters. "These guys still use castle and moat security. Break the front door, you can do anything. Is Zero Trust model for sure," Nicolay says while staring at his screen, stabbing away at his keyboard.

"No segmentation? What's in there, finance-wise? Bao sent me to look over their numbers," Yin asks.

"The online casino has a secure socket layer, appropriate gateway, and legit merchant account. Everything is working properly, but the office is not strong. Bao is finding business plans, but I cannot read Chinese. For sure, this is why he is sending you in here."

"He said something about a ten-year plan. Have you found their financials? Anything like banks or money transfers?" Yin asks. It sounds innocent enough to her, and she tries not to act overly interested in the plan, but any insights she can gain are bonus chips for her eventual meeting with Nigel Rainer.

"Maybe you see something," Nicolay says. Yin takes his seat, and Nicolay hovers over her shoulder. She slowly scans multiple pages, capturing bits and pieces with her eidetic memory. There are valuable names and locations of trusted individuals, but Dragonhead's more secretive data is stored elsewhere. "This is basic organizational information and project management files for legitimate businesses," she tells Nicolay.

She reviews additional documents and finally finds spreadsheets containing impressive numbers on his fishing businesses, cash outlays for a loan business, and a folio of income properties.

A final ledger leads to banking and investment information, and she realizes that the numbers deposited are far less than his other ledgers show. The numbers have nothing to do with hiding money, but they explain something Bao said earlier. The Triad has resources in China capable of converting $100 M into cash every week. It makes sense. The Triads run drugs, loan sharking, and other underworld enterprises, mostly in cash. None of it is reported. They need a money laundering system, and that's something valuable to them. "I don't see anything we should be concerned about. Let me know if you can find their private server, but I'm done. Do you agree?" Yin asks.

"Is fine with me," Nicolay says, reclaiming his seat.

• • •

At 7 pm, Bao joins Yin seated at Mott 32, the restaurant she's strategically selected for their meal. She stands to greet him and even gives him a weak hug, which pleases Bao. They sit. A waiter takes Bao's drink order, and they look at the menus. Bao is dressed smartly and looks around the room, possibly hoping people will notice that he sits with such a beautiful woman. They do. Yin has dressed to impress in a way she hasn't done since arriving in Singapore. While applying Li's makeup, she started crying and had to start over.

"How did it go with Nicolay? He says there must be another server," Bao says, craning his neck, looking for another drink.

"There is, but where? That's up to the two of you to figure out. All I saw was a disparity between what they report as income and what they have on hidden ledgers. You said they were able to convert crypto to cash?" Yin asks purposefully without interest.

"No problem," Bao says, laughing. "What you found in the books is nothing. The guy is worth billions. What are you having?"

"They brag about the applewood-roasted duck," Yin offers, trying not to push too hard.

"Sounds amazing. I'm in. Wine? Cocktails?"

Yin closes the menu and smiles. "Both. May I order?"

"I'm all yours," Bao says, apparently pleased with how things are going.

Yin signals for the waiter and orders an expensive bottle of wine, appetizers, and their entrees. She arrived early to position herself appropriately and frequently glances at the entrance during dinner. She casually places her phone on the table and taps the display. If everything goes as planned, Nigel will enter the restaurant in seven minutes. "There's one thing I've been thinking about. Next time you speak with Tu, ask if they need help laundering money."

Bao seems surprised at the suggestion. "Why?"

"These are the guys who were going to convert crypto to cash? If they are sitting on that much liquidity, why not put it to work? It's none of our business, just an observation," Yin says.

"It's like money in the till at a box grocery store, right? It just sits there making change. What do you have in mind?" Bao asks.

"They should look at currency exchange with other countries. I heard of a woman who flies big gamblers all around the globe. Maybe they could clear 50 million per trip to Vegas or Monaco. Let those other casinos worry about exchanging currency. Money goes out as cash and comes home digitally. We could also set up our exchange business in China and neighboring countries. There's always a way," Yin says, glancing up.

Bao's response fades into the background as Yin peers towards the entrance. As expected, Nigel Rainer enters the restaurant precisely at 20:00. She recognizes him from her sleuthing, and it's all Yin can do to continue her conversation with Bao. Nigel talks with the head waiter, sits, and receives a menu. As the waiter leaves his table, he says, "On second thought, I'd like a Harbor Dawn cocktail. Make it a double."

That's all Yin needed to hear. For the rest of their dinner, and until they leave, Yin does her best to remain hidden while barely paying attention to Bao, the narcissist, recounting one nonsensical story after another. Nigel sits on the far side of the restaurant, occasionally looking through the crowd, unsure why he is there, but he came. As far as Yin can see, he came alone.

Yin knows she's being surveilled at work, at home, and elsewhere. She hasn't seen any of her shadows this evening, but that doesn't mean they are absent. Among the many learning curves she rides, tradecraft has become a priority. What Bao doesn't fully realize, and Nigel can have no way of knowing, is the strength of her memory. She can recall faces seen for only seconds, days before, and mentally catalogs repetition in the seemingly random patterns around her—specific cars, joggers, people on the bus, even the way coworkers look at her. She follows a zero-trust policy with everyone, even those she believes are trustworthy.

"Do you want to talk about it?" Yin asks, changing the subject.

Bao needs clarification. "About what?"

"We both worked for the government, me for a short while and you for much longer. How did you get started, and why did you leave?"

"Who says I left?" Bao says with a grin.

"Okay, you still work for MSS. What's the arrangement?"

Bao laughs. "Just messing with you. I don't work for those fucks anymore. I still have contacts, just as you might. Have they helped you find your sister? I'm sorry. You're friend's sister?"

Yin tries to avoid reacting, but it's impossible. She nearly breaks down. Forged by her inner darkness, she musters the strength to keep it together. *He knows.* "Her name is Li. How long have you known?" Yin asks.

Glancing at his Rolex, Bao says, "About 40 seconds. No. Tu did background checks on all of us. You're twins. Your parents are dead. Why say it was a friend's sister? I don't understand. You lied for no reason."

Calculating where to go with this awkward situation, Yin uses fragments of the truth to manipulate Bao's feelings. "I didn't want anyone to know too much before I could trust them." She says, hoping Bao will take the bait. "I thought EEL could help me, and when you said you were opening the center to cater to a powerful Chinese family, I thought I could find out if the Triads took her by being on the inside. I'm sorry."

Those words hang in the air for a moment. Then Bao gives a curious response. "You were wise not to trust EEL, but you can trust me. Business comes first, though. I've already warned you about these guys."

Once again, Bao knocks her off balance. Yin lets the comment go.

"Twins?" Bao says. Yin finds his response challenging.

"Identical," Yin answers.

"What happens if you find her? Are you planning to leave? Because you and I have an agreement."

"And I'm honoring that agreement. Two different things, Bao. I'm excited by the work and want to find my sister. These are not mutually exclusive paths."

Bao lifts the napkin from his lap and folds it on the table. "I need another drink," he says, raising his arm.

Regaining balance after the conversation's surprising turn, Yin presses forward. "Listen, EEL or Bao, whichever is more likely to help me, my sister was taken. She looks just like me, and I need help finding her. If you help me, I'll stay with the project until the end. If you want me to leave, say so."

Bao laughs. "Whatever. My name is Bao. I run a data center. Like I said, stick it out, and I'll help you find your sister, but stay focused until the finish line. I'm serious."

As the waiter approaches, Yin softens, "I'm sorry, Bao. Truly sorry. Let's not talk about business or missing sisters for the rest of the night."

"What else is there?" Bao says and orders another round of drinks.

Across the room, Nigel Rainer finally tires of waiting and leaves the restaurant.

"Tell me about Silicon Valley. It must have been exciting," Yin says, just marking time.

For the rest of the evening, Bao controls his drinking. Yin sees him alternately looking at his cocktail and the waiter, sometimes raising the drink to his mouth and placing it again on the table without a sip. She listens intently to everything he says to reward him, often feeding his ego with words like fascinating, amazing, and cool. She needs to nurture this resource.

Bao is the perfect gentleman when sober. They ride-share to their destinations, Yin arriving first.

Bao steps out of the vehicle to say goodnight. Yin says she had a great evening, adding that they should make this a regular thing. Bao smiles broadly while approaching, but Yin doesn't let him kiss her. Instead, she briefly hugs Bao and retreats into the sanctuary of her walk-up apartment. If Li were waiting there for her, the twins would have spent the night laughing at Bao's bizarre mannerisms.

The next is just another day at the data center in every observable way. Bao and Yin nod at each other as they walk to their respective offices, but neither has anything more to say about the night before. Nicolay continues hunting through Dragonhead's network looking for access points to a second server farm they know must be in operation. Yin moves money around the globe, and Peter works on a call tree that may soon be used by terrorists.

Yin stares into space and wonders if Bao, knowing Li is her sister, changes things. It does not. She's desperate enough to accept help from whomever, even devils.

Because Nigel showed up alone at Mott 32, she believes he is anxious to meet. She promised that if he did, and he came alone, she would follow up with a place and time, but she didn't promise when she would notify him.

She waits until the end of her workday, takes Uber to Picotin-Fairways restaurant, and sits at the bar. She orders a glass of wine, logs into one of the phones she cloned, and sends a text. By design, Nigel barely has time to race out of his office or apartment and get to the restaurant. If he doesn't arrive on time, the Incense Master will leave. When sent, she waits.

Nigel arrives. Yin studies new customers for ten minutes and then steps into the parking lot, pretending to call a friend as she scans the lot for signs of someone waiting there—a van or other vehicle capable of concealing technicians, signs of Nigel being accompanied or followed, anything that does not seem appropriate.

When sufficiently convinced he is alone, she returns to the restaurant, sits at a table next to Nigel's, and orders. He waits patiently, checking his watch more often as time passes. She knows he is looking for a man in a green hat carrying a yellow bag.

"Would you like to join me?" Yin asks. Nigel looks confused as he sees her, but he controls his emotions. He is the perfect gentleman, yet he smiles as many men do when a beautiful woman shows interest. "I'd love to, but I'm waiting for someone."

"Pity," Yin says as Nigel turns away. When he's once again watching the entrance for the mysterious Incense Master, she pulls a green hat from her blue bag, flips the bag inside out to be yellow, and says, "How about now?"

Nigel turns, eyes widening. As surprise and recognition evoke an involuntary chuckle, he mouths the words, Incense Master? "Crikey. I didn't. I saw you there and—."

Yin interrupts his stumbling speech with a confident smile. "It's important that we talk. May I join you?"

The Deputy Chief rises momentarily to greet her, but Yin doesn't yet allow their eyes to meet. She glances at the waiter to indicate she has moved, arranges a chair, and gingerly places clasped hands on the table in front of her, eyes down until she feels fully attentive. When ready, she allows their eyes to meet.

Nigel has inched his chair forward and displays a state of readiness. He says, "I didn't expect—"

"A woman?" Yin consciously analyzes every word, gesture, and subtle reaction Nigel makes, assessing her counterpart's reactions and adjusting accordingly. She knows he will do the same. Many professionals in his position would already show signs of hiding a predetermined agenda. Nigel is open-faced.

"And quite young. We could go somewhere more private if you think it necessary, but you have my full attention."

"I doubt we will be overheard, and I've just ordered. This won't take long. Obviously, I am not a Triad Incense Master, but I need your help and have valuable information to trade. Think of me as your confidential informant. Is that the correct term? I work in a clandestine data center for one of the Triads, and we both know they have dangerous plans. In return for the information I can already give and will get, I need your help finding my twin sister. She was abducted in Shanghai."

Nigel's eyes divert momentarily as he adjusts. "How long has she been missing?"

"She was abducted early in the morning of February 13, Shanghai time. I've been hunting for her ever since." Nigel hears the story of being at MIT, returning to Shanghai on a mission, exploring the dark web, and ending up fortuitously embedded in a Singapore Triad data center. She openly admits to manipulating every step in meeting Nigel but carefully deflects her knowledge of Triad business onto others as if she's simply an observer at the center and has little to do with the actual work. Nigel comments more than once on the lengths she's gone through to find her sister, even acknowledging that the way she set him up was strategically brilliant.

"I'll need to verify a few things, starting with your sister's abduction, but you're unfortunately correct about us. If you'd walked in the front door looking for help, we'd have taken your story, promised nothing, and that would be the end. Good on you."

"Can I count on your assistance and discretion? To everyone you know, I am the Incense Master, a man in China who secretly feeds you critical information in return for your assistance in finding his friend's sister. That's it. Play by those rules, and you'll get every scrap of information I can find."

"You know I could have you brought in right now if I wanted to. We have to trust—"

Yin interrupts. "Three conditions. I need absolute anonymity and absolution for anything I tell you. The Triads will know if you run to Essex, especially if you use my name. Your organization's security is compromised in ways you don't understand.

"I also need assurance that you'll intervene if something happens to me. It could be some other agency or the Triad itself. I'm in a perilous situation, and you are the only person I can turn to in Singapore.

"Finally, I'll do my best to get any information you ask for, but if I say it's too dangerous, that's it. Trust me. If you raid the center, you'll get nothing. We are already under the surveillance of Triad goons. You'll feel the need to do something, but my life is on the line, and all I have is your word. Do I have your word, Nigel? These are dangerous people."

"I know what you're saying, but I can't effectively hunt for your sister without involving resources. Maybe I can go outside the agency."

"The time will come when you can do whatever you want about the center, but not yet. Be careful. The people I work with know more about you than you do about them. When you went to Australia, you stayed at the Novotel Geelong Hotel. The day you interviewed Dragonhead's brother, Essex took his son to a soccer game. When you returned, you sent your report to Essex and, inadvertently, to the Triad. The game has changed. Do I have your full attention? Try to go around me, and I'll quit working there and return to China."

Nigel appears shaken. With every word, his trust in the agency evaporates in smoke. "How is that possible?"

"I know this must be difficult."

"You don't know the half of it," Nigel says as confidence drains from his face. He turns away, hoping to hide how deeply unmoored he feels.

"I'll try to find out how they got inside, but I can't promise anything," Yin says. "They have some highly skilled engineers back in China. The main thing now is that we are a team. I will give you information, and you will find Li. I can see you're struggling to keep up. Incense Master is a woman, and your agency is leaking information. It's a lot to take in. Worse yet, she wants you to keep all this information to yourself." Yin is somewhat shocked by how much she just sounded like Bao.

Nigel laughs but seems okay with her teasing. "You're killing me here. What's the information?"

"Anonymity and absolution, correct?" Yin demands.

"I'll protect you."

That is all Nigel needs to say. "The Triads are planning something huge, which will occur within the next few months. They've moved over a half billion dollars US into the region through shell corporations. They are creating secret money cards to finance over one hundred individuals that possibly mean to do harm, and my fear, Nigel—and I can't yet verify this—there is a link between the Triad and a group of terrorists. I believe they are collaborating," Yin says, watching Nigel analyze what he's just heard.

"How do you know all this?" Nigel asks with a dose of disbelief in his voice.

Yin pounces on his moment of skepticism. "Listen, I know you are suspicious, but if you spend time determining if I'm playing you, it's time wasted."

Nigel looks at Yin with kind eyes. "I get it, but we have processes and ways of dealing with assets."

Frustrated, Yin says, "I'll spell it out for you. Mutual trust is necessary, or there's no point in moving forward. I need your help, and you need mine."

Nigel looks towards the neatly stacked bottles behind the bar and says, "Tell me how you know all of this."

"I've heard things and have even seen fragments of a list. Give me a week to get that list. Meanwhile, prove that you are looking for Li," Yin says. It feels wrong to withhold critical information, but she's thought about this deeply and believes she has no choice. She must remain in control of Nigel, not the other way around. To punctuate the point, Yin coldly stares into Nigel's kind eyes and says, "If you play me, I'll walk."

"Nodding, Nigel simply replies, "I understand."

As they leave, Yin realizes how stressful the encounter has been for them. She's planned this for nearly a month and laid everything on the line. Looking into Nigel's eyes confirms that he, too, feels the strain. His agency is compromised, and he's entered into a secretive agreement that defies everything he stands for as a member of the IC. In a way, Yin realizes Nigel has just lost everything. And Yin, better than most, knows what it feels like to experience loss.

"Do you know what my parents called me as a child?" She asks softly.

As if entranced, Nigel says, "No. What?"

"Yin Yin."

"Yin Yin. I like that." Nigel says.

Unaware of any underlying motivation, Yin hugs Nigel like a brother, fighting back tears. "Can you wait in the restaurant until I'm gone?"

Nigel is taken aback. Yin is a remarkable woman at a breaking point.

Most, if not all, people in his shoes would not trust Yin for a second. They would focus on her manipulations, but Nigel seems different. He's listened to her story, understood her plight, and felt her fear. "Sure," he agrees.

Confusing and dissonant emotions accompany Yin to her apartment. Emotionally drained, she needs to collapse onto her bed, but she's hyper-vigilant with adrenaline. If she had the energy, she would run through the streets of Singapore, celebrating her accomplishments. She's penetrated a Triad data center and recruited a Deputy Chief of Station to aid in the hunt for Li. Knowing she must rest. Yin stands disrobed in front of her bathroom mirror as steam from the warming shower fills the room and clouds her image. She hasn't felt this close to Li for days. Opening Li's lipstick, she draws a single Chinese character on the mirror in thick, bright red lines. It translates as *I love you with my actions*. Stepping into the shower, the beast within repeats a different mantra. Someone has to pay.

Chapter 25

Barwon Prison, March 15, 3 am

A compromised correctional officer nervously opens a door in the loading area of one of the prison buildings for three masked men. He guides them to the control room, where they overcome tired guards, strip off uniforms, and assume their roles. The fool who let them in changes his mind when the full intent of their mission becomes obvious, but it's too late. He's viciously attacked and left mortally wounded on the control room floor.

Their attack takes less than twenty-five minutes. During that time, they find and murder six of the Triad criminals captured by the Australian authorities, eventually leaving Chuanli in a pool of blood. The assassins are also contracted to eliminate the two that received special treatment, but thus far, TU has not found them.

When they finish their mission, the assassins send photographs, and Tu personally delivers the information to Dragonhead. "We have succeeded at the prison. The team has yet to identify where the traitors were taken, but I doubt they can provide much of value." He hands over confirming photographs taken by the hit team.

Jiao fans through the images until landing on the photograph of Chuanli's mutilated body. He stares silently for a long moment. "Did he suffer?"

Tu is unsure how to answer. The assassins had entered the man's cell, tased him, and after puncturing his chest multiple times, cut out his tongue and slit his throat. "Yes. He suffered."

Tu has read his superior properly. Jiao nods, sips his Scotch, and says, "As he should have. If the traitors had families, you know what to do."

There is an emotional precipice that only undercover operatives and confidential informants experience. For Yin, the apex of her journey comes when she enters the data center the morning after meeting Nigel. She is already an infiltrator embedded in a Triad data center to get information on their human trafficking operations. She is also now a spy for the Australian intelligence community. Self-taught in the art of tradecraft, Yin analyzed multiple approaches leading to her meeting with Nigel. Terms like OPSEC and SDR meant little in her previous life. These terms and concepts are now guiding principles required for survival.

She renewed her commitment to Li when she entered the bathroom this morning. She'd repeated her mantra in the mirror, doing her best to see herself as Li: "I love you with my actions." She repeated the affirmation several times.

Yin takes a moment to reflect on her situation at the data center. For a few months with SSSB, she assisted data analysts in China by cross-referencing information from European human intelligence assets with readily available online research. How brave some of those assets must be, living double lives. They risk their careers, deportation, imprisonment, or worse. Yet she's doing the same thing in Singapore, dancing the tango with Triads and the intelligence community.

Trust is not a traded commodity in Singapore. Yin mentally prioritizes her actions at work while logging into the network. Ever mindful, she glances up to see Bao staring in her direction from across the room. He stands in the doorway of his office. She nods. Bao nods back, then returns to his keyboard. Many of Yin's contacts in this new life are like Bao. They are mysterious, dangerous, and necessary. Bao is brilliant, generous with money, selfish with time, and socially inept. At the same time, he is her gateway to the underworld. The form of self-confidence Bao exhibits can be a weakness because it makes him so predictable.

A cathartic thought brings Yin to a complete stop. She rests her hands in her lap as pieces of the big picture come into view. Bao is a gamer, always hunting for the next level and a great win. Why is he in Singapore working for the Triads, to get a paycheck? Where's the juice in that? He loves the rush of power, but terrorism? Where is the win in that goal? Bao could care less about causes and ideology, so the only thing left is elevating the game. Viewed through the lens of what she knows about Bao, he wants to benefit from the chaos terrorism would cause, which presents a dilemma. What's her next move with Bao?

Tu is the most dangerous of her loose connections and possibly the best informed. He has a darkness about him, a dense, frightening aura, and that unmistakable look of recognition when their eyes met means she should stay as far away from that man as possible. The challenge is that Tu may hold the truth. Who else in her network has a better view of Triad activities?

Yin walks to the common area for a morning tea and greets one of her team members. She smiles broadly at him and offers encouragement, prattling phrases like good job, and keep it up, but these are layers of deception. The young statistician has landed the best job of his life. He smiles enthusiastically but has no idea that he is a simple smoke screen, a foil in a much larger story.

She, Nicolay, and Peter are insiders but also pawns. Like the eager statistician, they only see in fragments. They are all assisting a criminal organization with moving money around the globe. They support the theft of information from law enforcement agencies. They harden security for the Triad's digital assets, but to what end? Now, Yin fears terrorism. She reminds herself this is only a theory, but the thought angers her. How callous and malignant is it for Bao to use people this way, to use her! The rage of ten thousand dragons rises in her to counter the evil she perceives, but it's just a theory. She must be patient.

When Yin returns to her office, Bao is waiting. "Hi. My name is Bao," he says, smiling. "And I'd love to get dinner with you."

"You're funny. Are we good?" Yin asks, mimicking one of Bao's greetings.

"Why wouldn't we be? After dinner the other night, you said we should do it more often. Were you serious or just blowing smoke up my ass?" Bao says.

"Things are complicated right now for both of us. It could be a distraction given all we're trying to do."

Bao smiles and turns to walk away. "A girl's gotta eat. Seven works for me. I'll send details."

Yin is amused and wonders if Bao's approach works for other women. Resolved to get more tradable information, Yin accepts Bao's third invitation to dine.

• • •

Bao surprises Yin with a limousine. "You look amazing tonight," he says as she enters the limo. He's done everything possible to impress, which can only mean one thing. The limo, a new expensive suit, and reservations at a Micheline restaurant known for its fusion of French and Japanese cuisine all say that he wants more than a casual business relationship. Yin has become a challenge, which is right where she wants him.

"Thank you. You look nice as well. I like your hair like that," Yin says, referring to a closely shaven skull. Bao is mercurial, but tonight, it doesn't work. He's shown up as someone he is not.

Whitegrass restaurant is a strange experience for Yin and, apparently, for Bao. When she accepted his invitation, she'd expected a steak house or sports bar, with soccer matches blaring from television screens overhead, or even an Americanized pizza parlor. But here, the atmosphere is sparse, the seating minimalistic, and the restaurant is clearly meant for epicureans. They sit at a glass table in a pastel room. Portions are small, and though the amuse bouche, kanburi, poisson, lily bulbs, and cured pork with black truffle taste amazing, as does the aged cheese, Omi Wagyu, and milk-fed lamb, haute cuisine does not fit with Bao's world. Here, the focus is on each bite and the ritual of celebrating new and innovative ways to prepare food. More to the point, this is not an environment where Bao can drink to excess. Yin needs that to happen.

Sensing how uncomfortable Bao is in this setting, she says, "I know a bar where we can relax. Would you be willing to leave?" Bao's face brightens, and they call for the waiter. Bao hands the surprised man twice what the meal cost, and they leave for the Elephant Room.

"Fuck yeah!" Bao barks as they enter the sports bar. The establishment features colorful, spicy food, strong drinks, and warm décor rich with laughter and discussion. He is in his element.

Bao orders a massive Indian fried chicken burger with curry aioli and pickled onions. Laughing with the bartender, he describes their earlier dinner as an appetizer. He drinks two or three cocktails for every one Yin drinks. During Bao's eighth cocktail, their conversation turns to the big boss. Bao cannot help but brag. "I met Ji at his casino. We talk all the time now, the little fucker. He's smart but needs me, him, and Tu both. If it weren't for me, his 10-year plan would be dead," Bao says, looking at the floor and making a strange splatting sound like dropping a bowl of gelatin.

Yin laughs at his antics, which only encourages him to do more. It's the moment she's been waiting for. She says, "How can I help?"

Bao catches himself momentarily, as if he's said too much, but continues anyway. Speech slurred, possibly already blacked out, Bao says, "It's a secret, but they're going to fuck things up, okay? Screw it. What could we do with a billion dollars? You know everything is going to shit, and we're sitting on a billion to invest. *What would we do?* Know what I'm saying? Like money markets? Stock options? Should we buy up a shitload of land? Imagine chaos in the streets and violence on the television, like every day. You're the financial wizard. Lay it on me. What would we do?"

Yin wants to press and find out what he means by violence in the streets, but it's too soon. He's also used the word we—what would we do? "If we had a billion dollars? I suppose all of the above. We'd start with stock options and commodities like oil. Convert holdings to cash to take advantage of price fluctuations. There are short-term opportunities and long-term gains with the right strategy."

Spinning on his stool, nearly falling from the grand gestures he attempts, Bao says, "See? That's why I like you! You know shit, and you're beautiful. You're fucking beautiful, Yin. What would we do with a billion dollars in a world going to shit? We're fucked, you know? Bung-holed."

"We should go," Yin says, but Bao isn't paying attention. Instead, he pulls a phone from his pocket and stares at a message.

"Holy shit! He did it. The bastard whacked him."

Definitely blacked out. "Who?" Yin asks.

"He killed his brother right there in prison. How can a guy even do that? I mean, if the little fuck can do that to his brother, what are they going to do to me? Shoot my fucking face? Stab me in the guts? Fuck!" Bao roars and then makes gestures of apology to the bartender, issuing a hushing sound with an index finger pressed against his lips.

Yin touches Bao's shoulder, and they both laugh at his outburst. In a near whisper, Yin says, "What are you talking about? Who is in prison?"

Slurring his words, Bao replies. "The big guy's brother. They're fucking good at whacking people, even in prison. Next-level shit. He's sitting in a cell, and whap. In the blinkling of an eye you're gone, you know? Wait, that's not the right. Is blinkling a word?"

"I don't think so. The big boss assassinated his brother? When?"

"Who the fuck knows, like yesterday or something. You need another round?"

"I'm good. How can you possibly know this?"

Bao winks, and again, puts a hushing finger to his lips. "Nick has fucking awesome sauce. Cloned his phone."

"Tu's phone?" Yin asks, hoping this rant continues.

"Guards couldn't do shit. Know why?" Yelling, Bao says, "Because they are that fucking good at whacking people! Awesome."

Yin shakes her head and tells Bao to keep it down, but Bao cannot be silenced. Turning his attention to restaurant guests, he yells, "Message received! I'll keep it down."

The bartender and a large bouncer come toward them, but Yin stands and gestures that it's okay, that she will get her drunken friend out of there. She tells Bao it's time to go.

"Whatever," Bao says politely. He's not as gracious with the bartender. Spitting a drunken cliché, he says, "I've been thrown out of better shit holes than this one."

Yin apologizes profusely, pays the tab, leaves a generous tip, and steadies Bao as they stagger through startled guests toward the door. Waiting curbside for Bao's limo driver, he mumbles how beautiful Yin is and tries to touch her breasts. She'll have none of it but doesn't raise her voice. Instead, she takes his hand, rubs his head, and says, "I like your hair like that, Bao. You look nice tonight."

The move brings Bao fully into the present. He says, "I do. You look nice, too, but I have a question for you. What would you do if you had like a billion dollars and the world was going to shit?"

The limo driver takes Bao to his apartment complex. Yin accompanies Bao to his apartment, but he fumbles with keys, dropping them to the floor. Yin helps him into a sorrowful den of empty takeaway containers, spent soda cans, and beer bottles. There's a cluttered dining room table and sofa. Bao asks if she wants a drink, perhaps his final attempt to get her into his bed, but she turns him down with a simple gesture.

The man is lonely, but it's his own fault. Yin's inner dragon takes a break long enough for her to feel compassion for him. She guides him to a sofa, where he mumbles nonsense for a minute before passing out. She removes his shoes and drapes a towel over his torso. Before she leaves, she rubs his head one more time in the way a gambler might touch the belly of the coming Buddha before entering the casino. In Yin's case, it is not to gain luck or show admiration. Her touch rises from a darker place as if apologizing to the universe. If Bao thinks he can benefit from terror, she must destroy that dream.

Yin sends an urgent text through Nigel's burner phone while riding home. It reads, *We have to talk. Call now!*

The call comes instantaneously, and she picks up on the first ring.

"Are you okay?" Nigel asks immediately.

"They killed him, at least that's what Bao told me," Yin says.

"Killed who?"

"Dragonhead's brother Chuanli, the man in prison. I have more information for you, but my guy is scared. I think he is about to run. I may have to get out of there myself. Any progress on your end?"

"Are you sure? I haven't heard, but about Li, I may have a lead," Nigel says.

"May or do?" Yin snaps.

"We have a lead, okay? Someone recognized your photo. I can't tell you more now, but we're working on it."

"You can't tell me, or won't?"

"When I have details, you'll be the first and only person to know. My source is solid and willing to keep things away from the IC, at least for now. If your guy is about to run, we need to act," Nigel says absentmindedly.

"You say that a lot, Nigel. You say, at least for now, so I'm going to say it, too. At least for now, any raid on the data center will trigger a kill switch. You know that, right? You'll walk out with a burned box," Yin warns.

"I understand," Nigel says, his voice reassuring.

"If he can do that to his own brother—. Anyway, I'm still dizzy from alcohol, but might we meet now? I'll text you the location in a minute or two."

Nigel agrees, and Yin taps her driver on the shoulder. "Pull over at the next bar or restaurant. Thank you."

Chapter 26

Muhammad Ulul Khan just turned 41 years old. He was born beneath the flight paths of Husein Sastranegara Air Force Base, Husein Sastranegara International Airport in Bandung, Indonesia. He was never an athlete, was always self-conscious of his looks, and plagued with acne during the developmental years most boys discover girls, but he excelled in science and mathematics and aspired to be a pilot. He had goals and direction, which offset his low self-esteem. Like his father, he was a natural aviator. Muhammad learned to fly aircraft before he got his driver's license. While other children played soccer and went on first-person shooter gaming missions, Muhammad sat at the console of his father's flight simulator. He learned the difference between altitude and attitude, pitch and yaw, and could pilot both fighter jets and commercial airliners, at least in simulation.

At 15, he trained on a small biplane, and a year later, he not only flew solo but also graduated high school, a full two years ahead of his peers. In that same year, his mother's brother and sister-in-law died in Iraq during a series of cruise missile and air attacks known as Operation Desert Fox. Although President Clinton's Pentagon claimed the precision attacks yielded no civilian casualties, young Khan's cousin Omar is proof of the lies the West tells. Living an isolated Bedouin existence with little care of the turmoil in the world around them, an errant cruise missile made its way into their small camp, instantly killing both parents and leaving his cousin Omar burned and disfigured. The news devastated his mother. Mrs. Khan got the news while working checkout at Setiabudhi Supermarket and collapsed in sorrow, incoherent to the point where her supervisor feared for her life.

What followed was against Muhammad's father's wishes, but they airlifted Omar from Iraq to Indonesia and cared for him through multiple skin grafts and surgeries. The experience had a profound and lasting effect on Muhammad and his father alike. Omar referred to the incident as Clinton's little war in Iraq, meant to divert attention from impeachment proceedings against him, which lasted four days. The cost was Omar's family. Omar panics every time he hears an aircraft. Omar hated the US for what it did to him, and much of that hatred filled the young, impressionable mind of Muhammad Khan. Why had Allah allowed this? To what end had fate sent Omar to Indonesia?

After high school, Muhammad was approved for early admission into the military, no doubt with help from his father. He joined the Indonesian Air Force at 16 and was immediately selected to fly Northrop F-5s. Soon afterward, Russian-made Mikoyan and Gurevich or MiG-29's. He and his father flew on active duty together for a short while. The elder Khan was one of the experienced combat pilots who participated in the intervention in East Timor in the 80's and 90's. For years, his father's experiences in combat were relayed to his son so that young Khan could learn from the experiences of others.

The new millennium brought new forms of turmoil. Young Khan and his father fought an insurgency to free Papua and Aceh. Khan earned an exemplary reputation as a gifted aviator. However, throughout his military years, young Khan became more incensed by what the US was doing in Islamic countries around the world. His cousin's scarred body was at the core of his anger, a relentless reminder of what he knew to be global injustice.

2001 significantly changed the course of human history when Jihadists flew aircraft into the New York World Trade Center towers and the Pentagon. Their bravery and martyrdom proved that the great Satan was vulnerable. Only 19 men and their supporters had done what armies could not, struck the beast's heart. If they could take over planes, why couldn't the pilot of such an aircraft do something similar? He imagined that one day, he would have the opportunity and courage to battle with the West, a thought he'd never shared with anyone except his cousin Omar.

In 2006, Muhammad left the active duty ranks of the Air Force. He continued to fly military fighter jets part-time as a reservist, once again with help from his father. He moved to Kuala Lumpur in late 2006 to begin a second career in commercial aviation. In early 2007, Indonesia started a newly created state-owned airline named Inter-Asian Airways, and young Khan got in on the ground floor. He was only 24 years old. Flying fighter jets by day and commercial airliners by night, Muhammad Khan had the best of both worlds.

Six years into his commercial career, he met a butcher named Nasr. That initial meeting started a friendship that grew into various assignments over the following years. Captain Khan reveled in the feeling of power that came with belonging. His destiny seemed inevitable. He dreamed of having an impact.

Nasr came to him every month with requests—humanitarian flights to move refugee families from one country to the next, airlifting of food and supplies into conflict areas worldwide, and the desire for information on the capabilities of various commercial aircraft. Nasr's appreciation was profound, and he received excellent compensation.

Khan found himself flying various aircraft for the cause almost as much as he was flying commercially. Feeling overburdened by his flying commitments, he retired from the Malaysian Air Force in 2019 at an equivalent rank of lieutenant colonel at 36. He now had more time to make a difference.

Now, years into helping Nasr and the cause, earning money is no longer a concern. He has a sense of purpose and enjoys the camaraderie. So, he is more than willing to assist when Nasr asks him to fly a group of refugees to a remote destination in the Sangihe Islands, the eastern waters of the Celebes Sea.

Captain Khan rides the jump seat of a commercial flight from Kuala Lumpur to Sam Ratulangi Airport in Manado City, where he discovers that the twin-engine plane he is to fly carries displaced women. He hears them laughing together as he climbs into the aircraft, but as they see him, they become solemn and subdued. Lifting his hat momentarily, he greets his passengers. "Assalamu alaikum. Good news, I don't bite!" he says.

Nearly in unison, the women respond with *wa alaikum salaam* and are at ease. He hears them chattering together as they fly. One of the women even approaches him to ask about his career, how long he's been flying, and what he likes best about aviation.

Surprising Captain Khan, Nasr greets them on the island with a generous smile. He and Nasr haven't talked in person since Syhala took over deliveries. He takes them uphill in a golf cart to drink tea on a lanai overlooking the road, airstrip, and harbor. Nasr wants to know how the captain feels about their work so far. As they settle into small talk, Nasr asks Captain Khan if he has ever considered marriage. "Every man should have someone to hold at night, to cook for him and keep things nice around the house. You're not getting any younger, you know. You don't want to become lonely."

Khan laughs. "Loneliness is nothing, my friend. One becomes used to being alone."

"You're a successful, good-looking guy. Many women would want to be with you—the women you flew here, for example. I need to meet with them before we go back. I'm returning with you."

Khan has long since stopped worrying about his looks. Yes, he's successful. He can acknowledge this success as he sits with Nasr, enveloped in the glory of helping the cause, but good-looking? What is Nasr playing at?

Nasr and Khan take the golf cart downhill and spot the women sitting together under a sprawling tree. Nasr drives the cart up to the women and speaks to Khan about them as if inanimate storefront mannequins. "These women are all faithful, good cooks, and willing partners. I have business to take care of inside, but I'd like you to sit with them for a while, have something to eat, and see if one interests you. When I come back, you can tell me all about the experience. I'd also like you to meet someone before you fly home."

"You're joking?" Khan says in disbelief.

"I don't joke, my friend. Sit. Enjoy their company," Nasr says. Laughing at Khan's apprehension, he instructs the women to make the good Captain comfortable, leaving Khan dumbfounded, embarrassed, and offended.

Khan doesn't know what to say or even where to sit. He awkwardly lights a cigarette and tries to imagine what it would be like to be with someone who cares for him. "Sit with us," one of the younger women says. She's the one who showed an interest in aviation while in the plane's cockpit.

One woman takes his arm, another gives up her chair, and Khan is surrounded by curious, giggling women within seconds. Some appear to be as uncomfortable and embarrassed as he is, but they are warm, friendly, and full of questions—where does Khan live? What foods does he like? On and on. Laughing, one of the women asks if he is good in bed, but within the hour, Khan is the one asking questions. Not once does Khan say that he already has a love interest and believes she is also interested in him. These are refugees. Nasr's apparent plan to place one of them with him, saying he's a good-looking guy but probably lonely, only deepens his concern. Khan thinks Nasr has a generous heart, but in this case, he's misguided. Requests often follow lavish treatment.

Khan sees Nasr in the distance, making his way back to the group. He wonders if Nasr's matchmaking would continue if he knew how interested he had become in his niece.

By the time Nasr returns, Khan knows something interesting about each of them and more about himself. They come from Afghanistan, Pakistan, Yemen, Iraq, Bangladesh, and Sudan. Each woman is lovely in one way or another. Khan spends the most time talking with the woman claiming to be from Iraq. She claims to have grown up near where his cousin burned in the bombing. She claims to recall the incident, but Khan doubts her claim is valid. He is cordial and listens to her stories for a few more minutes, leading the women to believe Khan has made his choice. By the time Nasr returns, Khan has lost interest altogether. He strolls at the edge of the harbor, smoking cigarettes.

Further offending Khan, Nasr seems upset. "What are you doing? I leave you with women, and you look at fish? Take one to your home. That one from Anbar looks perfect. I can tell she likes you."

"Not for me."

"Then another. They will help you prepare with cooking, cleaning, and at night—"

"None of them. Please stop, but what do you mean, prepare? Prepare for what?"

Nasr smiles, shakes his head, and touches Khan's shoulder. "Talk of women can come later. First, I will introduce you to Almudir. We have a vital mission for you, my friend."

Chapter 27

March 16

When Nasr and Captain Khan enter the former fish processing plant, Khan presses the palm of his right hand to his forehead in disbelief.

"You can see it. See what we're building here?" Nasr says proudly.

Khan breaks into laughter. "You've built a hangar! A huge hidden hangar, I must say."

"Exactly. It's large enough for a 777. Well, almost. It will be ready soon, and you, my friend, will help us get a plane," Nasr says jubilantly.

Glancing at the airstrip, Khan's face shows both concern and surprise. "That's what the bulldozer is doing, extending and widening the runway."

"You didn't know, but you helped us calculate the required dimensions," Nasr says, patting his friend on the shoulder.

Khan's amazement turns to concern. "Stealing a plane won't be easy, probably impossible."

"We have money, resources, and lots of help. All we now need is you." Nasr says hopefully.

Khan ignores the comment and asks, "How long have you known about this plan? From the start?"

"No, no. Two months, maybe three. Almudir keeps us in the dark, but that's necessary, you see? Necessary. One thing at a time. That's him over there," Nasr says, pointing to a group of men at the far end of the hanger.

As they approach, Nasr calls out. "Let me introduce you to the amazing Captain Muhammad Khan!" He says emphatically.

"Assalamu alaikum," Khan says, embarrassed by the introduction. He stands as tall as he can, puffing his chest, but it's useless. Compared to Almudir, Khan is a twig of a man.

As they shake hands, Almudir says, "I've heard many good things about you. Very helpful to our people. What do you think of our project?"

"What you've accomplished is remarkable, but I have concerns. Nasr says you plan to steal a commercial airplane? That's nearly impossible," Khan says, knowing exactly where this is heading.

"We don't use that word, steal. Call it hijacking if you want, but we are going to liberate an airplane for the cause. We know when and most of how, but we need your intelligence and experience to fill in some of the gaps. First though, are you willing to train the pilots?" Almudir asks.

Khan seems thrown off by the request but says, "Of course."

"Excellent! We have a few hours for you to get acquainted. This way," Almudir says, gesturing toward a small office space on the far wall of the hangar.

Three hours later, Captain Khan emerges from the room. He's been working with two men on a flight simulator. Eyeing Almudir and Nasr walking their way from across the hangar, he recalls advice from his father to never be the one in the room who doesn't know the play. He never quite knew what he meant until this moment.

"Well?" Nasr asks.

"Your guys are not aviators. It could take months, maybe years, to teach them to fly a commercial jet. Flying at the low altitudes and speed required to avoid detection takes years of experience. When will you do this?" Khan asks as if he's addressing someone's fantasy.

Almudir's face showing disappointment as he offers a counterpoint: "They are very dedicated. What if we teach them on smaller aircraft first?"

"It's not just flying. Someone must get control of the plane, disable comms, work out the routes, and don't forget landing. Even veteran pilots would have difficulty landing a commercial jet on that runway. Very challenging, so please. Let's cut to the bottom line. You want me to do this. Is that right? Be honest," Khan says, looking at the narrow strip of runway, imagining the exhilaration of dropping out of the sky at close to 150 knots onto that ribbon of uneven ground. *What if it were nighttime?*

Almudir interrupts Khan's internal musings. "If you are willing, of course. You have great skill and faith. Whoever does this will receive enough money to live well for life—new identity, protection, and the eternal thanks of the All-Powerful."

Nasr quickly interjects, touching Khan's arm as if to warn him. "Can you help find the right pilot? You know many pilots."

Khan ignores Nasr and nods toward the little office. "Training isn't the solution. I'm not saying yes, but how would this work? If I diverted a plane midflight, which is the only possible way, I'd have to hide for the rest of my life. I'd need my cousin and wife taken care of."

"Of course," Almudir says.

"You like the woman from Iraq! I knew it!" Nasr says, patting Khan's back and chuckling.

Almudir practically whispers. "Quiet!"

"Not her. Someone else. Someone you may know," Khan says to Nasr with a smile. The comment stuns Nasr into silence, and Khan continues with Almudir. "You're building a hangar and clearing a runway, but your plan to train those men won't work. My grandfather lived to be 95. I am 41 now and could easily live into my late eighties. If you want me to do this, the price is $10 million US. I'll hijack the plane and map a route for the next phase. I can possibly even train your men for that mission. My only condition is that the passengers are somehow released."

"You say they cannot be trained," Nasr says, confused.

Khan and Almudir exchange a knowing glance. "I'll map a route for your pilots and train them enough to get the plane in the air. Do we have a deal, Almudir?"

"Ten million is a great deal of money. If you can bring a plane to this island without being caught, we can easily hide it and the passengers until ready. The passengers will be found after the final flight. That is the plan. Is it possible?"

"With a measure of luck, the right people in place, and guidance from The Omnipotent one, yes. It is possible," Khan says, smiling.

Almudir embraces Khan, kissing him on both cheeks. "Then we have a deal. We'll have to coordinate timelines. Approximately when do we act?" Khan asks.

There's a golf cart nearby. Almudir nods in that direction and takes a deep breath. "Soon, my brother. Soon. Before you fly home, Captain, let's discuss details."

Chapter 28

March 20

Nigel Rainer sits in his office reviewing case files. A sliver of sunlight illuminates the room through a screen behind his chair. His third coffee is nearly gone, and he still can't concentrate on his tasks. He ruminates on the frightening information Yin gave him and the subsequent list of money card recipients the Triad intends to send to men she thinks may be terrorists. After she left Bao in a drunken state the night they last met in person, they sat in a small noodle restaurant for a few minutes, then walked for an hour. He'd become even more intoxicated by her looks and entranced by her mental agility. Yin is levels above him. She expressed concern over a potential connection between Triad members and terrorists and laughed when he cautioned her about taking materials from the data center. She told him to put his phone in record mode and recalled the names of 124 money card recipients from memory, saying he could transcribe it all later. Alcohol was a factor, but something else had shifted in her psyche. Yin was less guarded and more forthcoming, as if her evening with Bao Gu had moved her more firmly into his camp. He trusts her.

He's never met anyone quite as capable or courageous. If Yin is this brave, he must step up as well. Protocol demands that he escalate this new information, which means returning to Essex. Yin wants a few more days, and her arguments are sound. Bao had told her the cards were for traveling repair mechanics, a way for some companies to cover costs in the field. It's not uncommon to manage expense budgets this way, but according to Yin, Bao predicted an international financial crisis caused by chaos in the streets. Though profiling is taboo, it was hard for either of them to ignore the cultural origins of many names on that list.

While walking together, Yin had been tipsy. She'd held Nigel's arm for stability, and they had a moment where Yin looked into his eyes, her face inches from his. She held the gaze as if expecting something, but he stayed the course, asking another question about the cards. Yin explained that a controller would adjust card limits in real time and that some recipients would receive multiple cards, making it more difficult for authorities to track their movement through purchases. No cards will be used more than once.

Yin needs three more days to get phone numbers for the card limit controller, but time is running out. Nigel needs a team. At the very least, they should surveil the data center to identify who comes and goes, but Yin said it would be foolish. He's given his word, but the list bothers him. Interrupting a terrorist plot is far more important than protecting his informant, isn't it?

Essex has no issue playing the numbers game. A team would be heading to the data center if Essex were in charge. He'd order a full assault and haul everyone encountered away as they tore the place apart. The Singaporeans can hold suspected terrorists indefinitely, and someone might break during interrogation. Still, Yin is inside the organization, and they need more information to expose any plot and eliminate potential threats. Nigel's gut says to give Yin the time she needs, and he trusts her intuition. He can simultaneously help find her sister.

As of three nights ago, Yin and Nigel operate on a schedule that facilitates coded messaging and the in-person exchange of information. Yin sets the date, time, and location for each meeting. Meetings occur in the open air of Fort Canning or MacRitchie Reservoir Park. Alternatively, she designates a restaurant or bar. This evening, it's Bukit Batok Nature Park off East Avenue, where they can talk as they jog.

It makes sense that Yin wants to control the meetings. Informants are often in difficult situations. Is Yin wholly transparent and trustworthy? Neither of them can honestly say that. He's promised not to monitor the data center, but he's already ordered remote surveillance. She claims to have given him everything she has, but that's not possible. Bits of information are reserved as bargaining chips. I's her style. Her inner dragon sees to it.

Nigel has walked the tech campus, identified available CCTV, and downloaded files on the data center. Every corporation doing business in Singapore requires that one of the principals be a resident. In the case of the Singapore Data Centre, they used a long-time resident named Hàorán Wu with a side business claiming partnership for a fee. He becomes their legal resident, a stand-in for foreign corporations wanting to open offices in Singapore. He probably doesn't do anything, but even so, Nigel orders a phone tap.

Nigel closes his office door and checks the time. Before heading to his meeting with Yin, he calls his CIA contact. When Wright answers, he says, "I've got something for you that comes with beers and a fat steak. Are you available tomorrow night?"

As the afternoon turns to evening, Nigel stretches in shorts and a T-shirt near the entrance to Bukit Batok Park. He arrives early, hoping Yin is not already jogging in the park below. While stretching his calves at the top of the long cascade of stone stairs leading to the park's basin, Yin approaches. Nigel is once again stunned at her grace and physique. He's seen her in business clothing and an evening dress, but today, her black unitard leaves little to his imagination.

As she jogs by, Yin says, "Possible tail. Catch up."

Any man's eyes might follow this beautiful woman as she passes. He watches her descend the stone stairs and shakes his head, as men often do when seeing someone so attractive, but he continues stretching for the moment.

As she nears the bottom of the long stairs, Nigel sees a short man walking quickly, turning the corner on a neighboring street. Not seeing Yin, the man speeds up. Nigel continues to stretch, carefully pulling his phone and speaking to no one about a car purchase on the other end. Instead, he uses his camera to capture an image of the stout individual as he comes closer.

They acknowledge each other with a nod. Nigel begins his descent with rapid footsteps, the other man at the top of the stairway scanning the park below. At the base of the stairs, Nigel quickly glances back to see that the man has gone, possibly to wait for her return.

Within a few minutes, Nigel catches up to Yin. "Did you see him?" she asks, slowing some so they can talk as they run.

"I think so. Are you followed often?" Nigel asks as he hands her his phone and shows her the picture he just took.

Yin glances at the photograph. "He's one of them. They seldom follow me this far, but there's a team of at least three. This one is probably looking for a vantage point right now. We'll have to speak quickly and then separate. Is there anything new on your end?"

"Nothing yet on Li, but I want to send your list to another agency. They won't approach anyone, but they may have the names in their database. I need a team on this and I'm not yet ready to contact Essex. You okay with that?"

"You'll keep me out of it?" Yin says, her pace quickening.

Nigel acknowledges the energy required to keep pace and is once again blown away by this machine named Yin. Controlling his breathing, Nigel says. "Of course. What about these guys watching you? Does anyone else in your family need protection? Parents, siblings, a lover in your life?" Nigel appears to be blushing as if he wishes he could take that last question back.

Yin scoffs while effortlessly increasing her pace, forcing Nigel to keep up. "Just Li. I've given you a lot, Mr. Rainer. It would be best if you reciprocated. We should split up."

Stung by her words, Nigel says, "I am making inquiries, but I need those numbers, Yin. Anyway, I'm sending a package to your apartment. I've instructed the courier not to leave without your signature." Nigel shocks Yin with a sudden burst of speed. Yin smiles to herself and slows to a jog, taking in the scenery. Within seconds, Nigel is out of sight, and her shadow arrives on a ridge above a stone cliff.

When she gets home, Yin opens her apartment door, drinks water, and is about to shower when her doorbell rings. A woman is at the door with a large plastic food bag under one arm. "Yin Chen?"

Yin confirms her identity, noticing that this driver has an image of her on her phone, apparently used for verification. The Deliveroo driver goes through the motions of getting a signature and whispers. "If you need help with this equipment, Nigel is standing by."

Locking the door before returning to her living room, Yin glances out of a window to see what she knows will be there. A young man down the street uses his phone to snap a photograph of the driver returning to her car.

Engrossed in tradecraft and clandestine meetings, Yin feels like a spy. Exhilarating and terrifying, she expects to find bulky surveillance gear and imagines sneaking into the center with listening devices or miniature cameras, which she would never do.

Yin opens the package. Nigel has sent a boxed dinner and a small tin of chocolates. Is he courting her? Nigel is single, after all, and asked if she had a lover. He's not unattractive, but that can't be it. She unravels packing materials, finding two things. A surveillance wand is rolled in parchment paper to look like a spring roll. Maybe someone has embedded devices in her apartment? The thought makes her more angry than frightened. If there are video cameras, they will see her checking the rooms. She doesn't worry as much about audio. She never has others in her apartment and will be vigilant while on phone calls.

A small plastic tab protrudes from the flap of a food container. Pulling it retrieves a miniaturized thumb drive, which is borderline insulting and problematic. Whatever is on the drive could have been dropped on a file transfer protocol server somewhere for easy download. Years ago, a standard hack was to drop thumb drives onto bathroom floors and corporate elevators where some fool might find it and then pop it into a workstation, triggering an exploit. Could sending her a drive mean he wants her to load information to it?

"You can't be that naïve," Yin mumbles, wishing now it was just dinner and a box of chocolates. She places the drive on her desktop, showers, and then logs into an email account she and Nigel share. Nigel has left her a draft email, which she reads with a sense of incredulity.

Inserting the drive into the USB of any networked machine does two things. It freezes access, locking the hard drives. A notification goes directly to an action team via WiFi or other means. If used, leave immediately, and I will move you to a safe house.

"He is that naïve," she mocks. Data centers at her level disable the USB ports for staff. Yin manipulated her way into one of the Triad's digital strongholds and coerced a Deputy Chief of Station into helping her find Li, but she's ended up with this? Nigel does not have the technical insight required for this mission. He's out of his depth without the support of internal resources. The realization is enervating, but ultimately not that important. He's a competent bureaucrat, if nothing else, a gateway to resources and information and an ally. Yin feels the respect she felt towards Nigel and the tendency to rely upon his partnership sink.

As always, she is on her own.

Chapter 29

March 21

Since the first time Syhala delivered food to Captain Khan, they've been engaged in an ongoing flirtation, and remarkably, Syhala hasn't recoiled. Her clothing is frayed at the hems. The sandals she wears need repair, and the handmade jewelry on her wrists, ankles, and around her neck are cheap beadwork. Occasionally, the scooter Syhala uses for deliveries won't start when she leaves, and she'll need a push start. Like many of Syhala's things, it needs replacing. But she is lovely, thoughtful, and full of life. Somehow, the strips of meat and seasoned vegetables he's received from Nasr for months taste better when she delivers them.

After only two days of deliveries since returning from his trip, Khan mustered the confidence to ask Syhala if she would cook for him. To conceal his motives, he offered to pay her as he did for the deliveries. She gladly accepted. When she cooks for him, she sings like a bird. The apartment fills with delicious smells and the sound of her voice. No matter what he's doing when she arrives, Khan sets it aside to be near her, always cautious, never advancing on his friend's niece, simply enjoying her company.

But after his island visit, he's changed. He feels emboldened. He hopes he'll have money when he's completed his mission and be off to a new life.

"Syhala," he says as she finishes cooking. "Can we talk?" Khan says.

Nervous, she sits with him at the kitchen table. "If you've grown tired of lamb, we can remove it from the list," she says. Among the things he likes most about Syhala are her attention to detail and desire to please.

"Not at all. I love what you prepare. It's just that I may be leaving soon and will miss you," Khan says, blushing.

"Where are you going?" she asks.

"I'm not sure, but your uncle asked me to complete a mission, and after that, I won't be able to return here. I want you to know—"

"My uncle?"

"Nasr." Khan says.

Syhala bursts into laughter. "I just call him uncle. He likes it when I toy with him, but Nasr is not family. He helped me find work. He is my employer and friend. Did you think—?"

"I did. I thought Nasr was your uncle."

"And now that you know? What?" She says playfully.

Khan blushes again, and nervously rises to his feet. He touches her hand as a childlike look of wonder sweeps across his face.

"So precious," she smiles. "You have feelings for me, is that true? Let me tell you something, Muhammad. I am so proud of what you've done for Islam, of who you are, your mannerisms, and your kindness. Even if you don't have feelings for me, I have them for you."

"You do?" Khan asks, dumbfounded.

"How could you not notice? I've been sending signals since the day we met. It's embarrassing how I change to look nice, cook, and sing for you. Until now, I wasn't sure you even noticed. May I touch your face?" she says softly.

Khan's eyes widen. His hands fall to his side, and she slowly lifts her hands to his cheeks. Even slower, Khan brings his hands to her hips and kisses her forehead. He says, "You've made plenty of food. Can you stay a while longer and eat with me?"

Syhala smiles, touches his lips with an index finger, and says she'd love nothing more before turning to get another plate. "Please, no! Let me," Khan says and slides a chair away from the table for her to sit. He brings a glass, plate, and utensils in silence because he has no words.

When the table is set, they pray together and eat. Syhala starts their conversation. "You've flown many missions for Uncle Nasr. What is different about this one?"

Khan chuckles. "I should call him uncle, too. Nasr works with other people. I can't talk about what is coming. I can say that I will be gone for a long while. They'll pay a great deal, so if someone wanted to come with me, maybe to one of the Caribbean islands or someplace just as nice, there would be enough money."

Syhala looks concerned. "Why would you have to disappear? What's going on?"

"I can't say, only that no one is forcing me to do this. I want to make an impact," he says.

"Because of your cousin Omar," Syhala realizes.

"And everyone else whose life has been taken or ruined," Khan says, happy to hear that Syhala recalls their discussion about his family.

In the silence that follows, Syhala appears to struggle for words. Pushing her plate to one side, she takes the captain's hands. "I'd like to help. Tell me what I can do."

Khan looks down at her hands, then into her eyes. "If anything happened to you, I could not forgive myself. It's best if you know nothing of this mission."

Syhala makes a show of pouting. "My uncle has told me all you've done for our people. I'm sure this is no different. When do you leave?"

"I don't know. Maybe in a few weeks. They'll let me know, but please, don't tell your uncle we talked. I'm supposed to keep this quiet. Hush hush, you know?"

"Of course," Syhala says as she approaches the living room and bedroom door. "This is a nice apartment."

"You can have it when I'm gone. I'll pay ahead." Khan says, hoping Syhala will spend the night with him.

Syhala smiles, her eyes moisten, and she leans forward. "I do have feelings for you," she says as she lifts one of his hands to her face.

Chapter 30

March 22

"Can we talk, uncle?" Syhala says to Nasr. He's been in and out of the shop so often that they barely have time to catch up.

"Quickly. What's on your mind?" He says, passing Syhala and heading toward the back of the shop.

"The captain. The captain is on my mind," she says, her playful nature gone.

Nasr stops and turns to face Syhala. "I understand. You're tired of making deliveries. Maybe we can get one of the boys to—"

"No. I must tell you something. I have feelings for the captain, and he for me. He's arranging for me to have his apartment when he leaves. I just thought you should know." Syhala braces herself for the impending sharp reply.

Nasr nearly drops the package he is carrying. "How is this possible? Where is he going?"

Realizing that she's made a mistake, Syhala quickly recovers. "He's going on a long trip somewhere. He doesn't talk about it with me, but somewhere for a long time. I'll stay in his apartment until he returns."

Nasr cannot shake the look of surprise until he laughs and points a finger at the ceiling. "This is the work of the All-Powerful One! I'm telling you, it's kismet. Your destiny. Are the two of you—you know?"

Syhala should be embarrassed by the question, but she is not. "Uncle! Of course not, but I would say yes if he asked me to marry. He's such a kind, good-hearted man. He makes a good living as a pilot. I think we could be happy together."

"Then, my dear, I am happy for you. If your father were alive, he'd be happy for you, too."

"Thank you, uncle," Syhala replies with genuine sincerity.

"Let me tell you something else," Nasr says, placing the box on a small wooden table and touching her cheek. "In the eyes of the Compassionate One, you are already together. Believe that. I believe it. Allah has brought two of his children together."

Two days later, Syhala moves into Khan's apartment. Captain Khan, delighted, finds he can whisper her name and derive joy from the mere recall of her face as he plots various routes on his flight simulator, no matter how exhausted he is. Khan is tired from his most recent airline trip to Beijing and back to Kuala Lumpur. It is his favorite route, but extracurricular activities have him questioning the pace and trajectory of his life. He is most happy when he is home. The apartment is filled with the aromatic scents of cumin, cloves, and turmeric and the soothing melodic tones of soft singing as Syhala cuts vegetables and scrambles eggs in his kitchen.

Early this morning, she did laundry and went to the market. Nearly every night, she tells him how much she loves being with him as sleep comes. He'd never imagined a woman like Syhala would want to be with him, even given her desperate circumstances, but Nasr was right. Having a woman like Syhala at his side day and night, believing she is as excited to be with him as he is with her, renews his confidence and fulfills the Prophet's plan. He walks taller at work, can better focus on everything he does, and sees a brighter horizon. But it saddens Khan as he knows this could be short-lived. If only he'd found Syhala sooner, things would be different. He would have told Almudir no. He gazes at her in the kitchen and wonders if he should tell her about the mission. No, he thinks. Lovely as she is, she can't know his intentions. Khan thinks about Syhala all the time. He massaged his airline schedule so that he'd have a week at home before his next Beijing trip. Time with Syhala is all he can think about.

As Khan adjusts the controls at his flight simulator for another run, his body vibrates with desire. They pray, eat, and sleep together as of the night before, albeit without physical intimacy. Khan worries she is only doing this to repay his kindness, but her voice, touch, and heart are sincere. A substantial financial reward awaits, or so he's been promised. He's not explicitly asked Syhala to come with him, but she has spoken about their future using exclusive terms. Perhaps they can find peace in Lebanon or Morocco together. His heart says they will be together forever, but his rational thoughts cast doubt.

"My love," Syhala calls out from the kitchen. "Will you join me at the table or continue at the machine?"

"I'll be right there," Khan says and picks up the well-worn printout of his flight checklist. They express their gratitude to The Beneficent One for their meal and eat silently when seated. Their silence is not born of discomfort but an acknowledgment of compatibility. They seem made for each other.

After a lovely supper, Khan excuses himself to rehearse at his flight simulator, and Syhala takes an evening walk so he can concentrate. Even if he experiences confusion or distress during the upcoming mission, everything must proceed flawlessly. That can't happen unless he plans for and practices every possible scenario.

Checklists are a necessary crutch. To test his memory, he sets them aside and closes his eyes. Chair flying begins with a visualization of every meticulous detail. Pilots fly by imagination while preparing for demanding flights, and to help engrain every move into second nature, Khan verbalizes boarding the aircraft. "I follow a preflight routine. I arrive early, hand chocolates to the gate agent, board the aircraft, secure my roller-board, and place my overnight bag in the space between my seat and the left bulkhead.

"I inspect the interior moving forward to aft. The catering truck arrives to replenish the galleys. A maintenance worker in uniform enters through the ramp rather than the jet bridge. He'll carry paperwork, but I only pretend to sign. He'll have replacement fire extinguishers, a small device, and a modified atomizer with a powerful but harmless liquid. I carefully pocket the device, and in the presence of flight attendants and any ground crew onboard, I approve of swapping out the extinguishers by pretending to sign a second document. I say, "Safety first." I pocket the pen.

"As the maintenance worker replaces the extinguishers, I distract the flight attendants with small talk and only return to the flight deck when he's gone. The First Officer and I execute preflight flows—before-push, start, after-start, and before-takeoff checklists."

Khan reminds himself that routine is necessary. It calms the mind, which is what flying is all about."

Listening for Shyala's return and hearing only silence, he mentally imagines the next steps. *We depart, engage the autopilot, and I suggest the First Officer take a break at the proper coordinates, which will coincide with our top-of-climb.*

Khan reviews his checklist. *No, I order the break, and while the First Officer is locked out and the flight attendant trades places, I announce that we are cruising at 37,000 feet and traveling on schedule. 15 seconds later, I must trigger an alarm by conducting an APU fire test. The flight attendant will not know what I'm doing but will be startled. I start the timer, put on my mask, and pretend to grab a mask for the flight attendant. I look concerned. Although not deadly, the chemical is powerful and will render me unconscious for hours if my mask is not secure.*

I hold the atomizer in my left palm and speak to the flight attendant through my oxygen mask. Because it's difficult to hear me, the flight attendant naturally leans in closer, and that is when I spray.

The announcement of reaching 37,000 feet signals Almudir's men to render the passengers unconscious. I wait two minutes, and if I have not heard the knocking pattern on my door, I decompress the cabin. Khan opens his eyes with the same dismay when first receiving the plan. He sets his checklist aside and shakes his head. Aloud, he says, "I can't do that. All those people!"

Khan focuses on a more positive outcome. *I'll hear four knocks at my door telling me the passengers are subdued. I start a rapid descent, then disable ACARS and the transponder while Almudir's men pull the circuit breakers for the satellite data unit, making my plane virtually invisible to air traffic control radars. Tracking systems will make the controllers believe we went down in the ocean. A Mayday call will reinforce the misdirection. After descending, I level off and fly the route that raises the least suspicion.*

Khan has finally memorized the procedures. Returning to the controls of his simulator, he rehearses the predetermined route toward the island destination. Khan's concentration breaks as Syhala returns from her walk. She is careful not to disturb him. He watches her move toward the bedroom, refocuses, and then practices this sequence several more times before joining her in bed.

Chapter 31

April 4

It's been two glorious weeks for Captain Khan and Syhala. During that time, he flew one Beijing trip for Inter-Asian Airways, but it was a perfect opportunity for a dry run. He spent the rest of the time in the apartment, practicing his flight or delighting Syhala's passion.

They stay in bed longer than usual, entangled in each other's arms. Syhala massages Khan's neck, whispering how grateful she is that they met, worried that this could be their last day together. Khan kisses her neck. Rising to a seated position and touching Syhala's shoulder, he says. "There are risks with every flight, this time more than any, but I deeply care for you so please listen to what I'm about to say." His eyes moisten as he continues. "Even if something happens, you will be taken care of. That is my promise."

Syhala is surprised. "Don't say such things. Nothing will happen. We will be together soon and go someplace far from here. That is our plan. That is our destiny," she says as they embrace.

Mundane thoughts and actions break up Khan's day at the flight simulator. Does he want lamb or hummus for lunch? Should he get gasoline for the car now or on the way to the airport? He'd planned to replace the kitchen faucet, but the replacement sits unboxed beneath the sink.

Before leaving for the airport, Khan gathers his belongings and gives his apartment one last look. His farewell to Syhala is difficult, but he mustn't waiver. If he does his part perfectly and the men in the passenger compartment do theirs, he and Syhala might be together again within a few days. He tenderly kisses Syhala. "I need to apologize because I've kept some things from you."

Concern floods Syhala's face as Khan hands her a piece of paper. "I said you can stay here, but that won't be safe. When I'm gone, remove anything that might link you to this place and to me, and go to the address on that note. Omar prepared everything for you. The rent is paid for many months. It can be your apartment for as long as needed, even if you change your mind about joining me."

"You're frightening me," Syhala says, puzzled by the turn of events. "You know I will do whatever you ask, but don't talk like that. We will be together soon. I believe it."

Shortly after sunset, Syhala accompanies Khan to his car. They are both emotionally drained and already living in the future. They embrace as if Khan were leaving for another day of work. He starts the engine, pulls into traffic, and brings his full attention to the mission.

Khan leaves his car in the employee lot for the last time and follows his routine—stopping for coffee, buying multiple bags of chocolate, and then walking to his gate.

Aisha will be the First Officer tonight. It bothers Khan intensely that she will be drawn into this betrayal, but he's trained incessantly for this possibility. Routine is his friend. He smiles and makes jokes while greeting her.

Captain Khan and Aisha check the flight plan on their iPads. Khan smiles. His dispatcher added extra fuel for the trip to Beijing. Captain Khan adds even more fuel to the legal limit, as he customarily does, then signs off on the flight plan. He chats with the customer service representatives and flight attendants gathering near the gate, creating a sense of normalcy. He hands out chocolate before taking the jet bridge to the plane.

As planned, he conducts his walk-through, taking his time until a maintenance technician arrives to swap out the fire extinguishers. The man's paperwork is a blur, but he signs it as flight attendants prepare the forward and aft galleys for flight.

Captain Khan hoped the First Officer would be a stranger. Aisha will be frightened by what happens, but he tells himself she will be released soon after the event. He takes comfort in the thought that she will be celebrated for her bravery when this is all over.

Inter-Asian Flight 957 lifts off Kuala Lumpur's runway 32 at midnight on April 5th and starts a lazy right-hand turn to the northeast over the South China Sea. Captain Khan and First Officer Aisha follow their routines to altitude. As rehearsed repeatedly, Khan calls the flight attendant via the intercom to arrange a bathroom break. When the flight attendant enters, Aisha leaves.

Khan triggers an alarm designed to frighten the flight attendant. A fire test on the Auxiliary Power Unit brings multiple red flashing lights to life, and his look of concern causes the young flight attendant to panic. Acting confused and afraid, he aggressively places an oxygen mask over his face while subtly palming an atomizer. He gestures wildly that the flight attendant should come closer, but he is intentionally unintelligible, causing her to lean into him for clarity. Khan clings to the front of her uniform as he sprays her face multiple times. She struggles at first but quickly falls to a knee, clinging momentarily to the armrest of his chair, face stricken in pain and panic. She struggles for breath. Her eyes water, lips quiver, and hands tremble with instantaneous fatigue.

Khan is alarmed by the flight attendant's reaction to the atomizer but remains focused. He disengages the autopilot and makes a public announcement, telling passengers that they have reached their altitude of 37,000 feet and should remain seated. He gives them basic flight information, then taps his clock and waits for Almudir's men to do whatever it takes to subdue the passengers.

Khan has tried on dozens of occasions to imagine how subduing the passengers is even possible. It took only three sprays for the flight attendant to slump on the floor between seats. If there is a gas potent enough to subdue all the passengers on this large aircraft, it must be a banned military-grade substance. The fire extinguishers the mechanic brought must all carry the same pressurized gas as his atomizer.

But as he glances down again, the flight attendant on the floor next to him doesn't look quite right. He wants to check her breathing and help, but a misstep in attention now could jeopardize the entire mission, so he turns away.

Captain Khan hears muffled but intense yelling and pounding at his door. He fights an urge to open the door and bring Aisha into the flight deck, but the mayhem lessens, pounding stops, and an uncomfortable silence follows. The door remains locked. Forty seconds tick by on his timer, then sixty. As instructed, he prepares to decompress the plane but knows he won't do it. Rows and rows of innocent people are onboard, many of them women and children. Eighty seconds, eighty-five—Khan's hands hover over the decompression controls, but he can't do it. He cannot deliberately kill everyone on board and has never considered what will happen next. Does he continue the mission? Will the passengers awaken and gain control of the plane? His mind feels numb, and his fingers tingle as he resigns to the fact that he failed. As his mind cycles through images of what he should do next, he is startled to attention by loud pounding on his door. The pattern of someone's striking repeats—four strikes, then four strikes again. They've done it!

Relieved, Captain Khan pulls the throttles to idle power, manipulates the yoke, and starts a very aggressive dive towards the ocean below—5,000, 10,000, 15,000 feet per minute, rapidly accelerating airspeed. He makes a panicked Mayday call for good measure.

"Mayday. Mayday. Mayday. Inter-Asian Flight 957 is experiencing a fire on board. The aircraft is full of—"

Captain Khan cuts off his transmission and then gets to work. He quickly disables all the tracking systems on the flight deck while closely monitoring the flight path. The aircraft becomes virtually invisible to commercial radar systems. Military early warning radar systems could be a problem, but his route will go unnoticed, at least for now. With communications disabled and radar mostly defeated, he sends the plane downward in as close to a vertical path as possible. He's only ever done this maneuver in fighter aircraft, sleek machines engineered for speeds above Mach 2, so as he descends, alarms sound.

The altimeter unwinds quickly as the Boeing 777-200 dives. Accelerating, he picks up speed—30,000 feet, then 20,000. The plane shudders during the maneuver, but Khan has done the research. He tested the limits on simulators and did not decrease speed until 10,000 feet, gradually leveling the aircraft into a horizontal trajectory less than a thousand feet above the ocean's surface. Khan knows this is where everyone will think the plane went down.

Everything is silent now, except for the hum of jet engines and wind against the fuselage. The men must have done their job with utmost efficiency. He pulls a printout of the new flight plan from his pocket and replaces the coordinates with those tested on his simulator. When complete, he turns on the autopilot.

Oceanic control begs for a reply, but Khan ignores their pleas.

As pre-dawn light begins to illuminate the horizon, Khan spots the island. The landing strip is a thin ribbon of road partially engulfed by a lifting fog. Visibility is perfect. His weather forecasting was spot on. As planned, he circles the island once to alert men on the ground before approaching. Below, he sees activity clustered around a bulldozer at the upper end of the improvised runway. Even a tiny error now could send him into the mountainside, potentially killing him and everyone on board.

Captain Khan begins slowing his aircraft while extending initial flaps, then starts a 180-degree turn to align himself with the runway. Thankful this is not the first time he has landed on the island; he slows to approach speed as he puts the landing gear down, followed by final flaps, putting the 777 in the proper landing configuration. There will be a four-mile straightaway. Captain Khan carefully watches his radar altimeter at 1,200 feet above the ocean, then methodically descends 300 feet per mile, slowing speed to 180 knots, then 150, until he touches down nearly at the harbor and brakes hard. After leaving the paved runway, the aircraft struggles for traction, bouncing on uneven terrain, but stops uphill within yards of the waiting men and their bulldozer.

Khan fights to control his breathing, stands, looks into the dim morning light outside of the window to his left, and sees Nasr urgently waving for him to come out of the plane. His oxygen mask obscures details, but he sees men on the ground applaud his success.

Khan quickly goes through the checklist for after landing and shut-down. He takes as deep a breath as his mask allows, then disconnects the hose so he can exit the cock pit, pinching the end of the hose as he moves. He encounters Aisha's collapsed body at the base of the flight deck door, and seeing her causes him to freeze. His instinct is to assess what happened, but the need to breath forces Khan to step over her and move to the exit. As he does, he scans the cabin. The grey pallor of the passengers and their limp bodies, limbs askew, tell him that something is not right.

Panicked, he disarms the exit door and forces it open. As he leans out, he removes his mask and inhales fresh air before shouting, "Nasr! They're dead! They are all dead!"

"No, no. The passengers are only unconscious. Come down, quickly!" Nasr insists as men hoist a long ladder toward him. With its improvised tow bar in place, the bulldozer moves into position at the front of the aircraft.

Khan looks over his shoulder at the horrific scene, but Nasr insists that he climb down immediately. "Now! We need to hide the plane. Hurry," he shouts, and Khan does as he's told.

At the bottom of the ladder, Nasr takes Khan's arm and leads him away as men in gas masks rapidly climb the ladder. "You have done a good thing. Very good, but we need to hurry. Come with me."

Khan feels lightheaded and nauseous, but they sit in a golf cart as the bulldozer pushes the plane back down the road toward the harbor and processing plant. Nasr drives Khan uphill toward the cabins, chattering about how well Khan has done, but Khan doesn't listen. Images of Aisha's body and the flight attendant's panicked face haunt him.

When they arrive, Almudir greets him with a hug and a kiss on both cheeks. Almudir has celebratory words for the captain as he offers tea and dates. Khan is weak. The thought of eating nauseates him, and he struggles to steady his legs. Almudir and Nasr sit on the lanai, watching the plane back into the hangar. The façade then closes around the fuselage, rendering it invisible to passing aircraft and satellites.

Unlike Khan, Almudir and Nasr are gleeful. They congratulate him and each other on pulling off something of this magnitude. A radio on a nearby table tells them that various search and rescue operations are underway. Almudir responds to one of Nasr's questions by saying they have all the debris they need. Khan is about to ask questions but instead forces himself to stand. "I need to check on my copilot."

"He's okay. Don't worry," Nasr says.

"Her, a woman," Khan says. "Her name is Aisha."

"Sit!" Almudir says. His tone is abrupt.

Nasr interjects. "Don't worry. I'll call in a minute or two. Please sit."

Khan sits. Nasr reaches for a two-way radio and calls. Within a few seconds, someone answers, and Nasr asks for the condition of the copilot. Moments later, the respondent says she is coming around and okay. "See there?" Nasr says. "She's fine, as are the other passengers. You did very well."

Khan is still visibly upset. "They all looked dead!"

Nasr says, "You are mistaken. It was only a strong sleeping gas. Even our men who were with you are asleep. Everything is going to plan. We will load them into the boats and bring them to safety when it is dark. They will be released once your mission is complete. You're going to be a very famous man, Captain. Those you care about most will be taken care of."

"And Syhala? She will be taken care of?"

A wry smile creases Almudir's lips while observing the exchange. Nasr quickly speaks. "Yes, yes. Your cousin Omar will see to her needs. Rest now. Have some tea. It will make you feel better."

As the two men sip tea and eat dates, Khan does not partake. The radio chatter continues. Nasr must detect doubt in Captain Khan's face. "You look tired, my friend. I'll show you where you can rest. The three of us can discuss what comes next at a later time."

"Next, I get paid," Khan says.

"Of course. You get paid, and we fly you anywhere you want to go. Now, though, you rest."

Chapter 32

April 5

Yin picks a place and time. The protocol now is that she travels along surveillance detection routes. The SDRs are relayed from Nigel to Yin, and she uses the route he gives her. Nigel explained in their last meeting that he has called in personal favors for countersurveillance during these rides. The primary job of his friends is to ensure they pick up any tail following Yin. They've also begun electronic surveillance of the routes, and though Yin is displeased, she assumes they are also watching the data center. She wouldn't be surprised if the man now renting the apartment across from hers is one of their technicians.

As Yin travels, she knows that Australian officers are stationed at various positions along her route. It's something of a game for her to identify these men and women, but so far, she has been unable. Either they are very good, or Nigel's resources are extremely limited.

"Recognize this name?" Nigel asks, pushing a scrap of paper across the table. They sit in the back room of a small family restaurant surrounded by empty tables.

The only name on the paper is Muhammad Ulul Khan. "If you're asking if I recognize him from the list, no. You already know that he is not. Who is he?"

"If you don't recognize the name, it doesn't matter. Let me know if it comes across your desk. Meanwhile, I need the information on their money card controller. You said—"

"I'm trying," Yin snaps, cutting him off in mid-sentence. She's angrier with herself than Nigel, but not because he is insistent. She's frustrated that she took on a task she's not yet willing or able to complete. Continuing, she says, "Sorry. I am trying. I don't think even Bao knows. Tu, maybe, but I doubt it. Who is Khan? Do you think he might be the controller?"

"Let's just drop it, Yin Yin. I'm just frustrated. You're doing your best."

Yin raises an eyebrow. "You called me Yin Yin."

"Did I?" Nigel says, looking embarrassed for revealing something akin to intent.

"I haven't been called Yin Yin for many years. I like it," Yin says, laughing.

"I worry about you sometimes. Maybe I could send a clandestine team into the building during the night? You could disable the alarm system before going home. We'll show you how, and no one inside will ever know you were involved."

Yin looks at Nigel disapprovingly. "First, there are cameras and motion sensors throughout the facility. The server room has an extra layer of physical security, and even if you could get through without proper credentials, anyone attempting unauthorized entry will trigger a kill switch. Should I go on?"

"Who handles backups?"

"The techs I told you about would know. Look for two Middle Eastern-looking guys in T-shirts. One has a long beard, the other a shaved head. The shaved-head guy carries a backpack in and out of the building, but it will be encrypted if they carry an external hard drive."

Nigel takes notes. "And these are the only guys with access? What about Bao? He's a hacker and was trained by some of the best in China."

"I told you not to poke around. He's very good at detecting things like that."

Nigel laughs. "We've had an eye on this character for a long time. He disappeared for a while, but here he is again, right in the heart of more nasty business. He worked for MSS right out of college. You didn't know that?"

Yin is skeptical that Nigel followed Bao before this year. Lying, Yin says, "No. I only suspected. I know he spent a lot of time in Silicon Valley. Is he still with them?"

"An agency friend says he couldn't handle the discipline and went rogue, but he has access to those servers, correct?" Nigel asks expectantly.

"He and the techs have physical access. Tu has a login, so he has remote access to select segments at minimum," Yin answers.

"You mentioned Tu before, and we're working on him, but it's hard to get intel out of China. You asked what I'd like you to do. Ask Bao if there are new names for the list. If not, tell him there was a mistake and resubmit. We're better positioned now to see traffic flowing in and out. It's a busy place."

Yin laughs. "You're investigating Bao's smokescreen. There's close to a petabyte of random information sitting in an Apache Hadoop structure. He's got thousands of active nodes, but it's just fluff. We move terabytes of data through Fiber Channel every hour to keep up appearances, so don't waste your time and resources hammering away at the big data. Have you noticed those for lease signs at the end of the building? It's a ruse. Bao has another set of servers in there, I believe. Much of what matters is done on a separate network, maybe there, on a rack in Europe, for all I know. He has tripwires everywhere. You're suggesting we attack a digital fortress. Are you familiar with ZTNA, zero trust network access? Never mind. I'm not saying we can't get some of what you want, but you'll get nothing without a guide or roadmap."

"You can do that? Are you willing?" Nigel asks impatiently, trying to keep up.

"It would be very dangerous," Yin snaps. "Any attack must come from outside, perhaps from law enforcement or an intelligence agency."

"If it's too dangerous for you, then it's out of the question, but it's possible for someone with your skill level. Correct?"

Yin can no longer hide her disappointment.

"What?"

"You don't seem suited for this work," she says in a matter-of-fact manner.

"Wow! I suck at my job. Please don't tell my mother," Nigel says, using humor to mask what is obvious to Yin. Nigel feels inadequate when it comes to digital security.

Yin touches his hand. "That's not what I'm saying. Not at all. You're great at your job but also a kind and honest man. A harder person in your position wouldn't take no for an answer. He'd force me to be the guide without thinking twice about my safety. I meant that maybe if you'd chosen a different career path, you would be happier."

Nigel appears shocked. "The elders do that. They call it soul gazing. You pluck overarching truths from the middle of a mundane conversation. I often think I should have become a simple fisherman and invested in a boat to work with my father. I miss—" he says and turns away before completing the sentence.

"Please don't hide who you are. When our parents and brother were killed in a car accident, I assumed the responsibilities of parenting. I thought I had to change into someone else to do that. Li stayed true to who she was and is. She's gentle, innocent, intelligent, and kind like you. Is Essex like that? Does anyone above you act like that? No, but look who's giving advice. I'm barely treading water, sinking into the dark shadows of the criminal underworld, and pretending I know what is best for you. Let me rephrase the response to your question. Can I be the guide or create a roadmap? The answer is yes, but the attack must appear to have come from outside. Connect me with your network engineers, and maybe we can come up with something. You could still become a fisherman one day."

Nigel laughs. "Forgive the pun, but I think that ship has sailed. My parents are getting older, though, and could use my support. When we wrap up this case, I'm requesting a sabbatical." Nigel's voice trails off, staring into a distant corner of the room.

"I hope it works out for you. Should we talk with your engineers?" Yin asks nudging Nigel back on track.

"I get it that the techs where you work are top notch, but we have very talented people. What makes you think they can't succeed without insider help?"

"In a word? Nicolay. There's nobody better at penetrating hardened digital networks. Knowing how to defeat systems tells you a lot about how to create them. Think like a gamer. You get through what you think is the firewall and find yourself in a room. Do you pick door one, two, or three? If you know to select door three, you enter a stairwell. Do you go up ten floors or down twenty? If you pick the right floor, you're in a lobby being questioned by a virtual receptionist, and on it goes until you win the game. However, a wrong answer triggers an alarm at every step, and you are sent back to the beginning. Meanwhile, Nick and Bao know you are there. They can watch every move you make. Security firms run challenges like this all the time. They open certain doors to fool you. If you make it three or four levels deep, they gather around a console somewhere and take bets on whether you can reach level five. In this case, it's not a game. Nick or Bao will come in behind you and game over."

"There must be a back door. You said it yourself. Bao thinks he's smarter than everyone," Nigel says confidently. It's as if he's entered the game for the first time.

"Maybe. We're nearly out of time. When can I meet your experts?"

"Let's do it. Let's do it right now. Let me make a phone call, and we'll go there together." Nigel smiles.

An hour later, after a lengthy, random SDR in Nigel's car, they pull into an alley in the Katong neighborhood and climb a narrow, dusty flight of stairs at the back of a historical building. Yin is introduced to Justin Wright, an African American who claims to work for the US State Department. He's accompanied by a wiry man from Noida, India, who went to the United States to complete his education. His name is Laksh.

Mr. Wright claims they are in Laksh's apartment, which seems unlikely. Except for a small sofa and the table, they sit at, the room is unfurnished, leading Yin to believe these men are as cautious around her as she is. "Where in the US?" Yin asks Laksh.

"University of Michigan and MIT," Laksh says.

"So, you know MIT's Executive Director for Computer Science. What was her name, Margo, Marjorie?" Yin says, deliberately confused.

"You mean Margaret? How do you know her?" Laksh asks excitedly. Yin feels an immediate kinship with Laksh, her trust strengthened by the fact that Laksh really did go to MIT.

"That's right, Margaret. Director Buchannan offered me a fellowship, but I had to turn them down."

"You should have gone! I'd like to hear about it, maybe compare notes, but let's get to it. Tell us about their systems."

Nigel and Justin do their best to follow the conversation for a few minutes, then step away to talk business. In the adjoining room. Wright gives Nigel a look.

"Stop it. She's an informant. Nothing's going on, so knock it off," Nigel says.

"The picture you sent was hot, but wow. There are two of them? I see how she might cloud your judgment," Wright warns, arms crossed, a wry smile on his face.

"You know what, you're an embarrassment sometimes. You really are."

"Me? I'm just saying be careful. The initial background check shows a connection with Chinese intelligence, and that's just what we found on the first pass. What did you think I was saying?" Wright asks.

"To be clear, Yin isn't asking for information. She's volunteering it. The missing sister is also legitimate, so there. By the way, thanks for the help."

"What can I say? I love steak." Wright says, eyes locked on the woman across the room.

• • •

After a half-hour of brainstorming, Laksh calls Rainer and Wright back to the table. "I'm sorry to report that we would need physical access and a lot of time to get everything you need out of the systems. Yin understands the problem very well."

"No way to hack in?" Nigel says. It's not a question as much as a moment of resignation.

"They would definitely know," Laksh replies.

"But it's possible," Nigel repeats.

Yin answers. "Getting information may not be the reason we go in. With a series of exploits, Laksh and I think it's possible to harvest a few files before being booted. I can't say what happens next, but they won't trash the servers if the attack is defeated quickly and critical data isn't compromised."

"Then why bother?" Nigel says in frustration. "There's no point if we can't get anything of value."

"Anything useful in breaching the firewall would probably come from an administrator. Am I right? They might figure out that Yin was involved. It's too dangerous," Wright says, surprising Nigel.

Yin is impressed with the observation, though she doesn't think for a second that Wright is concerned for her safety. She says, "Think of this as part one of a multi-part attack. I can observe Bao's reactions when Laksh goes in. The alert will come to his wristwatch. He'll log in to get details. It's possible I'll catch his password. Anyone can slip up while in panic mode, and Laksh says you guys have ways of capturing fingerprints. Maybe we can spoof his biometrics?"

Nigel is about to speak to that when Wright pulls him aside. "You haven't kicked this up the ladder, brother. Shit goes south, you go with it."

"I'm hoping you get authorization for this one. We both have skin in this game."

"She's your asset. We don't even know what's on those servers, man. I can't sanction a blind witch hunt," Wright says bluntly.

"She's our asset, not just mine," Nigel insists. We ask about the files and tell her what we want done."

"You're going to owe me at least twenty meals before this is over."

"And 36 holes of golf, but who's counting? What do you say? I need your help," Nigel pleads.

• • •

Yin studies body language from across the room and interrupts their conversation by calling out to them. "You two done telling secrets?"

Nigel looks to Wright. His hopes are confirmed as Wright turns towards Yin and says, "Before we go any further, you need to come clean on those files."

Yin looks at Nigel for help, but Nigel shrugs his shoulders. Yin is visibly disappointed in him. She leans back in her chair, crosses her legs, and gestures for Wright to sit. "First thing, I trade information for help with finding my sister. Full stop."

Wright sneers at her attempt to exert control and remains on his feet. "You don't call the shots here, honey—"

"Then we have nothing to discuss, honey," Yin snaps.

The staring contest lasts ten seconds before Wright says, "I get it about your sister. I have a sister, too. I agreed to help Nigel when he brought this to us. You have my word that we are working on that."

Yin lets the comment about his word slide by and says, "Then you may as well sit, Justin Wright from the State Department. This could take a while."

• • •

After hours of plotting a digital attack on the data center, Yin is driven home and goes to the neighborhood bar for a nightcap. It's late. The stressful conversation they had with Wright at the safe house makes her wonder if she disclosed too much about her data center involvement. Maybe they are stringing her along hoping to keep information flowing.

She still can't tell if Wright believes her motives. There were tells in Wright's mannerisms. He loves control more than anything and cannot help but use his athletic frame to seduce. She is far from trusting him but is satisfied Li's rescuers have entered the game.

Now it's time to decompress. It's a Friday night, the night of the week she and Li often went out to unwind. If she could return to the last night, she and Li spent dancing, she'd force Li to come with her to Cambridge. It might have saved her from the abduction. The weight she carries seems unbearable at times. Her caged dragon within speaks to her in a whisper, yearning for release. She's done this before, sometimes actually to enjoy some wine, twice in seductive clothing, hoping for something intimate. She doesn't know what she wants tonight except to be distracted and driven far away from her thoughts. It's no use. As much as she tries to free her mind, fantasy and reality collide.

She's imagined having someone snatch Bao off the street, restrain him in a soundproof room so she could interrogate the weasel, but Bao is being used just like the rest of them. He may not know where Li is, but he has leverageable information. Bao is weak to his core. A few hours alone with someone like Wright and he'd crack, but in what ways? If he fears prison more than the Triads, he will give them everything, but they are resourceful. It seems they can get to anyone anytime, a fact Bao emphasized repeatedly. He may fear the Triads more than the CIA.

Yin feels compelled to stick with Bao, the Australians, and even the CIA long enough to find Li and then vanish. She often imagines stealing money from the Triads so that she and her sister could disappear for a long while, and as she orders her second glass of wine, she admits to thinking too often this evening about Wright. She's seen men like him in American movies—confident, defiant, muscular, and mysterious. If she ever did connect with him on a sexual level, it would be an entirely different and possibly amazing experience. Recalling her nights on the town with Li, she smiles. Yes. If we ever hooked up, it would be a Friday night.

A TV above the bar draws Yin's attention away from her fantasies, showing images of debris scattered in the ocean. A header travels across the screen reading, *Debris field has been located from Inter-Asian Flight 957 in the South China Sea.*" Yin wonders.

An older Anglo woman interrupts Yin's thoughts by sitting beside her at the otherwise empty bar. She also orders wine, and they talk briefly about visiting the sights of Singapore as strangers often do. Yin sees the woman deliberately slip a small envelope under her napkin. Two minutes later, the woman's friend enters the bar. She momentarily places her hand on the napkin, taps her fingers a few times, saying she hopes Yin has a great evening, and then leaves.

When the bartender is distracted, Yin takes in her surroundings. The bar is nearly empty, and no one seems interested in her being there. She discretely slides the napkin in her direction and recovers the small envelope—her heart rate quickens.

• • •

When Yin returns to her apartment, she opens the envelope to find a pad of adhesive strips and a miniature camera with a microphone. Instructions show how to use the adhesive to capture the residue of fingerprints from smooth surfaces, and she presses her thumb into the side of a coffee cup. Her fingerprint is copied to the clear strip. Placing it on a dark surface makes the fingerprint even more visible.

The camera with a microphone was designed as a man's tie pin. Yin is unsure how to use it and conflicted over whether she should even try. Bao often brags about the radio frequency and spectrum analysis countermeasures installed in the data center. A note in the envelope shows that she's not the only one concerned. It reads: *This was the only option available on quick notice. Be careful.*

The device is little more than a small black orb with a metal stem connecting it to a coin-sized clasp behind clothing. Pressing the orb toggles the camera on, and pressing it again toggles it off. Given the device's size, color, and shape, Yin has the precise outfit to mask its visual presence, but the electronics are dangerous.

Chapter 33

April 6

Captain Khan jolts from a dead sleep into frightened consciousness—sweating, throbbing headache, and shortness of breath. He is on a cot in one of the island dwellings, and as he calms slightly, his eyes remain wide with fear from images of the flight attendant, his First Officer, and all those lifeless passengers sprawled in their seats on the plane. "It was a dream," he mumbles, but the realization doesn't comfort him. The horror he experienced in real life was not a dream—and it will stay with him forever.

"They're all dead!" he says aloud, but there is no one present to hear. In the aftermath of his dreams, he's convinced Nasr lied. There must have been a miscalculation with the gas mixture, or maybe they planned to kill everyone onboard all along.

Conflicting memories claw for attention. The plane was maneuvered into the improvised hanger. He'd sat for a long while with Almudir and Nasr on the big-house veranda, listening to chatter between search and rescue operations and scanning different frequencies for any indication that authorities knew where they were. When one of the search planes reported seeing debris on the ocean surface near where they lost contact with his flight, Almudir was exuberant.

Now, Khan sits upright in a dark room lit only by dim light emanating through louvered window shutters. He hears the hum of a refrigerator and slowly rises onto unsteady legs.

Khan's wristwatch says it is three am. He's been sleeping for five hours and still feels incredibly weak and tired, but his nausea has subsided. He drinks a bottle of water while standing in the light of the refrigerator's open door, then takes a second bottle with him out of the hut and into a cooling breeze that rises from the harbor below. As Khan relieves his bladder, he feels like walking.

The bulldozer he'd seen earlier is at work somewhere in the distance, and there is activity near the hanger. Perhaps Nasr was right. Perhaps they are moving the passengers now, loading boats to take them away in the cover of darkness. He feels compelled to talk with Aisha and somehow explain his actions, so he follows the road downhill toward the hangar, the harbor, and the activity.

As the hangar comes into view, he falls to his knees. Workers haul bodies from the hangar onto a flatbed trailer and an array of carts. The realization of what he's done, how he was duped into this evil, is seared into his mind. Taking a plane is one thing, but killing over 300 passengers and crewmembers is quite another. What now? How could he have been so stupid and trusting? He thinks of Syhala and wishes to touch her, but she's far away.

Khan understood what Nasr asked of him and accepted that some passengers could be hurt. He'd been more than eager to bring the fight to the enemy, but not the indiscriminate murder of innocents. He would never have agreed. Hiding from view in bushes near the road, watching the scene below, he sees that the bodies are being moved to an open pit near the bulldozer while others are being taken towards the dock.

Khan wants to yell, protest, and believe what he sees is unreal, but he can do nothing. He's been a fool. He agreed to hijack the plane. He agreed to train pilots willing to martyr themselves in that plane, but Nasr and Almudir lied to him. There was no miscalculation. They planned to slaughter the passengers from the start. What else have they planned from the start?

Stricken by shame and anger, Captain Khan observes from the shadows for a long while before returning to his hut. What will happen to me now? He alternatively paces in the small hut and lies on his cot in the predawn light. He hasn't yet been paid. He fears for both Syhala and Omar. They know too much. He tells himself he'll say no if asked to do anything else. He needs to reestablish control. They can't move forward with their plans without him. After pacing, tossing, and turning, he finally returns to sleep.

"Wake up, my love."

Khan feels a hand on his shoulder, hears Syhala's voice, and opens his eyes to see her leaning into him, touching his brow, and smoothing his hair.

"They're all dead," he says.

"I know. Uncle says it was a mistake. Something about the gas. It's not your fault, but I'm so proud of you. I'll see you soon."

Khan closes his eyes for a moment, but upon reopening them, she's gone.

Chapter 34

April 6

After receiving the camera and fingerprint strips, Yin got very little sleep. She gets out of bed for an hour to use her surveillance wand. She wands the walls, floor, and ceilings in near total darkness, spending extra time on light fixtures and near sitting areas. She moves slowly to be sure she's looked everywhere and feels confident when done. There are no listening devices. The activity calms her temporarily, but hypervigilance continues. She imagines standing over Bao's shoulder when Laksh and his team attack the data center, activating the camera during the few seconds he logs into the network and turning the camera off just in time, but she's never had the opportunity to stand behind an accomplished technologist during a login. It's not done. She imagines being caught and wonders if it would be Bao himself, or maybe Nicolay, who grabs her. Probably Nicolay. She returns to bed and eventually dozes, but even in sleep, her problems oscillate between hope and anxiety.

Yin, Nicolay, Peter, and Bao work seven days each week, but having gotten the center up to speed, Saturday and Sunday mornings are free. Yin rises in exhaustion and prepares, but she has a plan, and the first step in the plan is to confer with Laksh and three other cyber experts he's recruited to assist with the pending data center attack. At 8 am she executes another quick electronics sweep of her apartment then logs into secured communications provided by the CIA.

Continuing their earlier conversation, Yin shares information on server configurations and which segments may yield the most relevant information. Because access to folders is role-based, she lets them know which folders to explore first, encouraging them to hack one of her folders as a cover. Everyone in the data center can only see their own information and the relatively benign administrative information common across teams. In addition, Yin only has access to a project in which she works. Nicolay and Peter undoubtedly see other project folders, while Bao can access everything. Without sending any files, Yin has Laksh take screenshots of relevant information she's prepared. Secure Copy Protocol is used rather than SFTP to move information to remote locations, including Tu. She also shares the file settings she was exposed to during configuration.

Nigel is present in the meeting, though just an observer. Yin is his asset, but the subject matter is outside his expertise. His only input is to lighten the atmosphere by telling a story, and his story endears him to Yin.

"Can you record video or send static images of the server room?" Laksh asks Yin.

Nigel responds for her. "No. I'm not sure seeing the equipment gives us an edge."

"It's all right, Nigel," Yin says. His overwhelming concern for her safety is obvious in how protective he is during the meeting, and she acknowledges his apprehensions. Yin then goes on to describe the equipment behind glass walls in detail. Because Laksh asks, she describes how the software was configured during setup, all from memory.

As Laksh and his team talk offline, Yin watches Nigel watching her on the video display. She and he have both withheld information, her ensuring he is on the hook to find Li, him not discussing in any detail what his team or teams are doing about the Triads potential terror connection. She would do the exact same thing to protect critical information, and she knows he might hide information found about Li to keep her in the game.

"What are you thinking?" Yin asks.

"Honestly? I'm thinking how incredible your memory is. You rattled off operating system settings as if reciting a little poem."

Through their respective displays, Yin and Nigel gaze at each other. Yin smiles and touches her finger near the lens of her laptop camera. It takes Nigel a moment to understand, but he replies, their fingers touching in virtual space.

"You are right, you know," he says, breaking their silence. Their hands withdraw from the cameras.

"About what?"

"Everything probably, but specifically, I may be in the wrong profession. Last night, I dreamed of being on the water beneath a full moon. My father was putting out the nets."

"I'm glad for you. Last night, all I could see was me getting caught with a camera." For a flash, Yin's face hardens. It's only for a second, but the absolute outrage that someone would dare to take her sister, mixed with a commitment to wreak revenge, overtakes her. The transformation is physical—Nigel recoils.

"Are you okay?" he asks, but before she can answer, the techs return to the video.

"We have a plan. When do you want us to launch the attack?" Laksh asks.

"What exploits?" Yin asks. Laksh is unwilling to elaborate. Yin believes he works for the cybersecurity division of America's National Security Agency and not the CIA. If not him, then one or more of the other members of his team. That agency has a remarkable reputation for penetrating communications worldwide. She'll soon know if that expertise extends to networks hardened by hacking experts. Laksh terminates the video call, telling Yin they need time to plan but will get back to her.

•••

Trepidation has haunted Yin for weeks, surfacing in unexpected ways and with frightening, uncontrollable force. One minute, she's having a pleasant conversation with an old woman on her bus ride to work, and the next, she's rushing down the street, fists clenched, embroiled in an imaginary violent exchange with Li's captors. A persistent sense of foreboding has changed the pool of civility and restraint she always relied upon into bursts of anger and frustration. If she put her feelings into words, they would be laced with vitriol and despair.

Sitting on the edge of her bed, Yin realizes that her internal battle has little to do with an enemy. Fight, Flight, or Fold does not apply in the same ways she expects. She can't attack, fleeing would mean giving up on her hunt for Li, and if she allows fear to cripple her, she fails. Failing is not an option for the dragon inside her.

Rising to dress, Yin consciously decides to exact revenge. The emotional shift surprises her. Thoughts of revenge calm her emotions. She is no longer angry and frightened, just determined. Rationally, she risks everything by attempting to record information in the data center, yet she no longer recoils from the specter of being caught.

An app on her phone sounds. It's Laksh. "We're ready for the party on our end. Still coming?"

Yin is momentarily off guard, wondering why Laksh would call about a party, but of course. He's coding his speech in case of surveillance. She says, "We can talk freely. I just did a bug sweep. I'll try to catch him alone in his office, between 1 and 2 pm. When you see me online, work fast. I'm going to log into your portal and video conference. I'll need you to share your screen."

Yin logs into Laksh's secure portal and brings her laptop into the bathroom of her apartment. She wears one of Li's favorite nightlife outfits and gazes into the mirror with her laptop balanced on the sink. The camera orb outside her dress is virtually undetectable, hidden in clusters of black sequins. When she sees the image of her own laptop and apartment appear on Laksh's shared screen, she directs the wide-angled miniature camera by moving her shoulders left and right, up and down. She leans forward at the end of her experiment to record a video of the keypad. "Thank you, Laksh. Good luck to all of us." Yin toggles her miniature camera off as Laksh closes the connection.

Li wore a sleek outfit like this one the night she went missing, but when Yin packed for Singapore, this one was still in their closet. Anxious about what she will attempt, Yin lights incense. She bows at the shrine and laughs. "Demons don't light incense," she says aloud.

When Yin arrives at the data center, Bao has a coffee mug in hand. She's only waited for him to open the office once. He usually sleeps on the cot and nearly always heads into the bathroom with a toothbrush when she arrives, Today, he cat-whistles and calls out. "What up, girl? Looking righteous."

Yin laughs. "It's laundry day!"

If Laksh and the others were ready, getting him alone in his office now would be perfect, but it's not time. The office gradually fills, and Yin waits until lunch to make her rounds. She carries a tissue in one hand, her phone in the other, asking if anyone wants takeaway.

Her last stop is the server room, where the two technicians spend their time. She taps on the glass summoning one of the techs. When he opens the door she leans against the frame, pressing an adhesive strip onto the thumbprint door-lock device, and listens to the techs debate what to order for lunch. In the back of her mind, she wonders if the CIA will ever actually send someone through physical security measures, but it's not for her to decide.

After the takeaway is eaten, the afternoon continues, and Yin watches Bao's office, waiting for her opportunity. It comes when she sees him pick up the tennis ball from his desk. Between projects, he often squeezes it as if building muscle. Sometimes, he tosses it against the far wall and attempts to catch it on the rebound—game time. A wave of calm determination rushes over her as she enters.

"Can I have a minute?" Yin asks, standing in his door frame.

"Sure. Shut the door. What's up?" Bao says. Casually tapping her hidden camera into the on position, Yin approaches but doesn't sit. Instead, she rests against the corner of his desk. "I need advice."

"Whatever I can do."

"You may regret saying that, but I am getting nowhere hunting for Li."

Bao looks puzzled and says, "We agreed to keep that out of the office."

"I thought maybe you could ask Tu for help. Do you know the term Snakehead?" Yin asks.

Bao sets the tennis ball on his desktop and sends it rolling with the flick of a finger. "Jesus, Yin. Fuck of a big ask."

Carefully wording her reply, Yin says, "He seems to know a little about everything. I'm desperate. Maybe there's someone he knows that I could talk to?"

"I'm not saying give up or whatever, but she's been gone a long-ass time. Think! If you believe these guys had something to do with her abduction, which I do not, you're asking the bad guys to help." Bao's voice trails off, attempting to end the conversation by saying, "I'll think about it. That's all I can promise right now. How close were you two, really?" Bao asks, turning back to his laptop.

Yin wants to lash out. How can anyone be so callous and uncaring? "If she was your sister—" Yin says and is interrupted.

"But she's not. I don't want to be rude, but Tu has priorities, and your sister isn't one of them. Where are we on his projects?"

Yin is shocked that she didn't scream at Bao for speaking about Li that way, but she's being recorded. She talks about projects as if someone else does the work. Thankfully, before Bao can press for specific answers, his wristwatch beeps an alert. "Hold that thought," he says. Yin slides partially around the desk and leans forward to get a better camera angle as Bao taps a password into his laptop and presses his index finger onto a reader.

Algorithms monitor the network's entire attack surface, continually checking for anomalies. An anomalous event has triggered an alert. In her mind, Laksh hammers at his keyboard, grabbing as many files as possible. He'll have to act quickly, as specialized software is scouring event logs, comparing every entry to thousands of scenarios in a master database to see who or what is inappropriately accessing files.

Bao slaps the desktop with an open palm. "Fuck!" he says and jumps up from his chair to race toward the server room. Yin follows as Bao punches in a passcode and presses his thumb into the lock. She asks what she should do, but Bao doesn't acknowledge her.

"Disconnect from the Internet," Bao yells as he enters. As the two techs scramble toward the back of the racks, Bao tells Yin to bring Peter and Nicolay to his office. Yin's camera remains on.

By the time Bao returns to his office and closes his door, Nicolay has analyzed the attack. Rather than target the critical servers used to conduct business for the Triad, Laksh and his team conducted a broad probe of multiple networks, including Bao's smokescreen of a data center. As Bao and Nicolay begin digital forensics, Bao sends Peter to a neighboring business in the same building to see if their IT group has had issues.

When Peter returns, Yin realizes how carefully Laksh planned the attacks. "They got hit, too, but they're still scrambling to figure out what to do. Whoever it was probably hit the whole building." Attacking nearby businesses lessens the implications that whoever it was specifically targeted Bao's operation.

Within an hour, the story unfolds. Three attackers seemed to have hit them from Thailand, Bulgaria, and Australia, though none were trusted points of origin. Nicolay concludes that the last traceable block of IP addresses came from Australia. He recognizes one of the addresses from his penetration of a police station there while hunting for information on Chuanli and the other prisoners at Barwon Prison.

Bao paces in anxiety. "I don't fucking know if I should tell the big boss, or just restore our system with another layer of security."

"It won't look good if we try to tighten their security while we have a breach of our own," Yin says.

Bao rakes the palm of a hand across his forehead while apparently validating Yin's comment. He says, "They'd shut us down, so no. We don't say we were breached, just that the Australians tried. That's the right move. I'll have Tu tap in from a different machine. Nick can set it up while I make the call."

Nicolay leaves to modify security procedures. In addition to verifying the machine address of incoming devices and requiring the end user to enter a six-digit security code, they now require the authorized user to send a verifiable text message before attempting to log into the server.

Pacing behind a closed office door, Bao stares at the Inmarsat phone in an open desk drawer. Operational security dictates he only use this phone to call Tu at prescribed times. But this can't wait.

When Tu answers, he's gruff. "This is unscheduled. Is everything okay?"

"I need to talk to the man. It's important," Bao says.

"What for?"

"Listen, I don't want to explain this twice, so please. Just do it."

Moments later Dragonhead is on the line snapping at Bao, "What is so damn important—

Cutting off Dragonhead, Bao says, "Someone from Australia attempted to breach our firewall. They failed miserably, but I thought you should know."

A chilling silence follows. Bao says in a calm, measured voice, "They hit everyone in the building. It probably wasn't directed specifically at us."

Dragonhead won't have it. "Get things done and wrap it up. No more mistakes!"

The call ends abruptly, leaving Bao angry and with little choice in what he does next. Calling an old friend, he says, "How soon can we talk? I need your help."

Meanwhile, Yin goes to the women's bathroom and faces the mirror. "Are you still there? Get all of that? I need to know."

She receives a promotional message from a fake company touting a new financial instrument. Deleting the notification, she faces the mirror again and requests a meeting at 6 pm. This response takes longer but comes as another notification from a Foodies Singapore resource that she knows to be another of Nigel's deceptions. It informs her of happy hour specials at a restaurant near her apartment. Giving a thumbs up to the mirror, she toggles the camera to the off position. Just then, Yin receives another message on her phone. It's Haitao. She opens the message. It merely says, *Call as soon as you can. The police say they've reached a dead end.*

Yin knows leaving the data center right after the attack will look suspicious. Worried, she sends Haitao a message: *Can you text me? At work.*

His response leaves her dumbfounded. *The police say the city's CCTV servers went down explaining the abrupt ending to the last known whereabouts of Li.*

Chapter 35

April 6

Yin and Peter are sent home, leaving Bao and Nicolay to continue with forensics and security enhancements to the data center. Under other circumstances, Yin would be happy for the time away and looking forward to the large payment coming her way, but she's anxious to see the fallout of the attack, and she's experiencing a rush of conflicting emotions. As they leave, all Peter can talk about as they walk toward their bus stop is the pending bonus—how much he might get, what he'll do with all that money, and how he'll be so happy to get out of Singapore. "It's been stressful as hell, no?" he says.

Yin smiles, but she isn't thinking about money. Peter's banter doesn't require her to pay attention, and she may not even remember what he says. No matter how much she wants to, she can't tell Peter to shut up, that she can no longer listen to his dribble, or that she has far more serious things to consider. Her actions today positioned her squarely against Bao and the Triads. The Western Alliance intelligence communities know she is helping them, but she has a history with MSS. Finding Li through Bao's connection to the Triads has not panned out, and as they walk, a dreadful feeling of having gone too far takes over. If the Triads discover what she's done, no corner of the globe will be safe for her or anyone she knows, including Li.

Before calling Haitao, Yin wonders if she even needed to do what she did today. Maybe the police have found Li, and she won't have to do anything more in Singapore. There is only one way to find out, but Haitao doesn't answer. She leaves an urgent voice message and heads back to her apartment and notices what she perceives to be another tail.

Haitao finally returns Yin's call. Police discovered CCTV confirmation of Li leaving the club at 1:05 am. They know she boarded a bus at 1:17 am, transferred to a second bus at 1:42 am, but claim there is no additional footage.

"They think they were hacked," Haitao says. "How is any of this possible? Who would hack the police?" He asks rhetorically. Yin feels for him. He knows far less than she does. She can't say she's already seen all of it, including Li's exit from the bus near their home. The police would not give details explaining how the CCTV trail of Li abruptly ended before she departed that last bus. Yin has a short list of who may be responsible for the hack. She confesses that thread will only lead to some predetermined dead end and waste valuable time. Given everything that Yin has since encountered, she's not surprised. Her inner rage has matured—she's angrier about more than just Li's abduction now. It no longer matters how Li was taken, possibly not even by whom. What matters is where she is this minute.

The call with Haitao ends in the same way their other calls ended. Haitao will call if there is any news.

At 5:30, Yin begins the complicated routine of shaking surveillance. It starts with a taxi ride to the Paragon Shopping Centre mall. She's memorized the faces of those who have followed her and sees one of those faces in the reflection of a window. She eventually emerges from a side exit after moving in and out of stores. The driver waiting for her has logos prominently displayed in his windows, but he doesn't work for Uber. As he speeds away, Yin removes her miniature camera, places it in a small plastic box, and leaves it on the seat. The driver introduces himself as David, one of Wright's assistants. He seems chatty, but Yin refuses to engage him in conversation, except to say, "The CIA is chauffeuring me about? Things are looking up."

When they arrive, Nigel meets them behind the restaurant and accompanies Yin to sit at the back of the room. Wright stands as she arrives, and Yin recognizes two other faces from Nigel's team sitting at a nearby table, but they are true professionals and don't look up. She sits as Nigel slides a familiar sheet of paper her way. Two names have been circled. She slides the paper back towards Nigel. "They were on the list. What's up?"

Nigel's expression is grave. "Both these names were manifested on Inter-Asian 957. Our people should have more on their histories soon."

Yin's heart drops into the pit of her stomach. "Men on Bao's list were on the missing plane?" She asks as she rests her full weight on the table.

Nigel nods, and Yin feels somehow responsible. They may have intervened if she'd turned over information sooner, but she can do nothing now. She changes the subject. "Did you get what we need from the videos?"

"We didn't get much more than what you've already provided, but we have linked the data center to Triads and Triads to financing known terrorists. It will be easier to mobilize resources with those pieces in place, so the answer is yes, at least for now. Bao's reaction was telling. He knows things. Bao makes a call to the guy you know as Tu. Tu's boss was on the line, so we have solid actionable intel. They want Bao to wrap things up in a week. What do you think that means?" Nigel asks.

Yin chooses her words carefully. "You listened to Tu's side of the call? Be careful. You're not just surveilling them; Nick, Peter, and Bao are surveilling you. The data center is like an early warning system. I don't know how deep, but they are inside of law enforcement, ready to report the slightest hint of heightened activity."

"Which is why you didn't want us probing the center. We didn't," Nigel confirms.

"But you just admitted listening in on a phone conversation between Tu and Bao. If they catch on, we're done. Bao will move to deep cover," Yin says.

She occasionally glances at Wright, assessing his body language and trying to understand the dynamic between these two men. She's noticed the wandering eye she and Li laugh about and expects him to make flirtatious overtures at any moment, but how he looks at her now means something else. They've turned a corner, but in what direction?

Nigel says, "These guys are dangerous, Yin. I think it's time to pull you out of there."

Before Yin can respond, Officer Wright asserts himself. "There may actually be one more move. We're better positioned to warn you if they become suspicious, but it's up to you. Nigel is right. It's dangerous."

Turning on Nigel, Yin says, "I specifically demanded you not to spy on them, and you agreed."

Holding his hands up, Nigel says, "I honored that agreement. It wasn't me."

Yin's disappointment with Nigel is palpable. She deliberately looks from Nigel to Wright, who is clearly the man in charge.

"Here's how this works. If we have reason to suspect an individual, we go through channels, get authorization, and begin surveillance. The person this started with lives in the Middle East. We will eventually bring him in, but he is something of a hub. One of the people that contacts him, is Tu. We start surveillance of him, and as we said, Tu contacted Bao. We're aware of your situation, so we're holding off for the moment, but Nigel is correct. It wasn't him. No one has tapped Bao's phone. We didn't even know he was involved until we heard his voice on your recording."

Yin's leverage is slipping away. What new information can she possibly offer if she doesn't return? "I appreciate how dangerous it is, but I need a few more days to harvest financials. What files did you retrieve?"

Wright dismissively raises his arms. "We can't talk about any of that." Even Nigel seems surprised.

"Then we have nothing more to discuss," Yin says while standing in rage to leave. Her move startles one of the men in a nearby booth. He rises to intercept her, a move that speaks volumes.

"Wait," Nigel insists. He also stands.

Yin is desperate, frustrated, and furious. She nearly hisses at Nigel. "Go ahead. Grab me. I dare you. We had a deal. I help you, and you find Li. I've done everything you asked, and you've accomplished nothing. Just make sure I keep giving, right? That's it isn't it, no matter the risk." Her words cut Nigel deep.

"Sit. Sit down," Wright insists in a hushed but very firm tone. "We have information on Li, but damn it. Take a breath. No one is going to grab you. Sit."

Yin studies both men, Nigel looking defeated, Wright in a warrior's stance. Nigel pleads. "Please?"

Yin sits. "That should have been the first thing out of your mouths. I'm listening."

"She was smuggled to Cambodia, that much we know. At a minimum, we have a trail to follow," Wright says flatly.

Yin is flooded with conflicting emotions and still trembling from her near confrontation with these powerful men. She is also excited by the news of Li. Did Nigel withhold this information to keep her working? Did Wright? "How long have you known this?" she asks, directing her frustration this time at Wright. Her tone has softened, but she's still agitated.

"I've said that I had a guy looking for her. This is the guy," Nigel says, nodding toward his friend.

Yin feels her eyes tear and looks away before speaking. "Where is she now?"

Wright also sits and speaks deliberately "Now just hold on. Hear me through. We're still working on that, and I promise to keep you informed, but for now we need to focus on the data center. What financial information do you still need?"

"How do you know about Cambodia? Stop hiding information!" Yin says firmly.

"Hey, now," Wright replies, an edge returning to his voice. This isn't a fucking game were all playing here, all right? Li is in a tough situation. We all are, so we need to work together."

Wright's words about Li being in a tough situation shake her, but she goes silent.

Wright rubs the top of his head, sighs, and touches his eyes before speaking. "Okay. You think we're jerking you around, but that's just not true. I'll lay it all out for you when we meet again tomorrow, but it's not pretty. Prepare yourself."

"I've been ready for anything since she went missing," Yin says, folding her arms across her chest.

"You'll have it all tomorrow, I promise, but I need your focus right now. What financial information can you provide?"

Yin has remained cautious around Nigel. They know that she's involved with the underworld, but they have an unwritten agreement—her cooperation for immunity. The arrangement has worked well, but Yin hasn't had that conversation with the CIA. She says, "Let me put it this way. I trust Nigel, but you and I don't yet know each other."

"We can fix that. What information?" Wright repeats. He is visibly exasperated by her reluctance to be forthcoming.

"I help you, and you find my sister. It's that easy, but I need assurance that I won't end up in chains. How do I know the men above you won't change your mind? From my point of view, it's more dangerous working with the two of you than with Bao," Yin explains.

Nigel shakes his head in disagreement but doesn't speak. The intelligence community is notorious for having people high up in their organizations override those below them. It happened in China. It's happening here. Yin feels justifiably wary.

Wright does his best to bring the conversation back on track. "Nigel and I talked. From now on, he'll represent you to his people as one of my assets, but I call bullshit on us being dangerous. More dangerous than the Triad? Give me a break. Look at the poor bastard. Nigel sucks at golf, is dangerous off the tee box, but he's one of the good guys. I'm having you declared an in-pocket resource for me, which comes with immunity. If you haven't personally done something incredibly egregious, you're good. Does that work for you?"

Nigel silently watches Yin during this fiery exchange. The darkness he previously witnessed on the computer screen earlier today is stronger.

He's always thought his mother's talk about gifts was folklore, but he now understands. Yin interrupts his thoughts.

"Can I get that in writing?"

"No," Wright says flatly, but his straightforward honesty helps Yin trust him.

"It's legit. You still report to me, but Justin is standing by to help with anything we need," Nigel says, rejoining the conversation.

Yin reluctantly smiles. For reasons she cannot even explain to herself, she trusts Nigel and believes somehow that Wright will find Li. She looks at Wright, intentionally leaving Nigel out of the conversation, "It makes sense to me now, but I'd still like something in writing."

"Wouldn't that be nice. The thing is, who could you ever show that to?" Wright asks.

Still speaking to Wright, Yin says, "It will be documented somewhere in your systems, correct?" Knowing the request will go nowhere, she continues. "We'll meet tomorrow after work, but I need to go back, or it will look suspicious, especially after an attack. Honestly, I'm surprised Bao let Peter and I leave."

"Why do you need to go back?" Wright asks.

"There are approximately fifty shell companies funneling money to another twenty corporations created by a third party. I'll get you a list of everything within a few days.

"Twenty corporations? You've said there is a lot of money changing hands. What are we looking at?" Nigel asks.

"I only know what has moved through the data center thus far. There may be other funnels, but close to a billion dollars US. Some of these corporations deal in advanced weapons systems."

"Jesus," Nigel says, sitting back in his chair and deferring to Wright.

Yin can't serve two masters on this side of the fence. She's amused by Nigel's submission when there's an alpha dog in the room. Officer Wright is the stronger and more capable man. He's smarter, cunning, and the most likely candidate to be Li's savior. Wright respects assertiveness.

"There's a clear connection between the Triads and terrorists. It's a fact. Rescuing Li is my prime objective, but there is more at stake. I'm going back. Do what you can to protect me, but it has to happen. Agreed?

"Agreed," Wright says immediately.

Nigel is more reserved. He pulls a device from his pocket. "I want you to take this. Keep it on your person no matter what. It looks like a common key fob, but if you press hard for three seconds, I'll have people at your location within minutes. Give it a try."

Yin presses the button until an alert sounds on Nigel's phone. He pulls it from his pocket and shows her their current location on a digital map.

"We don't trust these guys, and I'm not only talking about the Triad bosses. I'm talking Peter, Nicolay, and your guy Bao. You shouldn't trust them either. The head of the Triads had his own brother assassinated, for Christ's sake. At least, that's how things look right now. They won't hesitate if they believe you betrayed them," Wright says.

Yin slips the fob onto her key chain. "I apologize for doubting you. Thank you, gentlemen. Keep me informed about Li. Anything else?" Yin refuses to make eye contact with Nigel, sending a clear message.

Wright picks up on the signal. "The flight that went down had six

Australian and four American citizens on board. We are participating in the analysis of the debris field they found near the missing plane's last known location. I'll have high-resolution images soon and Nigel thinks we should put your eidetic memory and powers of observation to work. The two names you provided makes some of us nervous."

"You think it was an act of terror?"

"It's too early to say. The flight was fully booked, yet air safety investigators found seats without bodies. People buckle up in crisis," Wright continues. "Analysts will review the images and fly to Kuala Lumpur if necessary to see the wreckage firsthand. Something doesn't add up. The short answer is, we don't know what happened."

"I'm not sure what I can do, but we'll talk again tomorrow," Yin says and stands. She wants to return, even if to secure a future for her and her sister.

The men stand, Wright beckoning for David to come forward. "You'll exit the back of the restaurant and David will drop you a few blocks from your apartment. Be careful, Yin. These guys are no joke.".

"Tomorrow, for sure. I'm sorry," Yin says, touching the cheeks of both men before departing.

All eyes follow Yin as she leaves. The men stand in silence, each believing they know what Yin's apology and gesture mean.

Chapter 36

April 7

Yin spends an extremely restless night alternately lying in bed, on her couch, pacing, and looking at her reflection in the dark windows of her apartment. There's a streetlamp glowing on the corner two doors down, which Yin finds somehow soothing. The refrigerator hums for five minutes, the compressor shuts off for three, and starts again before she turns back toward her bed.

Wright told her to prepare for the worst, that it wouldn't be pretty. The lack of sleep and pressures closing in from every direction press Yin toward despair. Her imagined dialogue in the mirror with Li has carried her from anguish to resolve and back again a dozen times, ending with Li's voice reverberating in her thoughts. "I'll hold on until you find me, but hurry."

Yin fights several battles simultaneously, with new fronts emerging daily. Why was the CCTV footage she saw scrubbed before the police reached it in their investigation? Yin can't let this go because it feels like a conspiracy. Hidden forces must be at work, and she's stuck in a vicious game, unable to solve a riddle of this level. She forces herself to review every memory of her sister's disappearance, every memory from the data center, everything Haitao has said to her. Unbidden, the memory of Tu's reaction to seeing her for the first time in the data center continues to resurface: his unmistakable look of recognition.

Bao is a masterful gamer. Had he anticipated she would run to the criminal underground for help when Li was kidnapped? Did he believe she would hunt for EEL? Why would he do that? He's a Triad pawn, just as she, Nicolay, and Peter are.

Eventually giving up on sleep, Yin showers and sits exhausted at her kitchen table, preparing for what will happen at work. She has Nigel's emergency toggle on her keychain and knows which files she will hand over, but she cannot help but wonder how her story will end. She's had these files for a long time. It's her insurance against the Triads, leverage on Bao, and maybe she just did it for the thrill. But knowing the CIA is hunting for her sister heightens her emotions even more. They know things and, like her friends at MSS, are capable. With their resources, they may actually rescue Li. How unbelievable that will be, but then what? Can she and Li return to their lives, jog in the park, and eat frozen treats? Will she hand Li off to Haitao and continue with academics in the West? She feels like a different person now, and this person can't imagine sitting in a classroom.

Engaged with her darker side and this criminal enterprise, she feels confident and focused. The academic identity she spent all those years developing didn't carry her through these ordeals: she, her new, emerging self, did. The problem is, will this more assertive self, survive? This feeling is probably what addicts feel when first introduced to methamphetamines. It's a high, a rush, but will her future collapse on itself, as happens to so many addicts?

While riding the bus to work, she makes the biggest decision in her life, a move that will change everything—she'll go for the money.

The financial information she promised to get from the data center has been on her private, secure server in the cloud for a long time. From the moment she arrived in Singapore until now, she's secretly captured every meaningful transaction on her phone, transcribed it from memory, and in a few instances, literally copied documents in communications to some of her shell corporations. Information is a hedge against Bao and the Triads. It's also a collection of bargaining chips to be used with Wright and anyone above him. That last thought seems strange and out of place. She subconsciously thought of Wright and not Nigel, as if some deep vein in her subconscious mind had already decided Nigel could not help her.

Her goal now is to secure some of those millions in Triad money for herself and Li. She rationalizes that every dollar withheld from terrorists is a win, but it won't be easy. Every cent is accounted for, audited, and triple-checked to ensure that the money she's charged with distributing ends up in the hands of the intended recipients, but those recipients. What if one or more of these sham corporations were to be discovered by authorities and their assets seized? Bao didn't bat an eye when that happened.

"Not now," Yin tells herself, but the idea of taking the Triad's money resurfaces repeatedly, accompanied by fabricated justifications. Li may need medical attention, psychological intervention, a treatment center, and certainly to live a stress-free life for an undetermined period of time. Whoever did this will pay. Li will say to move on, but Yin is not built that way. She wants to even scores, and getting even with major players like a Triad takes resources.

Staff report to work as usual, but the environment has dramatically changed. Late in the morning, Bao calls everyone into a meeting. He apologizes but claims they have lost financing and need to shut down. He meets one-on-one with everyone except for Yin, Peter, and Nicolay. By 3 pm, the data center is empty except for the four primary employees and network engineers.

Yin closely observes Bao's mannerisms and words for anything valuable to the intelligence community. When they have locked the doors, Bao meets with the remaining team. "On paper, we're still a viable company. Our smokescreen is intact, but the big boss wants us to wrap things up in a week to ten days. Pisses me off. I'd thought we'd get two years out of this gig, after which we could move on to bigger and better projects. They sure as hell need the help, right? But whatever. Screw them. Stick with me until the end, and I'll see you get the full two years in pay and enough extra to disappear for a while. These guys don't like loose ends. Understood?"

"We should just go now," Peter says, driven by fear.

"I can't stop you, but that's the deal. I need all three of you to help me wrap things up. I want Peter to shut down the public side of the data center. Tie everything into a tidy bow so we don't have the Singaporeans on our ass. Nicolay can scrub the server farm, and Yin has the biggest challenge. Dismantle all those shell companies and ensure that none of that garbage comes back on the boss. Meanwhile, I'm working on what to do next. Are you up for another gig? I promise it will be lucrative as hell."

Nicolay laughs and offers a thumbs-up while Yin and Peter smile and nod. "Okay then, get busy. The quicker we finish our respective assignments, the sooner we can get out of here."

Yin recalls the second evening she and Bao had dinner together, how, in a drunken state, he'd gone on about an escape plan. He's a gamer at heart, which means there is always a hidden back door, but his surrendering control is out of character. If Bao is concerned, the data center may be a dangerous place. If securing her financial future wasn't a possibility, she'd leave.

During the afternoon, Yin moves all but a few thousand dollars out of multiple shell companies. Bao asks why she doesn't just liquidate them, but Yin explains that officially shutting them down after having moved so much money through these companies will set off alarm bells. Leaving them on paper buys time. "It's better we just draw down the money and walk away."

Bao sees and approves the logic in her approach, so she continues with her transfers. Funds move from abandoned corporations into the five shell companies that have not yet transferred funds to the end recipient.

She intends to report these abandoned shell corporations to Officer Wright and Nigel, strategically avoiding companies that retain large balances. She doesn't tell anyone that she has contacted a banking institution for one of the corporations still in play, requesting that they freeze her assets until further notice. Why? She believes they have been hacked and need to assess the damage. On paper, Yin is named Ya Huang, Chief Financial Officer for the corporation, the woman who created the account in the first place.

"It's possibly nothing, but we cannot take chances. I'll get back in a few days," Yin tells the bank officer, a man more than willing to oblige a corporation with over thirty million in assets.

• • •

Yin takes an Uber to ION Orchard as evening descends and quickly hops into a waiting van at the edge of the parking lot. The driver takes her through a series of maneuvers to ensure they are not followed, then into the Australian Embassy. If she'd known this was the destination, she would have protested.

At the entrance gate, she is required to hand over her phone and any other electronic devices. Nigel explains that allowing a foreign national into the embassy without being vetted, especially one from China, is a huge deal in and of itself. Knowing she's surrounded, memories of what she's done for the Triads follow her through the security check and into a second-floor conference room where Officer Wright and three Australian aids wait.

"You okay?" Wright asks.

"I'm fine. I have the information. How do you want to proceed?"

Wright extends his hand to receive a thumb drive or whatever she has. "Hard copy is on my phone at the guard shack, but we can continue. You should record this," Yin says, pointing to Wright's laptop. Wright does nothing.

"I've got it," Nigel says. He activates record mode on his phone and places it on the table. With her eyes closed, Yin recites the names of financial institutions, account numbers, dates, amounts, and additional information. Nigel smiles and raises his eyebrows at Wright.

One of Nigel's dedicated assistants is named Jeffrey. He emphasizes his disbelief with raised hands and a shaking head. "No offense, mates, but nobody retains strings of numbers like this. She's playing us. Doesn't anyone see that?"

"She can, so just listen," Nigel says.

Yin returns to the recitation but is interrupted again by Jeffrey. "How do you know she's not making it up? It's crazy."

Nigel is frustrated with his subordinate and seems about to dress him down or throw him out of the room, but even Wright seems doubtful. For that reason, he throws up his hands. "We don't have time for this. Somebody give her a memorization task, but hurry up. We're wasting time."

Jeffrey ruffles through his briefcase for a spreadsheet and hands Yin a dense sheet of information. Yin shakes her head at Nigel while submitting to the challenge. Yin scans the printout, dragging her finger over some sections for a few seconds before handing it back to Jeffrey. "By column or row?"

"What do you mean? Oh. By row, I guess. What's in column A of row fifteen?"

Yin recites the content from all columns in row fifteen, which causes Jeffrey's face to blush and his hands to shake.

"There are 52 rows and 18 columns. You can choose any cell or just let it go. I don't have much time," Yin says.

Before Nigel has a chance to emphasize to Jeffrey to keep quiet, Wright interjects. "I guess she told you, buddy."

Getting no further pushback, Yin finishes reciting all critical data for the first account and asks if they need the articles of organization. "The officers are bogus anyway, but there may be something of interest."

"How many shell companies?" Nigel asks.

"Nine today. I can only get to a few of these at a time, and it's possible that some may have already been scrubbed, but it's a start." Within minutes, Yin relays all critical information.

Having lived up to her side of the deal, Yin says, "Now, what about Li?"

"It would be better if we just described things to you and brought you back when we have more information," Wright answers. "I'm sure your sister wouldn't want you to see this."

Yin doesn't hide her frustration. "It can't be worse than the things I imagine."

Officer Wright looks at Nigel, possibly for confirmation, and then says, "Wouldn't count on that."

They call an AV technician into the room, and he positions a monitor on a rolling cart at the far end of the table. Nigel orders everyone else out, and Wright sits on one side of Yin, Nigel on the other. "Ready?" Nigel asks.

Wright holds up a hand. Turning to Yin, he says, "As horrible as this is, please keep in mind that your sister is alive, and we are doing everything we can to bring her home. The video was captured on a phone by one of our investigators." He takes Yin's hand. She doesn't resist.

The technician presses play, and the video starts with file information, a case number, date, time, and an employee number before opening on a scene of Li sitting on a stool wearing a leather studded collar around her neck, above sheer lingerie. Yin viscerally reacts, gasping softly and stiffening, tears forming in her eyes. Li looks relatively healthy but has dark, sunken eyes and too much makeup. "Is she drugged? Has she been drugged?" Yin asks, staring at her sister.

"We don't see tracks, but it's likely," Wright says.

A man's voice in the video says she is beautiful. He asks what she likes. Li responds in an uncomfortably sexual tone, saying she likes it all and asking what he wants her to do. He wants her to take off the lingerie. Standing, turning slowly away from the camera, Li slowly slides it off of her body. Her head is turned back toward the camera, asking, "Like this, baby?"

During the next horrifying minute, Yin sees her sister completely undress and slowly masturbate for the viewer, saying how good it feels, asking if he wants her to go faster or slower, and moaning as if reaching climax. Choking back tears, Yin says, "Enough. I've seen enough. Who took the video?"

"We have a team embedded in the dark web. It's their job to infiltrate these kinds of sites, but getting a physical location is not easy. Like you, these guys know how to hide, and they are expensive. Sorry. That didn't come out right. That half-hour session cost $500, and these girls do five or six hours daily," Wright says.

"But that was your man. He told her to do all those things."

"Yes, he did. He knows how to blend in, which gets us into these places."

"What's the collar on her neck?"

Wright looks at Nigel as if to ask for an opinion. Nigel says, "That isn't just a fetish. It's a shock collar. Someone hits a button if the girls don't follow an order. The sadists deliberately ask for unthinkable acts to see them punished. We're doing everything we can to locate the webcams. It's just a matter of time."

"Then what? And she's a woman not a girl. Do we send in a strike team?" Yin asks.

"They call them CamGirls, their terms not ours. Most CamGirls do this kind of thing out of their bedroom for a little extra cash. As sexploitation sites go, this is among the most expensive. Li is worth a lot of money to somebody, which is good. It's in their interests to keep her healthy. If she does what they say, there's no need for drugs or brutality," Nigel says.

Wright answers Yin's question more directly. "Depending upon who has her, there are options. The last-case scenario is a strike team. Too much can go wrong. We have infiltrated some of these sites with undercover agents, but it takes too long. The most likely scenario is that we buy her away from whoever controls her now. It all depends upon what we encounter."

"Let's at least get a message to her. I can provide keywords. Let's buy her out of there. How much? Actually, it doesn't matter. Whatever it takes. What do I have to do?"

"The way it's done, we send in a man looking rich as hell, and in the middle of the session, he opens a briefcase full of cash, saying he wants her for himself. It could take weeks or months to negotiate a deal. I'm sorry, but we don't have the budget for that," Wright says.

"I just told you that money isn't a problem," Yin begs. At this point, she'll agree to anything.

"Only people with long histories in that world can make offers. The guy you heard on the tape has been deep undercover for years. If you have the money, I don't see why we can't try, but Li is earning what? Maybe six grand a day, seven days a week? My man Green says she's nearly untouchable."

"Listen to yourself. My man? The voice in the video telling Li to do those horrible things is your man, Green?"

"Sorry. It was a figure of speech, but please understand that everyone that deep undercover plays a part, and they protect their anonymity with names like Mr. Green or Mr. Doe. I don't have to know his birth name to believe he will do the job. Li is worth up to two million to the bad guys if she stays healthy. It's a lot of money. They might take a million-five, but we're talking big numbers," Wright says clinically.

"Whatever it takes. How quickly can we move?"

Wright turns to Nigel, but Nigel folds his arms. Looking at Yin directly, he says, "You're a student, remember?"

"Rich uncle," Yin says flatly. The cynicism in her voice is unmistakable, causing Wright to pause.

"Come on, mate. If she gets the money, can you make it happen? Get it green-lighted with the Chief?" Nigel asks. Both Yin and Nigel lean forward, waiting for the answer.

Wright fidgets, staring at his hands. When he looks up, he says, "Not in a thousand years, but I'll beg for a favor and see what we can do."

Chapter 37

April 11, late morning

Embezzlement is not something Yin ever considered, yet for days, she's inched closer to that possibility by configuring secret companies and accounts. Stress mounts, and her mental and physical well-being succumb to fear and fatigue, but she has moments of energy and clarity that rise inexplicably from a stream of despair. Yin has snapped at her coworkers twice in as many days for no logical reason.

To Yin, constantly revisiting the horrible images of her sister's plight and living in fear is nothing more than a distraction. She cannot control what is happening to her sister, only what she can do to rescue her. She focuses on a metaphor her father often used. He said that when the inner mind is troubled, Yin should close her eyes and hunt for a door to the outer mind until she feels calm. To her father, everything could be understood and processed by controlling the mind.

Sitting at her desk, Yin focuses on one of the small Buddha figures Li often venerated and imagines her sister bowing, lighting incense, laughing, and running alongside her through the parks in Shanghai. She touches the charm bracelet on her wrist, recalling another thing her father said when she was caught stealing from a neighborhood store. It was the first and only time she did such a thing, and she expected punishment, but his reaction surprised her. He took her for a walk. "People learn from bad decisions, but there is a limit. The limit for you might be eight, ten, or twenty. No one knows until it is too late, but learning from mistakes is a wonderful experience. The experience keeps us from making even worse mistakes in the future. Unfortunately, it is impossible to learn from mistakes once you cross that line. You've made one. How many remain? No matter what, Yin Yin, don't cross that line."

Yin calms her mind. The solutions she sees all frighten her, but soon, there is only one path forward. "No matter what," she whispers. Fear and restraint instantly fall away as Yin transfers eight million US from a Triad account into her own shell corporation. From there, she sends $1,200,000 to an account number provided by Officer Wright. It's as if she has just crossed mile 23 in a marathon, but the second she verifies the transfer, fatigue and despair return. Instead of imagining Li's rescue, she revisits her on that stool, the shock collar around her neck, and being forced to display her body in such a humiliating way. Being caught stealing from the Triads is a life-long death sentence for her and everyone dear to her, including Li. They are notorious for violence and long memories, but it's done. She has taken the money. Whatever her fate, the man Wright sends into the dark to purchase Li will have the funds for success.

• • •

As noon approaches, Bao comes to Yin's office carrying his laptop. He shuts the door and places the device on her desk before rolling a chair to face her. His expression is unfamiliar to Yin, as if the man has shifted into yet another identity. He gives his phone a fleeting glance. "You okay? You were upset earlier."

"Not exactly. Whoever we're sending all this money to hasn't requested payment from our corporations, and there's something else I just discovered. Two of the corporations have had their assets frozen. I don't know by whom and don't think I should push, but it isn't good. Someone is on to us. What do you want me to do?" Yin surprises herself with how easy it is to deceive even with high stakes.

"Fuck me," Bao says, but there's no pounding on the desk, none of his typical displays of temper. It's as if he expected the news. His eyes flicker back down to his phone. Disturbingly, his voice is completely calm. "Do you think the problem can be traced to the data center or their client?"

"The accounts were in Cabo Verde. If it was the locals, we'd be okay, but if it's Five Eyes? You tell me."

"How much?" Bao asks, glancing at his phone for the third time since arriving.

"Twelve million. There are still thirty across the portfolio, but if the recipient is compromised, any further interaction is risky. Are you expecting a call?"

Bao ignores the question. "What do you recommend?"

"That's a lot of money. I could try to consolidate or maybe get it back, but you know the risks as well as I do," she says.

"You know what?" Bao says, throwing up his hands and standing defiantly. "30 mill is nothing, I don't give a shit. Shut it down. We're out of here in a few days anyway."

"Are you sure? What about the big boss?" Bao has fallen for her ruse. More remarkably, he doesn't care about the millions of dollars lost. Thirty million is nothing, according to him. Thirty million is everything to Yin. The relief is instantaneous and overwhelming, but she feigns concern.

"Fuck 'em, right? We've moved plenty. Leave it to the fucking feds and shut it down. I'm serious. Shut it the fuck down and get everyone out of here."

"Now?" Yin asks.

Someone bangs on the front entrance door. "Peter, get rid of those people, we're closed!" Bao hollers. Turning back to Yin, he taps his laptop and says, "Now. As soon as possible. If something happens, I created crypto keys for you, Pete, and Nick. I appreciate everything you've done for me. Seriously. I hope we work together again one of these days."

By the time he's finished speaking, men in police uniforms rush into the lobby, yelling in broken English for everyone to stay where they are. Bao steps into the main room and glances at the back entrance as if considering a run, but the police race forward quickly, calling his name and blocking egress. Like Yin, Peter and Nick are in their respective offices, hands in the air. Yin feels strangely calm and alert, as if in a dream or stage play as she slides Bao's laptop off her desk and into a drawer. She could quickly initiate a kill switch on her laptop, fish the key fob out of her bag, and summon Nigel's team. Despite practicing deleting data hundreds of times, she stands calmly behind her desk. She'll be taken into custody, but she has an informant relationship with two powerful organizations, and she knows how to play that game. For a second, she wonders if her ruse has been trumped by one from Bao, but Bao's hands are also raised, and he turns his back to the police as they grab his arms, twisting them behind his back to apply cuffs. Staring at Yin's desk, he calls out. "You are in charge! You other guys know what to do. Long live Santana!"

Before Bao can say anything else, he's violently marched out the door, spitting expletives, leaving Peter and Nicolay shaken and confused. Peter frantically taps the keys of his laptop as Nicolay runs for the server room, but Yin stops both of them. She is the only one who can stay calm enough to process what just happened. "Wait. Guys! Stop a minute. Why didn't they take us?"

Peter looks up, then joins Nicolay and Yin in the big room. "Let's think a minute," Yin says in complete control.

"What's to think about? We kill machines," Nicolay says, but Yin counters.

"If we do that without reporting what happened, Tu will believe we betrayed him. It has to be his idea. See if Bao's SAT phone is still in his desk drawer." As Nicolay sprints toward Bao's office, she mentally races through options. She wants to preserve information for Wright and is aware millions of dollars are still in nefarious accounts scattered across the globe.

Nicolay brings the phone and hands it to Yin. She hesitates before placing the call. "If we do this right, there is something in it for all of us. Just before the police arrived, Bao walked into my office with this strange look and said money was set aside for all of us. I need an hour or two to find it, but first I call Tu," Yin says, with a don't argue tone of voice.

"How much?" Nicolay asks.

"We'll know when it's found. As soon as that happens, we trash the servers. Can we at least agree on that much?"

The men concur as Yin dials the only number in Bao's call history while placing the SAT phone on speaker mode.

Tu answers her call on the third ring. He sounds angry. "Why are you calling at this time of day?"

"This is Yin, not Bao. Something bad has happened, and we need to talk."

There is a moment of silence before Tu replies in an angry tone. "Put Bao on now!"

"Singapore police rushed into the data center just now and took Bao. If there is anything personal on the servers that you need badly, grab it quickly because we're going to scrub the hard drives and get out of here," Yin says.

Tu starts questioning Yin's assessment of their situation but perhaps thinks better of it. "One minute," Tu says. His voice is an odd mixture of panic and agitation. Yin assumes Tu is relaying the information to Dragonhead, but their conversation is muffled.

Nicolay and Peter wait nervously, looking to Yin for answers. Glancing at Bao's office, Yin instantly understands what Bao meant about Santana.

When Tu returns to the call, he says, "How long does it take to clean the servers?"

"We can clean everything in about an hour, maybe less," Yin responds, still staring at the Santana poster.

"I need twenty minutes to review files, then you delete everything and stay there for one hour. No trace. Do you understand? Stay there. I'll send a team to get you out of the city."

"Understood," Yin says and ends the call.

"You heard?" she asks, and in unison, Nicolay and Peter say they did. They look to the servers where the techs press their palms against the glass wall, waiting for instructions.

Yin says, "Tell them we spoke to the head office and to be prepared to scrub, but not quite yet. I need systems online to finalize transactions."

Nicolay informs the server techs as Yin carries Bao's laptop into his office. She flips through Bao's desk drawers before turning to the Santana poster. He wouldn't have been careless enough to use the word Santana as his laptop password, so Yin studies every square inch of the poster, finally focusing on the barely visible six-point type located at the bottom right. It reads, Copyright Parpit Productions, 2019 - Item Number: X-print19267.

Yin opens Bao's laptop and tries multiple password combinations before combining the word Santana with the Item Number, and she passes authentication. What she finds surprises her. There is only one file, and that one file is opened upon passing authentication. The text file's name is Read Me.

Yin,

I woke up this morning with a premonition that my time is up. I'd hoped I was wrong, but if you are reading this, I'm fucked. Below, find crypto keys for you, Nick, and Peter. Trash everything and go off the grid. I'll hold out for a while, but you know what's up. Everyone breaks under enough pressure.

Three blocks of code follow the shocking message, and Yin uses one of those blocks to discover it's worth $650k US. She knows Bao to be a self-absorbed narcissist, concerned only with himself. Does Bao have a conscience, or is he playing another of his games? Either way, she prints the page, separates blocks of code for Peter and Nicolay, deletes Bao's note, and commands a disk utility to reformat the hard drives and printer before setting the empty laptop on Bao's desk.

Bao is gone. Tu has said to delete everything. Who will know if she doesn't declare the remaining shell corporations to Nigel and Agent Wright? There is a term she recalls reading—the fog of war. During chaos, anything can happen, but there is little time to act. While returning to her office, she calls out. "Almost done, guys. It looks like we each get around 650k US."

Yin moves another $28.6 million out of Triad accounts into a shell corporation she created in Cameroon. Her thoughts tumble rapidly, triggering a sense of disembodied dark calm. When done, she tucks her laptop into her bag, slides the strap over her shoulder, and steps into the big room to hand Peter and Nicolay their crypto keys just in time to see three men approaching the center's front entrance. They move quickly and with obvious intention.

Yin recognizes Crooked Tooth, one of her frequent tails, but this time, he is with two other more frightening men. As they reach the locked door, she sees them pull out weapons. "Run!" she yells.

Yin runs toward the back of their office without waiting for a response from her coworkers or trying to explain. The glass door bursts open, and gunfire rips through the room. Yin runs, leaving the carnage in the data center behind her, moving as fast as she can across a hallway, down a multi-floor interior stairwell to a docking and loading area. Small bursts of gunfire echo behind her, so she keeps moving. She's taken this route to exit the building before, often spending lunch breaks in the facility's gardens. She runs as fast as her legs can propel her. The weight of her laptop flung over one shoulder is imperceptible as she moves swiftly towards the exit. The feral instinct for survival is weighing down on Yin like the force of gravity itself, the dragon inside of her propelling her forward. She notes a clenched right fist and almost laughs as if pressing harder will hasten intervention, but she keeps her thumb firmly pressed down on Nigel's emergency toggle.

She bursts through the loading dock's double doors with little concern for what might be on the other side. What's closing in from behind pushes Yin to her physical limit. She quickly scans the immediate area and makes her move. The utility road behind the data center building is bordered on her right by fencing but also leads toward a wooded park. Yin sprints for the park, dashes through bushes and under trees, over a footbridge, and past a gondola with the speed and agility of a spooked deer. She finally reaches a path she knows will lead her to Science Park

Road. A sharp branch nearly takes out her eye as she traverses the uneven terrain, but she manages to move her head just enough to take a glancing blow to her cheekbone.

Yin leaps off the narrow path behind a tree trunk and heavy foliage to catch her breath and strains around the side of the tree to see if she is being followed. She knows that if she follows the path and fence line far enough, she'll arrive at the entrance and driveway to the next building complex. Instinct tells her to run and never stop, but rationally, she is hidden from sight among the trees and foliage. She's pressed the button. Help is on the way, but how long will it take? A few minutes? Ten or twenty minutes? Yin's heart pounds relentlessly with the force of a caged dragon lashing at the inner wall of her chest. She wonders why she would cry while running and wipes her cheek. The shock of discovering blood completes an inner transformation, and she suddenly is a cornered animal, assessing escape routes. The decision to stay or go is made for her.

Crooked Tooth and another goon race toward her. They've reached the gondola and don't seem at all concerned by the sound of approaching sirens. The police will be focused on the building, leaving her vulnerable in the park.

Just then, her phone rings. Nigel is yelling to her. "I see you! Run to your right! Run now!"

Yin looks up, panicked, and sees Nigel's car on the road just beyond the corrugated fence line surrounding the park. She glances one more time back up the path toward her assailants and runs, knowing her life depends upon speed. Yin has always been quick but feels now as if running in slow motion. Her assailants give chase. Shots are fired, and bullets rip through the leaves and branches around her head as she breaks from the tree line and sprints for the end of the path, where

Nigel screeches to a halt. He throws open his door, pulls a weapon, and returns fire.

"Get in!" Nigel yells. Yin dashes to the far side of the car and glances toward the threat as she opens the door. Time slows. She sees Nigel fire his last rounds. One of the attackers is hit. His arms drop to his sides as the momentum of his run propels his lifeless body to the ground. At the same moment, Crooked Tooth stops running, clasps his pistol in both hands, bends at the knees, extends his arms toward them, and shoots. She sees the muzzle flash and recoil as if it were a still image to be seared into her mind forever.

As Nigel re-enters the car, a round from Crooked Tooth's weapon shatters the window, penetrates his right arm, and enters his chest. Two more rounds strike the car, but despite being critically wounded, Nigel manages to put the car in drive, floor the gas pedal, and leave a cloud of debris in the wake of their escape. He struggles to stay in his lane for a quarter mile before losing consciousness. Yin reaches across the console and grabs the steering wheel. The car rolls to the side of the road and slams hard into the curb. "Nigel!" Yin shouts, but he's unconscious and slumps awkwardly in her direction.

With considerable effort, Yin pulls Nigel from the driver's seat into the back and takes the wheel. "Nigel!" She shouts again and again, stomping the gas pedal and speeding away. There is no answer.

GPS guides Yin to the nearest hospital emergency room, an eight-minute drive, where she sounds the car's horn. The sudden stop and horn bring Nigel momentarily into consciousness. He points insistently to his pocket and attempts to speak, mouthing the word Wright and a four-digit number.

Yin tries to understand. "Call Officer Wright? Call on your phone?" "Your passcode?" she repeats the questions. Nigel nods once before becoming unresponsive, and the rear passenger door suddenly opens with a rush of air. Yin is pummeled with a barrage of questions. She gives medical attendants enough to act upon as they rush Nigel's gurney into the emergency room and stays long enough to relay Nigel's name and instruct them to contact the Australian Embassy, but fear prevails.

Covered in Nigel's blood and panicked that the assailants are tracking her movements to take her life, Yin runs from the hospital to Nigel's car. There are shards of glass and pooled blood on the driver's seat, but she sits, slams the windowless door, and speeds away. Crooked Tooth knows where she lives. Returning to the data center would be pointless. Where can she go?

Less than a mile from the hospital, she pulls into the back of a busy parking lot, retrieves her emergency Faraday bag from the laptop case she dropped on the passenger—side floor, and slides her phone in so it can't be traced. Using Nigel's phone, she enters the four-digit code Nigel gave her. She finds the number for Justin Wright. "Sup, asshole," Officer Wright says when he answers.

"Nigel has been shot," Yin says. Her voice is much calmer than she expects of herself, but heightened emotions accompany every word.

"Who is this? Yin?" Wright asks, his tone registering surprise and anger.

"Before losing consciousness, Nigel gave me his phone and said I should call you. It's bad. I need your help."

Silence.

"Say something, damn it!" Yin says.

"You're at the hospital? I'll send someone," Wright says.

"I left in his car. The assailants may be looking for me," Yin adds, feeding Wright's confusion.

"Assailants? What assailants? Nigel has GPS built into his car. Find his home and I'll meet you there. God damn it."

Fifteen minutes later, Yin turns into Nigel's parking lot, where Officer Wright waits. He points to where she should park and walks to her as she exits the vehicle.

"Jesus!" Wright says when he sees the intense amount of blood on Yin's clothing and face. "Were you hit?"

"I don't think so." Yin wipes away another stream of blood running down her cheek.

"Nigel was talking at the hospital, though, correct?" Wright asks, more panicked than Yin seems to be, obviously trying to get a feel for Nigel's condition.

"Not when I left, but they were wheeling him in. It was Crooked Tooth, one of my tails. I think Nigel got one of them, but I'm not sure. They had to be Triad," Yin says, feeling a new and strangely comfortable anger envelop her. Officer Wright talks. He may even be asking important questions, but the only thoughts registering in Yin's mind are focused on destroying the people who took her sister and tried to kill her. When she finally realizes that Wright has taken her arm and needs her attention, she hears him ask a series of questions.

"You're sure they were Triad?" Wright asks, leading Yin to his car. "How many were there? Did this go down at the data center? Was anyone else hurt? Which hospital? You know they could be tracking your phone. We need to deny that." It's all just noise to Yin. A blur.

"Faraday bag," Yin says absentmindedly, tapping her laptop case. As she speaks, Wright slides a blanket onto the passenger seat of his car, and Yin enters.

"Which hospital?" Wright asks as they pull away.

Yin takes a moment to control her heart rate, then turns to Wright and calmly says, "Gleneagles."

"You're sure it was that snaggle-tooth mother fucker?"

"It was. Yes," Yin confirms, then closes her eyes to revisit images from the past few hours.

While driving, Wright taps a key on his phone to place a call. "Jim? Yeah, it's Justin. Do you remember Nigel Rainer, Australian IC? He's been shot, big time. Get his status at Gleneagles ER, then have Elaine pull photos of the guys that were following our girl, Yin. And see if any other gunshot victims were admitted or reported."

Yin only hears Wright's voice during the call, the other person muffled and distant. "Yeah," he continues. "They were the shooters. Coordinate with SPF. They arrived at the scene within minutes, or at least that's what I understand. Science Park 2. One more thing. Ms. Chen needs protection. Emerald Hill if it's available. If not, let me know ASAFP, because we're on our way."

They ride in silence for a long minute, Yin's mind racing. It was panic that sent her to Wright. Perhaps she wouldn't have contacted him if she'd just taken a moment to consider options. He has an edge in his voice. "He shouldn't have let you go back there. Dumbass got himself shot." Wright says.

Yin feels the guilt of giving Nigel the cold shoulder a few nights ago, thinking a transition to Wright was the answer. *Be careful what you wish for.* She chastises herself.

Wright repeats himself. "You should never have gone back."

"Say what you mean," Yin says defiantly. "Say that I got your friend shot." Her eyes remain straight ahead, but her defensive reaction hangs in the air. Wright could be correct. She'd never once considered that infiltrating a Triad operation could have consequences for anyone other than herself and perhaps Li.

"If the shoe fits," Wright mumbles, then corrects himself. "Sorry. I shouldn't have said it that way. This guy Tu is responsible, not you. Did Bao make it out alive?"

"Bao? Bao wasn't there when the shooters came. The police had already taken him away. That was over an hour ago."

"Singapore police? You're kidding. They didn't take all of you?"

"No."

"Crazy day. I'll get in touch. I want to interrogate the crap out of that guy. We got your money, by the way, and I talked with my guy."

Yin allows something else to take priority over her sister for the first time. She says, "Will your people be able to tell us about Nigel? If he's going to be okay, I need to—"

Wright interrupts. "Someone will get back to us. Did you hear what I just said? My guy is going forward with your plan to get Li back. We have a real chance to find her."

"Thank you." Yin doesn't react as Wright expects. She should be jubilant at the news, but feels numb.

"You may be in shock," Wright says. "It's going to be okay."

"What is Emerald Hill?" Yin says, but her mind is elsewhere.

"A safe house. You'll be good there until we can get your shit worked out."

Yin turns directly toward Wright for the first time since getting into his car. She notices a touch of grey and a few wrinkles she'd not seen before, but he's still a chiseled, athletic-looking man, someone not to be trifled with. "I'd be dead now if it wasn't for Nigel. I was so mean to him the other night," Yin says, nearly breaking down.

"Hey. The man does what he does, all right? Nigel knew I'd take over, and he's right. We'll find your sister. It's okay."

"He got shot because of me," Yin repeats.

"Let's not think about that now. I need to focus on what comes next. The data center is gone. We'll see what SPF got out of Bao, and we may still get intel from the center. It's a murder scene, so there'll be an investigation. Someone will interrogate the shit out of the shooters if they have one. We'll need your help with a few things."

Yin knows Wright and his teams will eventually question her in depth about what she's done for the Triads. She's already given them self-incriminating information, and there is more they will discover. Her thoughts return to Nigel. He made her feel safe, and she took him for granted. These are different players with different motives. "Nigel and I have an immunity agreement."

"In writing? Never mind. I'll talk to the Aussies. Essex will get someone to take your case."

"I'll only work with you," Yin insists.

"You have a good reason for that? Essex a problem for you?" He turns into the Emerald Hill neighborhood.

"I can explain. I'm just. . . Nigel was hit in his side. The bullet went through his arm into the chest," Yin says, finally coming down from the chaos of survival adrenaline and choking back tears.

"Tough day," Wright says flatly, idling up to the gate of a town-home complex.

Wright taps a code into the system, the gate lumbers open, and he drives to a building in the center of the complex. "This is home for a while, kiddo. You can't ever go back to your place, but I'll have someone gather your things when we think it's safe. Key?"

Yin stares blankly, then, "Oh. My key." She hands over her apartment key, knowing there's nothing incriminating to be found there, and gives him the name and number of her landlord. "Nigel's surveillance wand is in there. We should get it back for him."

The townhouse is much larger than Yin's apartment was on Ann Siang Road. There is a large open living area connecting the living room, dining area, and kitchen. She sees a small backyard with a high fence and a walk-out veranda. Wright says she can choose between two bedrooms as he performs a basic security check. "WiFi is secure. Your ID number is also the callsign password."

"I have an ID?"

Wright laughs, pulls a sheet of paper from one of the kitchen drawers, and pens a long number either from memory or using a preset format. He also hands her his business card. "Call my mobile or go through the office. They'll want your callsign. Memorize it and destroy the paper."

Glancing at her ID number, she hands it back to Wright and says she's got it. Knowing she must remain valuable, she says, "Did the photos of that plane crash come in yet? If it's all right, I'd like to see what the investigators came up with."

Wright is surprised by Yin's sudden interest in some seemingly unrelated event. But he plays along. "NTSB acts like it's a done deal. The plane crashed, but the jury's still out on what caused it. With those two Iranians on board, who knows?"

"NTSB?"

"Sorry. National Transportation Safety Board is one of our investigative groups. Will you be okay for a while? I'm told there's canned stuff in the cupboards and beverages in the fridge. Someone will bring groceries later tonight, and my team will take care of your things."

"How will I know it's them?" Yin asks.

Wright opens one of the cupboard doors to reveal a short list of six-digit codes followed by a phone number. "I was about to say that if anyone comes knocking, it's not us. Call this number. What happens is you get a text four or five minutes in advance. The text will include one of these codes. Hope you like tuna fish," Wright says, smiling as he nods towards a dozen cans in the cupboard.

"Keep me informed on Nigel's condition. I'm really worried for him," Yin replies.

"He's tough. The two of you were close?" Wright gives Yin a telling look.

"If you're implying something romantic, it was strictly professional. He was like a brother to me," Yin says curtly.

"Come on now. You can tell me. But hey, stay inside, don't order takeaway or anything like that, and stay safe. Oh. I need your phone, both phones, actually," Wright says, snapping his fingers like he just remembered.

Yin pulls Nigel's phone from her pocket. It's still smeared with blood.

She hands it to Wright. "Mine can't be tracked. It's in the Faraday bag," she says, annoyed by the request and pointing to the bag.

"I won't ask why you have one of those. But I do need it," Wright says. His tone suggests not resisting this request. Since arriving in Singapore, Yin has kept secrets from Bao, the Triads, and multiple intelligence communities. She does a mental risk assessment, recalls nothing on her phone that could incriminate her beyond what they already know, and gives Officer Wright what he wants.

Wright receives the bag and turns to leave. "You just said to call that number on the cupboard door if someone comes unannounced. I'm also supposed to get a text, and most importantly, I will be Li's first call if she escapes or is freed. I need a phone," Yin says.

Wright reaches into his coat pocket, pulls out a burner phone, and tosses it to Yin. "Use this only to contact us. The other one will be back by end-of-day tomorrow. I'm unsure how we will handle you and your calls going forward but keeping you safe is a top priority. Stay inside. I'm serious about that one. Don't even think about contacting anyone." Wright's eyes shift from Yin's eyes to her laptop, still slung over her shoulder. "Go get yourself cleaned up. We'll talk soon," Wright says and steps out of the townhome.

Yin watches Wright walk away, firm stride, resolute, completely controlled, and already on the phone with someone. He flatly admitted he doesn't know what to do about her, and she doesn't know what to do about him. He's the one with leverage.

Yin rests her forehead and arms on the plate-glass door leading to the backyard and sobs when alone. The intense emotions and surge of adrenaline that supported her through the collapse of the data center and subsequent shootings has subsided. She endures repetitive, vivid recollections of the past hour—shattering glass, bullets smashing into and through walls, and the screams of her coworkers. Nicolay begs, and Peter yells, voices silenced by gunfire. Shots burst through the glass wall in front of the servers before turning in her direction.

She dashes out the back door. Footsteps follow her into the stairwell and echo through cinderblock walls as she runs. The chain of horrifying recollections cycles through Nigel slumped into her lap before they begin again, replaying in her eidetic memory as a loop she will undoubtedly revisit for years to come.

Chapter 38

April 11, late afternoon

Tu has worked within the Triads for most of his adult life as a guide escorting members and government spies across borders, as an enforcer, and later as the Yaba trade manager. For the past five years, he's been Dragonhead's right-hand man. He takes pride in managing large, complicated projects, and his position gives unprecedented insight into the motives and character of their leader. Even so, he stays alert 24/7. Working with Jiao is the proverbial tiger-by-the-tail scenario, and today, it is Tu's uncomfortable duty to report failure in cleaning up the Singapore data center operation.

"Is it done?" Dragonhead asks when Tu enters his office. He stands behind his desk, gesturing for Tu to sit. Tu reminds himself how he was promoted to Dragonhead's second in command all those years ago. He casually looks over both shoulders to see if anyone else is in the room, ready to take his place.

Dragonhead recognizes the gesture and dismisses it with a wave, saying, "It's good that you remember how you got here."

Tu does not sit. "It's done, but the woman had help and got away. It was a professional, and there's more. In the past week, she was able to slip through surveillance on multiple occasions."

"And you're telling me this now? What about our data?" Dragonhead asks, resting his knuckles on the desktop, veins in his forehead swelling into a roadmap that disappears into his hairline.

"I made sure we retrieved all critical files before sending in the shooters, and our two embedded technicians wiped the servers clean. Except for Bao and the girl, everything has been cleaned up. What would you like me to do?"

Dragonhead strikes the desktop with a closed fist and turns away. He often paces through the office while deliberating, which is what he does now. Tu waits, arms at his sides, his body ready to spring until Dragonhead returns to the desk. "You say Singaporean police took Bao? Find out where they took him and take care of it. We should have cleaned house the moment that plane was taken. Who helped the woman?"

"Our men managed to hit the shooter. Called him Tu'Ao, which fits. An Australian was admitted to a nearby hospital with a critical gunshot wound. I'll have more information within a few hours. There's more. One of our men was shot and killed, but we got to him before the police. There will be no trace of him." Tu allows that bit of news to hang in the air. "As to the larger project, Almudir's plans appear to be—"

"Sit down!" Dragonhead demands.

"I'll stand," Tu says calmly. He's seen how Dragonhead responds when people show fear. It never ends well.

Ji locks eyes with Tu momentarily, then nearly shouts in rage. "Unacceptable! Bao gets snatched. The woman has an IC contact. How in hell! Australians?"

Tu nods. "We'll know soon enough. Meanwhile, Almudir is going forward, but a weak man like Bao cannot keep his mouth shut."

"Bao knows what will happen if he talks. Plus, all that happened in the data center flowed from his money. I am more concerned with the woman. She handled money transfers, right? She was also rescued by the Australian, which means they were in direct contact. We should have applied stronger measures. Bao insisted—" Dragonhead says before being interrupted by Tu.

"Bao insisted! Bao? You run this operation," Tu says rhetorically, intentionally pushing the boundaries of Dragonhead's patience.

There is no answer. Dragonhead allowed Bao to lead him astray with his billion-dollar promise, and Jiao fell for it. Dragonhead continues. "I do not want that name spoken again. You know what to do. And as for the girl, we have her sister. Bring her into the open. What's her name?"

"The sister is Li."

Dragonhead moves towards his office window, his back towards Tu. He calmly says, "Almudir is the one that ties us to terror. He could bring us down. Where is he now?"

"On the island. He plans to disappear when the attacks are launched," Tu replies.

"You had that conversation with him, the one I instructed you to have?" Dragonhead asks while turning to face Tu. His face darkens in anticipation of Tu's reply.

"Yes. No witnesses," Tu replies, matching Dragonhead's cold tone.

"Other vulnerabilities?" Dragonhead returns to his view of the street below.

"We disabled tracking devices built into the weapons systems. Only a nation-state could do that. When the attacks are over, ICs in the region will go through every scrap of shrapnel until they identify the systems, but neither Russia nor China will admit they allowed their advanced weapons to be stolen by terrorists. It will appear to the West that

Russia or possibly even the CCP were behind these attacks. Whatever the outcome, there will be a period of intense distrust and posturing."

"The media will show the violence over and over," Dragonhead adds, as if reassuring himself that his plans are foolproof and today's events are just a minor inconvenience.

The stakes have never been higher for Jiao. Tu does what he can to reassure his boss. "Disruption will affect supply chains. Markets will fall. Land values and productivity will naturally follow suit as they always do after disasters. We are ready, Ji. Your plan is solid. Yes, Bao and Almudir are points of vulnerability, but only Bao knows how this is directly tied to us. I'm working on that," Tu says. It's a point he's made from the start.

"And the bitch?" Dragonhead asks, tone still icy.

"I did everything possible to contain the situation, Ji. You know that. Neither of us imagined that Bao would be taken. We've killed the servers, and no one made it out alive except for the woman. She may know things, but—"

"But what! Spit it out," Dragonhead demands.

"She moved money and had access to names, but that doesn't mean she will admit as much to anyone in authority. We could have initially used her sister to gain compliance, but the data nerd insisted on another course of action. My point is that it's all too late for them. Things are in motion."

Dragonhead looks confused, but only for a second. "Data nerd. That's a good description of Bao. You took care of my brother in prison. We have people on the inside, so it should be easy to erase him. Use the sister. See if this Yin got on a plane for Shanghai."

Tu is relieved that Dragonhead has moved from blame to problem-solving. "If he is in custody, he'll be taken care of within 24 hours. We still have a team in Singapore, and I've sent additional shooters to help find Yin Chen."

"If possible, take her alive and bring them to me," Dragonhead says, peering at Tu's faint reflection in the expansive window.

"I've sent word into the network. We don't know exactly where Li Chen is, but it should take no longer than 72 hours to collect her."

"And the man that helped Yin?" Dragonhead asks. The questions come more rapidly, which indicates the conversation is nearing its end.

"The man was shot. We are checking with hospital and morgue contacts," Tu responds.

"He might be dead? What about our men? You said there was a gunfight."

Tu has already explained this. "He was killed immediately. No trace. We're clean."

"Almudir has his warriors in position?" Dragonhead continues to pepper Tu with questions, probing for missteps.

"Yes, but we have no definitive times or locations. He says 200 men and women will participate. Weapon caches are in place Allah be praised, they will strike terror into the heart of Satan," Tu says with a smile, delivering his assessment with ease.

Dragonhead laughs, conceding that Tu is still worthy of the mission. "I hate these guys, you know? But they are useful. One more thing. I'm going to strengthen my personal guard. I don't trust Almudir."

"He has no idea who you are. He thinks I report to the nerd. But that would be a wise thing to do for any threats that might emerge. You might also consider becoming invisible for a while."

"When the attacks unfold, I may go inland. When you've taken care of everything, join me. Tu, don't fuck this up, understood?"

Tu nods and turns toward the door, but Jiao isn't finished.

"You've met Almudir face to face. Is he going to follow through on the attacks?"

"Almudir will carry out the attacks, but I fear he could go too far," Tu adds.

"What do you mean?" Dragonhead asks, suddenly defensive for the first time in this long volley.

Tu turns towards Dragonhead before leaving, concern on his stoic face. "We need strategic chaos." Tu pauses. He waves a hand through the expanse of the massive office and continues. "Men like Almudir live only to destroy, and we've given him a lot of money."

Chapter 39

April 11, early evening

Yin imagines hidden cameras and listening devices abound in CIA safe houses. There may also be cameras on the street and up the road, a compromised WiFi network, and surveillance measures she hasn't accounted for, but it's not normal to sit, to be idle, to have time on her hands and nowhere to be. She positions herself next to the countertop between the kitchen and living area, careful not to expose much of the laptop's display. She's fought for control with everyone she's met recently, the latest battle being between her and Wright. *He must believe I'm an idiot if he thinks he can track my moves,* Yin thinks as her fingers glide over the keyboard, but even this is unsettling. Wright has made a huge mistake allowing her to keep her laptop, or did he? The machine address is still useful in contacting and manipulating Triad shell companies. She has names, account numbers, and balances stored in her memory. They can see and follow any IP address she enters, but with a secured VPN, they cannot easily see what she does at those destinations, or can they? Have they been inside of her systems all along?

Yin feels repulsion as if the laptop she lives in has turned against her. Erratic patterns of exhaustion, bouts of anxiety, inner rage, and dreadful calm buffet Yin for the first two hours she is alone. She has never been this vulnerable. Without a written copy of Nigel's agreement, she's potentially doomed. Wright calls her an asset and says she now has immunity under his authority, but he also used the word if. *If there were no egregious behaviors.* Who defines egregious? Moreover, she is no longer a valuable informant in the Triad data center. Until a few hours ago, she lived on a razor's edge. She'd known from the moment she applied for the data center job that she might break laws and associate with underground elements to find Li. She couldn't possibly have known that was just the beginning. She has potentially funded terrorists through the suspicious shell corporations she created. She's manipulated everyone in her path, leading to the ultimate mistake of calling the Triads when Bao was taken. Now Nick and Peter are dead, Nigel had been shot, and she played a central role in all of it.

The most startling of her many transgressions is that she stole millions of dollars. *How long will it take the intelligence community to figure out what I've done?* Yin has already admitted to having enough money to buy Li's freedom, and as Nigel said, she's just a student. Consequences are inevitable. Past and future are transfixed in a moment of clarity. *This is what happens when I let go.*

Yet, letting go brought her to the finish line. If Wright is an honest man, Li is close to freedom and she has the resources to hide off the grid once they are reunited. Whatever the consequences, there is no turning back.

Yin recalls her last moments with Nigel as if trapped in a first-person shooter game. As the hospital attendants lifted Nigel's limp body from the car onto the gurney, she thought him dead. Blood oozed from his side, coagulating in his shirt.

Tears form as Yin recalls the unwavering kindness Nigel showed her, countered by thoughts of her curt dismissal of him when Wright got involved. For all his shortcomings, Nigel was trustworthy and dedicated to finding Li. Wright is far less trustworthy but incredibly competent. Yin pauses to mentally consider the balance sheet. Officer Wright has the competence and assets to find and rescue Li, but trust isn't easy for Yin. Trust comes at a price. What price will Wright exact for Li's freedom, and possibly for her own? Is she about to be arrested? She and Bao are not completely different in one way. They are both natural gamers. In this game, trust is not a given. Wright and his resources will all have to earn her trust.

• • •

Before falling asleep, she has another in a long series of imaginary conversations. Yin stands staring at the bathroom mirror, speaking as herself and answering as Li, gazing at the reflection. "I'm going to find you, my beautiful girl."

I know.

"Be strong. Someone is coming for you. Hang on."

Yin does not realize how true her words are. As she gazes into the mirror, 1,500 miles across the South China Sea, Tu makes a series of calls to pinpoint Li's exact location. The resources at his command are far more direct and effective than hunting for Li on the dark web, and Tu wields the extensive reach of the Triad with authority.

April 12

Yin makes coffee and oatmeal in the morning before returning to her computer. For the thousandth time in her life, she fears digital exposure. It's been a second thought in public spaces—coffee shops, university classrooms, offices where she's been on temporary assignment, even sometimes in her apartment. But sitting in a CIA safe house? She smiles at a personal challenge she dares not accept. Wouldn't it be cool, she admits, to access her cloud tools and buy crypto right now with stolen Triad money? If Bao were here, he'd accept that challenge in a heartbeat, but she knows better. "If Bao were here," she says aloud, mustering ingenuity and courage. She feels a rumbling from within and knows the real Yin would gladly accept that challenge.

Two hours into the morning, her thinking stops cold on that statement, and she repeats it aloud. "If Bao were here."

Yin reasons that if the Singaporean police raided the center and took Bao, they would have taken everyone. At a minimum, they would have asked questions, but they didn't do any of that, they just left. Moments earlier, Bao left money for her, Peter, and Nicolay. Had he known the Triads were coming to kill them? Did her calling Tu activate the hit squad or trigger the hit sooner than planned? Anger with herself for making that call shifts to Bao. He left her in charge. She was the last voice of authority heard by Tu. "You knew I would call, and you knew what was coming. Just another of his devious games," she says aloud.

Yin's battle flag unfurls, dragon crest, revenge leading the charge. A man capable of effectively manipulating people and events in an elaborate exit plan may have done more than she imagined. She feels less betrayed now than played, and it hardens her resolve. "If Bao were here? No. I am here."

Yin realizes that whatever in her nature kept her in a difficult and dangerous situation is also a force for extrication. She refuses to play the victim in Bao's plans. Mistakes were made. Yes, she wanted to find Li, but she was also entranced by the power and excitement she felt working for the Triads while informing the Five Eyes intelligence community of their intentions. A recollection of Bao yelling "Santana" at the top of his lungs leads her to an unnerving thought, and a smile creases her lips.

Before acting on her assumption and hunting for EEL on the dark web, she receives a text with a six-digit code in the message field. She mentally compares the numbers with the all-safe list in the cupboard and shuts down her computer.

The doorbell rings. She opens the door. Wright enters, accompanied by the young man she met riding from the back door of a mall to one of their clandestine meetings. A young woman is with them. They carry bags and boxes containing items collected in Yin's apartment. "We took most of your stuff to a storage facility, but here are the essentials. Get used to this crazy guy. He'll be your official errand boy for groceries or whatever."

"Hello, David," Yin says, recognizing the man. He smiles as he carries bags into the kitchen.

"If you want takeaway or need personal items, text David. He's your official go-for. Do I smell coffee?" Wright asks, clapping his hands together with enthusiasm.

Wright's assistants unload groceries into the cupboards and refrigerator and are dismissed. Wright grabs a mug and sits opposite Yin at the living room table when they are alone. "First things first. Nigel is alive. How are you holding up?"

"Will he be okay?" Yin asks, relieved.

"As you can imagine, it was touch and go for a while—shattered ribs, a punctured lung, and they had to repair some of the veins feeding the heart. There was extensive internal bleeding. If you hadn't gotten him to the hospital when you did, he'd be gone. He's a tough little bastard. They put him into an induced coma where he'll stay through multiple surgeries. It will be a long recovery, but we'll see him walking around someday."

Yin's eyes moisten as images of Nigel telling her to take his phone return, blood everywhere, his lifeless body spread on the gurney.

"You do have feelings for him. I can tell," Wright says, probing the defensive perimeter Yin has created in herself.

"Nigel saved my life," Yin says, annoyed by another suggestion that Nigel pursued her romantically. She can't tell if his motivation is an accusation or a proposition.

"And you saved him, but you know what I mean. Had him wrapped around your little finger. The guy would have done anything for you." Wright pushes, perhaps hoping Yin will divulge something unintended.

Yin shakes her head. "He would have helped anyone. He's like that. Are you? Do you have the crash investigation files?"

Wright smiles, but it's a mask. "In a minute. Let's go through a few things."

"Starting with Li," Yin says quickly. She's not in the mood to ever again be played in the way Bao played her.

"Exactly. My man is mission-driven. I approved the plan he will execute in a few days," Wright says.

"She may not have a few days. Hear me out. Li may have been taken as a bargaining chip to control me. Now that I am out of the picture, what do you think will happen?" The words hang in the air.

Wright taps his fingers on the rim of his coffee mug. "Has anyone attempted to use her as leverage? That's how it would have played out, don't you think? If the people you work for had her, they would have put you in a vice much sooner."

"This may sound ludicrous, but the first person I thought of when Li was taken was an underground hacker named EEL. EEL turned out to be Bao, a psychopathic gamer who wanted me on his team. He's capable of acting at that level, you know? Grab my sister, anticipating that I'd come running to him for help.

"Just before you arrived, I realized the SPF didn't take him. I think it was all a ruse. He knew I would contact Tu, and the call prompted the attack. I don't think he is in custody. I think he left me to get killed and went into hiding," Yin says.

Wright's eyes betray something that Yin does not understand. A moment of recognition? Perhaps he believes her, but he masks whatever flashed through his mind with a smile.

"What's so funny? He planned to have me murdered."

"I'm not laughing about that. I'm just. You're a hell of an analyst, you know that? I received some interesting information from our friends in the Singapore Police Force this morning. It wasn't them. They didn't raid the data center and don't have anyone named Bao Gu in custody."

Yin stands, alarmed. "Actors? He used actors or compromised SPF on his payroll?"

Wright shrugs his shoulders nonchalantly. "Who knows? It's possible the Triads staged the raid to get him out before the hit. Maybe he's still valuable to them, or they needed to be sure he wouldn't get away in the chaos. For all we know, he's diced into crab bait at the bottom of the ocean, or as you imagine, hiding somewhere."

"We were all valuable, and Tu sounded very surprised. I don't think he knew Bao was taken," Yin says, replaying the phone conversation with Tu.

"About that. You should have called us instead of Tu. Alerting him probably caused—"

"Say it. Your friend wouldn't be in the hospital if I hadn't called Tu.

I've revisited that possibility a thousand times," Yin says, standing and turning away.

"I didn't mean it like that," Wright says. "They never intended for any of you to walk away from that data center. If you hadn't called it in, maybe Bao would have."

Yin sighs, and Wright allows her to work through her emotions before returning to her seat. He sips his coffee and folds his hands before speaking. Yin sees this as guarded behavior, but she would expect nothing else. "Let me lay out what I do," he says gently. "I'm what they call an Operations Officer for the Central Intelligence Agency. We are a branch of the National Clandestine Service and have a heightened interest in this part of the world. To put it bluntly, I look for and work with human intelligence sources like you. You have critical and timely information. Nigel reached out because I have the budget, authority, and connections to make your information useful."

"Making me your in-pocket asset, as you said," Yin interjects.

"Something like that. I forward information to others in the IC. They take it from there." Wright finishes his thought.

"The intelligence community," Yin says incredulously.

"I could have said ICA, the Intelligence Collection Analysts, but we just say IC. They gather information from us and parse it into other divisions. These guys decide where the intel ends up, whether that be signals intelligence, analysis of images, or other groups. Even open-source data collection from the Internet, television, and other media sources is considered, but then you know all this, don't you."

Yin knows a recruiting pitch when she hears one. "Why do you say that? I'm just a student. Well, I was a student."

"Right. A student. You'd be a great language officer, but we can discuss that later. You asked for the plane crash incident reports. Normally, we don't share this information with anyone, but there were those two individuals on the manifest who connected with your lists, and that spells trouble. This is also something Nigel wanted. I'll show you the photos now and leave a link with you for later. Like I said, it's a lot to go through."

"I'm not interested in becoming an officer, but sure. We'll talk later." Yin stares at Wright's laptop, wondering what secrets lurk within.

Wright chuckles as he slides his computer across the table to Yin. "Riveting stuff."

As Yin swipes through dozens of photos showing floating debris from aerial views, a few taken while salvaging items into a boat, and many more taken from various angles showing debris collected into a hanger for analysis, Wright fills her in on what he's been told. "Flight 957 leaves Kuala Lumpur around 23:59 hours for Beijing. The pilot was Muhammad Ulul Khan. We're checking his background, but so far, there is little to indicate intent."

"Are there any other passengers on our list besides the two you already identified?" Yin asks, looking through photos of water-damaged seats and foam scraps.

Wright says, "Those two were from Iran. They both traveled one way and paid with cash. We're looking into whether they traveled under bogus passports. But I think it's safe to say they were involved."

"Foreign nationals seldom travel one-way to Beijing," Yin says flatly, noting what Wright didn't address speaks volumes.

"See? You'd make a great analyst. Anyway, 50 minutes into the flight,

ACARS sends its last message. Lumpur radar hands them off to Ho Chi Minh for their flight over Vietnamese airspace, and we get nothing after that."

"ACARS?" Yin asks.

"Sorry. Why the hell would anyone know this stuff?" Wright flips through notes on his phone and comes up with "Aircraft Communications Addressing and Reporting System. "ACARS helps controllers collect technical information about the aircraft, such as fuel reserves and basic flight progress.

"The pilot acknowledges the handoff to air traffic control in Vietnam, and then there's a Mayday call, which ends transmissions. The plane disappears from commercial radar. Even the satellite data unit goes offline."

"There was a Mayday communication? What did the pilot say?" Yin asks.

"The transcript is buried somewhere in this mess, but something about a fire and smoke.

"SATCOM goes offline, too?" Yin asks with piqued interest.

"You know more than I do. Yes. It's the thing that connects air and ground through radio frequency and satellites. The search has focused on the last known coordinates and expanded outward from there," Wright adds.

"What are the coordinates for the debris?" Yin quickly asks, scrutinizing a series of photos in her mind.

Wright returns to his phone and scrolls through the data, noting Yin asks for point after point without offering conclusions. They enter coordinates into a map on his computer and end at a spot nearly midway between Malaysia and the southern tip of Vietnam. Yin stares at the map for a moment, then begins retracing her path through photos. As she hunts, she says, "This will all be in the reports?"

"The route has been confirmed a hundred times over. The flight hits its waypoints on schedule and doesn't deviate until it disappears. What are you seeing?" Wright asks, giving Yin a little leeway.

Yin doesn't answer immediately, so Wright fills in the silence with his own conclusion. "I'm not sure where you're going but let me give this a shot. These two guys are on board with the means to take the airplane down. I'm not sure how they do it, but they create some catastrophe with explosives or maybe just by starting a fire. Who knows. But it would certainly support the Mayday call, and you're looking at the result. Maybe this is a prelude to something that's still to come. I'll give you that much."

"If these people were involved, I wouldn't see them simply blowing up an airplane," Yin says, but her focus is on finding the photo she'd seen forty or more images earlier. Her excitement has returned, and she becomes nearly giddy when she looks at the image. "That's it," she says aloud, turning the display toward Wright with a big smile.

Looking at a small section of what appears to have been ripped from a wing flap, Officer Wright acknowledges that he doesn't know what he's looking at or why. He says, "It's just a scrap of tin."

"There. Zoom in. See that bluish cluster?" Yin says.

"What about it?"

"Clavelina moluccensis. The common name is Bluebell tunicate, or Blue Sea Squirt, as my father called it. These are dried out but look like little bottles in the wild. Bluebell is a coral-feeding microorganism, understand? The coordinates you have are in the open ocean. The debris may be from a 777, but our plane didn't crash at those coordinates. The debris was placed there."

Wright zooms in and out of the photo. "How could you possibly ascertain all of that from one picture?"

Yin says, "That creature doesn't grow in the open ocean. There wasn't enough time for the wreckage to drift from warm coral reefs to this spot. See? The only possible conclusion is that the debris was placed there."

"That blue smudge could be from anything," Wright says, half in doubt, half impressed with Yin's confident deduction.

Yin continues but is clearly frustrated by Wright's look of incredulity. She wonders how he can proudly say he works in intelligence. "Someone deliberately placed that debris. Isn't it a bit curious to you that the debris is rather generic?"

"Generic?" Wright asks.

Yin sighs. "Try to keep up. None of this debris is specific to the flight at first look. This could have come from any flight. You yourself even questioned the finding of seats with no bodies.

"An operation of this scale would have taken years. Have your analysts verify my findings. I will concede that I don't know what happened to the plane, but I guarantee it didn't crash at these coordinates," she says.

Wright rolls his eyes. "It's a bit of a leap you're suggesting," he mumbles. "But I'll have my guys look into it."

"In context, there are many millions of dollars out there. Something big is coming. I can sense it. Have you traced funds from what I gave you? Who are the recipients?" Yin asks.

"What can you tell me about Dubai?" Wright answers with his own question, happy to move past the plane.

"Dubai? Nothing. Why?" Yin says, still staring at the images that reaffirm her belief.

"Has the name Rashid ever shown up?"

"If it's not on the list, no," Yin replies, looking up towards Wright.

"We've been watching this guy in Dubai for a long time, never able to prove anything, but we are currently cross-referencing what we know against the shell corporations the Triads created. We're getting a pretty good idea of where to go next. If your Blue whatever checks out—" Wright's voice trails off. He looks at Yin, unsure what to share with her.

"It will check out," she says.

Standing to face Wright, she continues. "Then what?" Her motivation is clear. Wright must see her as valuable. It's her only point of leverage keeping Wright motivated toward finding Li. He's said he is helping his friend Nigel, and hints that Yin could be a great analyst, but what really motivates him? She hasn't a clue.

"As I said, foul play may have had a hand in this crash, but it probably ended at those very coordinates," Wright says, masking his skepticism by turning away.

Forcing Wright to stay engaged, Yin asks, "Can I hang onto these photos? Maybe there is more the investigators missed. Something needs to be done about this."

Nodding to Yin's request, Wright continues for the door.

Yin stares at the side of his face in disbelief. "Now, Justin. Something needs to be done now! I can't believe you don't see this." Yin gestures a hand towards the images of the crash. Then, in a shockingly dark voice, Yin warns Wright, "It may already be too late."

Chapter 40

April 13

Junaid is a fiercely loyal military advisor experienced in clandestine operations. He and a dozen dedicated former Iranian soldiers are Almudir's enforcers, trainers, and leaders of smaller and extremely agile teams. Half of them served in special forces and are personally acquainted with the tactics used in conflict zones across the Middle East. They know how to assimilate into nearly any environment, hostile or otherwise. More importantly, they know how to train fighters. In Junaid's past experiences, he was always constrained by time, money, and resources.

Today's Battlefields are not the battlefields of yesterday or tomorrow, and the warriors that live and die in conflicts are as innovative in their approach to conquest and survival as anyone can be. Their lives depend upon adaptation.

When Junaid learned how much money he and his team had to work with, he turned his attention to the creative use of weapons in Ukraine's defense against Russia and lessons learned from the offensive tactics of Hamas in Gaza. In the 18 months before their planned attacks, he sent men to some of the world's most innovative military fairs and exhibitions, including the International Arms Fair in Nuremberg, Germany and an International Defense Exhibit in Abu Dhabi. In his opinion, the teams and tactics he's creating for this round of attacks will be unlike anything ever before.

Almudir gives Junaid total freedom in how attacks will occur but retains control of where. Inspired by the effective first-person view heavy-lift drones used in the Ukraine, he and his teams have dozens of drones capable of carrying projectiles from traditional launch platforms like rocket-propelled grenades to precise locations miles away. The Ukrainians used this tactic effectively against military installations and armored transports. He and his team have learned to use these platforms as autonomous weapons, unleashing new levels in terror.

As they review logistics this evening for the many attacks that will play out in the coming months, timing remains one of the biggest challenges. Junaid and five of his best men stand in the dim light of the island's big house with Almudir, revising last-minute details for sequential attacks across Southeast Asia. Their relentless alpha-male opinions collide as they review street images, topographical maps, and photos secretly acquired weeks and months earlier by their surveillance teams. Almudir listens attentively to the ideas presented by these experts, but only to a point.

As two of the operators argue over contingencies, Almudir kicks a table. "Stop. To our knowledge, none of the women gathering intelligence raised suspicion. They were properly trained, and the research was conducted long ago. Can we all at least agree on the principle of maximum carnage? If we hit soccer events, shopping malls, and nightclubs first, the police will be preoccupied. During the confusion, we take out communications, and—"

"No!" Junaid says emphatically. For the first time in two years of working together, Junaid openly challenges Almudir's desire to rain holy terror on soft targets. "We proceed as planned. Hitting soft targets in this region only turns the people against us. I didn't recruit and train drone pilots to bomb shopping malls. We have the speed, payload capacity, and distance to strike strategic military and paramilitary targets miles from their launch points. Everything is in position. We must hit facilities in Singapore with thermobaric tandem charges and booster explosives to disrupt civil communications. We take out military targets in Kuala Lumpur and Jakarta with fragmentation and tandem charges. Blowing up a nightclub or shopping mall isn't nearly as important as disrupting their military infrastructure."

Almudir is visibly enraged by Junaid's insubordination but allows him to continue.

"As for attacks in Jakarta, we follow the same pattern with this exception. When your 777 strikes the port, we swarm drones on local military assets and continue the attacks for the next few months."

"Where are these collateral targets?" Almudir yells. The two face off, but nothing happens. Instead, they push colored disks into various positions on maps and slash fat red Xs across targets.

Nearing dawn, the locations and timing of their assaults have all been decided, with one exception. Junaid dismisses his team so they can gather their things and catch a boat ride from the island, each man destined for a different location. When they've gone, Almudir turns to Junaid and says, "Don't ever contradict me in front of the men. Military targets are fine, but the path to victory must also destroy confidence in how they can protect the people, not just themselves." Seeing that Junaid is immune to his logic and tone, he smiles and says, "Please. Bring me Nasr and the pilot."

Chapter 41

April 13

Junaid brings Nasr and a reluctant Captain Khan to the big house, where Almudir greets them with a grand smile and tea before escorting them inside. Khan is defiant: "I've already told you. I won't train your pilots to kill civilians."

Almudir's face reddens, but he remains calm. "My good and faithful friend! If you had successfully trained my pilots as agreed, you would be on your way to the Bahamas by now. Though you failed in phase one, your concerns about unnecessary deaths make sense in the next, so here is what we will do. You pick the targets. Train pilots for the next mission, and we can part as friends. As he says this, he points to numerous maps of Southeast Asia stretched across tables and a few pinned to the walls. Some have bright red marks. Colored plastic disks rest on all of them.

Khan knows the two pilots Almudir refers to will never be ready for any mission involving the 777. The thought occurs that if he could train them at least well enough to escape the ribbon of runway leading to the harbor, the rest of the flight would be on them, but they could never possibly navigate over a thousand miles undetected. All those passenger deaths would have been for naught. "You think I am a willing martyr, that I believe heaven is sufficient reward for killing myself and infidels? I am not one of your zealots, but I will train your two pilots if that is what it takes for you to keep your word."

"Willing or not, whoever flies that plane will be honored for one hundred years as Shahid. Don't you believe it should be you? If you insist on training others, so be it. Now come. Look at the map. Where should we strike?" Almudir asks.

"I will only help you if you pay up," Khan says defiantly.

Junaid rushes forward and lands a palm strike on Khan's chest, dropping him on the floor.

Almudir looks down at a stunned Captain Khan who fights for breath, "Now you will help. We agreed that you bring us the plane and train pilots. You have yet to complete the second part of that agreement. Train the men, and you get paid."

Khan thought this through days ago. No matter what happens, he will soon die. The violence he just experienced and the struggle to regain breath is a prelude. He will continue the charade of training pilots until time runs out and Almudir loses his leverage. Khan would much rather fly a final mission than be shot in the head for resisting, but will Almudir honor his word? He's been given certain assurances and is included in picking the target, but needs proof that Syhala and Omar will be taken care of. That is the mission before the mission. While still on the floor, Khan laughs.

Nasr helps the captain to his feet. Almudir says, "I have a surprise, a rare opportunity to strike a high-value military target. My people are working on the details, but this is cause for celebration, not argument. Are you okay? Do you need water? Look."

Khan stands on shaking legs. Almudir leads him to one of his maps and moves a red disk onto the port of Jakarta. "This is where we are going to attack. It is a target-rich environment, but when I have the specific details in place, I think I know exactly which you will choose. In the meantime, plot a course and train my pilots for this destination," Almudir says, as his finger traces a potential route through the Makassar

Strait into the Java Sea and Jakarta. "You'll strike at night, and don't worry. I will pay whomever you wish—cousin Omar, Syhala, perhaps both. Your choice." Almudir pauses for effect, and it comes. He laughs. "Don't be surprised. Nasr told me all about this girl, so let's keep this civilized. Choose a recipient for payment. You have my word."

And there it is, Khan says to himself. Almudir has acknowledged that Khan must be the one to fly this mission, and he's right. He will continue training the other two pilots until he backs Almudir into a corner. Once Almudir has no choice but to deliver the payment, he will have Khan's full cooperation, not before.

Chapter 42

April 14

The average person has probably never knowingly surfed the dark web. They've not heard names like ARPANET or Freenet, nor have they ventured into Tor, let alone lurked in the Playpen. If asked about Satoshi, they may guess it to be sushi, but the dark web and cryptocurrency are inseparable, and if terrorists, pedophiles, drug dealers, illegal arms traders, tax dodgers, political activists, and whistleblowers need a forum, there will always be an encrypted digital platform available to them.

But that's why the CIA employs men like Green. And that's where Mr. Green is tonight, lurking on the site where he first found Li Chen. He has a dubious history and reputation of frequenting seedy cam-girl sites and forbidden auctions. As his coworkers at the CIA return home from work to have a glass of wine and talk to their kids, Green takes to his couch and the Internet with a plan and cash to burn. Though he has never attempted to purchase another human being, he knows what to say and how to say it in believable ways,

He's been fully engaged in this mission for days. To make up for his full-time dedication to one victim, three rookie CIA officers sit at computers in various cities in the US and Europe, tapping into the other website addresses where he's provided his credentials. Their job is to look through thousands of photographs showing women in lingerie, women in compromising positions, women with women, and men with men, hunting for matches to a grid of missing women. Complicating their work, many underground video parlors use bait-and-switch tactics. The image shown to users doesn't match the woman who shows up on stage after paying for time, but Green has been surfing these sites long enough to know and be known. Like whales in Vegas casinos, site hosts hunt for what they like. He wants a tall, slender, gorgeous Asian woman—the perfect China Doll.

Having paid thousands of dollars to reliable hosts, Green watched dozens of live women in brief one-minute trailers until, after days and countless man-hours of searching, he was shown a video of the cam-girl he believed to be Li Chen. Speaking with his host, he'd said, "OMG. I want that one." He's returned on multiple occasions and more frequently to create the allusion of serious obsession.

• • •

At the same time, in a dark office in a Macau casino, a cell phone flies across the room, crashing into the wall. Tu has been at it for the better part of 24 hours, trying to track down the girl he authorized the abduction of in Shanghai months earlier. He picks up another cell phone with only one number on it and is glad he's not in the same room as the recipient when he delivers his message.

Dragonhead answers. "At this hour, you'd better have something important."

Tu says flatly, "The sister hasn't been located yet. I tracked her from Shanghai to Cambodia, where she was sold. I have people trying—"

Dragonhead snaps, "They took it upon themselves to sell her?"

"Yes, against our orders. They'll be dealt with, but finding her is challenging," Tu says.

Dragonhead has no patience for this. His anger flies into the phone. "Find them both and take care of it. The next time you interrupt me, it's done."

Tu ends the call and sighs before unboxing another cell phone. It's going to be a long night.

• • •

Hours later, in Singapore, Officer Wright arrives at the safe house to show Yin another image of Li, saying they have contacted her captors and Green can pay to see her again anytime he wants. "The fee is steep, but he has to show how much he wants her time."

"What happens now? Did you get her physical location?" Yin demands answers.

Wright shakes his head, implying she's too smart to have even asked that question. "That's all I have for now, but we're working hard and getting close. My man Green will go through a kind of courtship process, and before you ask, it's not like it sounds. He'll visit her as often as possible without looking suspicious. Soft inquiries will continue whether the owner might be willing to negotiate a sale. He's rich as hell and head-over-heels. Green says it's just a matter of time."

"No one owns her!" Yin says, her rage tugging at its restraints. It surprises both Yin and Wright.

Recovering quickly, Wright says, "Bad choice of words. He'll deal with those assholes. Fair enough? We're not allowed to operate on US soil, but who knows where this stuff is hosted? We work with counterparts in the FBI and other law enforcement agencies, such as Interpol. You'll be the first person we contact when there's something tangible. I expect answers within a week."

Yin's impatience is uncontrollable. "A week is too fucking long. Can I talk to him? Maybe he carries something on his person that lets her know—"

Wright interrupts, "Green? No. The guy is buried so deep he barely talks to supervisors. Impossible. I probably don't have answers, but if you have more questions, I'd like to hear them."

Yin has dozens of questions, none of which Officer Wright could possibly answer. Is Li forced to have sex? What drugs is she on? She wants to know if the Triads are responsible, but there's little point in pressing. "Never mind. Let's move on. I went through the crash investigator's reports. There are 42 commercial landing sites and 16 possible—"

"About that. The analysts don't believe that a little smudge of blue is enough. I'm sorry," Wright says flatly.

Yin is less surprised than disappointed. "Why? It's clear as day. They are either fools or liars. Let me talk to them."

"Wow. Get over yourself. They didn't buy it."

Exasperated by what Yin decides is supreme incompetence, she doesn't bother going into other potential conclusions she deduced while further reviewing materials. She says, "Don't say I didn't warn you. There are 42 commercial landing strips within range, but none of them would be willing to hide that missing plane, so I started looking—"

"Yin. Please. They're looking at every possibility."

"Then maybe they should pay closer attention to what is right in front of their faces. So far, I am not impressed with the CIA. Is there anything else?" Yin snaps, folding her arms in a gesture of defiance.

"Come on, Yin. Don't be like that. We tried. I want you to look at the files we grabbed from those servers to clarify a few things for us." Wright opens his laptop, calls up a series of files, and slides his computer in her direction.

Yin reluctantly pages through documents, most of which are now irrelevant. She reads plans for Bao's data center, how the smokescreen would operate, and the relationship between the fake business and his real activities. Two files vaguely relate to long-term plans, but Yin cannot verify the content.

"What about this one?" Wright says, pointing to a word-processing document.

Yin opens the file. "What about it?"

"Scroll down. There's a diagram on page three."

Yin recognizes the workflow diagram and some of Bao's shorthand. She traces the diagram with a finger, beginning with an oval at the top of the page, commenting on various functions and decision points. "A project comes in from BB, which means the Big Boss. Bao evaluates the project here in this diamond and either returns it to BB for more information or forwards it to NPY, Nick, Peter, and me. From there, it flows into various project silos."

"And what's this one? DC to R?" Wright says, pointing to the last decision point before the diagram ends.

"I don't know what R means, possibly another diagram, but DC is Data Center. Bao used that term sometimes."

"Could R stand for Rashid?" Wright asks, making it sound more like a statement of fact than a question.

"The man you've been tracking from Dubai? I haven't seen his name anywhere."

"Doesn't matter. If you don't know, we can move on. What about this file?"

Yin opens the next file. While Yin scans the data, Wright says, "Its name is CZK Server.txt, and the title on the page suggests it is a passcode. The file itself is a massive string of random numbers."

"You're kidding, right? You don't know what you're looking at?" Yin says, thinking to herself again that the people she's met thus far give the intelligence community a bad name.

"You tell me," Wright says as if he knows the answer.

Yin laughs as she copies the text into a word processor, changes the text into mono-spaced characters, and adjusts the page margins. She says, "The thing about Bao is how smart he thinks he is. He doesn't fully understand the relationship between assembly languages and the OS, but when it comes to organizing people and big events, he's a puzzle master."

Wright watches Yin reduce the column width and count characters per line. When she's attained 50 characters per line, she quickly counts rows and hits return after the sixth character in the last line. The first character in the line below is a B. She repeats the process, ending a block that starts with the letter A, and asks Wright if he gets it now. "256 characters, separated by the letters B, A, and O."

"Crypto keys. I should have picked that up right away. You'd make a good analyst," Wright repeats.

"Liar. You knew exactly what you were looking at, and no, I'm not going to work for the CIA. You're a bright guy. Why feel the need to hide it?"

"Bao has a long history with cryptocurrency. Do you think he ever worked for APT1, Black-fly, maybe Double Dragon, or Unit 61398? Those guys are a pain in our ass if you know what I mean," Wright says, folding his arms and locking his eyes with Yin.

"What are you getting at?" Yin says, concerned her dark rage will leap out uninvited.

"Come on. You did some research projects in college. You must know," Wright says, fishing for a reaction.

"If you're suggesting I worked for those groups, you're crazy, and I have no idea what Bao did for them," Yin says dismissively. But Wright's expression clearly shows that he's not convinced.

"Whatever. Bao jumps from being a wonder boy for the Central Committee to gaming software in Silicon Valley. It's a pretty amazing leap, don't you think? He never talked about any of that?" Wright presses.

Yin is uncomfortable with his implications. "You know more than I do. Bao and I met online."

Officer Wright laughs. "Like a dating app? Come on. You had to know he was affiliated with MSS."

"Of course he was. I wouldn't doubt he left for California with their blessing, but that's not the Bao I know. A lot of young people do work for the government. Many also dream of getting out of there and living in other countries. If the Chinese were treated better in America, we would stay. Maybe the best and brightest minds in the world would be more inclined to help," Yin says, instantly wishing she could hit undo, but this new Yin says what she thinks, and it's usually accurate.

"Ouch," Wright says. "It sounds like you have some experience. You recently visited Boston, right?"

"What is this, an interrogation? MIT offered a fellowship, but you already knew," Yin says.

"Bao leaves Silicon Valley, and we find him again two years later operating an underground cryptocurrency business that caters to Russian oligarchs, arms dealers, and pornographers. He walked away with billions, and here he is again, at the nexus of Triad activity and terrorism," Wright says as if reciting a lecture.

"He hired me to work at his data center, and no. I didn't ask personal questions. Finding Li was my sole motivation until I discovered how FUBAR the place really was."

Wright bursts into laughter.

"You don't know the term FUBAR? Fucked up beyond—"

"I know what it means. I don't know why I should be surprised. You penetrated a Triad data center, cleverly enlisted the help of Australian intelligence, and had the courage to bring an underworld connection to our attention. It may be flattering, but none of that is hyperbole. You really should think about a career in the West."

"Does that recruiting tactic ever work? I'm not even thinking about the future until I get Li back, and I want nothing to do with geopolitics. No one in intelligence is trustworthy," Yin adds.

"Flattery exaggerates someone's great qualities. It's no exaggeration to say you're brilliant, but even brilliant people can get in trouble. You're brilliant on so many levels, but you're missing something. The Triads don't give up easily. They'll come for you and your sister. Work for us, and we can protect you," Wright says, gesturing as if there is no other choice, but his comments do not have the desired outcome.

"Anything else?" Yin says with ice in her tone.

"You must have at least considered working for MSS," Wright says, closing his computer.

Yin smiles. "Bao is devious like this, too, always with a hidden agenda.

You want to know if I am a spy or if Bao and I worked together for MSS. I wouldn't be here if that were true."

"Sorry. I just meant that it might be logical for you to want a position with them instead of us."

Yin shakes her head. "You assume too much."

"Bao is a person of interest. We know with high confidence that he was with MSS for a long while and may still be. SPF didn't take him, so where is he? You have similar backgrounds. You knew him before the data center. It's my job to ask questions like this, Yin. Where would you go if you were Bao?" Wright asks.

"I knew someone named EEL before the data center and only met Bao at the center, but one thing you mentioned could be important. Bao threw millions around like it was play money. He never complained that the big boss had tight purse strings, and if you knew him like I did, you'd say that was crazy." Her mind races through instances of inexplicable spending on meaningless side projects until her recollections yield a logical conclusion. "It's absurd to say this now, but what if it wasn't Triad money?"

Wright laughs as if pushed into a moment of recognition. "You're fucking great at this stuff, pardon my language." Sliding his laptop into a case and standing, he says, "I have meetings all night, but we could do something special tomorrow, a lunch meeting or whatever. Steak? Seafood? I know a place that makes amazing burgers."

"Whatever you're having," Yin says coldly. The last thing she needs is another round of questions from strangers, but she has no choice.

As Wright leaves, Yin senses how much he holds back. She loathes his tendency to ask questions when he already knows the answers, especially related to Bao. It wouldn't surprise her if the CIA had Bao in custody.

Chapter 43

Viewed from the street, the building Li is housed in appears to be a rundown, nearly abandoned hotel in a seedy section of Metro Manila. Rooms are supposedly available for rent, but when the occasional guest pulls up to the office, there are no vacancies.

All but the office and three rooms in this two-story facility are occupied by cam-girls working in 16-hour shifts, seven days per week. Food is provided. Laundry is collected weekly, and the women never see each other unless, by chance, they pass each other in the hallway. They spend their lives in small spaces built to look like bedrooms.

When Li was taken from the street just outside of her apartment complex, she was physically subdued. Wrists and ankles bound, she rode gagged in the back seat of a car through the streets of Shanghai to a harbor, lifted fighting into the hold of a large fishing boat with other taken women, and drugged.

Drugs enveloped her in a haze of confusion for what seemed like days. When the stupor lifted, she was no longer on the boat but in a dog kennel. Other trapped women were also in cages, their geographical location uncertain. To Li, the cage felt safe. No one could get to her. If she slept, she'd at least hear them unlock the steel door, and she had her own bucket in the kennel.

While on the boat, she'd been groped, spit on, laughed at, and embarrassed while using a shared pail for urination and defecation. The women were not allowed to speak, and the greasy men on the ship constantly threatened to *fuck 'em good*, but whoever was in charge didn't allow it.

That was not the fate of the other women, who, one after another, at the whim of their captors, were dragged to the deck for sex. They often returned bruised and crying.

Women returned from sexual encounters with information. They were heading for Cambodia, but another thought Thailand. They would be working at a factory. They were going to be prostitutes. Li soon realized that none or all of it might be true.

The boat docked somewhere in the night, and the women were taken to shore blindfolded, forced into a van, and delivered to the kennels. The experience was nearly too much for Li and even more devastating for two of the youngest women. Li screamed for help when a thin girl, also from China, began smashing her forehead into the cage door.

After days in the kennels, an older woman brought clean clothes. They showered, had tea and a warm meal. When they'd eaten, they were placed on couches and plush chairs. Li was no longer locked in a kennel. She scanned her environment for a chance to escape, but except for the older woman, her captors were all powerful men with sidearms and batons.

Men in business clothing arrived. They pointed, nodded, asked questions, and left the room empty except for Li and the old woman. The old woman smiled and asked Li if she would like more tea.

"No, thank you. What is happening to us? Where are we?" Li pleaded.

"We sell now. You get a high price. High price is better for you," she'd said in broken English, and Li believed for the first time in her terrifying ordeal that she would survive.The woman took one of Li's arms, and a muscular man took the other. They led her into a room the size of her kitchen in Shanghai, but this room smelled of sweat and sizzled with heat from professional video lighting.

Li was told to stand in the center of the room, face the camera, and do what she was told to do—nothing more. Paralyzed with uncertainty, she did.

An overweight, short, Laotian man wearing a headset issued commands to Li while receiving instructions from one or many remote participants. He was direct, impatient, and insistent as he told Li to turn around, remove her blouse, and finally remove all her clothing. Off camera, the man gestured for her to smile and look happy, which Li decided was in her favor. She was in a different world now, a commodity coping with a different set of rules.

It's been two months since her world was turned upside down, though Li lost track of days and weeks long ago. Sitting on a stool with an electric collar around her neck, Li believes that she is in the Philippines from the food she is served, the occasional voices heard outside her room, and the strange odor in the air she breathes. Her video guests, however, are from Europe, Latin America, China, Japan, and countries Li has never heard of. If she keeps men online longer, she gets small rewards. A good day might mean a new pillow. A bad day may mean receiving multiple shocks through her collar or getting chained awkwardly to her bedpost. The threat of the cage never ends. Any attempt to escape, which Li only tried one time, means another round of strong drugs.

Li speaks to Yin every night and morning by gazing into her small mirror. *I am weakening, sister, but I know you will come for me, so I hang on.*

Chapter 44

April 15

Yin expects Wright to show up with guests and more questions today. She receives the arrival text as expected and opens the door with uncomfortable disappointment. "Anyone order burgers and fries?" Wright says. He stands with two men, one of whom she recognizes instantly as William Essex. The Australian Chief of Station has Jeffery Haden in tow, the young man who needed proof of her memory. Yin gestures for the men to enter and follows them to her dining room table, smelling sizzled beef and deep-fried potatoes.

Wright places the food on the table and says, "I'd like to introduce—"

"William Essex," Yin says, interrupting Wright while extending her hand. She allows disdain for Essex to show. Yin is not a career intelligence officer, but she understands character. Incompetent leaders often make life difficult for their subordinates and blame others for their shortcomings. She'd seen many examples of that behavior in communications between him and Nigel. If she'd initially approached William Essex rather than Nigel Rainer, as she originally intended to do, she'd have gotten no assistance.

"Yin Chen," Essex replies, as his meaty paw grips her hand.

The edge in Essex's voice, even the pressure of his grip as they shake hands, says he doesn't trust her. The feeling is mutual.

Yin gestures for everyone to sit as she turns toward the kitchen for plates.

Speaking for everyone, Essex says, "That won't be necessary. Let me introduce Jeffery Haden, one of our Targeting Officers. Haden worked closely in support of Mr. Rainer. Jeffery will handle things going forward."

She is steps ahead of Essex. They've already met, so she says hello and smiles. Officer Haden smiles back.

Wright parcels out burgers and fries as they all get comfortable. Yin carries the burger and fries she receives to the kitchen and places them in the refrigerator. Wright calls after her. "You really should eat that hot."

Yin returns, "It smells very satisfying, but eating in front of strangers is impolite." It's not true, but she wants her full attention where needed most.

"Not where we come from," Essex says, and the two other men laugh.

"How can I help you?" Yin says, her speech guarded, stiff back, hands folded in her lap. She's been around many powerful men, some of whom know how to respect an equally powerful woman, but she no longer holds all the cards in this case.

Essex immediately tells Yin and the others that Nigel works for him and may have promised things he was not authorized to do. Yin and Haden are obviously going to work together under his direction, or so he thinks as he tells Haden to set a meeting, but Yin interrupts.

"How is Nigel? Is he out of the ICU?"

Jeffrey Haden is an open-faced, eager young man. He readily volunteers information. "Nigel's gone through three surgeries. They removed half of one lung. A few bone chips remain in his chest cavity, but things look promising. He was in bad shape when you brought him. We're all grateful."

Essex looks at Haden as if he's spoken out of turn, then addresses Yin.

"Nigel's condition is none of your business. Haden is now your contact, at least while Nigel is out of it. If you need anything, just let him know."

"Nigel sent me to Mr. Wright. I work with him now, so if there is anything you need from us, let Justin know." Yin says flatly. She perceives that the Five Eyes hierarchy has America in the lead. Until and unless Nigel returns to active duty, her best chances are with the CIA.

Essex becomes red-faced and flustered. "You're not in a position to tell us how this works, Ms. Chen."

"Nigel is a competent, caring professional. I'm sure his field notes are complete. I'm willing to meet with Mr. Haden if useful, but I won't work for you, Mr. Essex. I'm working with Mr. Wright now," Yin says, calmly returning Essex's sharp reply.

Essex turns to Agent Wright. "What the fuck, Justin? I'm sitting here with an asset we developed, and you turn her?"

"Officer Wright has nothing to do with my decisions. I don't trust you, Mr. Essex. The Triads have compromised you. If they find out I'm working with you or your team, they'll hunt me for the rest of my life. I can't risk that."

Essex becomes enraged. He cocks his head to one side as he throws accusatory looks at Wright, Yin, and even his startled subordinate. His reaction is so emotional that Yin can't tell if he will lunge at her or bolt for the door. The answer comes instantly in the form of a shout. "Bollocks! We run a very tight ship. Who do you think you are making accusations like that?"

And there it is, the power dynamic at play. There is a split second when everyone is startled, but Yin doesn't cower to intimidation. In a calm voice and through her delicate smile, she says, "I'm a 120-pound woman with no title, and you are a 240-pound man and Chief of Station. You have the power here; there is no need to shout. Please contain yourself, and I will tell you."

A telling glance from Essex toward the other men discloses fear. Having a cyber vulnerability exposed at a table with the CIA present could be a resume-generating event, so he does what many would do in his position: "You don't know what you're talking about. We have some of the best security in the world."

"That's true, but I'm not talking about the organization. You are the leak. It may not be deliberate, but there it is," Yin says. Confronting this powerful man with the truth is accompanied by a physical sensation she hasn't experienced since childhood. The words come from a place inside her that has grown impatient dealing with inferiors.

Essex turns to Haden and Officer Wright for support as Yin details his personal life and poor security habits. She can see that losing control of his emotions is possible but believes Wright would intervene if things became physical. Wright is athletic and muscular, watching the verbal duel with a knowing smile.

Essex involuntarily stands, then steps back in disbelief and rage, listening as Yin continues. "You're the weak link the Triads have watched for a long time." This last bit is a lie but effective. Haden and Officer Wright sit wide-eyed and startled but silent. Yin continues by quoting line after line from various reports she's stolen from his printer queue, never once saying how she got the information. She ends her outburst, saying, "Don't worry, sir. I won't expose you. Haden might, but fixing your security issues is not my job. If necessary, I'll work with Mr. Wright and Mr. Haden until I find my sister." Yin pauses and then decides to poke the bear once again. "It's people like you who get people like me killed."

Silence. The men look at one another as if a bomb has gone off. In the context of an intelligence community, Essex is in trouble, but Yin is unrepentant. She revels in the euphoric sensation of not bending to this powerful man. The intelligence community will interrogate her involvement in the data center. Without Nigel's protection, she's at risk. Vulnerable or not, she wants the men in the room to know she still has leverage and will use it as needed.

In the awkward silence that follows, Yin leaves for the bathroom. Her back turned, she calls over her shoulder, "Figure it out. I need a minute."

Yin is so emotional from the exchange with Essex that she wants to erupt. Despite her cool façade, the dragon within has become restless, and the reality of confronting Essex with the truth frightens her into shaking. She rests on the sink for support and waits, only daring to glance into the mirror again when she's calmed herself.

Yin is shaken. She whispers into the mirror. "Essex is not a monster, just incompetent. Look at what's become of me, pretty girl. I need you." But Li says nothing.

When Yin returns to the dining room, Essex is gone. It appears to Yin that the older, more experienced Officer Wright is counseling the young Aussie. Wright looks up. "You okay?" he asks.

Bowing slightly, palms together, Yin says, "Please accept my apology." She sits.

"Apologize? Oh, hell no. You tell it like it is, girl. The man needed to know," Wright says, grinning.

"Thank you," says Haden, as if he'd known Essex was weak all along. His face also suggests confusion about what to do with her information.

"Was that all? Introductions?" Yin asks.

"You sure you're alright? We can come back tomorrow," Wright says.

Yin forces a smile. "I have nothing but time today, and you have a job. I apologize for the outbursts, but I don't take well to bullies."

Haden chuckles through a wry smile. "He needed to hear it from someone, and it sure wouldn't be me. I say, good on ya."

Wright changes the subject. "My guy is pursuing Li. When he has something tangible, you will be the first to know. Fair enough?"

Wright receives a nod from Yin and continues. "Let's follow up on something you said about Bao. You suggested that it may have been his money. Expand on that. Is there any evidence?"

"Nothing you can take to your analysts, but there were tells. One day, he used personal information to separate crypto keys. On another day, he ordered me to send 18 million to a specific shell company. We'd drained all the funds allocated for that week. He didn't say, I'll get them to send money, which is what I expected. Instead, he opened his phone and cashed in a wallet. It was Bao's personal phone, and he didn't act like he was spending someone else's money. I don't have hard evidence, only a feeling. The amount that day was forty million US."

Haden gets excited. "Do you have any of those files? I need the names of those corporations."

Yin doesn't fully trust anyone in this room, but she trusts Wright more than young Jeffery Haden. "I've handed everything over to Nigel and Officer Wright. You can ask Justin."

"I'll bring you up to speed after this," Wright tells Haden before returning attention to Yin. "Bao earned billions in cryptocurrency. This new theory is that he approached the Triads and not vice versa. Is that correct?"

Yin has entertained the idea many times. "I don't know who approached who, but I believe some of the money was Bao's. He's a gamer through and through, and in his world, bigger is always better. It's a moot point. Whoever is behind this has wealth and bad intentions on a grand scale. We should focus on what they intend to do. Why would someone like Bao, who is not an ideologue, want to work with terrorists?"

"You still think the hijacked plane didn't go down at that spot in the ocean," Wright says, perhaps voicing the observation for Haden's benefit.

"I know it didn't. If you don't mind, I will eat the burger now," Yin says. She believes the intelligence community knows more about Bao's fate than they are letting on. Halfway to the kitchen, she stops, turns, and returns to the table.

"Remember something?" Wright asks.

"None of us know where Bao ended up. Might he still be in Singapore? Could he have left alone or been smuggled out of the city? I swear you guys know more than you're telling me, but with your permission, I'd like to hunt for him on the Internet."

Chapter 45

April 17

In the 1980s, the Chinese government eased travel restrictions, and Almudir's father took his family to Makkah in Saudi Arabia for the Hajj. It was a journey to cleanse sins and start fresh, but that wasn't the only thing on his mind. They never returned to China. Instead, he found menial work through the Bin Laden Group.

In China, he'd spoken often and loudly against the government. Living under the control of infidels didn't suit him. He told his family that Saudi Arabia was going to be different. However, like Bin Laden's son Osama, he spoke often and brazenly against the Saudi monarchy, decrying hedonist behavior and blaming everyone and everything except himself for the family's continued difficulties. There was never enough money. His wife and children were a disappointment.

Three years later, Almudir could no longer take his father's violence. He and two companions slipped across the border into Yemen with dreams of becoming holy fighters. A guerrilla training camp allowed him to fire an AK47, and that was all it took to transform young Almudir into a weapon.

In 1998, four men he knew carried out bombings in Kenya and Tanzania. He'd worked harder than anyone to go on that mission, but no one wanted him. Later, the attackers got caught. Two of them received death sentences. The other two life-long prison terms, but by then, Almudir had left Yemen for Khost Province, Afghanistan, where he trained recruits. In Afghanistan, he narrowly escaped death during an unexpected US military preemptive strike. Cruise missiles hit their training camp and a Sudanese pharmaceutical factory believed to supply nerve gas to the al-Qaeda network. The attacks led to massive growth in Islamist militancy and new ways for Almudir to serve the cause. He had experience. He had connections, and Southeast Asian groups wanted his expertise.

Tonight, Almudir and Junaid stand in the dim light of the big house on their remote island. A SAT phone rests on a table at Almudir's side containing numbers for each of his cells' leader. They are scattered into urban centers like Kuala Lumpur, Singapore, Jakarta, Bangkok, Rayong, Manila, and Padang. When the time comes the SAT phone will be used with caution to set his plans in motion. Five Eyes cannot imagine a coordinated series of attacks on this scale. He often doesn't believe what is happening himself, but Allah has been generous.

Nearly three years earlier, he recruited the philanthropist Rashid. Money had flown steadily through Rashid in his direction, but the small amounts meant he had to work frugally and judiciously. Then came the blessing. More precisely, an unanticipated contact named Tu set in motion a financial cascade of funding that started a year earlier and now flows like a spring mountain river onto the battlefield. Stickpins and colored disks attached to a dozen maps represent 20 cells and over 200 willing supporters.

Black disks represent hotels, ferries, entertainment centers, and resorts. Red disks show consulates they will destroy, and blue pieces cover military bases and radar installations. It's taken months to train and transport militants and their respective caches of weapons and ammunition into place.

Junaid races through plans, sometimes leading Almudir into confusion. Almudir stops him with a raised hand. "We increased support for teams attacking radar and telecommunications centers. Cyber-attacks on commercial radar installations in Singapore, Malaysia, and Indonesia will commence as they attack the physical infrastructure. This will hide the plane on its path to Jakarta. Is that correct?"

"That's the plan," Junaid says.

Almudir receives a secure message from one of his contacts. He reads it, laughs, and shoves nearly every disk away from Malaysia to the capital of Indonesia. "What are you doing?" Junaid growls.

"You specialize in violence, my friend, but forget to account for politics," Almudir says, pointing to the message he's received.

Junaid smiles at the text and flips through a stack of maps until he finds Jakarta. Tensions between China and the West have spawned numerous joint military exercises designed to improve readiness and solidify allegiances. The largest of these exercises involves the United States Navy and select allies. China, as do countries in the ASEAN alliance, also conducts exercises.

The message Almudir receives verifies a ceremonial end to another US Navy and Marine Corps exercise with the Indonesian Navy in the Java Sea. "Perfect timing," Almudir says, pushing Junaid aside to cover the Jakarta map in the dim light of overhanging lamps. "We'll strike while the dogs brag of readiness! Bring me the pilot."

Five minutes later, the door to Khan's hut is kicked open. Junaid laughs at the shock and fear on Khan's face as he motions for the pilot to follow. They say nothing during the walk from huts to the main building.

The room where Almudir waits has tables strewn in odd directions, each covered with one or more maps. Maps are also pinned to the walls.

"I have great news. Excellent news!" Almudir exclaims.

Khan ignores the maps and Almudir's proclamations. "I've held up my end of the deal. It's time you honor yours."

"Yes, yes, of course, but we do this first. You, my friend, are a strategic thinker and the only person here who can fully appreciate what we've discovered. Look at this!" he says, dropping both hands onto a large city map of Jakarta. Barely able to contain himself, he waves Khan closer and points.

"We have an opportunity to attack one of Satan's greatest weapons. The USS Carl Vinson is a powerful Nimitz Class nuclear-powered aircraft carrier coming to Indonesia for joint exercises. They are going to have dignitaries on board," Almudir says, holding his phone so Khan can read the text.

"They're going into the port?" Khan asks, surprise evident.

Almudir taps his chest and then points, smiling to the ceiling. "Praise to the All-Powerful."

Chapter 46

April 18, 7:00 A.M.

At Officer Wright's directive, Yin receives a text and lets Assistant

David Decker into Emerald Hill. "Hello again, David. Is this all you do? Drive people around?" Yin asks, smiling.

Decker smiles back. "New guy dues. They want you to pack an overnight bag. I'm taking you to the embassy. It's not for your safety or anything, just that Officer Wright is busy right now."

"Why can't I stay here and communicate online over a VPN?" Yin says, nodding towards her computer.

"Some names have shown up. They want to know if they mean anything to you."

Yin travels to the US embassy via an elaborate SDR. Counter surveillance teams are strategically placed throughout the route to see if Yin has grown a tail. Triads or other players are nowhere to be seen. She's escorted inside through a slew of security protocols. She's relieved of all electronic devices and then led to a small lobby—two chairs, two cameras, otherwise empty. Decker gestures for Yin to wait, enters a passcode, and slides his badge into a key lock. Minutes later, Officer Wright brings Yin to a small conference room. He shuts the door and hands her a list of names. Nearly whispering, he says, "We've found purchases of train tickets, gasoline, airfare, hotels, and groceries throughout the region. Some guy bought ammunition, for fuck's sake."

"You have them? Are they talking?"

"It may be too late. People on your list traveled into and out of Malaysia, Indonesia, and the Philippines. Thai border patrol stopped a guy crossing into Malaysia through Padang, but their watch order didn't specify terrorism. They claim he was a legit appliance repairman with work orders, equipment, and a corroborating phone number. They let him go."

"How many names are in custody?"

Wright's sigh is his answer. His look reinforces the collective sense that time is not on his side. "Threat levels have been officially raised at all endpoints. The region is on high alert, but we know where these people were, not where they are now. I appreciate that you've raised flags on this for a while. Something of this size should have been buzzing throughout the intelligence community from the fucking start. Forgive my language. Here's an update of your list, cross-referenced with card use. What are we missing?"

Yin studies the list for clues. She's been warning of the broad dispersion all along, but the urgency of this playing out in real-time is staggering. "The number of different countries potentially in play is worse than I imagined."

"Oh, it gets much worse. Now that we have better coordination, leads are coming in from everywhere. There was a midnight attack on an armory in Manila last month. The thieves made off with tons of equipment, including some nasty weapons. If there's anything else you can think of, we need to get out in front of this thing," Wright says.

"You still haven't found the plane," Yin says, crossing her arms defiantly.

Wright shakes his head as if disgusted, turns to the door, and then back to Yin. "There is a second debris field with verified bodies and luggage, so let it go already. I've got people waiting for answers, not theories."

"No structural elements, am I right? If they faked one debris field, they could do it again." Yin says.

"I have to go," Wright says while tucking the printed lists into a folder and heading for the door.

"When was this second debris field found?"

Buckling beneath the stress of the moment, Wright snaps. "Damn it. Who cares? Where they found debris doesn't matter. It's what they found. Known items. End of story. For all we know, the two mysterious Iranians probably brought it down as part of this whole—"

"I didn't ask where the debris was. I asked when. Calculate prevailing currents and you'll see what I mean—You can't all be busy. Have someone investigate." Yin hopes cold logic and glaring eyes will convince Wright, but he continues to move away. She follows.

"You gave me two minutes. What about Li? Did Green make the offer?" Yin asks.

Hand on the door latch, exasperation in his voice, Wright says, "He's ready to make the pitch, but shit. He went through $40K to locate her. If they ask for more—"

"Then we give it. I'll transfer whatever your man needs."

Wright tilts his head as if underscoring a point. "You and I both know where that money came from. It's the only solution for now, but we'll have to work that out later. I hope you know what you're doing because a bad guy somewhere is waiting for you to move that money, draw it down, spend it or whatever. You're risking everything."

Yin doesn't flinch. "Whatever it takes. Transfer funds to the same account? How much?"

"He didn't say, but a lot. They'll bilk Green for every cent they can get, and he'll need cash in a bag during the negotiation."

"I need my phone."

"We're not done with it."

"I need my phone to transfer money for Li's rescue. You promised. What's it been, nearly a week? Are you going to investigate the ocean currents or not? I've proven myself right enough times to be taken more seriously. You're running out of time, Justin."

Wright drops his hand hard on the doorknob. "They won't find anything, but sure. I can spare a tech or two for a couple of hours. Anything else, my queen?"

"I'll make sure Mr. Green has two million to work with. If he can't get the job done with that, something is wrong, and Justin? If there's change, I want it back," she says, touching Wright's shoulder with a smile. The surprise on his face is, to Yin, a victory. Having millions available to her has assured his attention. "And another thing. Thanks for your help. I need a run to clear my mind, but I'll stay within the complex walls."

"Don't mention it, but you can't go outside. I'll have someone show you to the fitness center."

Ten minutes later, Yin steps onto a treadmill. An absolute boulder of a man paces between reps on heavy weights at the back of the room. They nod at each other as Yin enters speed and elevation.

Her exchange with Wright returns to memory, adding to the long list of unnerving events. She stole from the Triads, or perhaps from Bao, survived an armed assault, told off a high-ranking Australian intelligence officer, and sent Mr. Green more than a million dollars of the money she only received days ago. Wright logically believes she liberated this money from the data center. None of this would have been possible months earlier. Is she wrong? She didn't create an inner dragon. It's been with her from the start. The dragon she was told to hide as a child is now an ally, and the ally needs a reward.

Yin imagines sleeping with the muscular man on the other side of the fitness center. He might be with Diplomatic Security or one of the Marine Security Groups. She smiles. He glances back, and she increases her pace, unwilling to look away from his glance. She and her sister would have called him a sly eye, a joke between them and a way to make light of oglers. But her daydream fades abruptly as she thinks of Li and how Mr. Green humiliated her in that video—Li sitting on the stool in lingerie, told to disrobe and masturbate, a shock collar around her neck. It's unimaginable that Green is also the man who will attempt the rescue.

She refocuses on her running, and her desire for revenge fuels a sub-six-minute mile. She's never run the mile in that time. Her mind is clear, and her body feels alive deep into the workout.

A wall-mounted television above the weightlifter is streaming CNA. Yin is familiar with Channel NewsAsia because she has often used it to improve her English reading skills. She follows the scrolling headlines, listens to the broadcasters, and imagines living in other parts of the world. Today, she reads of ongoing political problems in Malaysia and another set of sanctions against Russia for its invasion of Ukraine. That war is a wedge between countries for and against. It bothers her that China has sided with the aggressor.

Slowing the treadmill's speed and lowering its elevation as she prepares to end her run, the news shifts to Indonesia. A US Aircraft Carrier, Carl Vinson, accompanied and protected by a fleet of destroyers and other Navy vessels, will visit the Tanjung Priok port in North Jakarta.

According to the report, this affirms allegiance between Indonesia and the United States. Indonesian dignitaries will be guests of the commanding officer at the end of the exercise. The printed news feed says a second debris field was found, and Yin barks at the big man to turn up the volume. By the time he reaches the remote, the segment is over. "They won't pull into port, will they?" she asks.

The weightlifter seems pleasantly surprised that Yin is communicating. "Sometimes they do if the port can handle the displacement. Name's Clinton."

Yin gives her name and walks in his direction but is interrupted by one of Agent Wright's team entering the room. The woman, fit and in her early thirties, says Yin needs to follow her to the situation room.

"Can I at least change?" Yin asks.

"Please just follow me," she says and turns.

Dripping with sweat and having no time to cool down, Yin throws a towel over her neck and follows the woman to the meeting room door, where she knocks. Waiting, she turns to Yin and says, "You'll be fine."

"Who's in there?" Yin asks, but Officer Wright opens the door before the woman can answer and gestures for Yin to enter. She follows him into a tense room with alpha males of assorted ages. Most wear suits. She assumes these diplomats decide who will do what in response to potential attacks. Young assistants sit next to their middle-aged and older superiors in a pattern of old-young, old-young that extends around a large table. Introductions are brief—the UK, Singapore, New Zealand, and Thailand are represented in person or through video, as is a representative from the CIAs National Clandestine Services Counter Terrorism Center. "You already know Australia's Chief of Station, Mr.

William Essex," Officer Wright concludes, a wry smile crossing his face as he introduces the Australian.

"Gentlemen," Yin says, taking the only available seat, which happens to be across from Essex. Socially uncomfortable in gym attire, her cheeks still red from intense exertion, Yin presents a stoic face. Darts pass between Yin and Essex as their eyes meet, but Yin controls herself. She is no longer intimidated by men who use their physical stature as a negotiating weapon. She could crush this man's reputation with a few sentences but steadies her heart rate and emotional anger with a calming breath.

Officer Wright distributes a brief intelligence report on the data center, introduces Yin as an asset, verbally presents the group with a short history of her involvement and assistance, and invites participants to ask questions, many of which she cannot answer. They want to know who plans these attacks and where they will occur. The session is nearly over when Essex begins his somewhat personalized line of questioning. "Are the Chinese behind all of this?"

"The Triads operate primarily in China, but they are not China," Yin clarifies.

"But you worked for Chinese intelligence and this guy Bao Gup. Cyber?" Essex jabs, attempting to cast a shadow of distrust over Yin.

"Bao Gu, not Gup. Bao may have, but I was just a student. Like all students, I earned money on the side doing clerical work for the government, but I do not work for the CCP. I don't think Bao worked for them either. The man you need is named Tu. He is the key. Find Tu, and you'll learn a lot." *And so will I*, she muses. Yin has come to believe Tu was responsible for Li's disappearance. That look of recognition in Bao's office is unshakable evidence.

Papers rustle as men return to the page where Tu was listed. "You worked for the Triads, the Triads are now in bed with Terrorists, and you are right in the thick of it. You guys attempted to hack our systems, correct? You're a hacker?" Essex sharpens his knives, carefully planning his next move.

"We're off point," Officer Wright interrupts.

Essex doesn't let go. "Assisting at the time of an offense is a crime. You helped these terrorists set up their operations, and now you don't seem to know anything that's going on. Not a thing."

Yin is about to unleash another salvo in Essex's direction, but Wright intervenes. "Yin risked a great deal by reporting to us from the inside. Just so you all know, Yin brought this to our attention. Thank you, Yin. You can go."

Yin stands to leave, but the representative from Thailand holds up his papers. "It says you believe Inter-Asian Flight 957 was hijacked, not crashed."

"I know it was," Yin says flatly, sitting back down.

"But they've found bodies in a second debris field. All confirmed to be from Flight 957."

"Whoever is behind this is calculating and patient. They faked the first debris field. That they faked it once means they can do it again. Look at the current drift rate from the first debris field to the second. I find it peculiar that nothing in the first debris field is specifically tied to that flight. It could have come from any flight," Yin says, repeating an earlier fact she shared with Officer Wright.

Essex laughs, but the man from Thailand wants more information. Yin explains her thinking. "No structural elements were found in the first field, correct? No plane? The investigation shows that the plane left with extra fuel. Even so, when we rule out known airports, there are only a few options. Find Tu. He'll know where the plane is."

"What do you mean by structural elements? The wing or fuselage?" asks the man from Thailand. Yin is surprised he flew in for the meeting and is not on video conference but also encouraged, as he is the only person who does not summarily dismiss her ideas. She realizes this may be her final opportunity to bring resources into what she sees as factual danger.

Yin softens her tone and addresses him directly. "Structural elements mean anything needed for a plane to take flight. The aircraft can still fly without seats, for example. There were no structural elements in the first debris field. We've already addressed a second debris field was found. They won't find structural elements in either discovery."

Commotion envelops the room with multiple side conversations and crosstalk. Wright's frustration brings him to his feet, and even Yin is surprised by how menacing he looks when upset. "Let's focus on what is probable instead of what is possible. Resources are limited, and yes, Yin, we're hunting for Tu. Somebody, please check for structural elements in that second debris field."

Yin takes a chance on something that earlier seemed unimportant, even to her. "One final thought. Bao made an unusual trip less than two months ago. He returned with tattoos on his neck, claiming to have been at a concert in Bangkok, but I believe he met with Tu and possibly others. Upon returning, he isolated himself, in his words, to work on something huge. It might be important to find out where he went and who he met."

The man from Thailand is more intrigued by the plane than by tracking Bao or finding Tu. "Why are you so certain the plane isn't at the bottom of the ocean?"

Yin feels confident that explaining her logic will cause more people to take her theory seriously. "Please consider the following verifiable information. The first field contained generic debris and few material elements. One element showed a Blue Sea Squirt, a coral-eating microorganism that doesn't occur in open oceans. There's only one explanation for this.

"The second debris field had definitive evidence, including bodies and luggage from Flight 957, but no structural elements. If you compare the location of the captain's Mayday call with the location of the first debris field, it's almost directly below where communications were lost. Losing 37,000 feet over such a short horizontal distance implies a near-vertical trajectory. There would have been massive structural damage, and some of that structure would float. We should have seen life jackets, more seat cushions, and volumes of tiny debris caused by a powerful kinetic impact with the ocean surface, not to mention fuel slicks, tiny bits of plastic, foam, the list goes on. But none of that was found. Also, the debris was largely intact. Some, if not most, of it would have been destroyed beyond recognition."

Yin continues. "The second debris field was discovered after the initial search was called off, almost exactly where everyone predicted currents would have carried it. It was still mostly intact. Bits would have been floating there the whole time, some moving with the current quickly, other pieces buffeted by winds and moving more slowly. Isn't that suspicious to anyone? The grid search would have flown over the debris migration numerous times.

"The logical conclusion is that both fields were fabricated to deceive investigators. I'm not saying the plane will ever fly again, but you guys get paid to be suspicious. I'm showing you that there could be more to the story."

Her reasoning infects the room almost as much as her confidence. A flurry of questions ensues, but Wright thanks her, assigns one of his aides to investigate Bao's flight, and dismisses Yin, saying she may still be needed.

As she leaves, Yin hears Essex tell Wright that he wants her locked up. She is about to turn and attack, but Wright tells Essex to knock it off. It's a frightening moment to be this vulnerable. Nigel needs to emerge from his coma. Wright claims to have her back, but what does he want in return?

An hour after nearly decimating Essex for the second time, Yin sits on a cot in a small room provided by the embassy. A flat-screen television on the far wall is on, but the volume is muted. A news report tells Yin nothing she doesn't already know. A second debris field has been located from Inter-Asian 957, and investigators sift through the debris.

Another hour goes by while Yin entertains thoughts of fleeing, but this Mr. Green is supposedly close to finding Li. The CIA might not let her leave and will abandon the rescue mission if she does. Furthermore, Triad members are still looking for her. Their surveillance teams will watch the airport. For now, she's in safe hands right where she is. While considering all of this, one of Wright's assistants finds her to say she is needed.

This time, the situation room is empty of other government officials. Officer Wright sits with a woman and three men, Laksh among them.

Wright welcomes her back by saying, "You created quite the storm with your theories. What am I going to do with you?"

Yin ignores the comment as Wright leads her to Laksh's computer to watch a CCTV video recording. Standing behind Laksh, the video begins. Yin sees Bao and Tu join two other men. Wright points and says, "That's Bao, correct? With Tu? We have identified the Arab, but do you recognize the fourth guy?"

"Where was this recorded, and when?" Yin asks. It's impressive that within an hour or two, they would have found Bao and Tu together, or maybe they had this information all along and chose to withhold it from her. What else might they know?

"Sam Ratulangi Airport in North Sulawesi," Laksh says. "They arrived from separate destinations and joined for a chartered flight. We've asked our Indonesian friends to find out where they went."

"That's Bao, though?" Wright asks.

"May I?" Yin asks, gesturing that she wants to sit at Laksh's computer for a closer look, but instead, Laksh pushes the video to a large video screen at the end of the room and zooms in on four men. Wright and Yin step toward the larger image, and she realizes Bao was far more complicit in working with terrorists than she'd thought. She'd worried for him when taken by Singapore police. She even felt respect and sympathy when he left money behind, but being captured was a ruse. Her memory recalls the chain of events when the SPF took Bao. He'd come to her office. He left his laptop with her when they arrived. She'd contacted Tu. Men she associated with the Triads savagely attacked within an hour. The familiarity between Tu and Bao in the video is telling. She may never prove her assumption, but Bao may have worked with Tu to take her sister.

Officer Wright interrupts. "Still with us? What do you see?"

"Sorry. Silly hat and glasses, fake tattoos, it's an interesting disguise, but I'd recognize Bao anywhere. That's Tu, but I don't recognize the other men. Seeing them all together, it's likely Bao has been in on all of it from the start."

"Maybe. The four get on a plane together, but only Bao and Tu return. Tu flies to China, Bao back to Singapore," Wright says.

"What was the plane's maximum flight distance? Was it a seaplane?" Yin asks. Her mind races through dozens of photos she's seen of various airplanes, many of which appeared in documentation following the missing 777.

One of Wright's team members answers quickly, pushing a map onto the large digital screen, which shows a large circle with Sam Ratulangi Airport in the center. "The Cessna had enough fuel for 875 nautical miles. It wasn't a seaplane, and they were gone too long to have flown continuously. They had to have used a runway somewhere. We're looking into it."

Yin's mind races through the images and documentation shown her after the plane went missing. She points to a chain of islands within the Cessna's range of flight. "If the 777 isn't on one of those islands, I'll concede it has crashed."

Wright grimly turns to Laksh and says, "Let's at least rule this out."

"Already on it," Laksh says, his hands moving with fluidity.

Yin confides in Wright, desperately seeking someone she can trust. "I just know Bao and Tu took Li. We must find them."

Wright pulls Yin into a dark corner of the room. Whispering, he says, "Don't get me wrong, but you know more than you should. Some of my colleagues think there's only one explanation."

Yin feels a surge of rage and completes Wright's thought. "That I am involved in a terrorist plot? You know that's not true. Defend me."

Wright's expression confirms that he is one of those people, and Yin feels her options slipping away. Staring at images on the big screen, she says. "Why should I even stay? Do you know where Li is, or is that just a ruse to control me? Nigel wouldn't have lied. Would you?"

"You and I have issues, but trust isn't one of them. Mr. Green—granted, that's not his name—has a good chance of getting your sister. We have a better chance of rescuing Li than finding Bao."

"He'll be hard to find physically, but I know where to look."

"Don't bother," Wright says.

"Why would you say that? Of course, I'm going to look. He may have been in on the abduction of Li."

"There are things I'm not allowed to discuss. Case findings," Wright says.

"Not allowed, or is this another of your desperate—"

"Bao's dead," Wright says. He lets those words hang between them for a long moment. "SPF didn't take him. We know that for sure. Video shows him roughly escorted to an unmarked SUV with a bag over his head. There was a struggle then, bang. Double tap to the head," Wright says coldly.

Yin shows no emotion but succumbs to internal conflict. The sympathy she once felt for Bao fights for control with the anger she wants to unleash on the man. The Triads used Bao in the same way Bao used her. But that thought disappears in a cloud of dark rage. If he had anything to do with Li's abduction, a bullet to the head wasn't enough. He should have endured a long and painful end. She says, "If Bao is dead, we focus on finding Tu. Someone has to pay."

"They will," Wright responds, turning towards Laksh.

"One more thing," Yin says, interrupting whatever he would say.

"What now?" Wright asks, spinning in her direction. He appears frustrated to a breaking point, but Yin doesn't care.

"Show me the video."

• • •

Meanwhile, in Macau, Tu reports to Dragonhead that his men are close to locating the sister of the woman who escaped the data center. "We tracked her movement to Cambodia and then to the Philippines. There are only a few potential locations there. We are close. We should have confirmation within 24 to 36 hours. Even if we can't find Yin Chen right away, we'll have leverage."

Chapter 47

April 18, 11 A.M.

Captain Khan takes pride in being more intelligent than everyone around him, calm under pressure, and patient with those willing to learn from his experiences, just like his father taught him. Today, however, he is neither composed nor tolerant even though everything proceeds according to his plan. The only exception is that Almudir hasn't paid him, but this is to be expected. Khan finds himself seated at the simulator console adjacent to the mighty Boeing 777, frustrated and lost in thought. When he hijacked the plane, he had images of it being used as a weapon to accomplish something even more grand than what took place on 9/11. He sometimes envisioned flying this magnificent weapon into the enemy by himself. Those thoughts are strangely stronger of late. Captain Khan knows what pulls him towards flying this final mission—the USS Carl Vinson.

He initially imagined being thousands of miles away, sitting seaside in a comfortable cabana, watching the magnificent attack unfold on TV as any spectator would. His name would be used. Pictures would fly across the screen, but by then he would have grown a beard and donned glasses. Something to remain hidden, but this outcome was never truly possible. Captain Khan was never just a spectator.

"How could I ever have thought to entrust someone else with this mission?" he whispers to his flight simulator. The vicious attacks that disfigured his cousin Omar were launched from one of these US ships, or so he thinks. Striking and potentially sinking such a celebrated American weapons platform excites him. It's no surprise the men Nasr and Almudir recruited to fly the mission as martyrs are useless. They sit at the flight simulator, bickering as they disconnect the autopilot and descend too quickly over the Makassar Strait. The plane crashes into the ocean repeatedly before they can adjust altitude, infuriating Khan.

"No!" He shouts, his voice startling the men, causing the older of the two Iranians to spring to his feet in rage, fists clenched, but Khan doesn't flinch. "Sit down," he barks, pointing to the empty chair.

"I told him. Five hundred feet above sea level," the younger of the two Iranians says.

"AGL must be under 500 feet as you reach waypoint six. You should practically be surfing. Alerts should be blaring to pull up. Start again." Khan snaps, his patience at an end.

The older Iranian stares at Khan for a moment too long, causing the captain to shake his head and repeat his command. "Again."

Once the two have eliminated the last of his patience, Khan leaves the hangar in disgust and finds Almudir sitting with Nasr on the veranda of the big house. "They are ready?" Almudir asks, rising to greet the captain.

Still frustrated, Captain Khan barks his answer as he climbs the stairs to the veranda. "Not in a million years. You said that the ground radar will fail. Is that guaranteed?"

"Nothing is guaranteed, but we have two attacks, one physical and the other cyber. The cyber disruption was tested successfully in the Philippines on January 1, 2023. It proved to be a huge success. The airspace was chaotic, with no ability to track, identify, or manage the commercial airline traffic," Almudir says with confidence, then shifts focus and demands answers. "Why aren't the pilots ready? You said you could do it."

Khan throws his hands up in feigned frustration. "And you said you would deliver pilots. These guys aren't even qualified to fly biplanes, but I have an idea. How good is your mechanic with avionics?"

Nasr answers. "Very experienced. What is the idea?"

"To avoid ground radar, we must fly from the island through the Celebes Sea and skim the water of Makassar Strait and the Java Sea before reaching Jakarta. It's treacherous even for an experienced pilot. Ground radar is one thing, but the Automatic Dependent Surveillance-Broadcast system should also be dealt with. If your mechanic tears the ADS system out of one of your jets that frequent the island and can magically make it work in the 777, we could have an electronic signature of a chartered flight instead of our aircraft. Defeating ADS gives us a direct flight to Soekarno-Hatta Airport in Jakarta, within 10 miles of our target. I've flown into the area many times and can see this working, but only if we spoof automated surveillance."

Almudir stands to face Khan. "If the cyber-attack on the airspace works as planned, what you suggest will not be needed, but it might add a welcome layer of stealth." Concern envelops Almudir's face. "You say the pilots are not ready. Hurry up! Get them ready. The military exercises are nearly over, and our target will be heading into port at their conclusion."

Feeling this leverage, Captain Khan is practically immune to Almudir's threatening demeanor. He knew from the start that hijacking an aircraft would probably not be the end of his services. For many years, Khan considered crashing planes into Western consulates. He saw that as a potential end to his life. He even knew this moment would come when he hijacked the 777, but killing all those innocent passengers was too much. He was angry at Almudir and Nasr for being so uncaring, but just now, he sees things in a different light. The anger at these wicked men he's felt for weeks evaporates. They don't matter. Their actions don't matter. What matters is making a difference for his cousin and for Islam.

Captain Khan calmly takes a seat at the table. An unexpected sense of purpose replaces doubt and frustration. Buoyed by images of Syhala's lovely face and his cousin's fire-ravaged body, he says, "I want my payment to go to Syhala and Omar."

Almudir's face shows gleeful approval as if this is the proper outcome. "As it should."

"Are you sure?" Nasr asks.

Captain Khan's reply is crisp and unwavering. "They get paid before I depart. The Compassionate One will never forgive us for killing those passengers, but it's behind us now. If we can strike the great Satan, perhaps it will lessen our sins in the eyes of the Almighty."

"Their deaths were a miscalculation," Nasr says.

"Stop! Just stop it. I'm no fool. I'm just foolish for trusting you. Here are my conditions. One, we rip the ADS out of your weekly transit flight. When the time comes, it stays here overnight while we attempt to swap equipment into the triple seven before I leave for Jakarta."

"And the other condition?" Almudir asks.

Locking eyes with Almudir, Khan says, "Syhala and Omar must receive the funds before I proceed. I need proof, or I won't fly."

"You can trust us to pay them," Nasr says, but Khan pounces on the thought.

"Before I fly!" he repeats.

Almudir waves a hand at Nasr to be silent. Feigning concern, he says,

"Flying an aircraft here is risky. That must be well planned, and time is not on our side."

Holding firm, Khan says, "A man like you can always find a way."

Almudir considers the request. Long silence envelops the table. Finally. "As you wish. How would you like to proceed?"

"I'll compose a letter to Omar that you must deliver. He will understand my decision, and I trust him to care for Syhala. The letter will give account numbers for payment in Omar's name. A second letter will go to Syhala explaining my decision and how she'll be taken care of by Omar. She will be confused at first, but in time, living a life in comfort, she will understand. She may even celebrate what we are about to do. Pay them, and I will fly the mission, but know this. If I have any doubts, I will crash that plane into the ocean. All of this will have been for nothing."

Almudir nods. "That won't be necessary." Their eyes meet in a rare moment bound by faith.

Khan continues. "When we strike, the world will see that the US can no longer flex its muscles in our region."

"It won't only be your attack. Taking out radar and air traffic control systems will render us invisible. That is dominance. The West cannot possibly claim military superiority if they allow commercial planes to fly into their carriers," Almudir adds.

Almudir's eyes pierce Khan's soul. "Do you have confidence in the mission?"

Khan responds without hesitation. His delivery is professional, thoughtful, and, above all, honest. "The perfect flight has never been flown. I will have to make dozens of decisions, especially near the target, but yes, I am confident. I believe I can achieve near perfection on my end of this mission. I've practiced flying below the radar, at slow airspeeds, using terrain masking thousands of times in the simulator. There are issues with reaching the aircraft carrier that are beyond our control, but I am your best chance of success."

Khan recalls briefing a mission overview to one of his general officers during his days in the Air Force. "Even if we don't succeed with ADS, the element of surprise alone gives us a 30 percent chance of success."

Almudir's face sours as Khan continues, "If the cyberattack on the air traffic control systems succeeds, our chances rise to about 70 percent. But, if we accomplish ADS spoofing as well, I think we are nearer to a 90 percent probability."

Almudir seems pleased with Khan's appraisal. Keeping from him that he's already chartered a jet to arrive at the island to transport Junaid and Nasr, he says, "You are a true shahid. We are in a communications lockdown now, but I have ways to transfer funds, and someone will hand-deliver your message to Omar. What else do you need?" Almudir asks.

Khan laughs. "I want those two idiots away from the flight simulator so I can practice in peace."

"That is not a problem, but these men will fly with you. Think of ways they can help," Almudir says, pleased with this outcome.

Captain Khan is alone with his thoughts at the simulator an hour later. There's little need to practice now, but he enforces the discipline he's always known. As a former military pilot, Khan understands operational security but misses his conversations with Syhala. He wishes they could speak again before his death, then laughs. "I find the woman of my dreams and become a martyr?" Khan comes full circle, accepting the simple fact that this mission is grander than any one person. Perhaps things would have been different if she had entered his life sooner, but Syhala is a believer. She will understand his decision and one day praise his actions.

Khan reviews the plan, scoffing that the two Iranians might be considered copilots. The plane will carry 900 kilos of explosives and weigh nearly 400,000 pounds. When he strikes, the fuel tanks will create an awe-inspiring fireball.

There will be no turning back. Once in the air, impact with any solid object will trigger death and destruction. Khan knows Almudir's two goons will ride with him as a deterrent. That is of no consequence. Every professional aviator dreams of performing well on their last flight. Captain Khan's last flight looms on the horizon. Perfection is the ever-elusive goal. He gazes at the perfect aircraft in the perfectly hidden hangar. His reflection on the computer screen before him speaks with immense pride in what he is about to do—the perfect flight.

Long after sunset, Captain Khan returns to his sleeping quarters. He's going to die, and he is at peace.

As sleep comes, so does a recurring dream. He is in an airport terminal with First Officer Aisha. The dream jumps to the fast-approaching ground, and Aisha mouths the word, why?

Chapter 48

April 19, 7 A.M.

Yin, Officer Wright, and Laksh stand together in the embassy's information center. They are all tired from working deep into the night and the mounting stress associated with their tasks. Static satellite images flash across Laksh's display as he explores aerial views of islands in North Sulawesi, Indonesia. Most islands are too small, too mountainous, or have commercial airstrips surrounded by city structures. The established airports would have reported a landing.

Islands are reviewed and dismissed until they arrive at what Wright says is a dead end. Laksh scans several smaller islands but agrees with Wright.

"This is pointless. We have work to do, Laksh," Wright says brusquely.

Laksh turns to Yin with a sorrowful glance, but Yin is unconvinced. She urges him to take one last look at the fishing harbor a few islands earlier. "We agreed the runway was way too short," Laksh repeats.

"Please. Just go back. It was crescent-shaped, aqua lagoon, a bulldozer on the road a few hundred meters away, four outbuildings around a flat-roofed commercial structure, and a sliver of metal beneath the trees on the hill. There was a fishing boat moored at the dock," Yin insists. Wright reluctantly nods his approval as he checks his wristwatch.

Yin's ability to recall details no longer surprises Laksh. He cycles back through nearly a dozen images until zooming in on a plant and outbuildings near a harbor. "Come on," Wright says. "The road is too narrow. Even if they could land a plane there, which is impossible, there's no place to hide. It's over, Yin."

Even Laksh expects to see Yin deflate in defeat, but she appears to be excited. "No, it's not. I need historical images. Can you grab a previous image? Preferably 30 days at least," Yin says, her mind calculating all options.

Laksh is nearly as skeptical as Officer Wright, but there's something in the way Yin processes information that encourages him to continue. He enters coordinates into a database and pulls up static images of that specific island dating back 30, 60, then 90 days. The aerial photos show active construction. Images of the road show sections of excavation and widening, but the sections move from month to month, only to disappear into foliage. They are hiding their work. Yin also sees patterns in the layout, location, and construction of buildings.

"I'll have a team look through the operational database. It would be nice to know who owns that factory and rule it out," Wright says.

Yin is not interested in a database query. She's formulating one of her own. "What altitude are these images taken from? Low Earth Orbit?"

Satellite information is classified, so Laksh is obtuse in his reply. "Somewhere between 100 yards and 10,000 miles. Does that narrow it down? Why do you need to know?"

Yin laughs. "Find an image of a Boeing 777 from the same satellite vantage point and copy it."

Laksh enters coordinates for Manado City, zooms in on a row of parked commercial aircraft, and copies an image. "I'm not totally sure which are 777s but these look about right. Now what, overlay?"

"Drop it on those new buildings," Yin says confidently.

When oriented correctly, the wingspan and fuselage loosely fit the shape of the structures. With enthusiasm, Yin says, "That's it! That's where they took the plane."

"Those are separate buildings. I don't have time for this," Wright says.

"That's what they want us to see, but they are connected. May I?" Yin asks.

Wright approves, and Yin hunts through images backward from when Bao returned to Singapore after his mysterious trip with Tu. Nine photos into her search, she slaps her hands together and points at the display. "Isn't that a Cessna on the tarmac?"

Laksh magnifies the image until they make out the tail number. He saves multiple photos of the plane and raises his hand for a high-five from Yin while exclaiming, "Bingo!"

"Send those to print, Laksh," Wright orders, and as Yin enthusiastically hunts through more images, deepening her analysis, he touches her on the shoulder.

Yin turns her head and looks up at Wright with a knowing smile. "Like I said. Blue sea squirt."

Two minutes later, he raps loudly on Station Chief Sarah Hirsh's closed door and waits momentarily for permission to enter. Wright carries a digital tablet in one hand and the newly printed images of the island in the other. He thinks of the station chief as hands-on, so he places printed images on her desk. "I have something actionable on Rashid and the Triad connection. Laksh and Yin have identified where their Cessna landed. It's an island 200 miles north of Manado City, North Sulawesi."

As Hirsh looks through captured satellite images, Wright follows his boss by swiping through pictures on his iPad. "I'd bet dinner they're running operations from there, training camp or something. You see the sequence of lengthening the runway. Nobody hides that kind of work unless they have a secret, and you won't like this next part. Yin insists Flight 957 didn't crash as believed. I know it's crazy, but—"

"Impossible is more like it, but if this is where Rashid went, I'd consider sending something up the chain. Is there a request here, or just a status update?" Hirsh asks, getting straight to the point.

"Direct action. It's the only answer. We have Triads and terrorists traveling to this island together, construction taking place, and we still don't know who the fourth traveler was. Yin and Laksh think the construction masks a makeshift runway and hangar," Wright adds.

Hirsh laughs, but the longer she sits with the information, the more sobering it becomes. "Yin thinks? What do you say?"

"There are other interpretations, but linking Rashid with the Triads is credible enough. It is highly plausible that the island is a terrorist training area. Get me eyes on, and we may be able to interrupt their plans," Wright says.

"That would be extremely expensive. Have a seat so we can talk this through."

Wright and Station Chief Hirsh verbally review raw intelligence. The Triads sent hundreds of millions of dollars out of their data center. In at least one case, Rashid, a suspected funding conduit for terror, accessed those funds. He and the Triads flew together to the island, and on that island, there has been recent construction that may or may not indicate training facilities. As they talk, Yin's name comes up repeatedly. "You defer to her a lot, Justin. Over half of this intel comes from her analytical skills? Could she be playing us? Is she trustworthy, and more to the point, can she be turned?" Hirsh asks, her voice trailing off.

"I may have overreacted about the MSS connection. She'd make one hell of an analyst—phenomenal memory, bright as a laser, speaks six languages. Before coming to Singapore, she landed a fellowship at MIT, but she didn't take it," Wright says, clearly impressed.

Hirsh harshly interrupts Wright. "You didn't answer my questions. Can she be trusted? Can she be turned? Why did she turn down MIT?"

"My gut says she is trustworthy, but you know how that goes. Can she be turned? We have to try. Regarding MIT, she turned them down to find her missing twin sister. That's character."

"Could the missing sister be a ruse? Any chance a proverbial damsel in distress has taken you in? It's a bit convenient how easily she discovers intel," Hirsh says, playing the devil's advocate, as Wright knows she often does.

"I thought Nigel was thinking with his zipper, but we found the sister. Her name is Li. She was abducted from Shanghai and moved to an underground sex cam operation. Li is legit," Wright says.

"Let me guess. Ms. Chen searches for her sister, gets mixed up with the Triads, gets in over her head when she finds out what they are up to, and looks for help. Is that about it? Why wasn't I read in on this? Who authorized resources to hunt for the girl, you, or Nigel?"

"Nigel worked off-book. He got himself shot executing a rescue, then sent her in my direction before he went under. I contacted a friend to conduct the search for Li," Wright says, omitting the extent of the operation—and the illicit funds.

"Have you ever known me to micromanage as long as you color within the lines? I have your back, but this is sketchy. A brief would have been nice," Hirsh says.

"Sounds like you knew anyway."

"I wasn't born yesterday. How is Nigel doing, by the way?" Hirsh asks.

Relieved to move on, Wright says, "He may never work in the field again, but he'll live. Essex thinks Nigel gave her the info on lax security habits, but that's untrue. He wants Yin's blood for how she tore him up in a recent meeting. If I were Nigel, I'd never work under him again." His voice fades as he thinks about his friend.

Hirsh smiles. "Speaking of Essex, the Aussies are up my ass saying it was her that compromised their security. They want her. Are we going to comply?"

"If Nigel wakes up and wants her, maybe. But give her to Essex? No way," Wright says firmly.

"If this blue sea whatever and the fabricated hangar your Ms. Chen came up with are on target, we'll look like idiots if we don't proceed, but let's not mention that aspect in the writeup. Over twenty agencies looked for that plane, and none caught the anomaly. The training camp angle is enough to get the attention we need," Hirsh says thoughtfully.

"Around Yin, I already feel like an idiot. What's our course of action for Yin? As soon as she's on the street, someone will snatch her. If not the Aussies, then the Triads. They tried to kill her once. They'll do it again," Wright says, looking for support.

"To be determined. Right now, I'm more interested in rescuing the sister. What's the holdup?" Hirsh says, surprising Wright.

"The holdup is funding. Yin says she'll pay, but I'm sure it's black money. We'll have a lot of explaining to do."

Hirsh is tough as nails, but a woman nonetheless, a woman who understands what happens to women who the triads have taken. "My God, Justin. We'll deal with the money source later. Get the sister out of that hell hole. It's the right thing to do, especially if we want her working for our side. Anything else?"

Standing to leave, Wright says, "She's a bit upset because I gave her a phone, not hers. We can't have a foreign national with her background walking around the embassy with unauthorized electronics. Incoming calls will be routed."

"Makes sense. She'll get over it. I'll want you on the call with Langley, so stay close," Hirsh says, signaling the end of their meeting.

An hour later, Station Chief Hirsh and Deputy Chief Wright sit in a Sensitive Compartmented Information Facility video conference with staff at the CIA Operations Center in Langley, Virginia. Hirsh carefully presents their information to one of the operations officers who also sits in a SCIF, and her counterpart is very interested in learning that a known funder of terrorist organizations has traveled to an isolated island with someone high up in the Chinese Triads and a former MSS whiz kid. The analysis that Triads and terrorists may be working together spawns a round of follow-up questions that the team in Singapore cannot answer. Langley dismisses the assertion that Inter-Asian Flight 957 might be in a secret hangar on a remote island. Near their conference's end, the Op-Center asks if China might be behind the terror connection. "They are known to use Triad networks when it suits them, and having this Bao character in the mix implies a level of sophistication we don't often see. Any further thoughts, Justin, before we move this up the chain?" Hirsh asks.

"I have high confidence that the data center was a conduit for an excessive amount of money directed into terrorist networks. I have moderate confidence that bad actors are in Southeast Asia to carry out multiple attacks. We have plausible intel that the island is a component of these attacks, possibly even a training camp, but we need ISR corroboration," Wright says.

"And what's this shit about a secret hangar for a missing 777?" the Op-Center asks with a telling chuckle.

Hirsh gives Wright a look that clearly says *don't do it*, but he doesn't deny the possibility. "If I didn't think it possible, I would not have included it in the report. My gut says that the plane crashed, but the analytical capabilities of this source have proven to be exceptional. The main point is that ISR is needed."

"You're talking about Ms. Chen?" The Ops Center asks.

"Yes, sir. Yin Chen."

Their conversation continues for another fifteen minutes. When the call ends, Hirsh compliments Wright on the excellent work and says, "Now we wait. It could be a day or weeks. Operations will talk with the Director, and the Director will meet with the Secretary of Defense. Because we're calling for action on foreign soil, who knows? SecDef might even get the president involved. You mentioned in the report that the head of that data center is missing."

"Our analysts think he's dead. Based on CCTV images, I do too. But Yin seems to have doubts," Wright says.

"Is her doubt legit, or is she using that to keep us off balance?" Hirsh probes.

Wright shrugs. "It could be that. But she has a fraction of the information available to us and yet arrives at answers in half the time. I think she has doubts about Bao's demise. She wants to look for him in the underworld."

Hirsh thinks momentarily and then says, "I've seen the CCTV images, too. They looked authentic. Our analysts concur. But there's no body. Am I right?"

Wright leans forward to speak, then apparently changes his mind.

"What? If you have something, spill it."

"Yin thinks the video could have been AI-generated. I have no idea why she might think that, but there it is."

"Does this woman ever take things at face value? Christ!"

Wright lets his boss work through her thoughts uninterrupted. After a moment of contemplation, Hirsh says. "I can't tie up key resources just to watch her surf, but supervised access might be a good idea. Have your guy Decker sit on her and document her methods. I'm interested in seeing how the Chinese operate on the dark web. If she's as good as you say, there may be sites and methods we've not heard of."

As Wright stands to leave, he says, "She's not stupid. She won't give us anything she doesn't want us to know. But I'll have Dave sit with her."

Wright turns towards the door, pauses, and then returns to his station chief. "Don't get me wrong. Yin is hiding things from us, as we are from her—the source of her wealth, for starters—but it feels like she's on our side in this hunt. I like her instincts."

Station Chief Hirsh lifts her reading glasses from her nose and lets them dangle from the strap as she stands. "Do you like her instincts as much as her looks? Don't be so predictable, Justin. A smart woman can run circles around eager men."

Wright averts his eyes in embarrassment. He turns toward the door and leaves.

Two hours later, Wright sends his assistant to a meeting room with Yin and gives her access to WiFi through the segregated guest network. As he leaves them, Hirsh calls. "Operations pushed your information to the analysts and promised a quick turnaround. SecDef has a lot on his plate right now, so we must be patient."

"A quick turnaround could mean anything. We need that surveillance now."

"Patience, Justin. Patience. We've done our part. It's out of our hands."

Chapter 49

April 19, 11 A.M.

Almudir and Junaid are unwittingly fortunate. As analysts in Fort Meade decide whether to proceed with expensive signals intelligence, surveillance, and reconnaissance of their island, Almudir breaks communications silence and sends coded messages via sat phone to every cell in his network. The Five Eyes community does not immediately track these messages. He arranges to meet Captain Khan and the remaining workers in the hangar. A fishing vessel waits at the dock to transport the remaining 23 general laborers, two engineers, and the building contractors from the island to the Southern Philippines.

When Almudir and Junaid verify that everyone is present, he takes a position beneath the wing of the massive 777 and yells out, "Allahu Akbar!" A phrase that is repeated loudly multiple times by those who are present. His demeanor has changed significantly from earlier meetings, where he angrily urged everyone to work harder, faster, and more efficiently. Today, he is giddy. The world is about to burn, and Almudir tastes victory.

Pointing towards the jet engine behind him, Almudir praises his workers. "Look at what we have accomplished. In the past months, we have trained and equipped over 200 holy warriors, here and in other locations. You have transformed this aircraft into a formidable weapon that will strike the great Satan. But there is still work to be done. Soon, many of you will return to your families, knowing you played a critical role in this Divine mission. May heaven accept you.

"You've seen how hard our pilots are working. Let's acknowledge

Captain Khan and his two copilots who will fly this mighty weapon into the enemy. When you get home and see what unfolds, remember this. No man will ever again doubt our capabilities, reach, and resolve. "Allahu Akbar!"

The workers erupt once again into calls of how Allah is the greatest. Almudir continues. "Only the avionics mechanic and those essential for takeoff will remain. Everyone else, please gather your belongings and report to the dock. You are going home."

More cheers erupt.

Captain Khan is disappointed that the Iranians will fly with him. They are unnecessary and, in his opinion, will only get in the way, but as he approaches Almudir to protest, he is warned with a wave of Almudir's hand to remain silent. "When the crew is gone," Almudir whispers. He leaves for a private conversation with Junaid.

Within thirty minutes, workers load their belongings into the larger of two fishing boats as Junaid performs a head count. The jubilant workers exchange stories and congratulations until the last man is on board and below deck. Junaid waves farewell to the boat captain and returns to the hangar as the vessel disappears into the horizon.

Moments later, a sleek chartered jet arrives and taxis to the hangar to pick up Junaid and Nasr, each with final tasks to perform off the island. The chartered jet will drop both men off at Supadio International Airport in Pontianak, West Kalimantan, Indonesia, where Junaid and Nasr will board a flight to Kuala Lumpur.

The pilots disembark, greeting Nasr with laughter. They've flown many missions to the island, carrying people and equipment. They are helpful to the cause, but on a need-to-know basis only, and they certainly do not need to know what lurks behind the closed hangar doors. "Are we all set?" Nasr asks.

"It's going to be a long one. We have six hours to PNK and come right back here, correct? Where can my first officer and I rest when we return?"

"It's just the two of you, correct? Of course. Everything is prepared. Junaid will join us momentarily. He's making an important phone call. Do you need anything?" Nasr asks the pilot.

Junaid stands on the dock gazing intently at the horizon. He pulls a phone from his pocket and lets his finger hover over the send button as he recalls the faces of many of the workers he's come to know. There was the mechanic who kept their heavy equipment working, the cook, a former soccer player who had organized small matches at the end of the day, three carpenters, an electrician, a welder from Iran, and a dozen strong general laborers who spent countless hours working on the runway, all competent and faithful men. The thought that they will never again meet bothers him, but only until he hits send. As he does, the fishing vessel, somewhere between the island and the shores of North Sulawesi, explodes from the hull up, sending all on board in pieces to the ocean floor.

Moments later, Junaid arrives in a golf cart at the hangar for final coordination with Almudir. "Did you make the call," Almudir asks.

Junaid nods.

"Very well. It's been a long journey, my friend. Blessings upon you," Almudir says.

"My plane is waiting," Junaid reminds Almudir.

"Yes, yes. Who remains?"

"Hazer, the two pilots when they return, and three men to position the planes. My helicopter pilot will pick you up just after Khan's liftoff. Be ready. There won't be much time," Junaid says.

"I'll be ready. Now go, and make sure you hand deliver these," Almudir says, handing Junaid the letters Captain Khan wrote.

Smiling with dark intent, Junaid says, "It will be my pleasure."

They quickly embrace. No words are needed. Each knows what the other is thinking.

After watching his friend board the chartered jet, Almudir walks to the hangar office and finds Captain Khan practicing for his final flight. "May I watch?" he says. They sit quietly together for a time. The uncomfortable silence is broken moments later by the departure of the small chartered jet carrying Nasr and Junaid.

A dark smile, under a darker stare, Almudir says, "Don't worry. The plane will return."

11 P.M.

Hazer and two others finish placing the last of a series of portable solar-powered lights on the corners and at predetermined intervals down each side of the island runway in preparation for the return of the chartered jet. The lights were a contingency for the 777 in the event Captain Khan arrived on the island before daybreak. Now, they will serve the same purpose for the chartered jet. The moment the jet touches down, they will dispose of them.

The chartered jet returns on nearly perfect schedule at 11:48 pm. With Junaid and Nasr gone, Almudir greets the pilot and copilot. "You must be tired. I'll take you directly to the sleeping quarters and have someone bring food and drink," he says, smiling in recognition of the endurance run.

Almudir drives them uphill, thanking him often and profusely for the assistance. When they arrive, he opens the hut door and apologizes for the condition of the facilities. As the pilots step forward and take in their humble quarters, Almudir quickly fires well-placed rounds to the base of their skulls and sends a second bullet into their bodies as they fall to the floor. He holsters his weapon, closes the hut's door, and returns to the hangar without care.

Meanwhile, Hazer and his helpers rapidly disassemble the chartered jet's avionics equipment bay, hoping to transfer the ADS system into the 777. Captain Khan assists where he can, more concerned with whether his idea will pan out than his impending death. He is now completely dedicated to the mission. His flight pattern has to be perfect. What will happen when the nose of his aircraft finds the enemy? Will he close his eyes, yell that his creator is great, or remain laser-focused until impact?

"It is your lucky day, my friend." Captain Khan is surprised to hear Almudir's voice behind him.

Khan's reply is terse, nearly revealing his intense dislike for the man who dared lie about killing so many passengers. "And why is that?"

"The joint military exercises have ended, and our target will enter the harbor in Jakarta within a few hours."

Turning towards the mechanic, Almudir continues. "We're running out of time. Will you be ready, Hazer?"

The mechanic glances up momentarily, muttering that he will do his best as he pulls instruments and components from the chartered jet.

Hazer and Captain Khan have spoken quietly on multiple occasions and were about to do so again when surprised. Almudir doesn't like it when critical resources talk among themselves.

Like Captain Khan, Hazer has a deal to collect money when the operation is complete. Both men abandoned any chance of ever working again in the real world when they agreed to help with the hijacking. The mechanic has no leverage and is sure he will never collect. His attempt to secure prepayment for his family failed miserably, and he now fears for his life.

"We have things to discuss," Almudir says to his pilot. Captain Khan follows Almudir outside the hangar, subtly scanning the area, noting neither Junaid nor Nasr are present.

"As I said, the military exercises are complete. Observers will tell us when the carrier enters the port. How long do you imagine the carrier will be vulnerable?" Almudir has returned to his usual self. His attitude is fierce, menacing, and demanding.

"You should have included me while planning," Khan says.

"I have plans you do not know about. Just answer my questions. Timing is critical," Almudir demands.

"The ship will only be in the harbor for 24 to 36 hours. Exactly how long that will be is classified. If an attack is possible, they will stay in open water. Assuming they aren't scared off, the attack window is during the celebration with dignitaries. You mentioned fireworks?"

"Big fireworks. It's critical you time your attack accordingly."

"Of course. For reasons we've discussed, I'll strike during the grand finale. Your contacts will have to let us know that things are on schedule. We have alternate targets in case things don't work as planned, but I am 100% committed," Khan says, owning the moment as any mission commander would.

"Six hours flying time?" Almudir asks, pleased with Khan's acumen.

"We don't have the fuel for a six-hour flight. I must do it in four. It's more dangerous, but if Hazer is successful, I will arrive just in time."

"And this electronic box you speak of?" Almudir asks, pointing towards Hazer and his men.

Khan doubts the ADS spoofing will work but conceals his pessimism. "It's a complicated process involving machine addresses and software configuration, but I'm pleased with his progress." Kahn nods toward the small, chartered jet. "You should probably tow that jet out of sight."

"I will. Have you instructed your copilots?"

"You think someone has to be on board to watch me, but I don't need watching. I'm committed, and there's no possibility of landing without death and destruction. I want to strike the carrier more than you will ever know." Pride is evident in his voice.

"You say so now, but I have seen it many times how approaching death plays with the mind. You will have second and third thoughts. It's in our nature. Use them as spotters, lookouts, for inspiration, or anything else. It's not so easy to die alone. These men are more willing than you. Put them to work, if necessary, but they are going with you. That is not up for discussion."

Opening his phone, Almudir points to a screenshot of a wire transfer receipt. "As you requested, payment is made. Your cousin and Syhala will soon receive their letters. We have done our part. It's time you do yours."

Captain Khan takes the phone and studies the image before handing it back. "And no harm will come to Omar or Syhala?"

"My friend, that is up to you. Pilot the plane into the enemy's heart, and they will live long and happy lives." As he spits vitriol at Khan, Almudir's face twists into an expression crueler and more sinister than Khan has seen. "Fail us—No— Fail Allah! And the people you are so fond of will spend the rest of their days in unspeakable agony. You probably think I am ruthless. Junaid is much worse!"

"Speaking of your henchman, where is he and your sidekick?" Khan asks.

Almudir's reply is dark and menacing. "Who do you think has your letters? They have relocated to be close to those you care for. You know, to ensure they're taken care of."

Khan has been threatened dozens of times since arriving on the island. Somehow, the threats are more frightening when directed at the people he loves. He shudders, then locks eyes with Almudir. "My destiny is written in the heavens. Cowardly threats and coercion change nothing."

Almudir laughs. "Relax. Perform your task, and nothing will happen to them. Now, go get some rest."

Chapter 50

April 19, 11:55 P.M.

Mr. Green leaves his laptop to answer an expected knock at his door. "Took long enough," he says, inviting two young CIA agents into his apartment. They carry a duffle bag.

"I need you to sign off, but it's all here. $1 million. What is the status?"

Green unzips the bag, looks at the cash, and tosses it onto a sofa. "I'll make contact soon and get the ball rolling. If they go for it, I'll need assistance with the extraction. You guys have to be ready at a moment's notice."

"That depends on you. If Li is in the Philippines, like you think, we can be in and out quickly. But it will take time if she's nowhere near our teams. We are on notice and ready. The rest is up to you. Anything else?"

Green sees the CIA men out of his apartment and immediately contacts his underworld host. "You know that little Chinese treat? I want her."

"I'll get you another session," his host says.

"No. I mean, I want her for myself. I've got a half million dollars cash sitting here, and ten percent is yours if you can make it happen. I can't get her out of my head. Know what I mean? Delicious." Green says, always playing the part to perfection. He's often disgusted by what he encounters in the depths of humanity.

Silence ensues before the host replies. "I doubt the property is for sale but get real. She's worth three times that."

Green expects this response. Careful not to overplay his hand, he says, "No one is worth that much. 750 tops. I do have other prospects."

His host quickly snaps back, "Then I suggest you take your business elsewhere."

Green holds firm to his $750,000 offer. He has become an expert on reading others and knows exactly how this will end. "My offer stands."

His host's facade cracks first. "One million 250, and she's yours."

Green knows the next offer will close the deal or destroy his chances. "You and I know you'll never get more than I've offered."

"Then there's nothing further to discuss. Good luck finding something this nice."

Green stays committed to the outcome. "Bummer." He reaches forward to sign off.

His host flinches. "Hold on. I'm certain we can find something equitable. Make it a cool million and call it a day."

Green pulls back from the screen in contemplation and then says. "I don't know why I'm doing this, but sure. We have a deal. One million." Green reveals the suitcase full of money.

"Deal," his host says. I'll make the arrangements. Get back in one hour for details."

"I'll jet anywhere in the world to pick her up. The only thing I ask is that you handle this personally. It's important that she arrives in good condition. When can I have her?" Green asks.

"There are certain complications I'll need to work around. Like I said, I'll see what I can do and get back in a day or two."

"A day or two won't work. I'm arranging a party with clients. I tell you what. Let's sweeten the deal. If you can wrap this up within the hour, there's an extra ten grand in it for you," Green says, not wanting to give this guy any time to hunt for a better offer.

"You have a real hard-on for this one. Want another session while we wait for a decision?"

"You know me too well. Hell yes," Green says, holding back the bile.

• • •

Meanwhile in Macau, Tu places a long-anticipated phone call to Dragonhead. "We've located the sister."

Chapter 51

April 20, 4:30 P.M.

The setting sun casts long, dark shadows among the buildings adjoining the island runway. A sense of foreboding and solemnity fills the air of the hangar as Captain Khan methodically conducts an exterior inspection of his glorious 777. Repetition and habitual patterns are keys to success. He's done this exact thing thousands of times but treats it with special reverence as he knows it will be his last. He stands just outside the hangar and gazes at the sight before him. Captain Khan sees his beloved aircraft as a mighty beast that will forge a path on his final journey. He approaches the nose, ensuring the bulldozer and towing apparatus are properly secured before walking around the entire aircraft in a clockwise flow. He's deliberate in his manner, inspecting the landing gear, engines, under the wings, the tail section, and back to the nose of the plane before standing at the base of a ladder leading to an open door near the flight deck. "Was that even necessary? It's time to go," Almudir says impatiently.

"Everything is perfectly timed with the fireworks display, which ends in five and a half hours. If you are so anxious, why not join me and earn your spot in heaven Almudir?" Khan answers, implying that Almudir is nothing but a coward.

Almudir doesn't react to the cynicism. He places his hands on Khan's face and kisses both cheeks, showing respect for his brother in arms. Khan turns on his heels and ascends the ladder.

The two Iranians are already onboard. As Khan is about to close the door, Almudir yells. "Allahu Akbar!" but there is no reply, only the sound of Hazer dragging the ladder across concrete and the mechanical rumble of the bulldozer as the engine starts in preparation to drag the massive 777 uphill for departure.

After closing and sealing the door, Khan scans the cabin for a few minutes. The interior passenger compartment is familiar and inviting, though many seats have been removed and replaced by explosives and wiring harnesses. There will be no passengers today, but the weight of the mission is more profound than anything Captain Khan has ever experienced. Everything feels complete.

The hatch leading down to racks of computers and instrumentation needed to fly the plane remains open. Hazer has done his best to transfer the ADS components from the chartered plane into the commercial aircraft but quietly told Khan he doubts it will work. Every other request, however, has been fulfilled. The plane will travel in radio silence and appear like a dark hole in the sky. All exterior lights are still in working order, but Captain Khan plans only to use them for takeoff. He will fly the mission in the darkness Mother Nature provides, depending on unknown cyber experts to disable radar.

Almudir demanded that the landing gear be disabled as soon as it is retracted into the fuselage. Khan laughed when told this. Of course, Almudir would do everything possible to ensure the captain followed through on the mission. What Khan does not say is that those not willing to martyr themselves will never understand the brave minds of those who are.

Khan signals below that the parking brake is released, and he's ready for towing. He feels a slight jolt as the bulldozer begins pulling the beast from its lair. Khan begins his preflight ritual using the printed checklists as his guide. "Get comfortable, gentlemen. Grab a seat in the passenger compartment and buckle in. I'll call you when you are needed," he says to the redundant pilots, but they don't leave the flight deck. Instead, the Neanderthal he attempted to train produces a pistol and places it between his legs, glaring at Khan.

"You won't need that unless you intend to use it on yourself," Khan says defiantly.

When the aircraft is completely out of the makeshift hangar, Captain Khan silently repeats his mantra. *Routine is necessary. It calms the mind and minimizes errors.* Keeping with habitual patterns, Captain Khan briefs the Iranian copilots regarding the conduct of the flight. He routinely describes what to expect during takeoff, how they are most in danger as they pick up speed on the rough roadway, and what he needs them to do while he follows his circuitous route to the target. He then frightens the men by describing what will occur during the attack and how he needs them to be quiet during various segments of their practiced route.

He reminds the Iranians that they will fly low and slow, changing altitude and airspeed to manage time and fuel. He'll have to manage the fuel burn if they are to reach their target at the right moment. He emphasizes that he will be calculating many variables continuously throughout the flight. Distractions must stay at the minimum.

"This flight will be different than anything you have experienced on the computer or even in real life. If we don't follow the flight plan to the letter, military jets will shoot us out of the sky. We can only hope to be close enough to our target to complete the mission when we are discovered."

"But the radar will be disabled?" the younger of the two says.

"We can only hope," Khan replies.

The larger of the two Iranians shifts uncomfortably in the First Officer's seat. He doesn't know what to do or when to do it but doesn't want to appear weak and helpless. He reaches toward the console. "No! Touch nothing now or at any point during the flight," Captain Khan yells. "When I reach the target, I will tell you exactly what to do. I will advance the throttles for maximum speed and kinetic energy, flying just over the top of the terrain. I may need you as spotters, but until I say, do nothing. Is that understood?"

The younger Iranian, wanting to help, asks, "Spotters? Spotters for what?"

Khan takes a deep breath, trying to stay calm. "You will hunt for anything you think I need to know about. If you see other aircraft or tracer rounds heading for us, if someone fires a missile, and most importantly, if you see the aircraft carrier, that is what I need to know."

Satisfied that his preflight briefing is understood, Captain Khan experiences unexpected exhilaration. He opens the flight deck window to take in the Pacific air for the last time. He enters the route into the flight management system, knowing it is only a backup. He's already entered a highly detailed route into the handheld GPS device on his lap.

Khan yells instructions toward the bulldozer and wonders what will happen to the driver when they are away. The man has a family. Almudir is ruthless, and there is nothing he can do about anything or anyone he leaves behind. At least Omar and Syhala will have enough money to start over. Beyond the success of this mission, Omar and Syhala are his highest priority, but even their fate is beyond his reach.

Captain Khan runs through a series of checklists while the 777 edges closer to the runway. The pace of the towing process resembles that of a funeral procession and is unnerving to his two passengers. As Captain Khan prepares for departure, five time zones away, sitting in a weary apartment in Plovdiv, Bulgaria, a hacker sips Stolichno beer and devours a slice from the Pizza Lab. Two months earlier, his friend Nicolay sent code for this next hack. When the call comes, all he must do is run it, which he does, completely unaware that he is participating in the deadliest terrorist attacks in history. He taps the keys on his computer, finishes his beer, and turns up the volume on his television.

Simultaneously, every Flight Information Region's radar system from Manila to Jakarta and Western Indonesia experience a massive outage, including Aircraft Communications Addressing and Reporting Systems and Controller Pilot Data Link Communications, the primary means of control. In the dark, controllers cannot separate or identify aircraft. Initial media reports will indicate the failure is due to minor technical issues, but those who know better cringe in fear. This unprecedented outage is comparable to the airspace debacle in the Philippines in early 2023. Flights headed into the region get diverted to other locations. As for the hundreds of flights already in the affected airspace, it's too late. The mayhem begins.

Ibrahim tows the Triple Seven up the hill and positions it for takeoff before returning to the base of the hill and pushing the chartered jet off the runway and into the hangar.

When the runway is clear, Captain Khan runs through his engine start and before-takeoff checklists, like the professional aviator he's always been. The engines roar to life as threads of an ongoing question fill his mind. It ultimately wasn't Almudir's threats, intimidation, and coercion that put him in this situation. Yes, Almudir manipulated him, but he'd been so proud to fly refugees and supplies for Nasr. When hijacking Flight 957 was mentioned, Nasr ominously repeated that Khan didn't have to do it, but who else could have pulled off such a fantastic mission? He could have said these idiot pilots were ready for the mission and watched them explode before even getting off the island, but then what?

Junaid or Almudir would have shot him. No loose ends, right? Now in control of his own destiny, Captain Khan is ready.

Flight conditions are optimal. Khan clears his mind and engages the throttles. This will be like every other flight he's ever taken in the pursuit of perfection. He smiles, knowing the excess fuel he's asked for on every single flight over the past months has finally paid off. He advances the throttles forward through mechanical stops, the aircraft leaping in response, pushing the massive commercial airliner downhill toward the harbor on its glorious journey. Only then does he toggle on the lights illuminating the makeshift runway.

Engines roar as the jumbo jet increases speed along the narrow roadway toward the harbor. The Beast's wingtips nearly brush against the shrubbery that once obscured satellite views as the aircraft picks up speed. The uneven surface of the improvised runway causes the plane to shudder. When they reach flying speed, Captain Khan starts a slow, smooth, deliberate pull on the yoke and coaxes the Beast into the warm, humid air. The eyes of the Iranians widen with fear as they near the harbor docks. "Pull up!" One of them yells, but Captain Khan is steady, smooth, and, above all else, precise as he lifts the improvised missile into the air. They take flight precisely at 6 pm, four hours to the minute before the firework's grand finale in Jakarta.

Almudir watches the graceful liftoff while making a SAT phone call. Within seconds, the Beast's lights go dark, and all anyone can see is a vague but ominous silhouette gliding into the dusk. The landing gear retracts into the fuselage as the aircraft turns west and disappears, leaving the island in near silence except for Almudir's yelling. "We have much to do before we leave. Hazer, you will drain the fuel tanks of the chartered plane onto the hangar floor. Ibrahim, go to the office and destroy the flight simulator. Be sure to smash the hard drives. You two, ready the boat for departure. You know your responsibilities. Time is of the essence. We must leave within the hour."

When the work is complete, Almudir sends everyone to the boat and says he'll be along momentarily. He watches his friends hustle onto the vessel, hears the whir of helicopter blades in the distance, and presses a button on a remote detonator. The boat explodes, sending bodies and debris into the air as if in slow motion.

When he is safely in the helicopter and lifting off, Almudir begins pressing a series of buttons on his phone. Looking expectantly at his creation below, one explosion follows another, obliterating the big house, and the huts on the hill before converting their hangar into a massive fireball.

Chapter 52

April 20, 6:00 P.M.

Wright's young assistant, David Decker, leads Yin back to Meeting Room 6, essentially a large storage closet equipped with a table, four chairs, a presentation monitor, and carts piled high with AV equipment. Yin's attempts to track down Bao the previous evening and earlier today found nothing, but she's not finished. Decker says, "We have two hours."

"What's his problem?" Yin complains as she opens a laptop and immediately heads for the dark web. David slides a chair next to her as if he wants to observe every keystroke. She has access to the Internet through a non-classified IP router network and knows everything she does in digital space is recorded. He doesn't have to watch everything she does.

"Justin? What do you mean?"

"He praises my outstanding analytical skills, his words not mine, yet doesn't believe anything I say. You're a smart guy. The debris fields were faked. Anyone with a brain can see that, but he repeats that the plane crashed. He says Bao was shot twice in the head, which is probably true, but it is also possible that the video of his death was generated using AI."

"Why do you say that?"

"Bao hasn't worked out at a gym even one day. The man in that video fought hard and was physical until the end. The Bao I know would have used words to defend himself."

Decker lets Yin continue. "It wasn't Wright's idea to grant Internet access. How long have you worked for him? Is he as bad at golf as Nigel said?"

Yin asks. She's decided to exploit Decker's youth and inexperience. A strategy she was not ready to employ the previous evening.

"They both pretty much suck at golf. You play?"

"It's expensive," Yin says as she revives one of her old aliases to view underworld sites. Knowing every keystroke is recorded means this alias is burned, and she won't be able to use it with anonymity in the future, but none of that matters any longer. She makes light conversation for the first ten minutes of access while tapping into various websites. It is only a matter of time before she catches Decker inappropriately looking at her breasts. "Do you mind?" she says, throwing the young man off guard. Decker stands to stretch, escaping the embarrassment of being caught, which gives Yin time to check her messages.

Haitao has no additional information but wants to know where she's been and if she has any news. Neither question receives a truthful response. She types that she may be getting close, then feels sudden and profound dread. The emotion rushes through her frame like a panic attack but passes as soon as it arrives. Has something else happened to Li? She attributes the feeling to sleep deprivation and mounting stress and then is surprised by a message to her in one of the chat rooms.

"Find something?" Decker asks, leaning over her shoulder to see the display.

Yin doesn't respond immediately. Her mind races through points of contact with Bao, dating back to EEL. "I don't know. This message is from someone called Santana24. Someone is acting as if they are Bao," she says.

For reasons that Yin does not understand, Decker reads the message aloud. "I've been thinking a lot recently about balance, making things right, and Yin and Yang."

Hearing the words sends a chill through her spine. The message's syntax and formatting don't match Bao's style. The message fits so much of their relationship, but something seems off.

"Santana24 is Bao?" Decker asks.

"That's what someone wants me to believe. Yes."

"Dead men don't show up in chat rooms, so either he's alive or someone is using his identity. Either way, Wright should see this," Decker says, and pulls out his phone.

Yin interrupts by touching his arm. "Show me the recording of Bao's abduction and murder again. Maybe we can see something that was missed."

"I can't do that. If Bao is still alive—"

"You didn't hear me. I think this is a Bao imposter. For all I know, Justin sent it, but it's not Bao."

"The message didn't come from us. I can guarantee that. Play along with whoever it is and see where this goes."

"Not until you show me the video." Yin pushes her chair back from the computer, folds her arms defiantly, and throws a dark stare at Wright's underling while wrestling to control her frustration.

Decker responds by completing the call he started before her interruption. He waits uncomfortably until Wright answers. Yin can only hear his side of their conversation. "Will you authorize access to the Bao Gu video? We might have something here."

"I don't think she'll be happy with stills. We need the full video," Decker says, talking with Officer Wright but looking at Yin. It's as if Decker imagines he and Yin are teammates, so she gives him a thumbs-up gesture.

"Someone in a chat room pretends to be Bao, or maybe it is Bao. We need to revisit the video."

Decker smiles as the call ends and says he'll be right back. Four minutes later, he returns with a digital tablet, closes the door, and sits beside Yin. "You're not allowed to touch the tablet, but I can play it for you."

A deeper look at the video is deflating. The Bao in this video does fight his captors, but they do not appear to be quite as strong as she remembered them to be. Yin contemplates her next move and replies to the Santana24 message. She writes: *Yes. Let's make things right. I'm sitting in the American Embassy. Let's talk.*

"Why would you tell them you're here? You have no idea who you're communicating with."

"Neither of us do," Yin snaps, and then sees his point. She might have made a mistake. If the Triad is somehow using Bao's identity to locate her, she's just given them critical information.

Decker's hands rise to his face involuntarily, the young man wondering if he should call his boss again or wait to see what happens.

"How much time do we have?" Yin asks.

"Probably as much as you need, but at least another hour. I should get Justin in here."

Yin doesn't explain the familiar dread she felt earlier. Instead, she brazenly changes subjects. Placing a hand on Decker's knee, she pleads. "I need help. I sense that something has happened to my sister, so if you know anything, please, please tell me." Yin is ready to beg, but a new message appears in the chat. Santana24 writes: *Get out of there now!*

Chapter 53

April 20, 6:45 P.M.

Decker is stunned by Yin's insistence that the embassy may be in danger of an attack. Yin is so insistent about warning his boss that he leads her through the hallways to the situation room. They burst through the door to find Wright busy with his team.

"We close doors for a reason—"

"We have to evacuate the facility," Yin says with emphasis. Bao or someone pretending to be Bao made contact. There is going to be an attack here—an explosion or something. Everyone should leave!"

"What are you talking about? Bao is dead. We've been through this," Wright snaps.

"Fine, he's dead, but that doesn't negate the warning I received from someone posing as him." Yin recognizes what happens in her body as she loses control. Her muscles tighten, her face becomes flushed, and she grinds her teeth together between outbursts. That's happening now despite trying to stay calm.

Decker interjects and tries to explain, but Yin's rage dominates. "I just contacted someone pretending to be Bao. They warned me to leave. In the context of all that is happening, it can only mean one thing. This place is on a target list. You should evacuate the complex." As she says this, others in the room look to Officer Wright for direction. Some darken with concern.

"Hold on. Who exactly did you communicate with? What exactly did they say?" Wright asks impatiently.

Decker interrupts. "It was a chat room, someone named Santana24."

"It's a handle either Bao or someone who knows him very well would use," Yin says in exasperation. "Why are you just sitting there? The last time I received a warning like this, the data center was attacked," Yin insists, baffled by the inaction.

Wright is clearly annoyed with Yin. "Give us the room. David, you stay," he says, and the assembled team members do as he asks.

When they are gone, Wright turns to Yin, who has her hands defiantly placed on her hips, waiting for action. "She also thinks something has happened to her sister," Decker says, then backs away from the conversation with palms raised after receiving threatening glares from Yin and Wright.

"First of all, you can't just get in my face whenever you have a wild idea."

"Idea? I've given you facts. The plane didn't crash. It's on that island, and an attack is coming. Even if Bao is dead, this person is warning me to leave. Am I a prisoner or an asset? It's clear you're not going anywhere, but you should let me leave. Someone, and I'm not ruling out Bao, no matter what's on that video, is warning that something will happen, and I think it will happen soon," Yin says, urgency and darkness rising from somewhere deep in her psyche.

"And why do you think something has happened to your sister? You like facts? How about this one. Green successfully negotiated a price, and a team is heading her way for extraction. That's what we've been doing in here, monitoring the situation. Get out of here and let us do our job." Wright yells.

Yin's knees buckle and she catches her weight by grabbing Decker's arm. "Don't lie to me. Please don't lie. I won't survive another lie. Do the Triads know where she is? I need to talk to her."

Wright is visibly concerned by her reaction. Yin's eyes are instantly red and moist with tears. She appears to be on the verge of mental collapse. He says, "It's going to be okay. It will all be okay. There are protocols in place. As soon as we have her, you can talk."

"Don't bring her here, not here. What about the safe house? I've done all I can for you. Bring us to the safe house. I beg you. Not here," Yin pleads.

"We won't bring Li here no matter what. She'll need medical attention first and foremost."

"A hospital? We look exactly alike. They are looking for me."

Wright raises his hands in surrender. "Make one phone call for us, and you can go to the safe house. David will take you. When Li is safe, we'll connect you. Deal?"

"Phone call?" Yin says, her surprise evident.

"Satellite phone. I want you to call Tu," Wright says, expecting some of Yin's rage in response.

"They tried to kill me. Why would I do that? Why provoke him? This is crazy."

"We have our reasons, and we'll tell you exactly what to say. Keep Tu on the call as long as possible, and that's it. David will take you to the safe house."

Fifteen minutes later, Yin sits at a table with Chief of Station Hirsh, Justin Wright, and a small crew of technicians. She's given final instructions and handed a sheet of talking points. Bao's satellite phone is among the artifacts seized following the attack on the data center. When the techs are ready, she places the call.

Three rings. Four rings. Yin throws up her hands, mouthing the words, no answer, but then Tu's voice comes on the phone. "Who is this?"

"You tried to kill us all, but you missed me, you bastard," Yin says calmly. Her body is motionless and unruffled, but she wants to yell.

There's a moment of silence before Tu replies. "I don't know what you are talking about, but you have a lot of courage contacting me."

"I know about the money, the terrorists, the island, and the weapons. If you want me to stay silent, it will cost you." Yin pauses for effect. Her talking points include asking for one million dollars US to be sent via cryptocurrency.

Wright stands in front of Yin, swirling his fingers to keep the call going. Everyone expects her to begin a financial negotiation, promising anything to extend the conversation, but Yin cannot help herself. "And my sister. I know you took my sister. Return her, or I go to the authorities."

"Go to the authorities about what? Whatever you did or did not do in Singapore was for your friend Bao Gu. Where is he? You said the police took him away. Was that a lie? There may be a reward if you tell me where he is right now."

Yin's inner dragon begs for release.

"You have my sister, and I want her back now!" Yin screams, alarming everyone present.

A long pause shows Yin that she's triggered recognition. "I don't know anything about some sister, but if I were in your situation, I'd want to see her alive. Bringing foolish conjecture to the authorities could be unhealthy for everyone. If you think I have your sister, offer a trade—your life for hers."

As Tu says this, Yin's face turns to pure rage, and she springs to her feet, staring at Wright, who also stands and points to one of his technicians. "If you hurt her—"

"You'll do what?" Tu laughs. Before ending the call abruptly, he says, "Stay silent for a few weeks, and I may send her home. Go to the authorities, and I will slice the skin from her body in front of you. Inch by inch."

When Tu disconnects, Yin screams and lunges at Wright. "You lied to me!"

The muscular man easily restrains Yin, loudly denying Tu's claim. "Yin! Stop! Tu lied to you. He would tell you he has Li no matter what. I'm telling you, he does not. We are bringing Li home. Just stop. I promise."

A dark guttural scream escapes from deep within Yin. "If you are lying, I will destroy you!"

Chapter 54

April 20 6:55 P.M.

A private plane delivers Triad member Ming Dao to Butuan-Bancasi Airport in the southern Philippines. He tells the pilot to wait at the airstrip for as long as it takes and climbs into a waiting van of mercenaries. Ming's instructions are straightforward. They will drive to Bayugan City and meet with the men who control Li Chen. Tu has warned these men to hand Li over, but if they don't accept Tu's ample payment, Ming will take her by force and keep the payment for himself. Whatever it takes, they are to return to China with Li Chen.

The cluster of buildings at the address provided appears uninhabited except for dim lights illuminating windows at the back of the facility. The air is thick and humid, vegetation unruly. The buzz and chitter of insects accompany the armed men to a back door where they observe two young men playing cards and drinking Loshan through an open window. Ming decides the guards were not hired to protect the facility from intruders. They are there to ensure no one leaves and are not a threat.

Ming knocks hard on the door, startling the two young men. One of them picks up a machete and comes to the door, dropping it immediately when confronted by pistol muzzles. Ming states his business with force. "Dragonhead sent us. I need to talk with your boss. We've come for the girl." One of the mercenaries translates Ming's broken English into Cebuano.

"No girl here," the frightened man replies. Ming has no patience for nonsense. He grabs the guard's throat, prompting him to point toward a door.

The steel door opens onto the head of a stairwell leading downward. They descend into a hallway lined with locked rooms and encounter another guard, or perhaps the manager and enforcer. The man looks up fearfully from a computer console.

Ming shows a photo of Li on his phone, as one of the mercenaries tells the confused and frightened man that Dragonhead sent them and asks forcefully where she is.

The man holds up his hands in surrender, speaking rapidly, his gestures implying that he either doesn't understand or can't comply.

Ming is incensed. He sends his mercenaries down the hall, believing the man a liar. They move from room to room, throwing doors open to look for the woman in their photo. Unable to locate her, Ming returns to the man at the video console and presses his pistol into the man's throat. "Where?"

Perhaps confused or finally admitting where Li is, he points and holds up two fingers, implying room two. Ming grabs him by the back of his neck and pushes him down the hallway. The manager enters room two first, followed by Ming. Seconds later, a woman screams, and two shots ring out. The young men from the floor above reappear. A short gunfight ensues, followed by more screaming—then silence.

• • •

Tu drives the Cotai Strip in Macau to Jiao's casino and pulls into his reserved parking spot. He sits in his car, contemplating options for over ten minutes. Bad things happen when he reports failures, and he's had to do that too often of late. Now, he must report the failure to retrieve Li Chen from the Philippines. Guests pass by on their way into or out of the casino every few minutes. When he places the call, Jiao will ask him to come to the office. If he yells when Tu enters, all is good, but Dragonhead may sit behind his desk, looking disappointed. He'll ask if Tu wants a drink. Tu will say no and be told to sit. Tu will remain standing, but sitting or standing won't matter. If he is right, his replacement will emerge from the corner of the room, probably someone he knows well, and even trusts. Pounding on his steering wheel multiple times doesn't satisfy his frustration. Instead of making the call, he snaps his phone in two.

Chapter 55

April 20, 7:10 P.M.

Concern and action reverberate throughout the Five Eyes community, and resources mobilize as urgent conversations occur at the intelligence community's highest levels. The island everyone is now concerned with is a potential terrorist planning, staging, and training site. The outlying possibility of finding the missing Boeing 777 hidden there has implications far beyond 9/11. Everyone spins into action.

Earlier, the Director of the CIA asked the Director of National Intelligence, and the National Reconnaissance Office to begin collecting satellite images of the island. Simultaneously, the US Secretary of Defense tasked the Chairmen of the Joint Chiefs to plan a raid. Actions on the ground fall to the US military, and it's the Chairman's job to decide who will carry out these missions. In the South Pacific, that is the commander of all Pacific forces, INDOPACOM.

INDOPACOM directed its subordinate units with a planning order. Final tasking fell upon the 31st Marine Expeditionary Unit (MEU), commanded by Colonel Scott Campbell, to plan a raid for a possible threat found on a small island two hundred miles south of the Philippines. Expeditionary Strike Group Seven, comprising the ships that house the 31st MEU, steamed toward that destination.

Now, Satellite and U-2S flyover images flow into the National Reconnaissance Office, where they are collated from both sources. Analysts report a massive fire in the island's buildings, prompting the Secretary of Defense to issue a green light to INDOPACOM and the 31st MEU to execute a raid on the island.

Captain Khan is just over one hour into his mission when the raid force leaves the helicopter dock of the USS Bonhomme Richard. Two F-35B Lightening Fighter/Attack aircraft provide additional reconnaissance and help determine the best locations for a Maritime Raid Force to land. Four MV-22 rotary-wing Ospreys, housing 60 fully armed and combat-capable Marines comprise the landing force, relying on aerial surveillance to give them appropriate landing zones. At a maximum airspeed of 300 knots, the raid force will have boots on the ground in less than an hour, but they will not be alone. They will have air support for whatever comes.

F-35 pilots push their throttles forward within minutes of launching, accelerating beyond Mach 1. Sensors on the F-35s forward images of the island to a secure facility within minutes, and the Landing Force Operations Center receives an image of multiple fires in various dwellings. Two C-130 Js are put on strip alert at Clark Air Base to provide aerial refueling for the Ospreys and F-35s if needed.

As analysts review their findings, it becomes obvious that an improvised runway on the island could become the primary landing zone. A second LZ is located further away, allowing the raid force to get on the deck clean if there's opposition. The F-35s flight lead, call sign Smoke 01, reports that multiple explosions likely started fires in the main structures near the harbor and atop a hill. Analysts confirm his assumptions. Though the fires have nearly run their course, smoke and ash continue to rise. Neither the onboard sensors nor the pilot's visual inspection show movement, so they ascend to 15,000 feet to continue reconnaissance and be ready for close air support if the raid force needs them.

By 8:00 pm, the lead element of the raid force has landed on the abandoned airfield. They move swiftly through the objective, the raid force commander noting smoldering buildings in multiple locations, bodies on the ground, and evidence of devastating explosions. When the threat status is lowered, the balance of the force lands, and a process called Sensitive Site Exploitation begins. Trained personnel comb through every square foot of the site, sending images and audio recordings to the commander's attention through secured communications.

Each element has an execution checklist that includes identifying signs of a large commercial aircraft. Voice reports on top of voice reports detail the destruction encountered. The charred remains of two pilots in uniform are found in a badly burned-out hut, remnants of a boat and lifeless bodies are found near the dock, and aircraft parts, seats, and other evidence of a commercial aircraft are identified in a structure they believe doubled as a hangar destroyed by recent explosions.

The raid force commander summarizes their findings in a voice report. "We've got a badly damaged business jet in the large structure with some avionics boxes ripped out. Seats, galley equipment, and other debris are strewn throughout the hangar."

He exploits the main building for further information and then heads uphill in the same golf carts Almudir and Junaid used to move back and forth.

The most disturbing reports come late. Fresh tire imprints run the full length of an improvised runway. Elements on the ground confirm that a large commercial aircraft recently departed, elevating the operation to the President of the United States.

Chapter 56

9:00 P.M.

In Macau, Dragonhead paces anxiously in his casino office, alternately gazing down at the Flor de Lótus Estrada on which his office building resides and stepping again to his communications software. He's desperate to hear from Tu, to learn if the attacks planned for the night are on schedule. He mutters repeatedly that if Tu fails again, he is a dead man. Billions of dollars ride on the success of Almudir's attacks. Dragonhead has positioned all his financial assets to maximize his returns after the attacks. It is year five of his ten-year plan, and there will be no year six if this doesn't work.

Moreover, he worries day and night about leaks. His primary technical advisor, Bao, let him down. How could anyone hack into their secure data center? It doesn't make sense. They must have had inside help.

"The woman!" he yells into his empty room, throwing an empty scotch glass against the wall. She might have enough information to unravel the entire plan, and she's missing. The men Tu sent for Yin Chen failed him. Has Tu also failed? He should have already heard from the man regarding the sister.

Breaking protocol, Dragonhead types a message into the email drop he and Tu use to communicate, a draft to ask Tu if their plans are on target.

Tu responds almost immediately. But Dragonhead doesn't know that the CIA has compromised his email account.

Based on the few examples they have of Tu's writing, the CIA replies with the following message:

Success, though A needs clarification about which destination he should visit. Do you have preferences?

Dragonhead is flummoxed, angry, and disappointed. Why would Tu ask him for his input so late in the game? These are the questions Dragonhead wanted answered when he returned from the island. And now this! Without considering the message or its authenticity, he stabs at his keyboard: *Why does it matter? Consulates, ships, who cares? Get them moving and sweep the streets afterward.*

Dragonhead pours three fingers of scotch and goes to his inner office to watch for news of the attacks. As he waits for word on devastation throughout Southeast Asia, he thinks of all the money he will make in the aftermath and checks his accounts, but his computer locks up. A frowning face icon appears on his computer's frozen display. Dragonhead stabs at the keys without avail, slamming both fists down onto his keyboard, snapping it in two. "The nerd. That son of a bitch!"

Chapter 57

9:05 P.M.

Yin is inconsolable. Wright and Hirsh attempt to reassure her that everything possible is being done to rescue her sister, but she has lost patience. She wants proof, but there is none. Frustrated with what Wright calls her irrational demands, he orders Decker to take her to the safe house, where he will stay with her until receiving further information. Yes, she wants out of the Consulate, but everyone should go. The dismissive tone in Wright's voice and their lack of action, infuriate Yin.

Yin's inner dragon ensures that she believes no one. She and Decker ride in silence, Yin unable to fully calm herself, Decker speechless out of fear he will upset her in such a small space. The demons developed during the ordeal of hunting for Li have grown teeth. She is sullen, distant, and defensive. "Is there anything I can do for you?" Decker asks, his voice timid.

"Like what? You're an errand boy with no authority." Yin knows her words cut, but maybe this is what it takes to get an honest response. "If they really have my sister, where are they taking her? What is her condition? How can I get in contact with her? Answer any of those questions, and we'll get along fine."

Decker doesn't answer, and Yin barks at his silence. "Like I said, useless. I want to know if Li has been freed. It's a simple question, but no one has the answer. Do you? No, you don't. Why is that?" Yin demands, twisting in his direction and leaning forward.

Decker looks at her with pleading eyes, but she is even more insistent. "Why is that?"

The tension expands for blocks. Yin's mind is so crippled from what she's been through that she doesn't know what to think. She contemplates submitting wholly to her caged dragon and pounding her fists into the dashboard, tearing at the upholstery, and screaming into Decker's face, but she doesn't do or say anything. Of three options available to her in the confines of the car, fight, flight, or fold, she chooses the latter and turns toward the window in bitter silence.

At the safe house, Yin drops onto the couch and nearly cries. Everything she has gone through, all the threats, narrowly surviving a shoot-out with the Triads, having to argue with Nigel and later Wright, it has all been excruciating. All these people lie for a living, but there is nothing more she can do. If they are lying about Li, it's over. Her resources are incapacitated, dead, or missing. She closes her eyes, takes a deep breath, and tries to summon Li. Nothing. She cannot even imagine what Li has gone through, and the rage returns. Wanting to be alone, she asks Decker for a huge favor.

"Anything," he says, happy not to be yelled at anymore.

"Can you get me a pint of lemon ice? It may sound strange, but it makes me feel close to Li. It's her favorite thing in the whole world." A forced tear rolls down Yin's cheek.

Decker looks away in defeat. "I'm not supposed to leave you alone."

"See? An errand boy. That is all you are to them."

Throwing up his hands, Decker seems to change his mind. "Promise not to leave? It's still dangerous for you. Don't open the door for anyone, no matter what, until you hear me knock and say I've got ice. Can you do that?"

"And potato chips? Li loves chips."

Decker stands to leave, saying, "Wright can never know."

Yin follows him to the door. As he reaches for the handle, she takes his arm and kisses him on the cheek. "Thank you."

Decker looks perplexed. "I shouldn't say this, but you're wrong about Justin. You think he doesn't pay attention to anything you say. The military is running a mission on the island, non-essential personnel at the consulate have been sent home, and he's asked Langley to do a frame-by-frame analysis of Bao's death video. Just because he can't tell you everything doesn't mean he's not listening."

"That's good to know. But look at what it took to get his attention. I had to beg and badger. If you want to help, question someone about my sister's status and let me know what's going on. I deserve to know."

Decker pauses, searching for the right words, but comes up empty. "I'm not in that loop. You probably know more than I do. I'm sorry I don't have more."

Yin's inner dragon wants to lash out, but she says, "I'm not in the loop, either. All I can say is that I don't believe a word that comes out of their mouths."

Decker heads for the door. Turning to Yin he says, "For what it's worth, I do."

Yin plans a hasty escape when Decker is gone and gathers essentials for her getaway. If Tu has Li, or even worse, if she is dead, there is no reason to stay. She's thought for days that Wright and the CIA are playing her and their next move will be arrest, but what if she is wrong? What if they are close to freeing her sister, and she's vanished into hiding when Li arrives?

Doubt pervades every thought. She stands immobilized by indecision in the center of the living room, bags over her shoulder, remembering that she should take her laptop, but it's too much.

Yin carries her belongings into the bedroom, drops them on the bed, and goes directly to the bathroom mirror. She rests her weight on the wall, hands propped on either side of the glass, staring into the reflection. She says, "You're the only one I trust. Tell me you are still alive. Please speak to me. Where are you, pretty girl?"

No answer.

Chapter 58

9:15 P.M.

The path of Captain Khan's final flight has taken him nearly 1,000 miles from the island, through Makassar Strait, and into the Java Sea. It's been the most grueling flight of his life. He has methodically calculated and recalculated his fuel and timing to ensure success. At times, he flew at 10,000 feet. He sometimes dipped below 2,000 feet, a flight perfectly planned and executed to arrive undetected and on time. Precision increases his chances for success. Precision cuts down on mistakes, but precision also takes nonstop focus and abundant energy. So far, he's been nothing but precise. He knows many things are beyond his control, and he can only do his part. And he has. Perfectly.

Captain Khan completes the target and fuel calculation once more. He smiles. It's all coming together as planned. He still has 200 miles, roughly forty-five minutes of flying time to go before he reaches his attack profile. Fatigue sets in and is exacerbated by endless questions from his restless passengers. He puts an end to their disruptions by yelling as loudly as he can. "Quiet! Your chatter will ruin the mission." It's not necessarily true but yelling creates an element of conflict on the flight deck, increasing his blood pressure enough to temporarily renew energy and focus.

The detailed route plotted on his handheld GPS and the general overview he programmed into the flight management display performed flawlessly. Autopilot and automated throttles kept the airspeed fixed at 250 knots, and he maintained predetermined altitudes precisely through all waypoints. He conserved fuel for the flight and physical energy needed during the highest-risk segments of his route. Every pilot recognizes the danger of clicking off autopilot and cruising in darkness 1,000 feet above the ocean's surface. During tense periods in their flight, the Iranians sat in absolute silence, hoping not to be discovered or crash, but he made it through the Strait without incident. The chaos in the commercial airspace above has been a divine gift and Khan hopes it will last until he reaches the target.

Darkness envelops his craft, autopilot is re-engaged, and Khan's thoughts drift momentarily towards Syhala. He hopes Almudir will keep his promise, but he never did have control. Syhala was a faithful, short-lived companion who aided him in preparations. Her cooking and lovemaking made life delicious and exciting, and he hopes her kindness and loyalty will be rewarded in heaven. It would be so gratifying to see her face when Omar hands over his letter, but he will never see her again.

He glances at the time on the GPS device and is returned to the moment. He expects Almudir's cyberattack to last for ten hours, his flight to end in four, but he doesn't control any of that. Monitoring frequencies on two radios for news about the radar outages indicates that the promised mayhem continues. A repetitive frantic chorus of *Say your position, Say your altitude*, and, the coup de grâce, *Mayday Mayday Mayday: FUEL*, continue. Dozens of aircraft request diversion instructions. The demand overwhelms controllers allowing his 350,000-pound projectile to proceed unnoticed.

"I wonder how he did it," Captain Khan says aloud.

"Did what?" one of the Iranians says.

"Nothing." He wishes he knew how Almudir knocked out radar without destroying physical radar installations. As a former military pilot, he can't imagine any other way. He should have studied cybersecurity. Who helped him? It's the perfect distraction. Chaos in the airspace above creates doubt below. No military unit wants to fire on a commercial aircraft mistakenly. What a marvelous plan, Khan admits.

With practiced ease, Captain Khan flies at 300 knots and at low altitude for the remaining 45 minutes of his final flight. He has one primary target, with two alternate locations. The crown jewel of Carrier Strike Group Two, specifically the USS Carl Vinson, is currently anchored in Jakarta for a historic visit. That's his prize. She is vulnerable. Ships in the strike group are scattered in various regional ports, leaving CVN 70 unguarded. Host nations protect their harbors but are primarily concerned with surface threats. Every minute that passes without being discovered increases the probability of success.

If forced to abandon his primary target, the American Consulate is nearby. Tani Monument Park will be easy to spot, even at night. Khan weighs levels of mission success. Exploding anywhere in the port of Jakarta will send a stunning message but hitting a US aircraft carrier with 60-plus aircraft and thousands of service members aboard would be spectacular. He has no doubt that the dignitaries on board deserve death as well for supporting the United States.

"Have you decided?" one of the Iranians asks. The man smokes cigarettes incessantly, but thankfully, not on the flight deck.

"Allah will decide," Khan says. "There have been too many incidents where a hard and fast target has gotten pilots into difficulty. We have over thirty minutes to make that decision. Pray that we don't get intercepted before reaching land."

The 777 creates a faint shadow on the smooth ocean surface as it flies through the moonlight. Oceans look so different at this altitude, mirrorlike tonight. He's flown within hearing distance of a dozen ships thus far and expects to see many more as he closes on Jakarta, but even if they report a low-flying plane traveling in darkness, he thinks the message will be lost in all the confusion. If he hasn't been reported yet, it is too late.

Khan decides with less than fifteen minutes of flight time remaining. He switches charts and enters specific coordinates into GPS for Jakarta harbor. He is so close now that the message will be delivered even if the enemy blows him out of the sky before he reaches the carrier. *Even your powerful navy is vulnerable.*

As the Captain prepares for his final attack profile, his nerves flutter. He will fly low over the city, where even the US military will hesitate to fire upon him. He's accomplished so much already, and at each step, he worried he would fail. That hasn't happened. He successfully hijacked Inter-Asian Flight 957, causing incredible concern and confusion. He was able to evade detection and land on a narrow ribbon of uneven ground carved from a remote island, and now he is minutes away from using the hijacked aircraft as a missile. The story of Flight 957 will be completed, and his name will live on in the chronicles of human history for decades to come.

9:45 P.M.

Based on the raid force's exploitation of the island, and the CIA's ability to access Tu's shared email account with Dragonhead, Consular Generals throughout Southeast Asia go on high alert. Security teams arrive at each embassy, barricades are fortified, nonessential personnel go home, and the military prepares for potential assaults. Local police receive warnings of imminent danger. In the estimation of the State Department, they have done all they can to prepare on short notice. Officer Wright knows it won't be enough.

The US Navy's Carrier Strike Group Two Commander, Rear Admiral

Arnett, has just been notified by his intelligence section of the alert. A 9/11-level threat without specific targets is troubling. He listens intently to his intel chief's briefing while mentally cataloging essential tasks. Amidst the final moments of celebrating a hugely successful security cooperation exercise, Admiral Arnett looks to the skies with concern, aware that this would be the worst time to be hit with an enemy strike. He has dignitaries on board, fireworks will surely degrade the attention of his crew, and he is reliant on Indonesia for protection. He shakes his head. Although the odds of elements in his strike group being attacked are minimal, he orders the Captain of the USS Carl Vinson to work closely with the host nation's military. Radar operators should scan for rogue aircraft, and the weapons systems crew should ready the CWIS aerial gunnery system as a precaution. Everyone must exercise restraint. Considering the airspace outage above them, they can ill afford to shoot an innocent commercial airliner out of the sky. So much can go wrong in moments like this.

The Admiral's concerns are well placed, as his carrier is vulnerable while anchored in the harbor. However, he rests on his crew being well-trained and doing all they can to protect their ships and each other, spreading the word to remain diligent and not be distracted by the celebration. He wants to get through the evening, leave the harbor, and head for their home port of San Diego.

The Admiral scans the flight deck of his 100,000-ton ship, taking in all the festivities and verifying that weapon systems are online. FINEX, the Final Exercise of security cooperation training among various regional nations, ending with dignitary tours, speeches, and dinners, has gone seamlessly thus far, but as the fireworks show nears its grand finale, the Admiral receives an urgent report of multiple shipboard radar systems experiencing degraded operations due to multiple phantom radar return anomalies.

• • •

Captain Khan guides his Beast across the southern coast of Indonesia, using terrain to mask his intention to reach the port. He slows his airspeed to 200 knots as he approaches land to lessen the threatening posture his aircraft may exhibit. He listens intently to the VHF radio and smiles at the confusion in the airspace. Air traffic controllers and pilots alike are distraught.

Khan continues his low, slow, and stealthy approach overland from the south, where he can mingle among regularly scheduled commercial air traffic, all of whom are distressed. The Iranians riding with him act as spotters and offer prayers to harden their resolve. Captain Khan needs no help with his resolve. He only seeks calm, and when the moment comes, he methodically pushes his throttles full forward and starts his attack run.

Chapter 59

An hour before Captain Khan started his final attack run, a fishing boat exited Singapore Strait for Changi Bay on its hour-long journey toward the Johor River. Singapore has one of the most heavily trafficked ports in Southeast Asia, and the fishing vessel navigates slowly between tankers and cargo ships to the entrance of RSS Singapura - Changi Naval Base, where guards in the tower watching over the harbor warn them off.

Although dark, the guards can see smoke emanating from the small vessel. The ship's captain answers on his radio in a confused state and mutters about a fire and injured crew. They are lost and desperate. "Please don't shoot us," he insists. "We need help."

The guards restate their warning to turn around as if the plight of the boat and her crew is irrelevant. The boat captain pleads for them not to shoot as he begins a long circling move to port, making it appear that they are turning. However, as the vessel's aft section faces the warships in the harbor, men on the boat throw open a tarp and wildly unleash a barrage of well-placed surface-to-surface rockets and missiles.

Having rehearsed dry-fire procedures dozens of times on the island, the four men know exactly how to proceed as they attack the RSS Intrepid Singaporean stealth-class frigate and other targets. Two men fire rocket-propelled grenades at fuel stores, while the other two aim and fire sixth-generation anti-tank wire-guided missiles. The ATGMs hit the Intrepid's bridge and vertical missile launching system, causing extensive damage to weapons platforms.

One of the RPGs strikes a fuel supply, creating secondary explosions that significantly increase its impact. In contrast, two additional RPGs reach buildings in the harbor without causing much destruction before the fishing boat is fired upon. The Singaporean Navy obliterates the Jihadists with STK 50 machine gun fire. The rounds rip through the hull, causing it to list and the threat is quickly neutralized, but only after causing extensive damage to nearby ships and harbor installations.

While the fishing boats attack in Singapore, Nasr drives a rented van through the streets of Kuala Lumpur, delivering women he's come to love to their final destinations. These are the same women he brought to the island to meet Captain Khan and participate in training. He loves and admires them so much that he frequently cries as they exit his van. He was supposed to be the strong one, the firm voice of commitment, but when they depart in suicide vests laced tightly around their torsos, he nearly loses emotional control. No one says goodbye as they disembark, murmuring prayers.

Almudir entrusted Nasr with this important mission. He predicted that Nasr's calm demeanor would keep the women in check but instructed him to be firm if they wavered. He was wrong. The women don't need him, they need each other. They wear vests with pride, while Nasr hides tears in shame.

When the final suicide bomber steps onto a street corner, Nasr parks the van and weeps until startled by a blast in the near distance, then another and another—seven in total in as many minutes, each triggering additional police and emergency sirens. The women went to shopping centers, nightclubs, and transportation hubs. Two were in uniform. The woman dressed as a police officer intended to walk into a station, the nurse an emergency room.

When asked why he shouldn't also martyr himself, Almudir insisted Nasr continue running his butcher shop as Almudir's eyes and ears in the city until needed. Tonight, he is to drive the explosive-laden van to the shop of a friend who will dismantle the equipment and hide it from authorities. The remaining explosives will be used in a week or two is what Nasr was told, but he is grief-stricken. He studies himself in the rear-view mirror and wonders how he arrived in this situation. He wanted to be like Almudir and take the fight to the enemy, but tonight his eyes were opened. These women are the true warriors. They've proven their bravery and accepted the ultimate sacrifice. What has Almudir done but boss everyone around and send women to their deaths without compunction? He's been a fool.

He looks at the spare vest in the empty passenger seat. What choice does he have? Reciting a prayer for strength, he engages the gears of his van and drives slowly through the city. He looks again into the mirror and sees a coward staring back at him.

Overcome with emotion, Nasr accelerates the van and banks it hard to the left, directly toward a busy thoroughfare with upscale malls and luxe fashion boutiques. As the hood of his van plows through glass, he presses hard on a detonation button. His is the eighth and largest explosion in Kuala Lumpur this evening. This is the most violent night in recent history, but Almudir isn't done with Kuala Lumpur.

A second round of attacks is planned two weeks out, and a third will follow soon after. Sporting and entertainment venues, shopping centers, open-air markets, and cloistered western housing complexes are just a few soft targets on his list. Success or failure in the follow-on attacks means little to Almudir. He has one goal in mind. He wants to disrupt the influence of Europe and the US in Southeast Asia absolutely and permanently. His twisted calculation is that the West will no longer be trusted to protect its regional business and social interests. The Western influence on transportation, commerce, and public policy will end.

Chapter 60

Before Nasr made his fateful decision, Junaid moved into position on the south side of Kuala Lumpur. An unplanned eighth explosion in the distance could only mean one thing. At Almudir's insistence, he is to deliver a message and equipment to Captain Khan's cousin Omar, then accompany Omar to meet Syhala before joining his militant friends in Singapore. However, there are two delicate tasks to complete.

Junaid protested vehemently at first, saying that Captain Khan's desire to pay these two people was blasphemy, but Almudir reassured his faithful friend before divulging his plan.

Junaid arrives at Omar's flat and sees him sitting on his stoop. He approaches and greets him. Omar returns the greeting. Both men are shocked by the other's appearance. Junaid considers the grotesque scars visible on Omar's face and body, and Omar picks up on the dark nature and menacing presence of his unannounced visitor.

"You are Omar, cousin of Muhammad Khan?" Junaid says. He maintains eye contact to avoid staring.

"I am. And who are you?" Omar asks, guarded.

"Your cousin sent me. He and I spent a lot of time together recently," Junaid says, trying not to divulge too much until trust is established.

A surprised Omar lets his guard down and says, "You've seen my cousin? Where is he? How is he doing?"

Junaid is impatient. "I'm sorry. Things are in motion, and time is short.

I need you to help deliver a message to Captain Khan's fiancé, Syhala. He wanted it this way, and she doesn't know who I am."

Omar takes a long, hard look at his visitor and says, "He's done it? Did he take the plane? I knew it." He smiles and nods in trust. "I will take you to Syhala."

Both men get in the car. Omar moves with slightly more fluidity than usual. His pain has subsided as he relishes his cousin's success.

The drive to Syhala's is short. "So," Omar begins, looking to Junaid. "Where is my cousin? Where is Muhammad Khan? Tell me."

Junaid has been thoroughly briefed on Omar and knows he believes in the cause. "He will be a hero for the ages. He has accepted the mission to martyr himself." Junaid pauses for effect. "He is flying a plane to strike at the very heart of our enemy. He wants you to explain his sacrifice to Syhala."

"Explain? How do I explain such a thing to one who may not understand?" Omar says. He sits in deep thought for a moment.

"Your cousin is a hero. Read this. It will help you explain things to her." Junaid says, handing Omar two notes as he nears the next stop in a carefully planned sequence of events.

Omar reads the two notes ostensibly written by his cousin and looks up. "He's going through with this? He's going to be a martyr?" Omar confirms, smiling. Even though his face barely moves, his eyes show pride.

Junaid does not answer, and the car is silent as it pulls up to an apartment Khan arranged for Syhala to hide in until his cousin could come for her. Omar exits the vehicle and slowly makes his way to the front door. He knocks four times. The door slowly opens, and before he can say anything, Syhala invites him to enter.

"Muhammad sent a message to both of us. I could explain, but it's best if you read it alone," Omar says, not knowing how Syhala will react.

"He is back. He's here in the city?" Syhala asks hopefully.

Omar shakes his head in reply and silently hands Syhala the note. He watches her reaction, prepared to offer solace if necessary. Syhala trembles as she reads. "He sent you to say this? I don't understand. We were going to—"

"Yes, you do understand. We all understand bravery. Let's do what he wants and leave immediately."

Syhala steps around Omar and peers into the night at the menacing figure waiting by the car. Stiffening her back, she turns to Omar and says, "I need a few things before I join you."

"Quickly," Omar urges. "We don't have much time."

Syhala returns with a backpack and laptop strung over her shoulders. They join Junaid in the car, Omar taking the front passenger seat, Syhala entering behind. They quietly ride until Junaid pulls to the curb and idles the car. "What are we doing here?" Omar asks.

Junaid ignores him. He smoothly pulls a pistol from a holster, carefully keeping it hidden until the right moment. Turning to Syhala, he slowly extends his arm. Omar spots the pistol, eyes wide and paralyzed by fear. Continuing the deliberate motion until his arm is fully extended towards Syhala, Junaid says, "Just in case."

Syhala refuses with a simple shake of her head. Junaid continues. "You have done well sister. May your loyalty find reward in heaven."

Omar is puzzled by the comment as Junaid asks Syhala if she is ready, further confusing him. Junaid gives Omar a look of disapproval, causing him to be silent.

Syhala exits the vehicle without hesitation and walks with purpose into a crowded police station. Junaid drives off, turns at the end of a block, and speeds away. As he drives, he checks his rearview mirror and explains. "Syhala worked for a man named Almudir. The two of them worked on a plan to ensure that your cousin had the support needed for his mission."

Omar stares at the dashboard in front of him, stunned. Junaid touches the man's shoulder. "It's not like that. She wants to be with your cousin forever."

An explosion rocks the streets behind them. Junaid finishes his thought. "And now she will be."

Junaid and Omar share a quiet moment as they drive to their next stop.

There is one more task to fulfill before Junaid plans his egress. He carefully sizes up Omar and determines he is worthy. Having heard the eighth explosion, he has little choice. He drives Omar down a familiar street and stops in front of an old butcher shop. "This is your new home. You will make a great butcher. Work hard and remain faithful and loyal until you are needed. Here are the keys."

In Singapore, five of Junaid's friends prepare for a significant attack on the American Consulate. These are highly trained former Iranian operatives, friends Junaid fought, bled, and nearly died with on numerous missions. Junaid's most trusted friend, Hassan, hands each of the warriors thousands in American dollars after last minute preparations in a vacant warehouse. Their target is the American consulate, and for them, timing is everything. Unlike suicide bombers, these men intend to fight again.

Hassan drives in one van while the other warriors ride stoically in a second van filled with exotic weapons, including RPGs and multiple shoulder-launched guided missiles. One mile from the American Consulate, Hassan, acting as forward reconnaissance, determines the coast is clear and joins the rest of the team in a parking lot. They reaffirm their plans. Then, one by one, the men leave Hassan with a dozen drones capable of carrying powerful heavy explosives up to three miles. Hassan is an expert in drone flight. He's programmed six first-person viewable drones to deploy independently and drop munitions when ordered. For the next few minutes, he launches his arsenal into the air. They fly undetected to stationary positions a thousand feet above the American consulate and hover in midair.

Hassan checks the time, lights a cigarette, and waits as he watches multiple consoles. At five minutes, he starts the van. The first explosion occurs. He clicks the van into gear. Driving through nearly empty streets, he presses button after button, dropping explosives onto buildings on the consulate grounds. As he releases each bomb, he throws the drone's console out of the window until he is at driving speed without any further weapons.

Hasan's fellow militants fire their weapons into the compound and abandon the launchers before being picked up by the vans. The attack takes less than ten minutes from the first explosion to the last. The vans are abandoned twelve minutes later. A third vehicle distributes the attackers to preplanned locations throughout the city. Some will wait weeks before attempting to leave, but Hassan has other plans. Hassan will await Junaid's arrival, then board a fishing boat. The two men will ride out the aftermath at sea while preparing for the second and third phases of the attacks.

Before parting company with Almudir, Junaid wondered where the boss would go. He has long since ceased asking Almudir about his plans, but if he had to guess, Almudir would travel to Northern Pakistan, then slip unnoticed through the FATA into the haven of Afghanistan, where he would plan his next attacks.

Richard Giudice

Chapter 61

9:57 P.M.

Unknown to Captain Muhammad Khan, the prelude to his grand entrance was executed flawlessly and in perfect synchronization. The regional attacks hit the news cycle moments before entering Jakarta. A bomb exploded at a soccer match. A group of four riflemen charged a police station, and a surface-to-surface missile was launched at the air traffic control tower of the airport. Khan experiences a surreal quality washing through his body in the final moments of his attack. Months ago, he didn't expect to fly directly into fireworks and certainly never expected to aim a commercial airliner at a colossal aircraft carrier's flight deck and bridge. He experiences fleeting images of his entire aviation career culminating in the moment, but his memories, calculations, and emotional sensibilities don't keep up with the sheer velocity of action.

The lights of Jakarta are a ribbon of shoreline twenty miles ahead. It's impossible to believe the USS Carl Vinson does not have his aircraft under close watch, but if he can make it to the city, and approach his target from populated areas, they may be less willing to attack his plane. Firing weapons over populated areas is counter to policy. He travels in darkness, steering slightly away from the harbor, heading toward city lights. Above, he sees multiple aircraft circling, waiting for instructions, hoping they do not fly into each other. "Perfect Cover," Khan says aloud. His Iranian copilot stares at him, unable to comprehend how the stars have truly aligned for this fatal moment.

Captain Khan keeps a strip of terrain between himself and his target as he passes from sea to land. Looking up from his GPS device for the final time, he sees the fireworks over the harbor. His timing is perfect.

Military and civilian celebration planners would not have accounted for fireworks being packed with radar-jamming chaff. When dispersed in the air, each bundle confuses naval shipboard radar systems, rendering them useless. Attack elements work in concert with confusion in the airspace. The element of surprise, the cloak of darkness, the airspace cyber-attack, and now the chaff cloud floating through the port will give Captain Khan the chance he's been waiting for all his life.

Peering through the 777's windscreen, Captain Khan sees what he's been searching for. The USS Carl Vinson is in sight. He banks hard in the direction of the harbor and points the nose of The Beast directly at its prey.

Throttles fully forward, the 777 accelerates past 300 knots to 350 as he descends to 400 feet. At 400 knots, traveling nearly seven miles per minute in a terrifying path over the building tops of Jakarta, the aircraft begins to buffet from exceeding maximum speed limitations. The Iranians pray loudly and cheer him forward, and for a blessed moment, they all trust they will reach the Carl Vinson.

Captain Khan estimates they will reach their target in one minute and thirty seconds. Things proceed in slow motion. Khan's mind processes every nuance while his heart races in disbelief that he may succeed. Suddenly and without warning, tracer rounds emerge eight miles from his target like threads of deadly light. His aircraft is too big for evasive maneuvers. All he can do is guess the proper elevation and press hard toward his target. He'll be hit. He'll die, but if he calculates everything correctly, elements of the plane will survive long enough to plow into the aircraft carrier. One minute short of his target, munitions punch holes in the left wing, and his number one engine bursts into flame, shredded by naval gunfire. The nose of the aircraft yaws hard in the direction of his lost engine. With all his might, Captain Khan counters the yaw with his right rudder while struggling to keep his wings level and stay on target, but at this speed, the aircraft groans in protest.

Four miles from the target, more tracers find the plane's wing. The crippled 777 leans hard to one side. They suffer from multiple surface-to-air defenses, and Captain Khan can do nothing but grip the yoke tightly with both hands, hoping to control his aircraft. It can't be done.

Two miles to impact, still traveling at nearly 400 miles per hour and an altitude of 200 feet, he is rocked by an even stronger force. The aircraft yaws hard to the right this time. He's lost flight control and waits to see if momentum carries him to victory. The Iranians shout prayers at the top of their lungs, panic on their faces. Captain Khan tunes them out and prays for only one thing: perfection. He closes his eyes and releases the yoke. He's closing in on the USS Carl Vinson at a fantastic rate of speed. His work is done. His elusive perfect flight is nearly complete. It's in the hands of the Almighty now.

The final image flashing through Khan's mind as the impact of multiple 102mm rounds from a Phalanx Close-In Weapons System triggers all 2,000 pounds of explosives on board, is that of Syhala climbing into bed with him on their first night. As he leaves this world, he whispers, "My love, I'll see you soon."

Chapter 62

In the small, sparsely furnished living room of the Emerald Hill CIA safe house, a television relentlessly covers the carnage unfolding throughout the region. Decker sits transfixed in an armchair, shaking his head in utter disbelief. Yin, questioning her decision not to flee, sits half reclined on a sofa, shifting her eyes and thoughts from Decker to the television to an unpacked box of her things in the corner of the room. She is conflicted on so many levels. One moment, she watches events unfold as if a movie, glad that she isn't crushed under rubble or dead. The next, she wants to yell at someone for not preventing these attacks. Five Eyes is supposed to be oh-so competent, always on top of things, and fully prepared to act at a moment's notice. In her experience, that hasn't been the case, and she obsesses over men like Tu and Bao. She came so close to dying at their hand, and yet, it's possible she was warned to get out of the consulate by the mercurial gamer. In her present state of mind, all men live in the Essex category. If the Triads don't get her, men like Essex will. And if she doesn't agree to work with or for Wright? What then? She practically fought them to get out of the consulate, narrowly missing the vicious attack. They'll think she was part of that as well, just because she received that message.

Decker receives another call, the sixth since arriving, and steps into the kitchen. Everything Yin sees looks dark and evil. She's in her darkest moment and sees no way out. Men took her sister. Nigel and Wright claimed to do everything possible to find Li, and this sophomoric young idiot in the kitchen claims they have succeeded, but they haven't delivered. If the two million dollars she sent was used to buy Li's freedom, and if she is free, where is the proof? Is she even still alive? Worst of all, Yin does not feel Li's presence.

A series of expletives emerge from the kitchen, snapping Yin into the present. She leaps up to see if Decker is okay and sees him staring out the kitchen window. Yin goes to him, touches his shoulder, and asks if he's ok.

"They didn't make it. I should have been there."

"Who?" Yin asks, anger resurfacing as she thinks Decker may be referring to her sister.

"Charise, Ted, and the guys at the front gate, 26 dead so far, and they expect more by morning. No one has seen Wright and they think Hirsh is buried in a pile of rubble. I should have been there," Decker says, eyes cast towards Yin as if looking for answers.

"I'm sorry," Yin says.

"You warned them. I heard you. How did you—"

Before Decker can finish his thought, someone pounds loudly on the front door. There is no text, no call, and no notification whatsoever.

Decker pulls his weapon and orders Yin to take cover behind the kitchen counter as he goes to the door. Frightened and shaking, she hears him call out for identification and then nothing. She's unsure whether to look over the countertop or squeeze into the cabinet below the kitchen sink, but she does neither. Instead, Yin prepares for the fight of her life.

Suddenly, she hears Wright's voice in the other room. Wright is explaining in hushed tones what happened at the consulate, who survived, and who didn't, but says nothing about Li.

Yin hasn't felt Li for some time and knows Wright has the answers.

She submits wholly to her rage and sprints from the kitchen with teeth clenched and fists ready to attack.

Decker sees her first. Wright turns and is stunned by the darkness rushing toward him from across the room. With only seconds to react, he extends his right arm towards Yin's menacing form, at the end of which is his cell phone.

Yin nearly stumbles to a halt as she hears Li's voice. "Stop! What's wrong, pretty girl? Control it. I'm here."

Yin stares at her sister's face on Wright's phone. Unable to form words, she reaches both hands towards the screen, grabs Wright's phone, and won't let go as she falls to her knees and sobs uncontrollably.

Wright lets her take his phone to the sofa. Li is on a hospital bed with an IV in her arm, tears in her eyes, and the softest, most beautiful smile imaginable. They cannot take their eyes off each other as Li says, "We never gave up. I knew you would come for me, and you knew I would hang on. Don't cry. It's going to be okay. I love you, pretty girl."

Epilogue

For weeks on end, media outlets around the globe show footage of the final moments of Inter-Asian Flight 957. Images show fireworks exploding in the night sky above Jakarta as volley after volley of tracer rounds hunt for their target. The ominous 777, once thought to have crashed in the South China Sea, erupts into a ball of fire less than a half mile from the USS Carl Vinson. Shrapnel from the blast flies in every direction.

According to one news source, nation-state-level support may have enabled the attacks. Another report warns of escalating tensions between the US and China.

Of course, a third report suggests investigations are underway at the highest levels in a multinational effort to unravel what took place and ensure that something like this never happens again.

"Hollow promises," Nigel Rainer mutters to himself as he clicks off on his television remote. Following four weeks in an induced coma and after six surgeries to repair internal organs and bullet-torn ribs, Nigel arrived in a convalescent home for rehabilitation. A month later, he was wheeled into a courtesy van and driven to the airport: destination, Australia. His injuries are such that he may only be allowed desk jobs from this day forward, but his parents have been at his side throughout. He is happy to be with the two people he trusts most but sad that he is no closer to affording his father's dream boat and joining him at sea.

Inevitably, his thoughts drift towards all that has occurred during his recovery. Depressed about his physical condition and frustrated that he doesn't have access to the information he once took for granted, he sits dejected in his parents' home, sorting through the remnants of his life.

He receives a surprise text. It reads:

> *You saved my life. It's the least I can do. Don't you dare turn this over to the authorities! It's yours, free and clear. Take a walk on the wild side.*
>
> *Get well soon—much respect.*

The message ends with a link, which Nigel hesitates to open, but does. The page he opens has a photograph of a green hat, a yellow bag, and a comical boat. He laughs.

Scrolling the page, he finds instructions for manipulating cryptocurrency and a 256-character private key. He stares at the key for the longest time, thinking of Yin and all the questions he wishes he could ask her. There is a note of finality in Yin's words that draws a tear from his eyes. He'd thought they would meet again and discuss what happened that day and since. Now, he wonders if he will ever see her again. He learned that his friend Justin followed through on a plan to rescue her sister and succeeded, but bad actors still hunt the twins. Did they go back to China? Did Yin accept the fellowship at MIT? He acknowledges concern fueled by his immense feelings toward Yin.

Wright has called twice. He said Yin saved a lot of people and would have saved more if he'd acted on her analysis. There was awe and regret in his voice. Nigel replied with a signed immunity document he intends to enforce, no matter what Essex says. There are few people in his life he'd fight for. His parents and Yin are among them.

Following Yin's instructions, Nigel logs into the listed address and relays the key. Emotion nearly overwhelms him as Yin's gift approximates $1,500,000 US. He looks up from his computer and fixes his gaze on his father, who snoozes in the chair across from him. At peace, Nigel closes his eyes and drifts into sleep.

• • •

At an undisclosed location, Li Chen recovers in a hospital bed with her sister at her side. Plans for an uncertain future are discussed but most of their time together is spent in silence. David Decker taps Yin on the shoulder, indicating it's time to depart. Yin and Li embrace, neither wanting to let go. Yin is escorted from the hospital by a CIA entourage led by Decker. Decker's phone rings. Yin hears one side of the conversation.

"Yes, I have her. I'm not sure. Ok. Is he cooperating? Good."

"Was that Wright? Did they get Tu?"

Decker doesn't answer directly, but smiles.

• • •

In an undisclosed location on the outskirts of Singapore, Officer Wright and two interrogators pull the hood off of a very important prisoner. If he could, Wright would do the interrogating himself, and it would be long and painful, but he says, "I'm going to leave you in the capable hands of my friends here, but I wanted to look into your face and let you know that I am the guy who took you down. If you ever want to see the sunlight again, you'll have to convince these guys that you've given everything you know, and then they will have to convince me. Think about that in the coming months and years."

Tu's initial response is silence, but already Wright can see wheels spinning.

• • •

Nine thousand eight hundred miles away, in a small Argentinian village, Chaosmaster83 logs into Overwatch 2 and engages in a first-person shootout game with one of the players he encountered two years earlier. They trade shots, insults, laughter, and messages:

Chaosmaster83: *What'd I tell you, dipshit? I'm unbeatable.*

Player: *In a game maybe, but in the real world?*

Chaosmaster83: *Haaaa. Both.*

Player: *If I didn't know better, I'd say you were cheating.*

Chaosmaster83: *In this game or the other?*

Player: *Haaaa. Both.*

Chaosmaster83: *You bet your ass both. Taking the sister was a stroke of genius. I wish I'd thought of that one, but those points go to you. Knowing how she'd react was priceless. Bailing on the MIT campus and crawling to EEL for help was perfect. But the rest of it was all me, brother. Feeding her clues, the list of names, the two Iranians on the plane, like anyone would be that stupid. The money movement, the meeting on the island, the two debris fields, and my favorite, the Blue Sea Squirt.*

Player: *How the hell did you know she'd go for that?*

Chaosmaster83: *I wanted her on my team when I realized she hacked me. Remember when we had our guys break into their apartment to check things out?*

Player: *Yeah*

Chaosmaster83: *Her screensaver, man. Full of marine life and this little sea squirt thing. There were a few photos of her and her sister. They went diving and crap with their parents, so I figured she'd know. I'm always gaming, my brother.*

Player: *But you almost overplayed your hand.*

Chaosmaster83: *No way. I was in control the whole time. Okay, the Aussie guy got shot. That took me by surprise, but it was just a glitch. That CIA dude picked up the ball and ran with it. They nearly stopped Almudir where I needed him stopped. Control the chaos, right? I am the master. My plans worked.*

Player: *You're going to owe your friends for getting you out of there?*

Chaosmaster83: *Unfortunately, yes. But I'll deal with that later.*

Player: *And the girl. Kill her off? That would be epic.*

Chaosmaster83: *Hell no! I'm keeping her in the sandbox for the next game.*

Player: *Speaking of which, I've already lined a few things up for that, but winning the next game seems virtually impossible. Do you think you can get her to play again? I mean, if you're not going to end her, does she suspect you had anything to do with her sister? That could come back to bite us.*

Chaosmaster83: *I doubt it, but anything is possible, but hey, man. I've got to go. Later.*

Player: *Later man.*

Logging off Overwatch 2, Bao opens another can of Red Bull, mixes it with vodka, and throws the empty can across the room at a trash can.

"Damn, girl. You went to the Consulate? Smart move, but I hope you got out of there."

Taking a long pull from his drink and then licking his lips, Bao says to an empty room, "Let's see how you handle what's coming next.

Made in United States
North Haven, CT
18 July 2024

54962061R00283